To regain her birthright, she must be a match for a king. . . .

When she knew that the king was asleep, Reawen exhaled a slow breath. All of her body ached now. Gingerly, she eased from her hiding place. Her legs felt so stiff that she feared she might stumble and fall. She waited, breathing deeply and flexing her knees slightly, until she felt strength and control return.

After a last worried glance at the sleeping king, Reawen focused on the crown on the table next to him. Softly, she approached the table. When she stood at its edge, the water domis stretched the liquid ball she still held into a thin sheet between her hands, then spun it into gossamer threads. Deftly, she wove the strands into a fine, flexible net. As a child, Reawen often had captured birds with water nets and then laughingly set them free. Now she intended to recapture her birthright—the domi stone her mother had so carelessly lost.

Once I have the stone back, she told herself, I'll never let it go.

Other TSR® Books

GREENFIRE

Louise Titchener

GREENFIRE

First Printing: December 1993.
Printed in the United States of America.
Library of Congress Catalog Card Number: 92-61107
ISBN: 1-56076-685-9

9 8 7 6 5 4 3 2 1

TSR, Inc.
P. O. Box 756
Lake Geneva, WI 53147
U. S. A.

TSR Ltd.
120 Church End, Cherry Hinton
Cambridge CB1 3LB
United Kingdom

To John, for all his patience.

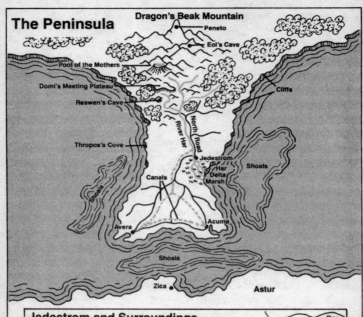

The Peninsula

Dragon's Beak Mountain
- Peneto
- Eol's Cave

Pool of the Mothers

Domi's Meeting Plateau

Reawen's Cave

Cliffs

Thropos's Cove

River Har

North Road

Jedestrom
Har
Delta
Marsh

Shoals

Canals

Avera

Acuma

Shoals

Shoals

Zica

Astur

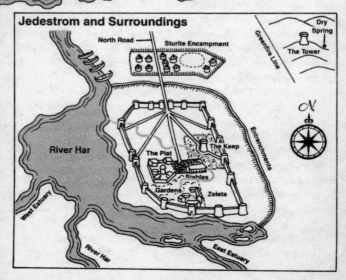

Jedestrom and Surroundings

North Road

Sturite Encampment

Greenfire Line

Dry Spring

The Tower

River Har

The Plat

The Keep

Entrenchments

N

Stables

Gardens

Zeleta

West Estuary

River Har

East Estuary

Chapter One

"We're nearly there. I can see the crest just ahead."

"Yes," Reawen agreed, following as the straight-backed older woman climbed nimbly over the face of a boulder. They had been scrambling up the side of the sacred mount all morning, yet Gris wasn't even breathing hard.

Then Reawen drew her own breath sharply. They had left the screen of trees and the thin silver ribbon of the waterfall behind. Now, together, they gazed down into a barren stone bowl, which looked as if a giant's thumb might have scooped it out of the mountain when the earth still sat cooling. Staring back at them from the base lay the bland blue eye of a lake.

"That's it," Gris muttered. "The pool of our mothers."

Reawen, her mind full of dread, awe, and longing, said nothing. Into those sacred, bottomless waters Nioma had vanished more than a decade before. Reawen knew that she would seek oblivion in them when her time came. But, for now, they were to be her testing ground.

"Come," said Gris as she began the descent over the sand-colored stone. "Since you are determined, we might as well get it over with."

Ignoring the sudden tremor in her legs, Reawen stiffened her spine and followed. Soon both women approached the bald lip of the rock surrounding the lake's consecrated waters. Gris knelt and made the required sign of obeisance while Reawen did the same. The two remained silent for a moment, taking in the eerie quiet of the place. Not even the wind disturbed its stillness.

"It waits," Gris explained unnecessarily, her gruff voice echoing off the stone walls. She looked up into the girl's shadowed eyes, and for a moment the old woman's gaze held uncertainty. Then her expression hardened. "Are you ready?"

Reawen swallowed, then nodded and bent her dark head, holding her long hair back so she could clearly see the water's opaque surface. Slowly, she dipped her arm until the waters covered her flesh to the elbow. Closing her eyes tight and locking her teeth, she waited. The sound of her pounding heart filled her ears. The minutes crawled by and nothing happened. Finally, Gris heaved a long sigh, and some of Reawen's tension eased. She opened her eyes and stared at Gris in wonder.

"It has not rejected you. You are in the true line of the domi." The older woman held up her own scarred hand and arm. "You can see what happened when I tried it. I failed the first test. For you it will be safe. You can begin now."

Containing the joy of her triumph, Reawen started with her earliest lessons. Scooping up a handful of water, she willed it to stillness. Though she opened her fingers, it remained a solid shape in her palm. With a smile on her delicate features, she gave it form—a flower, a leaf, a butterfly, a fluttering bird. Bringing her other hand up, she wove the water in glittering strands between her slim fingers, crafting a web. When the filaments were in place, she held her arms up and spread the web. Taut, it captured the sun's brilliance and threw it back in a thousand tiny prisms of color.

Her gray eyes concentrating on the brilliant hues, she repatterned the strands to form pictures. For Gris's amusement, she recreated the cave, almost a week's journey from here, where she and the older woman lived. She depicted scenes of woodland places they had traveled through, fires they had built, and finally the high silver waterfall guarding the rim of the bowl where the sacred pool lay hidden.

Gris nodded in satisfaction, smiling a little now as Reawen proved the ease of her mastery. The girl had learned well.

Reawen went on to other lessons. She formed the illusion of rain over the still surface of the lake and then produced waves.

Lifting her sculpted chin, she built the waves higher and higher until the lake took on the appearance and sounds of a storm-tossed ocean in miniature.

"That's enough," Gris said sharply.

Reawen looked up in surprise. The craft had absorbed her so completely that she had forgotten herself. She let her hands fall, and instantly the lake went as still and flat as before. Inquiringly, she studied Gris.

"The time has come to try the past and see for yourself how the power of the domi came to be lost." Gris dug a tarnished silver comb from her pocket and handed it to Reawen. "This was your mother's. You may recall her face well enough. Still, holding this will help."

Reawen accepted the comb and then looked thoughtfully down at the water's blank surface. Nioma's was not a face one forgot easily. The last time she had seen her mother, Reawen had been not quite four. Still, she remembered the domis of the Peninsula's inland water and her legendary beauty.

Reawen smoothed her free hand flat over the taut surface of the lake. It darkened, bulged slightly, and then a picture formed. It was Nioma, lying full length on the grass beside a stream, her body tangled with one whose golden curls were as bright as her own.

"That's him?" Reawen asked expressionlessly.

"Yes, that's Brone."

The girl cocked her head, studying the entwined couple. She could see them both clearly. Nioma lay flat on her back in the grass, her arms clasped around the youth's slim waist, laughing up as he bent over her. On her head glimmered a silver circlet set with a large, pale green stone.

"He's as beautiful as she," Reawen commented.

"Yes." Gris sighed restlessly. "It's what Nioma said. From the moment she saw him bathing in her favorite pool that cursed morning, she was besotted. She had never seen a man whose beauty equaled hers. They could be brother and sister, she used to say."

Reawen frowned and turned away from the scene on the surface. For most of her life, her mother's betrayal of the sacred trust had been the driving force of her own existence. "How long were they together?"

"A week."

"A week only? Can it have taken him only a week to destroy a power we have held for centuries?"

"No," Gris rasped. "Don't turn away from the image, Reawen. Watch it. You are here to learn."

Biting her lip, the girl swung her head. The couple on the grass had altered their position. The beautiful young man brushed his lips against Nioma's white neck and murmured something into her ear. Flushed, her lips parted with excitement, Nioma opened her eyes wide and laughed. Laughing still, she reached up with one bare arm and carelessly swept her silver circlet from her brow. In the next instant she had placed it on the young man's golden head. He smiled with satisfaction while she lay back to admire her handiwork.

Reawen's eyes narrowed. She thought she could detect a slight tensing of his shoulders, a barely perceptible curl of his mouth. But perhaps she only imagined these signs. Certainly, Nioma saw none of them. As the golden youth bent to kiss her, the welcoming smile on her face shone radiant and unshadowed.

Reawen shivered, and a knot tightened in her stomach. "How could she do it?" she burst out. Instantly the picture in the water darkened and vanished.

"You've broken your image," Gris accused furiously. "Retrieve it at once!"

Reawen lowered her eyes, inhaled deeply, and pushed the anger and hurt from her thoughts. Gradually, as Gris had taught, she restored herself to tranquility. When the core of her mind matched the stillness of the sacred lake, she passed her hand over the water. Again, the golden heads merged in a long kiss, the limbs twined in restless ardor.

"How?" Reawen asked quietly. "How could she?"

Gris sighed. "My sister was always careless, a creature of whim and caprice. But it was more than that. You must try to understand, Reawen, if you want to act on this vision. For if you refuse to see clearly, the knowledge you have gained here will weaken you, and believe me, you will need all your strength in this enterprise. Nioma's beauty was such that no man ever willingly walked away from her. She had many lovers. In the end, it was always she who tired of them, never the reverse."

"Even my father?"

"Even he," Gris confirmed.

"Will you not tell me something of him?"

"There's nothing to tell. He was but one of the crowd who worshipped her. Little wonder I can hardly remember him." The older woman shook her head. "Ah, but it was always so. How could one such as she imagine there existed a man her beauty couldn't enslave? When your mother gave the boy the green stone, she never dreamed he would betray her."

"It was she who betrayed her trust and my birthright," Reawen retorted angrily.

"Yes," Gris agreed. "But Nioma paid dearly for her error."

Reawen's gray gaze returned to the scene. The two bodies sprawled limply in the grass, apparently asleep. In the next moment, however, the youth rolled slowly away from the dreaming woman. Freeing himself from her arm, he surveyed her flushed face with a look somewhere between pity and scorn. Rising to his feet in one fluid movement, he brushed the loose bits of grass from his flesh and walked away. He took the circlet's green stone with him and did not turn back to look at the curving white body he had abandoned on the grass.

Reawen watched until he had disappeared behind the foliage, and then her considering gaze returned to her mother's face.

"She's so beautiful, so young there. It seems impossible, looking at her, that in a year's time she became an old woman seeking her death in this pool."

Gris shrugged and explained tonelessly, "Nioma gave away the stone. It was that which conferred youth on her, as it has upon all the water domi who came before her. Without it she withered like autumn fruit caught in winter winds. Lasting youth would be your destiny if you had the power of the stone. Without it, you will age as quickly as any mortal."

While the image faded, Reawen returned her gaze to Gris. The older woman hunched back on her heels, her graying hair straggling in loose bands around her bony shoulders. Her pale green eyes questioned Reawen's.

Summoning all her courage and determination, the young woman declared, "The stone is mine. Before the year is out, I will have it."

"It won't be easy."

"I know that."

Gris's gaze probed Reawen's. "You will require all your strength in this quest. For you may not have only Brone to deal with. He has a wizard, I'm told, a formidable student of magic who's counseled him for many years."

"It matters not who counsels him," Reawen answered simply. "I must claim my stone, for without it I will be denied my birthright as water domis."

Intently, Gris scrutinized her. "You must be very cool if you are to succeed."

Reawen's eyes looked back at her, clear as rain. "I will go to Brone's court in Jedestrom, and there I will be cool and quiet and dangerous. Before the year is out, the man who betrayed Nioma will be stripped of his power, and the green stone he stole will rest in my hands where it belongs."

* * * * *

A light tap sounded on the map room door. Turning away from the cabinet he'd been about to unlatch, Brone greeted the signal with a curt word. The heavy barrier, carved of finest lanken from the Peninsula's untamed north, swung open on silent hinges, revealing a coltish youth with straight brown hair cut long over prominent ears.

"Albin!" Brone's grim expression turned welcoming.

"You sent for me, Sire?"

"Indeed, I did. How long since you returned from your mission to the Gutaini?"

As he bowed low before his king, worship glowed from the youth's hazel eyes. "A week, Sire."

"Long enough to bathe away their scaly stink and to rest and refresh yourself. Not long enough to put on flesh, I see." The ruler's critical gaze roved Albin's gangly length. He laughed. "Well, no matter. You'll fill out soon enough, I expect. In the meantime, I have another task for you, a much more pleasant one."

"What is it you wish me to do, Sire?"

Brone dropped into a chair and stretched out his long legs which, like Albin's, were clad in dark hose. Over them, he wore a white silk tunic girdled at the hip by a gold band. The design on the band repeated his crest, a boy crushing four entwined snakes with his foot. Albin's tunic was of green wool. Only a serviceable knife embellished the plain leather belt he wore. But the king's distinctive crest had been embroidered in white on his sleeve.

"Killip has been badgering me for a reed player. None here at the Plat suits her. You know how fussy my mother can be in these matters." Brone rolled his eyes. "You are to search one out for her. Take all the time you need. But for my sanity's sake, bring back a musician skilled enough to suit my lady mother. That is, if such a wondrous creature should happen to abide on the Peninsula."

"I will do my best, Sire."

"I know you will, and right now I envy you."

At the startled expression that came over the boy's animated face, Brone chuckled ruefully. "Perhaps you envy me. But let me tell you, Albin, there are times when I would give my soul to be your age again. It's a wonderful thing to be young and free of care and to be setting off on just such a lighthearted venture as the one I have assigned you."

When Albin had bowed himself out, Brone's grave expression returned and, with a sigh, he stood. Lifting his hand, he brought his fingers to the golden band on his forehead and touched the weight he'd borne for the past fourteen years. One by one, his fingers found the four gems embedded in the precious band. First was the obsidian that had belonged to Driona, domis of the Peninsula's earth. It felt heavy, rich and unfathomable, like the lady herself. Next his fingertips crept to the simmering ruby that he'd wrested from Taunis. Appropriate to the Peninsula's domis of fire, the stone glowed with an unquenchable inner heat. Then Brone touched the cool white diamond that had empowered Eol, domis of wind. Finally, the ruler's hand found Nioma's emerald. As with Eol's gem, it felt cool and mysterious.

Sighing again, Brone let his exploring hand drop. Reluctantly, he turned his thoughts back to the task he had set for himself that morning. He went to a cabinet and withdrew a leather case. After opening it, he unwrapped a smoky glass disc and placed it on the table. He sat before the disc and slowly began to concentrate on the single point of light just at its center.

The glass fogged over, darkening to charcoal. The dizzying vertigo customary during these sessions seized Brone; he felt as though he might tumble into its murky depths. He tried to ignore the sensation, his eyes narrowing to indigo chips as they focused on the image materializing beyond the clouds within the disc.

When the image sharpened and filled the glass, a metallic

gray gaze returned Brone's level stare. "I wish to warn you of danger," Faring stated without preliminary.

Brone eyed the stony, lined features of the wizard's face. "What danger is this?"

"You have enemies, and they ally themselves against you," Faring snapped. "The land you've welded together with *my* aid"—he paused to emphasize the possessive—"is now ringed by threats. If you don't wish to be assassinated before the summer is out, you must tread with care. I know for a fact that the domi conspire to destroy you. The sooner you wed to make allies of the Sturites, the better."

Brone leaned forward. "Which of the domi conspire against me?"

"I sense a dangerous force moving toward Jedestrom, and you are its target. I cannot identify it as yet. But since Nioma is dead and Eol too capricious to be a menace, it must be either Taunis or Driona."

Brone shrugged. "That pair has plotted against me from the first, and their machinations have come to nothing."

"Even so, they are nothing to make light of. While they live, you aren't safe," Faring declared. "You should have followed my instructions and dispatched all four of the domi when you had the chance. Mark my words, someday you will pay for your careless chivalry."

"I did what I would with them. I took the sources of their strength and had some sport along the way."

"Sport," Faring hissed, his angular face darkening visibly. "You sported well enough with those two whores!"

Brone tilted his golden head and curiously studied the image in the reflector. Though Faring's tirades no longer intimidated him, the workings of his mentor's convoluted mind remained a puzzle. More than a dozen years earlier, something had moved the wizard to instigate the events that had catapulted the Peninsula into overwhelming change. But Brone could not guess what that something might have been.

Now he stared into Faring's angry eyes. "What would you have me do?"

"I would have you be alert for spies and traitors. The danger, of course, will be greatest during the time of your nuptial Choosing, when strangers flood Jedestrom."

Curtly, Brone agreed to heed his advisor's warning and watched as Faring's image faded from the reflector. After the glass had gone blank, Brone continued to sit before it, staring abstractedly at the polished surface of the table on which it rested. Like all the furniture in the Plat, it was fashioned from the rare hardwood, lanken.

Brone ran a finger over the black, even grain. Lanken was in high demand. Its export accounted in part for the dramatic rise in fortune the Peninsula's economy had enjoyed since he'd come to power. But it was the discovery of rich veins of wistite—an ore prized for the manufacture of weapons but relatively rare on the mainland—that had made the Peninsula more than a backwater in the affairs of the continent's motley assortment of quarreling nations.

Brone pushed back his chair and wrapped the reflector in its protective black velvet cloth before sliding it into the tight-fitting leather case. Closed, the container was glossy with age and deeply worn around the edges. It gave no hint of the value of the object it concealed. The king gazed thoughtfully down at it for a moment, weighing it in his hands and remembering how Faring had presented it. It had been the wizard's parting gift on the night he'd left Jedestrom to immure himself in Peneto, the stronghold of wizardry beyond the Peninsula's northern border.

He'd promised to continue to help and advise the young king from across the miles, and he had certainly kept his word. In the early years, Brone had been grateful for his teacher's frequent communications. But lately he'd been receiving them with less enthusiasm.

After stowing the case, Brone prowled toward the opposite

side of the room. A large map of the Peninsula and the lands surrounding it decorated the wall's buff surface. To the west, beyond the mountains, dwelled the Gutaini, a reptilian people with a rapacious history. To the east, the Chee, a city-state of wily merchant sailors famed for their cunning and their exotic tastes held sway. They traded in everything from the Peninsula's wood and metal ore to slave girls kidnapped from distant and mysterious lands.

Brone's eyes shifted to the central section of the map where black borders outlined Peneto. Then his considering gaze dropped to the curving shape of Sturite land that faced the Peninsula's southern coast.

On the map his kingdom looked like a small, defenseless animal caught in the jaws of a predator. It was ironic, Brone mused grimly, that until he'd stripped the domi of their power the Peninsula had been immune to outside threat. As a wilderness dominated by a quartet of violent and unruly demigods, it had offered little temptation to invaders.

Now the situation was vastly different. Under his progressive rule the Peninsula had grown rich—a tempting prize for its grasping neighbors and, consequently, a playground for spies. Now, according to Faring, one such spy, plotting his demise, moved toward Jedestrom with some plan of action. Who might this new intruder be, and where might he be lurking at this very moment? Brone's gaze roved the map, seeing only markings to indicate rivers, forests, valleys, and mountains. Nevertheless, his eyes narrowed before skipping over a patch of woods that lay some twenty leagues north of his capital city.

* * * * *

Between the roots of a willow that clasped the mossy bank of a brook, Reawen lay sleeping. On the pillow she'd made of her arm, she moved her head restlessly. Her dark brows puckered as if she sensed, even in her sleep, that she was being watched.

Turlip was watching her.

A few days earlier, the dirty little thief had slunk into a nearby village and begged a meal from an elderly widow. The old woman had taken pity on his ragged condition and given him what he asked. But that earned her no sympathy. While her back had been turned, he'd hit her over the head so hard she'd fallen to the floor and did not move again.

While she'd lain at his feet, dying, Turlip had stolen all the food he could carry, as well as her small stock of coin. When he'd tried taking one of her geese, however, the creatures had raised such a ruckus that several villagers had come running. They'd chased him into the woods, where he'd stayed, unde-tected, to eat the poor widow's meat pies before resuming his journey toward Jedestrom.

Turlip still feared a meeting with the rough village men. Even more, he feared a chance encounter with the king's guard. What if they questioned him and learned the truth about his mission here on the Peninsula? At the very thought, Turlip cringed.

But the thief's natural cruelty emerged like a freed cork when circumstances placed *him* in a position of power over another. He'd spied this pretty young girl lying alone and unprotected and had licked his lips at the thought of amusing himself with such a dainty prize. He pictured her naked beneath him, weeping with pain and terror, begging for mercy. The thought gave him intense pleasure.

"Oh, my, what a pretty little thing we have here," he whis-pered, drooling.

At the sound, the pillawn resting on a branch high above Reawen fluttered her wings and screeched a warning. It came too late. Turlip had stolen out of the shadows and, quick as a mongoose, seized the young woman's bare ankle.

With a gasp, Reawen opened her eyes and stared up into a snaggle-toothed leer.

"Oh, my, even prettier awake than asleep, and now she's

mine!" Turlip cackled and ran his grime-caked hand along Reawen's satiny calf.

"Take your hand off me!" Reawen cried and tried to yank free of his unwashed paw.

Turlip's evil grin only widened. "Now, now, missy, the jig's up. There's no one about but you and me to hear you yell."

Accustomed to silence from her long years living with Gris in the secluded forest, Reawen had no intention of screaming. However Turlip soon discovered that the pretty kitten he'd captured was actually a wildcat, lithe and strong. With one arm she swung at him fiercely, slamming him just behind the ear. He involuntarily loosened his grip a bit, and Reawen seized the opportunity to grab frantically for her traveling pack, which concealed her hand knife.

The thief recovered quickly though, and lunged after the girl, closing a hand solidly around her throat. Just then, a screeching fury descended from the skies and sank its razor-edged talons into the back of his neck.

"Yieeeee!" he howled, releasing Reawen to reach back and try to push off the winged tormentor busily shredding his flesh.

Instead of running off, as Turlip imagined that any self-respecting maiden ought, Reawen leaped up, seized her pack, and drew out her knife. "Peck out his eyes!" she cried to Cel, her attacking pillawn, as she advanced on the miscreant.

"Aieeee! Stop, stop!" he howled again more loudly. As he galloped off into the trees to escape the young woman and her blade, the avenging pillawn still clung to the back of his neck, pecking madly.

Finally Cel, having released her hold on the fleeing Turlip, fluttered back to her mistress. Reawen thought her companion's musical voice sounded quite agitated as the bird's question rang through her head. *Are you well?*

"I'm fine." Reawen brushed dirt and twigs from her plain woolen dress and combed fingers through her long dark hair.

"What about you?"

I'll be fine once I get the taste of that horrid fellow out of my mouth, Cel replied. As she settled onto her mistress's shoulder, she clicked her golden beak distastefully.

Reawen laughed. "He can't have been worse than those worms you sometimes peck up."

Oh, much worse! The worms are delicious by comparison.

Reawen stroked the bird's downy head and smiled into her grape-colored eyes. "That was a narrow escape. Thank you, Cel. You are the best pillawn in all the world."

Cel delicately nuzzled her young mistress's cheek. *Perhaps we should hurry away from this spot. That nasty fellow might come back.*

"You're right. Let us go."

While Cel fluttered above her, Reawen hoisted her pack and resumed her long trek. As she trudged through the forest on feet that were sore from the many miles she'd walked, she reflected on her journey. It had been longer than she'd ever conceived and a disturbing education. Reawen had discovered that all her years of living alone, with only Gris and Cel and the woodland animals for companions, had been no preparation for the world beyond the mountains.

She thought of the villages she'd passed through, the men and women she'd seen laboring in the fields, the bands of travelers on the roads. Most of the people she'd met had been surprisingly kind to her. Sensing something special about this slim, quiet, simply dressed girl, they'd offered her shelter and food. Some, however, hadn't been so nice. Once before in a lonely spot she'd been set upon by a tramp. Then, as now, Cel had come to her rescue.

Affectionately, Reawen glanced up into the morning sky at the pillawn. High above, she floated from tree to tree like a small white cloud. *How lonely and frightened I would have been on this long pilgrimage without my bird's company,* she thought. She smiled wryly, recalling Cel's fluttering insistence on coming along.

The morning wore into afternoon, and shadows lengthened.
Reawen paused now and then to pick berries and thought with
distaste of having to catch yet another fish for her supper. At
least here in the woods that option was open to her. What
would she do to sustain herself when she reached Jedestrom?
she wondered. With every day that brought her nearer the
king's capital, she grew increasingly nervous. She'd never seen a
city and had no idea what Jedestrom would be like. Would
there be rivers and trees? Regardless, her destiny was to go
there, find Brone, and come up with a way to recover the stone
he had seized with such cruel trickery.

Cel drifted down from the heights. She gave a little warning
trill in Reawen's ear and led the way toward a grove of maples.

Glancing about anxiously, Reawen followed with care. A
moment later she heard the snort of a grazing horse. Like a deer
scenting a hunter, Reawen froze and strained every sense.

Silently, Cel flew through the leaves to reconnoiter. When
she returned, her words whispered in the mind of her mistress.
*The horse's master is asleep on the grass. Come have a look. He appears
harmless enough.*

Reawen relaxed when she saw the boy. Cel was right; with
his long, straight brown hair and sprinkling of freckles, he
appeared harmless. Then she saw it, the band around his arm,
which she had learned to recognize in one of the villages. This
was a king's messenger.

Reawen's first impulse was to flee. But after a backward step
she reconsidered. Might not this chance meeting be fortuitous?
With a significant glance at Cel, Reawen stole forward. After a
moment's hesitation, she settled cross-legged on the grass
behind the boy's sleeping form and composed herself for the
mindtouch. She was not yet a true proficient at entering the
thoughts of another—it was not a natural domi talent, but an
acquired skill that Gris had only begun teaching her. Reawen
would not have dared attempt the mindtouch on anyone fully
awake, but she was skilled enough to unlock the messenger's

unguarded thoughts.

Eyes closed in concentration, she willed her mind to receive the thoughts of the slumbering boy. Beneath fuzzy layers of disjointed dream images, Reawen easily perceived the strong sense of purpose emanating from the messenger regarding his mission for the king. He's a dutiful one, Reawen thought, as she sifted through the wafting mental images. A few minutes later she opened her eyes and, after shooting a sparkling smile up at Cel—who'd perched on a branch to watch—headed for a creek that she'd passed a short way back to cut herself a choice reed.

* * * * *

When Albin began to hear the music, he was still dreaming of horses, swift steeds in many colors racing across a sea of meadow grass.

Earlier that day he'd begun to think he would have to return to Jedestrom empty-handed. For, though he'd traveled many miles and visited every village along the way, he'd found no reed player skilled enough to suit the needs of so demanding a lady as the queen mother.

Discouraged, Albin had stopped at this grove, tied his horse to a convenient tree limb, and fallen down on the grass to consider his problem. Without his realizing it, sleep had come, and he found himself running free with the colts in a sweet-scented meadow. He saw them pounding soundlessly across the open field, all different colors, their manes flying in the wind. Almost imperceptibly, a sound began to intrude into his dream. Sweet music played a counterpoint to their noiseless hooves.

Even as he slept, Albin's eyebrows drew together in concentration, and he struggled to hear the thread of melody that began to fill his mind like a promise. The phantom horses faded away, and he opened his eyes to stare dazedly up at the canopy of leaves shading his head. The music seemed to expand within him, rising and falling in a bittersweet song. A tremor passed down his spine, and he struggled to his elbows and looked around. His eyes widened.

A girl sat on a rock next to the stream that cut through the far end of the clearing. She wore a loose white shift of rough wool, and her long black hair hung straight to her waist. Her head was bent to her instrument and her face was turned away, so all he could see was the delicate outline of cheek and forehead. She played a reed with the effortless skill of an accomplished artist.

Entranced, Albin got up and walked toward her. He was unaware that two pairs of eyes watched closely. One pair, beautiful and amethyst-colored, belonged to Cel. The other, squinting balefully from behind a thick bush several yards distant, belonged to Turlip the thief.

Chapter Two

As Albin's horse, Grassears, clopped along a broad road, Reawen leaned forward and asked, "Why did you name your horse so strangely?"

Albin pointed to the tufts of hair sticking up from his animal's pointed ears and grinned lopsidedly. "Because he's like me. He always looks as if he just woke up after spending the night in a haystack."

Reawen had to chuckle, for what Albin said was exactly true. It had been two days since he'd introduced himself and asked her to go with him to Jedestrom. "I know the queen mother has only to hear you, and she will want you for her reed player," he'd pleaded.

As they journeyed, the two young people took a liking to each other. At least, Albin had certainly taken a liking to Reawen, though it seemed to him that since they'd met he had done nothing but answer her questions.

"Are there always so many travelers on the road to Jedestrom?" she asked after a cavalcade of merchants driving loaded mules straggled past.

"Oh, yes. People are always hurrying down to the capital to trade their goods. It's not just the wistite and lanken that they bring. The weekend markets are huge now, overflowing with stalls for every craft and food you can imagine. And some you can't," he added with a chuckle and a shake of his shaggy brown head.

A quartet of helmeted soldiers trotted the opposite way on horses far handsomer and swifter than Albin's furry-eared beast.

"Those weren't merchants!"

"Of course not! Those were part of the king's guard riding

forth on some mission or other." Albin shot a curious glance over his shoulder. How could this strange girl seem so wise and yet be so ignorant? From the moment Albin had wakened to the enchantment of her reed playing, he'd felt there was some deep and intriguing mystery about Reawen.

Far from clearing away that mystery, traveling with her had only deepened the riddle. Take her dress, he thought. Her rough wool shift was no better than a peasant's. Yet she bore herself like royalty. "Where did you say you came from?" he asked once again.

"From the north."

"It must be very far north indeed if you don't recognize the king's guard. They're everywhere these days."

"Why?" She leaned closer. "Does Brone send them out to punish his people?"

"Punish? Of course not!" Albin was indignant. "The guard roams the countryside to protect, not punish. What was the name of this northern village of yours?"

"No village. I was raised alone by my aunt."

"She must have been a hermit."

"Yes, I suppose she was. We kept to ourselves and saw few strangers, at any rate."

"That explains it," Albin declared. "No one who knows any-thing of the king and his ways would imagine him punishing his people."

Much to Albin's regret, Reawen drew back so he no longer felt her warmth against his spine. With her long, straight ebony hair and clear gray eyes, she was not beautiful in the way of the apple-cheeked, golden-haired maidens of his village. Yet he felt himself attracted to her. All day her scent had been in his nostrils, a cool, grassy fragrance that made him think of brooks and flower-edged woodland pools.

"You certainly are the king's loyal subject," Reawen remarked shortly.

"And so should you be—and everyone else!" Albin retorted.

"For myself, I've every reason to be loyal. I was a simple farmer's son, destined to spend my life milking cows and breaking my back behind a plow. Then, thanks be to kind fortune, King Brone saw me riding races at a fair and invited me to court to be his messenger."

"A great honor, no doubt."

"It *was* a great honor," Albin insisted, disliking her tone. "As for the Peninsula, only look around you," he continued with an expansive gesture at the busy road and lush, peaceful fields to either side. "Since King Brone took the power from the domi, he's brought his people ease and prosperity."

"But at what cost? He seized his power unlawfully."

"Unlawfully?" Albin snorted and swiveled his head to shoot Reawen a disgruntled look. "You wouldn't speak so if you weren't so young and hadn't been raised by a hermit."

She shot him an irritated look, thinking that she was probably older than the young messenger.

"Well," Albin returned, reading her expression, "then you should remember what it was like when the domi ruled. For farmers like my father, it was nothing but chaos and uncertainty. Those who neglected to appease Taunis and Nioma were punished with drought and fire and flood. For a whim, Eol amused himself by blowing newly planted fields to bits. And Driona!" Albin shook his head. "Lazy, slothful, unreliable! If you don't remember, then surely your aunt must have told you about the ways of the domi. Living in the north as you did, you might even have caught a glimpse of what I'm talking about. It's said what's left of the four are hiding in the mountains there, plotting to come down and wreak their havoc on us all over again should King Brone weaken."

Albin felt his passenger stiffen and draw back from him even farther, almost as if she resented his words. Was he doing the right thing by bringing her to the Plat? he wondered. "Listen to me and take my advice, Reawen. If you want to be the queen mother's reed player, you'd best not talk of the domi or say anything ill of the king. He's beloved by all his people, but doubly so at court, where he's worshipped almost like a god."

Reawen just glared at the back of Albin's head. Foolish boy! she wanted to shout. Your king is no god, nothing but a deceiver, a usurper, and a thief who needs to be punished for his crimes! But the words died in her throat, for at that moment they crested the top of a gentle rise. In the valley below she saw Jedestrom spread out before her.

"Oh!" she exclaimed.

The city's white buildings and blue tile roofs sparkled in the afternoon sun. Poised like chess pieces, tall copper-sheathed towers caught the light and sent it bouncing back into the cloudless sky. Between the roofs, narrow lanes and broad avenues rayed out from the main gate like the spines of a fan. Arrow-straight, they ran to the river Har, where wide bays girdled the metropolis on two sides.

"Beautiful, isn't it?" said Albin. "I have ridden up this hill a thousand times. Yet whenever I come upon this view, it's as if I'm seeing it for the first time." His heart rose into his throat as he gazed in wonderment upon his home city.

"It looks so clean and new."

"Jedestrom is clean and new," Albin answered proudly. "Before King Brone ruled, this was all hovels. After he took power, he knocked all that down and built it back up the way you see it now. Jedestrom is a testament to the new age of peace and prosperity our king brought to the Peninsula."

Reawen was too filled with confused emotions to answer. As Albin guided Grassears down toward the city, her legs tightened against the animal's warm flanks, and she looked around with wonder and apprehension. At every step the road seemed to thicken with new life. People of every description, and some beings who did not look human at all, crowded the teeming thoroughfare.

"Who are they?" she whispered when a group of grayish-skinned creatures jostled past. They wore only loincloths, and the gold, snake-shaped ornaments that wound up their scaly arms looked almost alive. Even as Reawen watched, she saw one of them kick a dog out of his path with careless cruelty. He hissed with satisfaction as it limped off, yelping.

"Those are Gutaini merchants. For sky's sake, Reawen, don't stare at them and draw their attention. They're all too easy to insult and have tempers shorter than a sneeze."

Inside Jedestrom the crowds doubled. Mule- and ox-drawn carts piled perilously high with vegetables, straw goods, pots, and woven mats vied for passage room with elegant, gilded vehicles pulled by liveried servants. Soldiers on horses and beggars on crutches rubbed armored knees and ragged elbows. A thousand voices shouted, cajoled, complained, called out bids, and hawked their wares. Soon Reawen's head began to ache with the noise and color and confusion of it all. Despite her earlier irritation with Albin's royalist opinions, she clung to his narrow waist tightly.

On the far side of Jedestrom, close to the river, lay the king's palace, a sprawling complex of low white buildings called the Plat. After Albin guided his horse within its gates and across its wide cobblestone courtyard, the noise and confusion of the city died away to a distant hum.

"The king will want to see you, of course, but for now I'll take you directly to your new home." Albin slipped down out of the saddle and caught Grassears's bridle. Then he looked up into Reawen's anxious eyes and smiled encouragement. "Don't look so worried. Everything will be all right. Her majesty is very kind, and you play like an angel. I'm sure when she hears you she'll want to keep you with her, and you'll have a fine home at the Zeleta."

"The Zeleta?"

Albin rolled his eyes. "I forgot, you don't know anything about anything. The Zeleta is the palace of Killip, the mother of King Brone."

"Doesn't the king want his mother in the same house with

him?" Reawen asked in wonder. Nearly all her life, she and Gris had lived together in a tiny cave. It seemed unimaginable that a mother and son should have separate houses when the houses were so huge.

Albin chuckled. "That's not it at all. King Brone and the queen mother are very close. In fact, he often goes to the Zeleta to take his meals with her. When he married, her majesty asked for a separate palace so she might establish her own court and give the newlyweds privacy."

"Brone has a wife, then?"

Sadly, Albin shook his head. "Three years ago Queen Leana died in childbirth. This spring our ruler will take a new bride in the Choosing."

Grassears stopped to nibble one of the wildflowers poking up between the tightly packed cobblestones, but Albin urged him forward. "Come on, you old four-legged gasmaker. Pib will give you plenty of good hay and oats in the stables." He glanced back at Reawen, and a grin lit his warm hazel eyes. "You'll like the Zeleta. I'll leave you with a friend of mine. Quista will take fine care of you. And when you're settled in, I'll come to visit you, so you needn't worry that you'll be lonely."

After a few paces, Albin, Reawen, and Grassears had disappeared around the corner of a building. Through a crack in the thick wall surrounding the Plat, Turlip watched. When he lost sight of his quarry, he grimaced. Scratching beneath his grimy shirt, he shot suspicious looks to either side of him before scuttling away toward the river. "We'll meet again, dearie," he muttered with sour breath. Like a skinny gray water rat, he vanished between the tall weeds that lined the shore, his small skiff hidden behind the greenery. "You just wait and see if we don't!"

* * * * *

Arant's bright red braids whipped, snakelike, and his thick shoulders gleamed with oil and sweat. "Do you yield?" he hissed as he slammed his opponent to the floor.

Small but defiant to the last, the pinned Chee glared up into the Sturite prince's feral green eyes. The young Chee knew there was no point in speaking, for he'd seen what had happened to the other men of his pod taken in the Sturite raid. Fodder for Arant's carefully orchestrated wrestling matches, every one of them.

"Not talking, eh? Well, we'll make that a permanent condition." Arant signaled a pair of muscular young slaves who, like him, were clad only in loincloths. They needed no further instruction, for they had been through this routine many times. Matter-of-factly, they stationed themselves on either side of the feisty prisoner's head and pinned his arms and shoulders to the floor.

A smile curled Arant's lips. He leaned back on his haunches and drew a wickedly sharp knife from the belt at his waist. Slowly, enjoying himself, he pressed its point to his victim's throat.

The Chee boy refused to close his dark eyes, but a glaze of resignation came into them. Already, in spirit, he was with his gods, the dog-headed Pronar and Detris, the sea mother.

Arant shoved the point into the boy's windpipe. A film of blood bubbled forth, but the Chee did not die. Under Arant's sweaty weight, the boy's chest went on heaving.

As he watched his prisoner's tortured features, Arant's cruel smile widened. "How does it feel to stare Death in the face and know you cannot avoid him?" he whispered. "How does it feel?" He leaned forward and sliced the boy's throat from ear to ear. "Meet him, Chee!"

Arant rose from the limp body. "Get rid of this garbage," he told the slaves briskly. Accepting a silken cloth from one of them, he swabbed at the blood staining his hands. Then, with no more than a brief glance at the audience of soldiers and other servants who'd been observing the unequal match, he tossed it away and strode from the gymnasium.

A twisted figure in a dusty black cloak glided after him. "You wished to speak with me this morning, my prince?"

With barely disguised contempt, Arant glanced down. "I did. Follow me into the steam baths where we can have some privacy."

Twenty minutes later Thropos, wizard to the Sturite court, huddled on a smooth wood bench, his lower parts wrapped only in a bulky towel. Stunted and hunchbacked, he had disrobed most unwillingly. But even he could not endure the heat of the baths in a wizard's robe.

Opposite Thropos, Arant lounged naked and very much at ease. He was a tall young man with an impressive barrel-chested physique. His blunt-featured face would be thought handsome by many. Arant certainly considered it so himself. He eyed Thropos's misshapen white body with disdain. Unshelled, what a miserable little insect this wizard turned out to be. Yet Arant knew he could not dismiss the wizard so lightly. For the twisted man possessed power—power that could be dangerous, but might also prove useful.

"You've not chosen sides about this proposed marriage between Brone and my sister. Now's the time to speak plainly. What think you?" Arant demanded.

Clutching his towel, Thropos shifted uncomfortably. "Yerbo is anxious to see it go forward."

"My father is old. Likely, he'll not live to endure the results of Fidacia's bedding by our smooth-tongued enemy."

"Your father's years persuade him to think about his country's future from a selfless perspective. He's weary of war and convinced that an alliance between Fidacia and Brone will bring peace and prosperity to both nations."

"More likely it will bring dishonor and disaster to the proud city of Zica."

Thropos put his fingertips together. "The marriage has

much to recommend it. Brone's kingdom has grown rich and powerful."

Arant pounded the side of the bench beneath him. "And will grow even more rich and powerful at my expense if this bad bargain goes forward. I'll not stand for it!"

Dispassionately, Thropos studied the violent young man opposite him. Recently, Brone had visited the Sturite court on a diplomatic mission. During his stay he'd publicly humiliated Arant by besting him in a wrestling match that had been Arant's idea. Now the Sturite prince regarded the Peninsula's ruler as a bitter rival. He wanted nothing more than to stamp him into the earth, as he had crushed all his other foes. But from what Thropos had seen of Brone, he judged that would not be easy. "Fidacia is agreeable to the union."

Arant sneered. "My sister is a silly child of eleven. What does she know beyond her dolls? She dotes on our aging father and will do whatever he tells her. No!" Vehemently, Arant shook his head, and again his braids whipped around his heavy head like scarlet vipers. He leaned forward, seized the wizard's wrist, and stared a challenge into his hooded eyes. "I'll cut her throat before I'll allow her to rear yellow-haired brats to challenge my power here in Zica. And you will help me."

"I am your father's loyal servant. I have been that from the day I came to Zica and he took me in."

"If you are wise, you will see that the time has come to switch your allegiance. Yerbo will be dead before long, and I will succeed him." Arant straightened. "Besides, if the rumors mean anything, you have good reason to hate Brone yourself."

"Rumors are rarely reliable. It's not Brone I hate."

"No, it's Faring, which is a sniff of the same ill fragrance. For as you and I know, Brone is nothing but Faring's puppet. It was Faring who taught him how to challenge the power of the domi. It's Faring who still pulls his strings. It was Faring who crippled you. Because of what he did, you couldn't go back to Peneto. Isn't that right?"

Thropos had gone rigid. His dark eyes burned within his pallid face, and the hand attached to the bony wrist that Arant still gripped had curled itself into a claw. "We had a disagreement, which resulted in my deformity. That much is true."

Releasing his hold on Thropos, Arant lounged back. "Well, little wizard, now is your chance to take revenge. Help me prevent this marriage. Destroy Brone, and you will rub his puppetmaster's nose in defeat. What say you?"

"I told you before, I owe my allegiance to your father."

"My father is a candidate for the grave. Give me your answer, wizard, and make it the right one, for I have you alone and naked in this place. Be warned that if what you say to me in the next few minutes fails to please, I'll make sure you never walk out of here on your own legs."

At that Thropos drew himself tight. "I may be naked, but I'm not without power, as you well know or you wouldn't be seeking me for an ally. Neither you nor anyone dares to lay a violent hand on Thropos!"

The two stared at each other, Arant's green gaze swimming with ferocity and resentment, Thropos's dark eyes hard and calculating.

It was Arant who looked away first. "I mean you no harm, wizard. I only seek your aid."

"Then show less arrogance when you sue for it."

Arant ground his teeth, but delivered no more threats. "What answer do you give me?"

"None yet. I must study the matter, for such a decision will have grave consequences. In the meantime, my hotheaded liege, try not to do anything foolish."

* * * * *

"Silver is your color, not gold." Quista surveyed her handiwork. "That silver girdle is a shade closer to your eyes, and the blue brings out the fine texture of your skin."

Before the tiny serving girl, Reawen stood in a gown of sky-colored linen caught at the shoulder with a silver clasp worked in a delicate flower design. Quista had drawn her dusky hair back with handsome silver combs and wound a silver girdle about her narrow waist. Even Reawen's feet were encased in silver-painted sandals.

"Now you are fit to entertain the king and his mother," Quista declared with satisfaction.

"The way you've fussed over me the whole afternoon, I should be fit to entertain a convocation of deities!" Reawen protested. She felt awkward in all her new finery and longed for the freedom of her woolen shift.

"You're not a peasant child wandering the countryside anymore. You're a royal musician and must look the part," Quista declared with a laugh.

"I was a lot more comfortable dressed as a peasant."

Vehemently, Quista shook her red-brown curls. "Listen to you talk. I know you're just nervous because the king is coming to have dinner with his mother tonight. You needn't worry. You've already pleased the queen mother with your reed playing, and that's what counts."

"Then it doesn't really matter whether her son approves of me or not?"

Quista patted Reawen's shoulder. "You needn't fear that her majesty will toss you out if the king doesn't like you. Why, even if King Brone thought you were a terrible musician, he'd defer to his mother, and she's accepted you into her household."

Reawen glanced down at her new finery. "Then why are you fussing over me as if you were going to try to sell me at a fair?"

"Only because the Choosing is coming up, and I wanted you to make a good impression," Quista said archly.

"The Choosing?" Reawen quirked a slim dark eyebrow at her new friend. "I still don't understand what you're talking about!"

"Bat's teeth! Reawen, sometimes you sound as if you spent your entire life in a cave. Surely you must know that later this summer the king will choose a bride."

"Yes, Albin said something about that."

"The Choosing is a ceremony where all the fairest maidens in our land—and from many other lands as well—vie for the honor of being the king's bride. Can't you see why it might behoove you to make a good impression on King Brone?" Quista winked suggestively.

"We're only servants here at the Zeleta. Surely you can't mean that he might choose one of us?"

"Life and hope ride the same donkey. That's how he singled out Leana, his first bride. She was just a village maiden with a buxom figure and a pretty face. If poor Leana hadn't died in childbirth, she'd be sitting on the throne next to him this very minute. Albin's all very well, but why should we girls settle for a bumpkin like him when there are bigger fish out there to be caught?"

"Now I really don't know what you're talking about," Reawen exclaimed. "What's Albin got to do with the Choosing?"

Quista shrugged. "Nothing, perhaps. Maybe it doesn't mean a thing that he's always finding excuses to come over here to the Zeleta so he can make moon eyes at you."

Reawen shifted from foot to foot. "Albin is just my friend, that's all. He doesn't make moon eyes. He tells me things. For instance, Albin told me that the king has already picked out a Sturite princess for his next bride."

"So the gossips whisper, but who knows what waits around the corner?" Quista darted forward to adjust the folds of Reawen's gown. "Ah, yes, now that's a better drape over your breasts. It never hurts to make a good impression."

* * * * *

That evening in the Zeleta's pretty pavilion, Brone and Killip sat enjoying a leisurely dinner. "You look tired," Killip said, leaning forward to touch her son's hand.

"There's been much to attend to."

"There's always much to attend to." Killip sighed. "It's not the business of court that makes you tired." She eyed the gold band around Brone's head. "The stones grow heavy."

"They were never light, Mother."

"No, but in the beginning you wore them much more easily." She shook her head, handsome and golden like her son's, though now the gold was threaded with white. "With every passing year the domi stones weigh you down more."

Casting his napkin on the table, Brone mocked her gently. "Surely it's not as bad as all that. I'm still a young man, not the dried-up ancient you make me sound."

A frown on her gently lined face, Killip gazed through the pavilion's lavender columns into the moon-frosted garden. She swept a hand in an all-encompassing gesture. "I wonder what your father would say if he could see all this."

Brone waited until the serving maid had removed their dishes. "He'd be proud of what we've accomplished, I hope."

"It's not *we* in the sense of you and me." Killip fluttered long fingers. "It's you and Faring who've made these changes. I fear that your father would not have liked Faring."

"Faring is not a particularly likable man."

"Strange and powerful, frightening even, but not likable. Oh, yes, you're quite right." Still frowning, Killip poured herbal tea into their thin cups. As she watched the fragrant steam rise from their gold rims, she murmured, "I remember the first day Faring appeared at our gates. Your father had just died, and I was so miserably lonely."

Killip fell silent, her soft blue eyes growing misty. Brone watched her, reliving that day himself. He had gone to Buw, the weapons master, for a lesson in the broadsword. But Buw had been too busy to attend him and sent him away. As he'd straggled back from the practice yard, the young Brone kicked at clods of dirt and mused unhappily that if only his father were still alive, Buw would have found an hour to spare.

"Your mother and her servants are struggling, lad," a deep voice had announced suddenly. "They haven't the time or the energy for you now. But I do. Take my hand, and you will learn more today of swordplay than you ever dreamed."

The boy's head had jerked up, and he stopped moving, as if his feet had suddenly petrified. At first the tall, thin figure standing before him had struck fear into his heart, for the man's long, dusty black cloak made Brone think of an enormous crow, or even a morcaw, that terrifying bird of death that sometimes circled the skies foretelling of evil times to come.

But then Brone's gaze had locked with Faring's, and he was lost. The wizard's penetrating gray eyes seemed to draw out his soul and read it like a page of freshly inked script. The king suspected now that Faring had snared him with a spell. But even without his magic, the wizard would have won him easily enough, Brone thought, returning to the present. After his father's death, Brone had been adrift. Faring had offered him a firm hand, a ready counsel, and, finally, a purpose that seemed heroic and noble.

"After your father's death, everything just fell apart," Killip was saying. "I didn't know how to be both father and mother to you, and so when Faring offered to take over your instruction, I agreed. Despite his austerity, he seemed knowledgeable. I never dreamed his teaching would lead you to conquer and dispossess the domi."

"Nor I. But he soon fired my ambition and set my steps on that path."

Killip set down her cup and gazed earnestly across the table. "Tell me truthfully, my son, do you ever regret what happened? Do you ever wish that man had never found our door and you had grown up to be only a tribal chieftain like your father before you?"

Brone took a moment to consider his answer. "Not when I see how happy and prosperous our people appear—then I have no regrets. Yet I will admit, there are times, moments late at night when the waking world is a distant dream. I look up at the indifferent stars and feel my burdens clamping down on me like an iron fist, squeezing the very life out of me. At those times, I would give much to return to that day when Faring appeared at our gate, so I might set the dogs on him and never again see his cold face."

When the words were out of his mouth, Brone regretted that he'd spoken so openly. He had no wish to worry his mother. To lighten the gravity, he plucked a pink rose from a bush growing nearby and presented it to her with a flourish. "Why do we spoil our excellent meal by speaking of such matters? Have you forgotten that you lured me here with the promise of special entertainment?"

"Oh, yes, indeed!" Brightening, Killip signaled a servant. "You've yet to hear the wonderful reed player that your Albin brought me. She's a delight. I'm most grateful to you for sending the lad out to find her for me. Ah, here she is!"

Brone turned his head in time to see a slim girl glide forward out of the shadows.

"Her name is Reawen," his mother informed him. "Isn't she lovely?"

"Indeed she is," Brone agreed, studying the girl. "Very lovely."

Reawen, her gaze fixed on Killip's son, emerged from the dark corridor where Quista had stationed her. It was one thing to see Brone in the water images, quite another to see him like this. So this was the man who had ruined her mother and stolen her birthright, she thought. This was the man she must somehow vanquish.

Usurper though he was, Reawen had to admit he bore himself like a king. This tall, commanding man with brawny shoulders and legs like the trunks of young oaks looked nothing like the pretty, soft-skinned boy who'd tricked Nioma. His face was heavier, his jaw squarer. Deep lines grooved his forehead and ran from nose to mouth. The stones were never meant to be worn by a human, Reawen thought with a twinge of satisfaction. They are sucking at his strength, making him old before his time.

Her gaze lifted to the band around his head and fixed on the four jewels decorating it. Her eyes sought the green stone, and her heart constricted. She could feel it calling to her. Was it a trick of her mind, or did it brighten and wink seductively? Reawen's hand tightened on her reed, and as she lifted it to her lips she renewed her vow. Soon, soon, the green stone would be hers.

Chapter Three

In the tallest tower room of the Sturite castle, in a well-worn chair specially carved to accommodate his twisted back, Thropos sat still as stone. Through his one dusty window a thin finger of sunlight struggled to illuminate the crowded bookshelves lining his walls. They contained volumes on every subject from asps to zerkchane, a subtle poison made from ingredients found only in selected swamps.

Above Thropos's head hung dried herbs: mugwort and valerian, comfrey and stinking hellebore, oak galls and liverwort. At his side, beakers, vials, measuring instruments, and a tellingly empty cage littered a table. Stacked in corners were many other cages. They came in a variety of sizes and were made of different materials. Some were metal, while others had been carved from wood or woven out of reeds. All were filled with the small, hapless animals upon which Thropos liked to experiment.

Occasionally one of the imprisoned creatures would whimper or mew. Thropos paid no mind. He'd centered all of his attention on the ragged, filthy, unshaven specimen huddled at his feet. It was Turlip the thief.

At last there came a lull in Turlip's whining recitation, and Thropos spoke. "So, Taunis has heard of Arant's discontent and seeks an alliance against Brone." The little wizard tapped his sharp chin with the point of his forefinger. His fingernails were almost as black as Turlip's, for, though Thropos could weave the most exacting spells, he rarely wasted effort on the mundane details of personal hygiene.

"This is interesting—very interesting. Even more fascinating is this tale you bring me of a girl with a pillawn."

"Pillawn?" Turlip scowled, never having heard the term before. "It was a monstrous white bird with eyes the color of ripe plums and cruel, sharp yellow claws. And it talked, I tell you, I could hear its bird voice in me head! After it ripped me poor back to shreds, it flew back to this girl and bragged of its evil doings."

"A pillawn," Thropos mused aloud. "They're rare creatures, virtually extinct and generally regarded as mythical. The story goes that, eons past, earthtenders bred them to be the companions of the demigods—the domi."

"Earthtenders? Never heard of 'em."

Scorn flickered in Thropos's hooded eyes. "Perhaps you should consider broadening your education."

"Stick me nose into a book, you mean?" Turlip snorted. "Now what good will that do me when I can't read?"

"True." Thropos sighed. "Let me add to your lamentably tiny store of knowledge, then. We know little of the early days of this world we live in, for those who made it left no records. Still, stories come down, stories of benevolent creatures who cared for the young world, tended it as if it were their private garden. For want of a better name, we call them earthtenders. The earthtenders disappeared long since, and nowadays precious few domi walk their preserve. Tell me more of this girl, Turlip."

Careful to cast himself in the best possible light, Turlip described his encounter with Reawen. He ended his story with what he had seen of her first meeting with Albin.

"Must be I followed those two for fifty leagues," he exaggerated. "Warn't easy stealin' rides on farmers' carts, and sometimes there was none to be had. Me poor feet in bloody rags, me belly empty, and me back achin', I trailed 'em through the city and right to the very gates of King Brone's Plat. I did it at the risk of being hanged if'n the guard what roams so cursed free these days should catch sight of me."

"Thieves who cannot resist lifting purses in Jedestrom

should take care to do a better job of bashing in their victims' brains. That way they wouldn't be able to give incriminating descriptions," Thropos murmured distractedly. He pushed himself up out of his chair, stepped over Turlip, and wandered to the jumble of cages stacked in the corner. As he peered into the topmost one, the baby clodle inside it gave a terrified squeak and huddled against the back bars, shivering.

Thropos smiled thinly. "When next you have business in the city, I'll provide you with a disguise. That way you needn't fear Brone's guard will haul you before a magistrate and hang you for villainy. Now, have you the slightest idea what this Reawen's purpose was in going to the Plat?"

"To be the queen mother's reed player. That I heard the first night, when young missy and the boy was sittin' around the campfire roastin' a rabbit and talkin'. While they was eatin' good, I was holed up in a prickly laurel bush, practically starvin'." Turlip, who'd shifted around to keep an eye on his master, scratched his crotch and then his wart-covered nose. "I ain't had a decent meal since, neither."

Ignoring this unsubtle hint, Thropos turned to gaze at his spy reflectively. "According to your story, they spent two days on the road. During this time, did the girl show the king's messenger her pillawn?"

Turlip shook his head so emphatically that a shower of greasy dandruff rained down from his scanty locks. "Never. The whole way down to Jedestrom, the bird hid high in the trees. I had to be sneakier than a green snake not to be spotted by it, I did. It never noticed me," Turlip added proudly.

"Commendable." Thropos's clever dark eyes glowed like banked coals flickering red behind a layer of ash. "So this girl is now housed in the Plat, close to Brone. And she has a pillawn for a pet. Interesting, most interesting."

He slid a hand into his black cloak, drew out a small leather bag of coins, and tossed it at his informer. The bag had not been tightly closed, and some of the coins scattered on the floor. While Turlip scrambled to gather them up, Thropos watched in sly amusement and talked at the back of the little thief's scabrous head. "I want you to go back to Jedestrom and keep an eye on this young lady of yours. Oh, and tell Taunis that I will meet with him. I wonder if our fiery friend might be able to shed some light on the identity of this mysterious Reawen. I shouldn't wonder if he could. To make communication between us easier and faster, I shall give you a spell that will summon me."

Turlip glanced back over his shoulder. "You mean magic that will take you from here all the way to the Peninsula?"

"That's exactly what I mean."

Turlip, still scuttling crablike on his knees, didn't get the chance to reply. The door to the tower room crashed open and Yerbo, the Sturite king, strode in.

Once a brawny warrior with a full beard of wiry red curls, he was now gaunt and gray. His leather tunic hung loosely over his shriveled belly, and his shoulders hunched forward as he walked. Nevertheless, with his eyes—cat-green like those of his two children—blazing fury, he still presented an impressive figure.

"Tell me what you know of my hotheaded fool of a son's doings!"

Thropos blinked. "I know nothing of the prince's activities. What's happened, my liege?"

Yerbo made to lunge forward, but his leg, weakened by an old injury, failed him. He staggered and then, with a frustrated groan, leaned heavily on his wizard's littered experiment table. "It's a contest to see which will kill me first, my years or my damnable offspring. When I'm not trying to tame Fidacia of her headstrong ways, I'm having to deal with my son's stupid atrocities. I've just received word that Arant has confiscated a trio of warships and sailed off with his followers for gods-only-know-where to do gods-only-know-what mischief."

* * * * *

Long before the first light of dawn, Reawen knew sleep had
fled and would not be coaxed back. She slipped out of her bed
and stood in her short shift, looking at the river through her
open window. It glimmered beyond the furred outlines of the
trees, a distant brightness. Its cool breeze fanned her cheek, and
with her sensitive ears she could hear its lapping, feel its currents flowing through her veins in the familiar, rhythmic
summons.

After padding across the room, she gathered her long gown
from a stool and slipped it over her head. Then she reached for
her short knife. In the corner Cel slept, her head buried in a
folded wing. Though Cel flew away to hide during the day, she
always floated into Reawen's room at dusk to spend the night
with her young mistress. Smiling gently, Reawen decided
against disturbing her pet and tiptoed past.

Outside, velvet darkness cloaked the garden, and the fragrance of the dew-wet grass saturated the night. Only a faint
gray streak over the tallest trees warned of dawn's approach.

Purposefully, Reawen made her way to a special place she
had found, a Y in the tributary fronting the Zeleta. It had a
neglected bend thickly screened by an unclipped hedge so
passers-by could not see it from any of the buildings or adjoining garden paths.

On the other side of the hedge, Reawen shed her long over-
gown and left it in a heap at the water's edge. Her shift reached
to just below her thighs. She would have liked to remove that
also, but feared some fisherman might spy her from the opposite bank, though at this hour such a thing was unlikely.

All her senses on the alert, Reawen stepped noiselessly into
the river and breathed deeply. She reveled in the river's tranquility, the silky slide of the water over her flesh. Last night,
Brone and the nearness of the green stone he had worn had
upset her. To be so close and yet unable to reach out and claim

it, to have to entertain the one who had stolen it and now held it prisoner—

Already, I have been too long among these people, Reawen told herself. Though she liked the queen mother and Quista well enough, the Zeleta's dull routines filled her with impatience. How can these women stand such confinement? she wondered. Their sheltered way of life bored her. It fogged her brain just when she needed it clear and sharp to formulate a plan of action. To her dismay, since her arrival in Jedestrom, she'd been able to think of none.

Glorying in freedom and activity, Reawen swam out through the deep part of the river to a muddy delta where the reeds grew thickly. Here, partially screened, she slid her hands along the surface of the water. As if it had been awaiting her summons, a shimmering liquid ball leaped forth and came to rest in her palms. "Ah," Reawen murmured with a long, happy sigh.

She could not remember her first lesson in watercraft, for Gris had begun her training when she was very tiny. Every morning the old woman had led her to the stream that bubbled outside their cave. There they had worked on the craft. Even as a small child, Reawen had not minded the long hours of instruction, for once she'd dipped her hands in the cool clearness, she'd felt she was home.

"The waters of the Peninsula are part of you," Gris had crooned, "part of your body, part of your blood. They call to you, and you call to them."

"But this is only a tiny stream in the woods," Reawen had objected one day when she'd felt fretful. "I've never seen the waters of the Peninsula. I've never seen a river or the ocean it flows to."

"It matters not," Gris countered. "This stream is like a vein in the body of our land. Once you have dipped your hand in its water and shaped it to your will, you have comprehended the whole. And it will have comprehended you. Always remember that. You will be domis of water, and the domi are owned by their elements as surely as they are their masters."

Reawen had understood Gris's meaning, for she had learned early that she could not be away from the craft for long. Tensions would coil inside her. Their tight knot could only be eased by the weaving of water between her fingers. Now she smiled down as her hands shaped webs, and she felt some of the constriction in her chest loosen.

When Reawen grew tired of holding webs up to the light to admire the rainbow colors trapped in their prisms, she began to create more complex forms. Transparent butterflies and elaborately finned fish sprang from her fingers, then many-pointed stars and crystals with a hundred glittering sides. She amused herself by sending these skittering along the river's surface to explode in high showers of glistening spray.

Pink and gold streaks feathered the sky, and birds commenced twittering from the dark foliage on shore. Reawen caught a flash of white and smiled. Cel had followed her after all.

The pillawn lit on a willow branch overhanging the water and gazed disapprovingly at her mistress. *My great-grandmother used to say, "Robins trying to pass as wrens should keep their breasts hidden."*

"All right, all right. I'll get back before anyone notices me."

You had best do exactly that. What if the king saw you weaving water? He comes here sometimes, when he's had a restless night.

"Does that happen often?" Reawen asked, much interested.

Often enough. He's troubled, that one.

"Good. He deserves to be."

Cel cocked her head. *Last night for the first time you saw mother and son together. Did you not think them a handsome pair?*

Reawen trailed her fingers in the river. "I've already made my mind up about the queen mother. I like her. She's a fine lady, though indolent and spoiled. Brone I could never like, no matter how handsome his looks."

He liked you. I watched his face while you played. His eyes lit.

"You're imagining things."

Human faces leave very little to the imagination. For instance, right now you are blushing. Clucking softly, Cel flew to the top of a tall tree, where she settled to preen her feathers.

Reawen stood waist-high in the water, scowling up at her. "I'm not human."

Until you have your stone, you are all too human. You are as weak and vulnerable as the least of them.

"I gather you have no very good opinion of humans."

On the contrary. Given the shortness of their lives and the frailty of their natures, I hold their accomplishments in high respect.

"Is that really true?"

Of course. I have never lied in all my life, and I have lived a very long time, Cel retorted softly. *For that very reason, I'd like to see you gain your stone. The bounty of power and years it will confer on you is infinitely preferable to the sad lot of a human.*

Troubled, Reawen unfolded her knife and turned away to search through the stand of reeds. If she was going to be here a while, she would need more than one reed—and a hastily constructed one, at that. Selecting reeds, however, was a tricky business. Reawen's requirements were exact, so it took almost an hour to locate stalks straight and unblemished enough to serve. By the time she had cut a half dozen and bound them together, the sky had cleared, and the sun peered over the horizon. She was about to swim back to shore with her bundle when a tingling along her spine told her she wasn't alone.

She leaned close to the water so the curtain of her loose hair fell past her bent arms and around her waist. When it hid her hands from whoever watched, she moved her free palm over the river's surface until a picture formed. It was Brone. He stood alone by her discarded clothes, gazing in her direction. A grin inched across his mouth. Swiftly, he unlaced his shirt, pulled it over his head, and dropped it next to her gown. Before stepping into the river, he casually removed the gold band from his forehead and set it down on the pile of clothing.

Reawen's heart flapped like a captured bird. How could the usurper be so careless of his stolen treasure? She did not have long to reflect, for Brone was stroking rapidly in her direction. The opportunity was so perfect, she almost fainted with excitement.

As the king's arm reached out toward her, Reawen swung sharply and sent up a stinging spray to blind and confuse him. Slipping past his grasping hands, she cut through the water like a quicksilver arrow. She was in her element. No human could outswim her. In a moment she gained the shore and darted toward the pile of clothes, her eyes fixed on the crown. Force would not take the stone, but perhaps it could be found.

In her haste, Reawen misplaced a foot and slid on the mud. Even as she tumbled, her hand reached and her fingers closed around the metal band. "Eieee!" she yelped, for in the confusion she had touched the red gem and the contact seared through her arm like a bolt of lightning. The next instant a steely hand flipped her over. She lay gasping on her back, staring up in alarm at Brone.

"Are you all right?"

Reawen opened her mouth and then shut it again.

"Let me see your hand." The king took it in his, spread the fingers wide and examined the angry red stain spreading across her palm. "I'm sorry. If you're left with a scar, it will be through my carelessness. I should never have dropped my crown where you might touch it trying to get your gown. But—" Brone cocked his head, loosening some of the drops of water in his gilded hair and sending them raining down on her—"I had no idea you could swim so fast. I've never seen a girl flash through the water like that. You swim like a damn fish."

Reawen goggled, wide-eyed with incredulity. Did he really believe that she had touched his crown accidentally? What a blind fool he must be! "It burned me."

"There's a binding on it. No one may touch the crown but me. You're lucky it didn't do even more damage." He favored her with a sudden smile that smoothed away the harsh lines of his mouth and set his blue eyes dancing. "I can make the pain go away. There's a healing ointment. I'll have it sent around to you."

"Thank you." Reawen tried to withdraw her hand from his, but his fingers tightened.

"I can't let any harm come to Killip's divine new reed player. My mother would snap my head off."

"I'm sure she would never do that. You—you flatter me."

"Not at all. Last night your skill beguiled me. So," he added, eyeing her appreciatively, "did your beauty."

Reawen became conscious of her near nakedness, the way her wet shift clung to her body. "I must dress now and return to the Zeleta."

"It's still early. Excepting the gardeners and cooks, you and I are probably the only ones awake. Do you make it a habit to come to the river before dawn?"

"No, I only came this morning to cut reed for instruments." Again she tugged at her hand, and again he retained it.

"You could do that any time of day. Why so early?"

Reawen's gaze drifted to his crown, which still lay next to her, tantalizingly near. "I—I couldn't sleep."

"Nor I. All night I tossed on my bed, unable to close my eyes. Can you guess why?"

"A king must have many affairs of state that trouble him."

Brone laughed, and even Reawen would have admitted that his laughter had charm, though it was wasted on her. "Indeed I do. They were not what troubled me last night. No, my pretty child, what troubled me last night was you."

"Me?"

Brone's blue gaze caressed her. "As you must know, my wife died years ago. Though I have taken a mistress or two for ease, the truth is, since Leana's passing, I have not really wanted a woman. The sight of you last night changed that, for you are very lovely, my dear." He reached out to let his forefinger glide softly down her cheek. "You are like the white roses that grow in my mother's garden. I have always had a weakness for white roses. Will you come to me tonight?"

Like a fascinated bird, Reawen stared at him. She knew what he was asking, but could hardly credit it. "I am your mother's servant."

"I know, but perhaps she will share you with me. If you come to me, Reawen, I will be good to you. You will never again know want. Your life will be one of pleasure and ease. I give you a king's word on that."

"Soon you are to choose another for your wife."

He shrugged that off. "I don't speak of marriage here. Surely you are not too young to understand my meaning. Marriage for one of my station is a matter of politics. But though it is hard to be a king, there are advantages. One of them is that, so long as he is discreet, a king may love and bed where he chooses. I would choose you, Reawen. What is your answer?"

His confidence in her glad agreement was plain to see. Perhaps if she'd been what she pretended, a simple village girl with a gift for music, she might have leapt at the chance to be such a handsome king's trifle. No doubt any other unmarried woman at court would have, and perhaps even some who already had husbands. But I am no simple human maiden, Reawen thought proudly. I am the last of a long and noble line of water domi. I would scorn to have this thief, who seduced and betrayed my mother, lay his hands upon me.

Sharply, Reawen tugged her fingers from his. Grabbing her gown, she scrambled to her feet. "I am too young to be anyone's concubine," she declared, and then fled through the hedge, leaving Brone to stare after her in astonishment.

Several minutes passed before the king roused himself from his amazement. As he donned his shirt and slipped his crown back over his head, he contemplated Reawen's surprising rejection. It wasn't that he was vain. It was just that he'd never experienced failure with a woman. Since he'd become king the problem had been with refusing them, not luring them to him. The minute he'd seen his mother's lissome reed player, Brone had found her attractive. However, since she was Killip's, he'd had to wrestle with his sense of propriety. Coming across her in the river this morning, with her wet shift clinging to her slim young body, had settled that issue. Killip's or not, he wanted her.

As Brone strode back toward his quarters, he puzzled over Reawen's rebuff. Like the girl herself, it intrigued him.

The band around his head came alive with energy and wiped the issue from his mind. At the familiar signal from Faring, Brone hastened his step. Back in his rooms, the king withdrew the reflector from its case and, clearing his mind of all else, sat down before it to consult.

The clouds within the disc parted, and Faring's face gazed out. A deep scowl puckered the wizard's brow. "Why have you taken so long to answer my call?"

"I was bathing down by the river. What is it? What's wrong?"

"You're under attack," Faring replied crisply. "I have seen Acuma. The city is in flames!"

* * * * *

That night, Reawen stalked the length of her room, checked and then retraced her steps.

Why do you pace back and forth like a trapped griffon? Cel inquired. *Hasn't the salve the king sent you soothed your hand?*

"Yes, the burn's all but gone."

Then quiet yourself. You're making me dizzy.

Reawen glanced at her pet. Cel perched on top of a tall wardrobe. From the fluffy depths of her folded wings, her amethyst eyes peeped out at Reawen humorously.

"I'm anxious," Reawen said.

Obviously.

"You were right to remind me of how weak I am without my stone. Since I've been here at the Zeleta, I've done nothing constructive to regain it. Somehow I have to make a plan, but what, what?" Reawen wrung her hands.

When you turned down Brone's invitation to become his mistress, you threw away the perfect opportunity. My uncle was a thousand years old and steeped in wisdom when he said a clever woman who nests with a besotted male can take anything of his that she wishes.

Reawen glared. "I couldn't do that. Have you forgotten what he did to my mother?"

He took the green stone from her. Avenge her by taking it back in the same fashion.

"He made love with her. Knowing that, having seen the image, I couldn't let him do the same with me!"

Why not? Cel inquired mildly. *It isn't as if Nioma didn't sleep with anyone she fancied.*

"I don't fancy Brone, I hate him. Besides, I am not like my mother." Head down, Reawen resumed her tigerish pacing.

Are you afraid of losing your virginity?

"No, of course not. Domi do not fear such things."

You are no domis yet, my girl. Far from it. Right now you are just a frightened child crying at the moon.

"Maybe, but when I have my stone, things will be different."

If you want your domi stone badly enough, you will be sensible and take Brone up on his offer. Besides, you're no longer a child. Time to stop being so squeamish and learn how to handle the opposite sex.

"Never, if sleeping with my mother's false lover is where I have to start! There's another way, there must be." Reawen shot the pillawn a sharp look. "You spend the days all about the royal gardens. Have you picked up any bit of information that might help me?"

Cel lifted her wings, then dropped them. *There was some sort of commotion early this morning, but I never learned what it was about.*

"Pillawns are supposed to be mythical creatures, you know. I hope you keep yourself well hidden."

I do. Cel grew haughty. *Even if one of the gardeners should catch a glimpse of me, he'd never believe his eyes. Humans are too unimaginative to see anything except what they've decided is real.*

Reawen sighed and turned to the door. "Being cooped up in this place has filled my brain with cobwebs. I must get some fresh air. Will you come with me out to the garden?"

Not I. Cel settled more deeply into her thick feathers. *There are too many owls about at night, and they care nothing for myths.*

Outside, the evening breeze lifted a tendril of Reawen's hair and cooled her cheek. The full moon cast a silver radiance over the curving hedges and raked stone paths around the Zeleta. As Reawen paced along she inhaled the sweetness of the ever-blooming roses that lined the path. Yet, their scent didn't calm her. She thought of how Brone had compared her to a white rose, and she quickened her step. Since he'd surprised her down by the river she'd been jumpy, irritable, constantly wracking her brain for a solution to her problem.

"Psssssst!"

Reawen jumped.

"Don't be afraid, it's only me!" A lanky figure slipped out from behind a tall yew and shot her a mischievous grin.

"Albin!"

"Shhhh! I'm not supposed to be here at this hour, you know, except on official business."

Very glad to see him, Reawen lowered her voice. "I thought you were out of town on a mission."

"I was. I just got back this morning."

Reawen pretended to pout. "Then why didn't you come to see me earlier?"

"I wanted to," Albin said seriously. He gazed at her warmly. "All the time I was away, you were in my thoughts. I kept wondering how you were getting on here. Tell me now, how are things with you?"

"Oh, fine." Reawen knew she couldn't tell Albin about Brone's disturbing offer. "The queen mother has been as kind as ever, and I like Quista more and more every day. It's only that I'm still a stranger here, and sometimes I get lonely."

"Of course you do." Albin came forward. "Would you like to sit a moment?" he asked, pointing to a stone bench.

Reawen nodded, and, after they'd both folded themselves down, Albin asked, "Did you think of me while I was gone?"

"Of course. You're the best friend I have in Jedestrom, and I wondered what you were doing, who you were seeing. Now that you're back," she added brightly, "you'll come visit me and tell me all the gossip, won't you?"

Soberly, Albin shook his head. "This very night I must be off again, Reawen. That's why I took a chance on sneaking over here. I wanted to see how you were and say good-bye."

"But why must you leave so soon? Has something happened?"

"Acuma's been attacked."

"Acuma?"

"You know, the port city to the south."

Reawen had only a vague idea of that part of the Peninsula's geography. Nevertheless, she nodded sagely. "Oh, yes. Attacked? By whom?"

"The rumors say Sturite renegades. Early this morning the king learned of it and rode south with a fighting force. I'm to deliver some maps to him."

Reawen straightened and clasped her hands in front of her. If a battle were to rage in this Acuma and Brone were in the thick of it, his crown might be lost. What if her stone were lost with it? "Oh, Albin, take me with you!"

"What?" Albin looked aghast.

"Take me with you. I promise I won't be any trouble."

"You're a girl, Reawen!"

"Well, of course I'm a girl. What has that got to do with anything?"

"I'll be on a king's mission, traveling fast. I can't be responsible for a girl in a war zone. There'll be refugees, soldiers, maybe even enemy soldiers. Besides, you have to stay here. Now that you've accepted service with Killip, you can't run away!" Albin looked outraged at the very idea.

"I'm a servant, Albin, not a slave. I came here willingly, and I can leave in the same fashion."

"Not when I went to so much trouble to find you and the queen is so pleased with you. Besides, where else would a friendless girl like you find such a good home?"

"There are more important things than a good home. It's boring here. Every day is like the next, and I feel confined."

Albin stared at her as if she were out of her mind. "Boring? But you have every luxury. Look how fine that silk dress is. You've even got silver combs in your hair. Reawen, what is it that you expect from life?"

She could see that Albin would never understand. Nevertheless, she went on imploring him. She put forth every argument she could think of except the real one—that she wanted to be near Brone's crown in hopes that some accident might throw it in her path. Or, at the very least, so she could see that no one else got it.

Albin said no to everything. Finally, angered by her persistence, he stalked off without ever saying the good-bye he'd come to deliver in the first place.

Alone, Reawen sat fuming, twisting her fingers and scowling at the moon. Then, with an oath, she got up and hurried to her room. A few minutes later she came out again trailed by Cel. The two flitted through the garden to the washhouse where all the Plat's laundry was done. There Reawen filched a messenger's tunic and a pair of hose like the ones Albin wore. After she'd changed into this outfit, she tucked her long hair under a cap and made her way to the stables. She arrived just in time to see Albin ride out.

You don't know the way to Acuma, Cel whispered in her

mistress's mind as they watched him and Grassears cross the courtyard. *How do you propose to follow the pesky lad without his noticing?*

"I'm not going to follow him, you are," Reawen answered. "Whenever he takes a turn in the road, you'll tell me. That way I'll be able to stay far enough at his back that he won't see me, and yet I won't get lost. Now, be off, while I go pick out a gentle horse."

Chapter Four

Acuma, which sat at the closest point across the strait from Sturite land, presented a tempting target for pirates. Indeed, it was the aggression of the seafaring Sturites that made the most compelling argument for Brone's marrying Fidacia. The union would, Faring contended, make her people allies rather than foes. The warlike Sturites would strengthen Brone to face the enemies hovering around the Peninsula from the north.

A raid by Fidacia's countrymen when Brone's engagement to their princess was all but announced—that was a bad omen. As Grassears jogged over the rapidly flattening terrain that dropped toward the sea, Albin puzzled over the meaning of the attack.

When Brone's secretary had instructed Albin to leave for Acuma, he'd called the marauders "Sturite renegades." Who might they be? Surely Yerbo would not sanction a raid when his only legitimate daughter was on the point of being betrothed to the Peninsula's ruler. Albin knew factions in that unrestful country opposed Fidacia's betrothal. Earlier that winter he had been present during a negotiating session in Zica, the Sturite capital. In Albin's opinion, it was a city whose barbaric splendor in no way made up for its disdainful want of the most basic human comforts.

Shivering in its unheated palace, Albin had looked with nervous alarm at the red-bearded Sturite nobles. All of them were well over six feet and went about carrying hunting eagles no more fierce-looking than themselves.

Around Zica's council table, bitter opposition had been raised to the marriage Brone and Yerbo were negotiating. The leader of that opposition, Albin recalled, had been Arant,

51

Fidacia's temperamental bastard half-brother.

Arant had made an indelible impression on Albin. After Brone stared Arant down at council and later bested him in a trial with sword and knife, the Sturite prince's bloodshot green eyes had blazed with malign fury.

Thropos was another member of the Sturite court whose image remained imprinted in Albin's memory. In his charcoal robe, with his wizened figure and twisted back, he'd reminded the boy of an evil crow. The weakness of his body had been more than offset by the poisonous cunning stamped on his bloodless features.

With a shudder, Albin recollected the chill the mere sight of Thropos had sent racing up his spine. He knew that, like Faring, the wizard was a product of Peneto. He'd heard rumors that Thropos had left Peneto in disgrace, but for such as Albin, the goings-on at the wizards' stronghold buried high in the northern fastness remained shrouded in mystery.

Turning his thoughts back to Acuma, Albin chewed on his lower lip and wondered again what the raid meant. Surely Yerbo had not approved it. The Sturite king seemed anxious to wed his daughter to Brone. Might such a breach of treaty etiquette interfere with the nuptial celebrations that were to climax the harvest season and ensure the Peninsula's future tranquility?

Riding on, the youth discarded his ponderings and began to look about him with interest and appreciation. He had traveled to the southern quarter of the Peninsula before and could see that, under King Brone's guidance, this part of the country was experiencing rapid development. The roads were paved with stones, and new settlements with market centers had sprung up.

As Albin left Jedestrom farther and farther behind, the thick forests and lush fertile valleys that characterized the north and central sections of the country gave way to a gently rolling landscape of sand, scrub, and rock. The land, no good for farming, was crisscrossed by a network of waterways that led to the port cities the king had established in the early years of his reign. These rivers bore lanken to the south for export. When veins of the prized wistite were discovered, Brone had dotted the area with forges. They processed the valuable ore before sending it farther downriver to the bustling harbors.

The industry had made of the south a populous and commercially active area, quite different in character from the agricultural north. The roads were busy, and as Albin pushed farther along his route, he began to see survivors from Acuma clutching their belongings and staring around them with haggard faces.

These distraught refugees jammed the inns. Albin had to stop at several places before he could find dinner and a corner in which to sleep the night. While he ate his meal in the dark recesses of a wayside common room that evening, he listened to the talk swirling around him.

"They swooped down on us like vultures," complained one elderly merchant with stubbled cheeks and bloodshot eyes. "No warning, just out of a clear sky their war eagles dropped to rip at innocent people in the streets. Then their cursed blood ships rammed the piers. Sturite warriors, crazy with that potion they swallow before a battle, spewed out like demons. They hacked to death everyone in sight, sparing neither women nor children. The buildings—all in flames!" His voice broke, and he passed a trembling hand over his soot-streaked forehead. "Warehouses full of grain and cured lanken went up like oil." Tears began to roll afresh down the man's cheeks. "All of my life's work was in those buildings, and now they're nothing but rubble!"

"Aye, but our ruler will deal with those devils," another man offered.

"Too late to save my ships and warehouses," the merchant muttered into his winecup, refusing to be consoled.

"Cheer up, friend. The king wasn't too late to catch those

Sturite fiends at their dirty work and wreak havoc on them. Surely that's some compensation for a barn full of bread dough and logs."

Albin scrutinized the speaker with interest. Above his ordinary woolen trousers and stained leather tunic, his darkly sunburned face was memorable. A thick brown beard covered the lower half but, above a strong beak of a nose, shrewd, sherry-colored eyes peered out from under bushy eyebrows. Those hard-bitten features belonged to one who had seen the world, Albin judged.

Fascinated, he resolved to stay alert in his corner to see what should happen. To his disappointment, the remainder of the evening proved dull. While the man who had spoken with such harsh humor lingered over his wine, gazing for long periods of blank reflection into the fire, the others who had filled the common room drifted away. Some went to share a corncob mattress, while others rolled themselves up on the floor in lieu of a bed.

When none remained awake but Albin and the stranger, the youth marshaled his courage. He picked up his own half-finished drink and approached the other traveler.

"Will you share a cup with me? I journey to Acuma in the morning, and I'm anxious to know what I shall find there."

The stranger turned his grizzled head and eyed the young man in silence.

Nervously, Albin hurried on. "I overheard you speak earlier of the battle between our king and the Sturites and would be glad of anything you might tell me."

The traveler's gaze lit on the thick leather pouch the boy carried over his shoulder. His mouth relaxed into a faint smile, and he gestured at an empty seat. "King's messenger, are you?"

"Why, yes."

"Ah, well, I know it's no easy task to serve a fighter in times of war. I'll tell you what you'll find in Acuma. Death, burned buildings, and Brone wreaking vengeance."

"Then you can say for certain that the king has put down the raid?" Albin asked eagerly.

"Oh, aye! Your master is a soldier. I've seen many in my time, and I'll tell you—the man impressed me. He swept down on the raiders like a wind from the seven hells and cut them to pieces before they knew their arses from their knees. He trains his archers well. They shot those hellborn eagles out of the sky like so many ripe plums. It's clear Brone keeps his men disciplined, and that's worth praise, for, while Sturites are warriors by nature, Peninsulans are not." He shook his head. "Most of us are happier milking a cow than trying to fit our hands to a weapon."

This was true, Albin acknowledged. Talk of violence on such a scale as had just occurred in Acuma made him feel slightly ill.

"Somehow Brone has made soldiers of a pack of farmers," the stranger went on as if talking to himself. He rubbed his furred chin and chuckled ruefully. "It's twenty years since I left to seek my fortune in a leaky ship that was shelter to three times as many rats as sailors. I did well enough and saw a bit of the world into the bargain. But I'm beginning to suspect I'd have prospered more if I'd stayed home and leaned my weight on a hoe."

Albin smiled. "Where are you bound, and what may I call you?"

"Call me Phen," the man replied genially, and the two fell into conversation over fresh cups of wine. As the night grew older, the boy learned that, if his new acquaintance's wild tales were to be believed, he had been everything from a sailor to a mercenary in lands Albin hadn't even known existed.

"Oh, I've knocked around," Phen agreed. He took a deep swallow from his mug and wiped his mouth with the back of a calloused hand. "I've seen the ins and outs of the world, and I've learnt a trick or two that I surely didn't know when I was a stripling pitching sheep's dung on my granda's holding up north. But apart from the scars on my back and the little I

carry about in my head"—he tapped his temple significantly—
"I'm no richer than I was the day I stowed away on a Chee
trader's galley bound for open sea. Truth to tell, that ship
smelled no sweeter than my old barn. I would have done better
to have stayed put and had some advantage from the milk and
honey Brone's rule has brought."

"It's not too late for that now," Albin declared. "Under King
Brone's leadership, our prosperity will surely continue. A clever
man such as you can still make his fortune."

While his hand toyed with the grip on his earthenware mug,
Phen gazed at Albin quizzically. "I've seen the world and you
haven't, boy. The Peninsula is but a bone surrounded by snapping dogs. Now that it's without the protection of the domi,
the beasts will soon fall on it and tear it to pieces."

Albin's eyes widened. He'd been privy to this argument
before, but somehow hearing it from Phen gave it extra impact.
"The Peninsula can defend itself."

"Not if its enemies ally themselves, as sooner or later they
will."

"King Brone has the domi stones in his keeping. He can use
them if need be."

Phen arched a thick eyebrow. "Can he? To be sure, they were
on his brow when he stormed Acuma. Fine they looked, but I
saw no sign of his making use of them. And surely that would
have been the easiest way to topple the Sturite ships and confound their eagles. No, he took the place with military
strength, not magic."

"He used them in the early years," Albin argued. "My parents saw him quell a forest fire with them. He changed the
direction of the wind."

"Did he now?" Phen's dark eyes narrowed while he emptied
his mug. "Has he used them in recent years?"

Albin frowned. The stones were the Peninsula's history and
its mythology. In his blood, he knew the land's fate was bound
to them. Yet, though he'd seen them almost every day

gleaming on the gold band the king wore, he had to admit he'd never seen King Brone use their power.

Phen, who'd been observing Albin narrowly, twisted his mouth. "Well, if he can make them his servants then perhaps the Peninsula will go unmolested. If not . . ." He let the sentence trail off ominously.

"When King Brone marries the Sturite princess—" Albin began to counter.

Phen cut him short with a harsh laugh. "Surely you are not so naive! Do you really imagine that a marriage to one of their redheaded termagants will keep those flame-haired murderers out of our boundaries? No, I'll wager it will only make sinking their fangs into us more convenient. What's more," he said, laughing again, "I ken your Brone is coming to some very similar conclusions for himself. No, my boy, it's the stones and only the stones that can keep the Peninsula safe from its enemies. I'll wait and see. If the king can command them as you say, then I'll stay on and look for my future in the land of my birth. But if he can't"—Phen emptied his last cup and pushed back his chair— "then I'll be off on my travels again, and the stars help me, because my bones are getting old for the wandering life."

With that, the outspoken adventurer rolled himself into a well-worn blanket and stretched his burly body out near the fire. In another minute his lids closed, and he began to snore loudly. But Albin remained awake long into the night, staring at the embers on the stone hearth with troubled eyes.

In a far corner, rolled into a dark blanket hiding her from view, Reawen did the same. She'd followed Albin into the tavern and overheard all that Phen had said. It gave her much to think on.

* * * * *

Phen had made so deep an impression on Albin that he was still mulling over the older man's words when he rode slowly into Acuma the next afternoon. He found the place much as its refugees had described it. Yet hearing of a disaster and seeing it for oneself were altogether different things.

The smell of death hung over the stricken city. Corpses yet littered the side streets, and all around, charred timber protruded from half-burned buildings. In the harbor, the havoc the Sturites had wreaked was even more shocking. The rigging of wrecked trading vessels still moored to the docks slapped and whistled in the breeze like death rattles. Those ships that hadn't been torched had been stove in by the metal rams attached to Sturite warcraft, protrusions cast in the shapes of screaming eagle heads with long pointed beaks. In a ghastly counterpoint of death, a pile of half-burned Sturite war eagles that had been shot out of the air by Brone's archers lay stinking on the end of one of the quays.

Brone's troops had been at work clearing the area, but storage buildings still lay in ashes, blood staining the cobblestones around them. As Albin took stock of this destruction, a cold hard ball of rage formed in his gut. How he hated these murdering Sturites!

Slowly, he guided Grassears into the open square, where a crowd of muttering survivors had gathered. Many limped and wore bloodied bandages. Despite their injuries, they milled around the edges of the open area with their eyes fixed to the action going on there.

Once he had taken in the scene's meaning, Albin, too, became riveted. In the center King Brone, grimly magnificent with the brassy sun glittering on his close-cropped curls, stood in command. He wore leather battle armor, and a bloody gash above his eyebrow remained undressed. On his forehead, the golden band holding the domi stones caught the light.

Arrayed in a semicircle at his back was his personal guard. Directly before him, hanging from a row of gallows that stretched across the entire central area of the harbor, dozens of Sturite bodies dangled in a grisly parade of death. Albin's heart began to thud. Hastily, he tied his horse to a still-standing fence and edged through the murmuring throng.

"What's happening?" he demanded of a woman who clutched a sleeping baby to her breast. At her questioning look he added, "I've just arrived from the capital."

She gazed up at him with flaring eyes and then switched her attention back to the macabre necklace of gallows. "He hung them all. Every last murdering whoreson left alive after King Brone's men swept down on them," she muttered. "May they roast in the seven hells!"

"Aye," the old man at her elbow injected. "And he made their bastard leader watch it all. It took the whole of yesterday to force Arant's band to build their own gallows and all of this morning to hang them one by one. Now," he went on grimly, "King Brone's men will row Arant back to Sturite land trussed like a pig for slaughter. They'll dump him on the shore as a bridegift for Fidacia." He cackled at the image. "I wonder what the little wench will make of it."

Instead of answering, Albin pushed toward the front of the crowd for a clearer view. When he got it, he almost wished he'd stayed back. Much as he'd thought he hated Sturites, the sight of their dangling corpses sickened him. Averting his eyes from them, he focused on Brone. The king's mouth was clamped tight. Expressionlessly, he watched while a half dozen of his soldiers tied Arant hand and foot.

Jibing laughter rippled through the crowd. Albin didn't join in. He could see the ferocious hatred in the fiery Sturite prince's eyes and, remembering Phen's words, felt a premonition of trouble to come.

"Arrogant cur!" Arant shrieked at Brone. "For this outrage, I curse you! You shall rue this day, and Faring will have no power to save you. Fidacia will never warm your bed. I'll take the Peninsula from you. You'll not live to see a son command those baubles you wear round your head."

Brone's stony gaze didn't flicker. "Gag him and remove him

from my sight."

The king's men quickly followed his order, dragging Arant to the waiting galley. One by one, they cut down the Sturite bodies and piled them around the renegade leader. Then, into a crimson sunset, they rowed his blood ship out to sea and pointed it in the direction of Zica.

For a long time Albin stood staring at the incredible sight. Finally, he turned away and looked directly into the face of one who had been as transfixed by the terrible scene as he. "Reawen!" he cried. "What in sky's name are you doing here?"

She was buried several layers back in the crowd behind him. She had muffled herself in a cloak and had a cap pulled low over her head to hide her hair, but none of that fooled Albin. When she saw that he'd recognized her, she pivoted and elbowed her way through the throng.

Gritting his teeth, Albin pushed after her. "Reawen, stop! Where do you think you're going?"

Ignoring his frantic calls, she dashed across the square to one of the narrow streets that corkscrewed away from the harbor. Albin was on her heels. Where the twisting street she'd used for an escape route dead-ended, he caught up with her. He seized her elbow and swung her around to face him. "I thought I told you to stay at home in the Zeleta."

She tried to pull away, but when he wouldn't let go, she drew herself up haughtily. "You don't tell me what to do. And the Zeleta isn't my home."

"It's your home as long as you're the queen mother's reed player. Does her majesty know where you are now?"

"Before you recognized me, nobody knew where I was."

Completely flustered, Albin glared down at Reawen. Defiantly, she gazed back at him. The cap covering her hair had been knocked askew so several long, ebony locks escaped it. Dirt smudged her cheek, and one of her stockings was ripped. Yet, despite her grubby outfit, she held herself like a queen. Albin suddenly felt strangely in awe of her, as if she really were some sort of royalty. Shaking the ridiculous notion aside, he demanded, "Where did you get those clothes?"

"I took them from the washhouse."

"You mean the washhouse back at the Plat? That's stealing!"

"I left my gown. Fair exchange."

Albin sputtered, at a loss. "You followed me all the way down here, didn't you!" Though, how she could have done that without his being aware, he couldn't imagine.

"Yes!"

"Don't you realize how dangerous it is for an unprotected girl to wander around in a war-torn countryside?"

Reawen glanced meaningfully at her captive arm. "So far, you're the only one laying rough hands on me. Besides, dressed this way, I pass as a boy."

Albin stepped back and snorted. "Anyone with eyes can see that you're not a boy." He cocked his head and studied her. He had to admit that she was certainly slim enough to pass for a lad. "Well, perhaps if I didn't know you, I might not notice, as long as you kept your long hair out of sight," he admitted grudgingly. "At least, I suppose that must be the case if you've gotten this far without being molested."

"Just let anyone try to molest me!" Shooting him a cocky grin, Reawen began straightening her cap. "I was even in the tavern with you last night."

Albin gawked, then rolled his eyes. "I can't understand you. Most girls would give their teeth to have a safe place at the Zeleta with a kind mistress like Killip. Why would you jeopardize that to run into danger and see all this horror?"

Reawen's expression sobered at once. "It is horrible," she whispered. "But I'm glad I've seen it. Now I know what your king is really like."

Albin stiffened. "What do you mean?"

"Oh, Albin, he's cruel!"

"King Brone's only done what was necessary to protect his kingdom. Surely, even you can see that."

"I can see that it bothers him not one whit to spill blood in the cruelest fashion."

Albin raised his hands and then let them drop. "There's no time for this. Reawen, we need to talk about getting you out of Acuma." He glanced around. "I have some papers to deliver. It shouldn't take me more than two hours. When that's done, I'll meet you back here, and we'll figure something out."

Reawen tossed her head. "Who said I wanted to leave Acuma yet? It's fascinating here, and there's much to be learned."

"Reawen, please!"

"All right," she agreed reluctantly. "I'll be here, but I'm not promising to go along with whatever plan you hatch for me."

When Albin strode off, Reawen watched with a mixture of relief and anxiety as he left. Having Albin hovering around was like being smothered by a mother hen. He was pompous, over-bearing, narrow-minded. Yet she felt safe in his company; the defiant front she'd put up for his benefit was just an act. Since leaving the Zeleta, she'd felt anything but confident. It had been all right so long as Cel stayed with her. But when they'd come within a mile of Acuma, Cel had sensed the nearness of the Sturite war eagles. *I have to turn back,* she explained to her mistress before flying off in the opposite direction. *They'd tear me to pieces if they caught me.*

Acuma itself had been a horrible shock to Reawen, the burned bodies, the hangings, the stench of death. Isolated in the mountains with Gris, Reawen had never imagined terrible realities like these. Such things couldn't happen if the domi had their stones, she thought. Perhaps Albin is right, and there were times when some of us were capricious. But if we still ruled the Peninsula as we were meant to, the Sturites would never have dared to attack.

Yet she was glad to have seen Brone in his warrior guise, so very different from the playful man who had trifled with her on the riverbank. Seeing his harsh treatment of the Sturites reminded her of how ruthlessly he had taken her stone. It underlined her resolve that she must be equally ruthless in getting it back.

For the next hour, Reawen walked the streets. As she moved through the muttering crowds, she listened to what people were saying to each other and tried to get a grip on her own feelings. All the talk was of Brone and his deeds. No one spoke of the domi, for it seemed they were no longer of any consequence in the lives of the Peninsula's people.

As this sank in, Reawen felt small, alone, and forgotten. On the other hand it was exciting to be in a port city. Inevitably, her steps took her back to the harbor. For many long minutes she stood on the edge of a deserted quay and stared out at the ocean's tossing waves. The Har was the largest body of water the young water domis had seen before this. Reawen belonged to the Peninsula's streams and rivers, yet she felt herself drawing strength from the ocean and knew that, before she left this place, she must pay homage by bathing in the Great Mother, to which all waters flow before they are reborn.

"Oh, Gris," she whispered under her breath as she knelt to dip a hand into the salty coldness lapping at a mossy piling, "it's just as you said. All the streams, rivers, and oceans are part of me. Because I know one, I know them all. Still, I wish you were here with me to see this." Reawen lifted a wet finger and touched it to her lips. Then she closed her eyes. A moment before, she had felt alone and frightened. Now she felt calm. It was almost as if Gris herself had whispered a reassurance.

Precisely at the time agreed, Reawen returned to the spot where she'd pledged to meet Albin. She was beginning to fear that he'd forgotten her when he finally came along wearing a frown.

"I was afraid you might not be here."

"You're the one who's late, not me."

He wrapped his hand around her elbow. "Come, let's find a tavern where we can talk over a mug of ale and a bite to eat. I'm famished, and so must you be."

Reawen nodded. She hadn't had much coin to bring with her and hadn't eaten since morning. When they'd found a quiet corner in an inn and Albin had ordered up drinks and meat pies, he fixed a worried gaze on her. "I've just come from the king. He's sending me to Peneto, and there's no way I can take you along."

"Peneto! That—"

"The stronghold of wizardry," Albin confirmed curtly. Though he wouldn't admit such a thing to Reawen, the king's surprising command frightened him. Of course, he would never dream of disobeying it. "I don't know why I'm going, but it must be important. To my knowledge this is the first time Brone has sent an envoy to Faring since they parted."

"And you have no idea what the purpose of your trip is?" She glanced at the pouch secured to Albin's waist. "Do you carry a message to Faring?"

"Yes, one that I will guard with my life, as all messengers are sworn to do."

"I suppose you've never peeked at any of the dispatches you've carried."

Albin drew back, affronted. "Never!"

Reawen would have given much for a look inside his pouch and toyed with the idea of trying a mindtouch. But she gave that up as useless, since Albin probably didn't know what he carried. She shrugged. "Then I guess I'm on my own."

"No, it's too dangerous. Listen, I've spoken with Pib, a friend of mine who's one of the horsekeepers in the king's camp. He's willing to find a place for you. All you'll have to do is keep that hat on your head and learn how to groom horses."

"Groom horses!"

"I know it's not a job for a girl, but you're the one who decided to trick yourself out in hose and jerkin. At least, disguised as a stableboy, you'll be able to travel safely back to Jedestrom with the army."

Reawen opened her mouth to refuse such demeaning work

and then thought better of it. If she were with Brone's army, she'd be able to keep an eye on him and her stone. "All right," she said demurely. "It's sweet of you to worry about me, Albin."

Impulsively, he seized her hand. "I know I haven't spoken kindly, but it's not because I don't like you. I have a special feeling about you, Reawen."

"You do?"

"Yes, I—" He blushed bright red. "I'll tell you about it when we're both safely back at the Plat."

* * * * *

The next forty-eight hours told Reawen how little she liked the life of a stableboy. Fortunately, Albin's friend Pib was an amiable fellow who treated her with tolerant kindness. But even Pib's good-natured camaraderie couldn't make her like the smelly, dirty, backbreaking work.

As far as Reawen was concerned, she saw far too much horse manure and far too little of her stone. The glimpses she caught of the king were rare, and always at a frustrating distance. What's more, she had to take the cuffs and insults of rough soldiers and other stableboys. Added to all that was the constant fear of having her sex discovered.

The second night, as she sat huddled in the shadows near the fire, a bully named Bort came swaggering up. "What's yer name, little girlface?"

Reawen gazed up at the tub-bodied, sweaty-faced Bort in alarm. "My name's Robin, and I'm not a girlface."

Bort grinned nastily. "Oh, yes, you are. Just look at that creamy skin and those big eyes. Why, you could pass for a girl any day. Let's take off that cap and see if you really are one."

Bort darted a grimy hand at her cap, but, quick as wind on water, Reawen leaped to her feet. In the same motion, she drew her wicked knife, which she'd kept hidden in her belt, and brandished it. "Leave me alone or you'll lose a finger," she hissed.

Bort's jaw dropped in surprise. Then his meaty face turned red. "That's a big, bad knife for a little girlface. Bet you don't even know how to use it."

"Try me. You'll soon find out."

Bort took a step forward, but stopped when Pib hurried up and planted himself in front of Reawen. Pib was a hulking young man with a mop of strawberry-blond hair and pale green eyes. Though he was a loyal Peninsulan, his grandmother had been Sturite, and his coloring testified to the fact. So did his massive shoulders and hamlike fists. "Leave my stableboy alone, or you'll deal with me," he warned Bort.

Bort backed off. Elaborately, he shrugged. "No need to go getting all violent. I was just kidding with the pretty lad."

He walked away then and didn't approach Reawen again that night. But she knew he *wasn't* kidding and that she'd come very close to losing her cover.

"You'd better get rid of that hair," Pib warned her the next afternoon. Reawen knew he was right. A moment earlier it had tumbled out from under her cap one time too many. With an impatient swipe at her sweaty forehead, she stepped back from the horse she'd been rubbing down and inspected her grimy, straw sprinkled hands and clothes. "I've got to have a good wash. Phawww! I stink!"

"Then do it now and get rid of that hair. And don't let nobody see you," Pib warned. He shook his head. "I should never have let Albin talk me into this."

Word had begun to circulate that Brone was preparing to return to Jedestrom on the morrow. A small fighting force along with engineers and carpenters would stay on to help Acuma rebuild in safety. But the bulk of the army would move with the king to the capital, and Reawen along with it. That means this is my last chance to bathe in the sea, she told herself as she left the stable enclosure.

After looking around to make sure no one was taking any notice, she threaded her way to the other side of the horses and headed for a rock-enclosed beach near the camp.

Twice before she'd stolen off to swim there, but on each occasion she'd found soldiers using the place and had had to sneak back, disappointed. This time, however, no one was about.

With a little thrill of excitement, Reawen clambered over the rocks that shielded the spot from view and hurried down into the sandy cove, where sun sparkled on the waves. Above, white seabirds played in the breezes. They made Reawen think of Cel and miss her company. Still, she felt glad that her pillawn was safe in Jedestrom, happily hiding in the king's garden.

After one last glance to make sure she was truly alone, Reawen shed her cap. Her black hair tumbled down, and she withdrew her knife. A few minutes later, her locks lay in a heap on the sand. They'll grow back, she told herself as she hid the hair under some pebbles. Truth to tell, she felt surprisingly little regret. The lightness around her head was most enjoyable.

She'd always thought that her hair was straight. But when she glanced into a tide pool close to shore, she saw that, without the weight of its length to drag it down, her hair had begun to curl. She touched a curving tendril and watched it spring back against her ear.

Reawen didn't linger to admire herself. The whoosh of the sun-warmed surf in her ears was far too seductive. With a final glance about to ensure her privacy, she pulled off her dirty tunic and leggings. She intended to carry them with her into the water. She could pin them down under a rock and wash them after she'd cleansed herself. With a little cry of joy, Reawen hoisted her bundle and ran into the waves.

They received her as if they knew she was their own. The moment she sank into their salty depths, her spirit soared. "Tell me your stories, O Mother of Waters," she whispered as she dived down to examine the tiny, brightly colored fish swimming at the base of the rocks. "Teach me your sacred secrets."

The Great Mother heard her plea and answered. She clasped

Reawen close to her smooth, dark bosom, and suddenly, the young domis found herself breathing the salt water as though it were air. Thrilled with this new power, she dived deeper to search out the wonders the waters kept hidden from the eyes of the surface world.

Easily, Reawen swam through a cavern lit by creatures streaked with phosphorous. At its end, she stopped short and gazed at a kindly old man, with a mane of white hair and the bluest of all blue eyes. He beckoned her closer, his eyes sparkling as he offered her a smooth stone of swirling greens and blues. A storyrock! Reawen thought, delighted to have one of the fabled underwater treasures in her hand. She held the stone to her ear and listened, enraptured, to a tale as old as the ocean itself, from when the sea was home to wondrous ancient creatures. She grinned in childlike excitement at the man of the storyrocks.

When she finally turned to leave him, the gentle old man called a sleek green larfin to carry her back through the cavern on its smooth back. As they neared the sunlit surface, the larfin introduced her to the Pleons, beautiful sea girls made entirely of foam who drew their energy from sunlight on water. They floated close to the domis, singing to her melodies of their birth from star stuff and of the Dreamking who led them. *We are all the stuff of his dreams,* they crooned. *Even you, Reawen. Even the king who has stolen your stone.*

"Then perhaps the Dreamking will dream it back into my hands," Reawen whispered, not quite believing them, for they spoke of things she didn't understand. The Pleons laughed their tinkly laughs and shaped themselves into a hundred different foam forms before her eyes. Glittering snakes twined into fish with gorgeous long fins, which suddenly exploded all about Reawen into many-winged butterflies and graceful, plumed birds from paradise.

Enchanted, Reawen listened to their songs, watched their dance, and forgot everything. It wasn't until a cloud dimmed the sun hours later that she troubled to surface and glance back at the shore. As the Pleons melted away from her, the young domis saw Brone standing on the sand, staring out over the water as he twisted and untwisted a length of her freshly cut hair between his fingers. He didn't look like a dream. He looked all too real.

Chapter Five

Inside his tent, Brone confronted Reawen. "What in fury's name possessed you to do it?"

She stood before him, sodden clothing clinging to her body like seaweed. Her hacked-off hair curled around her head in wild, salt-stiffened clumps.

After spying her from the beach, Brone had made her cover herself decently, which had been no easy matter. Reawen had had to dress herself standing chest deep in the ocean, her hose and tunic tossed this way and that by the pounding waves. When she'd finally staggered up onto the sand, he dragged her back to the camp.

"I was dirty. I needed to bathe," she answered defiantly.

"I'm not talking about your dip in the sea. I'm talking about disguising yourself in this way, deserting my mother, and sneaking around after my army!"

Reawen met Brone's angry gaze and noticed how worn he looked. Before this, she had seen that the stones were not resting well with him and that he appeared older than his years. Now, perhaps because of what he'd just gone through with the Sturites, perhaps because of the gathered weight of his worries, she saw an even more profound exhaustion in him.

A wisp of compassion stirred inside her, but the memory of his cruelty to her mother quelled it. Through the currents of her blood, Reawen could feel the green stone summon her. If the four gems in Brone's crown were draining him of his vitality, it was only because he had no right to wear them, she reminded herself.

"I wanted to see the war with my own eyes," she declared. "When Albin told me he was coming down here, I followed him."

"Albin!" Brone scowled. "Was any of this his doing? Did he suggest that you get yourself up like a stablehand and put on this masquerade?" The king's hand swept an encompassing arc over Reawen's shorn locks and bedraggled hose and tunic.

"Oh, no! Albin never knew that I followed him. And dressing like a boy was my idea." She had no wish to get Albin into trouble when he'd shown her nothing but kindness.

His expression highly dissatisfied, Brone gazed at her. Then, after closing his eyes for a weary instant, he signaled a servant. "See that she gets something dry to wear and, when she's properly covered, serve dinner for two."

Some time later Reawen was led back to the king's tent with her hair neatly trimmed and combed free of salt. The servant who'd attended her could find no women's clothes. Instead, he'd provided clean hose, a tunic, and a long, red velvet cloak, which covered her from neck to toes.

"That's better," Brone said with a smile, for plainly his mood had mended in her absence. "A pity to hack off all those lovely black tresses." He cocked his head and considered her hair. "But I have to admit it's rather fetching short that way."

Reawen eyed him in wary surprise.

"What have you been eating all this time?" he inquired almost genially.

"Whatever the stableboys get. Crusts of bread, soup, and an occasional meat scrap."

"I hope they treated you well enough."

Reawen shrugged. There was no point in mentioning Bort's bullying, she supposed.

"Well, you shall dine better than stableboys tonight. Sit."

A table had been covered with a fine white cloth and set with a variety of foods. There was dressed fowl, cheese, and bread. Reawen's gaze passed over these and lit on a worked silver bowl brimming with succulent fruit.

"Emberries!" she exclaimed despite herself. "They grow only in the north. How do you have them here?"

As Brone watched her settle herself on a chair and draw her robe around her, his smile grew warmer. "My steward has a genius for such small miracles. You're fond of emberries?"

"Very," Reawen admitted, her mouth watering. The round green fruit was a special weakness of hers. She hadn't tasted their tart sweetness in many weeks, not since leaving Gris and her home in the mountains.

Musingly, Brone watched while she eagerly plucked several and popped them into her mouth. He picked up a wrought silver ewer and poured her a goblet of dark red wine. "You are a strange young woman," he said as he passed it to her. "I should be angry with your presumptuous trickery, but on reflection I find myself flattered instead."

"Flattered?" Reawen stopped chewing and blinked at him.

"A motive for your odd actions has occurred to me." He leaned closer and his white teeth flashed. With his head mere inches away, Reawen felt the pull of her stone so strongly that it took all her strength to keep from reaching out to it.

"Perhaps," Brone mused, "you tricked yourself out like a boy and followed me to Acuma because you were worried for my safety."

Reawen almost choked on her mouthful of emberries.

"Perhaps," he continued, "you thought better of my offer and came here to be close to me so you could tell me of your change of heart."

Reawen's appetite, even for emberries, deserted her. She swallowed and replied, "You are mistaken, Sire. I do not wish to become your mistress, if that is what you are thinking. I had been taking care to keep my presence hidden from you. If you hadn't found me bathing, you would never have known that I was here in your camp at all."

Brone's genial expression cooled and his mouth folded into sterner lines. "Then why did you come? It couldn't have been merely curiosity about war. I don't want to believe that you are so coldhearted you wished to see death and destruction." He paused then, sizing her up thoughtfully. "You and Albin are of an age for flirtation. Is there something between you two?"

Though she had no appetite for it, Reawen sipped her wine in hopes that it would warm her hands and melt the ball of ice in her stomach. "Only friendship. And you are wrong about my motives. I did come because I wanted to see what war was like," she lied.

Brone regarded her coldly. "Then you are a very strange young woman."

"Yes, I guess I am. I've never been content to hide in the house like other girls." That much, at least, was certainly true. "I wish to know life, and I can do that only by seeing it in all its aspects, even those that are cruel."

"You actually wanted to see the carnage in Acuma?"

"I wanted to see what was happening." She cocked her head. "I was there when you hung the Sturites. It *was* a cruel and sickening sight."

"They were a vicious band of marauders who deserved their fate."

"Another king might not have dealt out such harsh punishment. By showing mercy, another king might have avoided making a lifelong enemy," Reawen said, thinking of Arant.

"So now you are not content to be an adventuress. You set yourself up as my advisor. Well, let me tell you—if such a king as you describe ruled the Peninsula, his enemies would soon eat him alive. I'll tell you something else. No king wishes to hear his decisions criticized by a serving maid." As Brone toyed with his own brimming mug, he stared at her hard. "You are a very unusual young woman, so unusual that I begin to wonder if I have taken you too lightly."

Reawen felt herself go pale. "What do you mean?"

"I mean it occurs to me that I have allowed you into my mother's household solely on Albin's recommendation. At times such as these, blind trust is foolish. As soon as we return to Jedestrom, you will give the details of your background to my secretary so he can verify them." He smiled at her to soften the words. "I don't really believe that you are a spy, Reawen. But I have to be sure."

*   *   *   *   *

Outside the king's tent, a shadow lurked close enough to overhear Brone and Reawen's tense conversation. "Lies!" Turlip muttered before scuttling away into the night. "Pretty missy will tell him nothing but lies." Turlip pictured Reawen's dark hair and soft white limbs and licked his lips. Then he remembered how she had scorned and beaten him, how her nasty white bird had scratched his back to ribbons. His beady eyes narrowed. She'll be sorry, he thought. They'll both be sorry. Before this is over, I'll have her all to myself, and that bird will be dead.

*   *   *   *   *

"I hope we haven't lost the way," Albin muttered.

Behind him, Waylo guffawed. "I never heard anyone talk to his horse as much as you. Tell me, messenger, has that donkey-eared mutt ever answered back?"

Albin risked taking his eye off the steep trail long enough to shoot an irritated glance over his shoulder. Waylo had removed his helmet to scratch the thatch of unkempt hair that sat atop his bovine face.

Brone had assigned the soldier to protect Albin on his long journey through the northern mountains. Despite Albin's fears about the trip, he would have preferred to go alone, for all Waylo had done was torment him with his clumsy teasing and slow him down by wanting a stop for liquid refreshment at every tavern they chanced to pass.

Now that they were finally in the mountains, which shut the Peninsula off from the continent, there would be no more taverns. All day they'd toiled upward on an unmarked route that grew increasingly uncertain. "On a perilous trail such as this, my life depends on Grassears's surefootedness," Albin said. "I'd talk to him all day to keep him friendly and alert. You'd do well to baby your mount a bit, too, friend."

Waylo shrugged thick shoulders. "A horse is but a dumb beast. I grant if ours should bolt on us now we'd be in a pickle, though." He scowled at the treacherous trail, with its loose rock and sheer drops into ravines so deep the bottoms were lost in shadow. Around them, the silence of the tree-studded mountains seemed to gather like storm clouds. "I hear there are giant wolves in these parts, great slavering creatures half the height of horses. I hear they like to eat men alive. Hope we don't run into any."

Albin hoped so, too—devoutly.

"It's said," Waylo continued, "that the domi still roam free somewhere in these mountains. I wouldn't care to meet up with any of them. It's certain they haven't been in a good mood since Brone made off with their stones."

Waylo chortled at his own joke, but he hadn't amused Albin. "Nor I," he agreed fervently. It was one thing to discount them when you were safe in Jedestrom. Here alone in this wilderness, the thought of an encounter with dispossessed domi was quite another matter.

"Of course, they're probably all dead and gone by now."

"Probably," the boy agreed. But even as he said the word, a shiver of premonition ran up his spine. He glanced back in time to see Waylo dismount and sag to the ground with his back against a boulder.

Albin pulled up on Grassears's reins. "Why are you stopping?"

"Time for a drink," Waylo replied with a wink. He hauled a wineskin out from under his arm and uncorked it.

"We stopped to eat no more than two hours past," Albin protested. He glanced up at the sky. "I don't like the look of those clouds. "If the first storms should hit us in these mountains, we'd be in for serious trouble."

Ignoring the messenger, Waylo held up the skin and shot an arc of red liquid into his open mouth. After wiping his lips on his sleeve, he groaned with satisfaction. Then he turned his head. Reluctantly, Albin had dismounted. With his feet planted wide apart and his arms akimbo, he stared angrily down at Waylo.

"Relax, boykin," the soldier drawled. "There's no one watching us here, except maybe leftover spirits from the wild time before the domi ruled. They do say the last of those still hang about in these mountains. But even if it's true, they're not going to tell on us. So who's to know if we take a day or three to reach Peneto? As for storms, that's out of our hands."

With a heavy sigh, Albin settled down on the ground cross-legged and leaned his back against the same rock supporting Waylo's. Obviously, the soldier had no intention of moving until he was ready.

"That's more like it. Now, tell me, what's it like to be the king's messenger?" asked Waylo.

"Exciting, interesting, sometimes frustrating."

"Keeps you busy, does he?" Waylo offered the wineskin to Albin, who declined it in favor of the water canteen he carried at his belt.

"He does, indeed." Albin thought of how he'd rushed down to Acuma, only to have Brone tell him he must hurry back north on this dangerous journey. Again, a shiver of apprehension coursed through him.

"Not too busy that you don't have a girl, I hope." Between long swallows of wine, the soldier winked a bleary eye.

"No one special at the moment," Albin replied stiffly.

"Now, that's not what I heard. I heard you had your eye on that new little reed player of the queen mother's."

"If you're talking about Reawen, we're just good friends."

Waylo guffawed. "Is that the truth? Well then, boy, I pity

you. I've seen the girl, you see. Neat little figure and all that long black hair." He smacked his lips wetly. "Wouldn't mind a go at her myself. Course, I'm not the only one who admires her, and I don't expect I'd stand much of a chance with my competition."

Albin glared at his companion. "Who are you going on about?"

"Why, the king, of course."

"The king!"

Waylo roared. "Close up your trap, you young boob. Why are you so surprised? For all that he wears that fancy crown, Brone's a man like any other. Word is he's had his eye on your Reawen, too."

"But he's to be married."

"That don't mean he couldn't have a plaything on the side, like."

Albin jumped to his feet. "Reawen's no plaything. You don't know her at all. She's not like that. Now, shut your mouth and let's get out of here."

"Yes," a voice hissed behind them. "Get out of here and leave me in peace."

Albin gaped at the speaker and Waylo leaped to his feet and stared behind him. The voice had come from the boulder they'd used for a backrest. A mouth had appeared in its rough, hard surface, and two angry little eyes. For another few seconds Albin and Waylo gawked. Then they dashed to their horses.

* * * * *

Hours later, shadows thickened around the two travelers. The temperature had dropped like a lead weight, and the trail had grown so treacherous that they couldn't even be certain they were still on it. "I've had enough of these damned mountains," Waylo growled. "It's high summer in Jedestrom, but here it's cold as a wizard's arse." He climbed off his horse and leaned his bulk against the sheer face of a rock. Then, with a start, he shot it a suspicious look and stepped away. "What I wouldn't give for a warm fire in a tavern and a mug of ale."

"If you hadn't drunk all your wine earlier, you'd have it to warm your belly now," Albin pointed out.

"If I hadn't let you lead me by the nose, I'd be somewhere safe instead of in these cursed mountains. I wouldn't be surprised if you've lost our way."

It was a fear that Albin shared. "All I've got to go on is a set of directions and my compass." He pointed to the small instrument he'd been keeping balanced on the pommel of his saddle. "We're still heading in the direction its needle points."

"For all that's worth. Now we know it's true that wild magic from the earthtender days still lives in these hills." After the boulder had joined their conversation back up the trail, the pair encountered a tree stump that tried to trip them with its roots and a log that turned into a hissing snake, which nearly spooked their horses over a cliff. "What's to say some crazy spell hasn't affected that compass of yours? And now that the sun's gone down, it's getting colder by the minute."

Albin swallowed. Much as he hated to admit it, what Waylo said was true. Until this day, Albin hadn't really believed the stories about magic in these mountains. Now he had no choice but to believe. It wasn't friendly magic, either. The things that lived and grew here were inimical. He felt as if the very earth he stood on wished him ill. And, when you couldn't trust a boulder to keep silent, what could you trust? A distant howl pierced the stillness, and Albin felt the hairs on the back of his neck jerk upright.

"Wolves!" Waylo exclaimed. "What do you have in mind we do now, little boy?"

Albin supposed that the soldier was right, the cry must have come from a wolf. Yet it had possessed an eerily human quality to it, and that made him even more anxious. If boulders weren't really boulders in this place, then wolves might not really be wolves. Even if they were wolves, that wasn't good news. "I recommend we push on 'til we've found a spot where we can make camp and build ourselves a fire."

"For once you talk some sense, hay hair," Waylo declared and snapped his whip across Grassears's rump and then his own horse's flank.

Though they picked their way upward for another quarter league, they found no likely camping spot. "Soon we won't be able to see our hands before our faces," Waylo growled. "Then what's to do? Spend the night standing still, afraid to move? Much good that would do us in this infernal wind. Any worse and it'll blow us both into that crevasse yonder."

The wind had certainly risen strongly, Albin thought. Earlier in the day there'd only been a light breeze. Now gusts eddied along the path and whistled through the gaps between rocks, as if they were some not-very-musical giant's teeth. "Maybe we'll find a spot to turn off around that bend," Albin called back.

Waylo merely muttered something about "a fool's mission."

Shivering inside the sheepskin vest he'd donned earlier, his teeth chattering as a frigid blast whiplashed his face, Albin brought Grassears around a tall outcropping. On the other side, they stopped dead.

"Whore's teeth!" Waylo exclaimed.

"Good evening, gentlemen. You've chosen an ill night for travel, I fear."

Albin blinked, hardly believing his eyes. Darkness had almost fallen, and the individual perched atop a rock just ahead seemed more like a phantom than anything made of flesh and blood. In his ragged, flowing cloak, he was tall and gaunt to the point of emaciation. Yet he looked far from weak. Around a face of strange and unearthly beauty, his white hair stood out like a halo composed of rays of wiry light. Beneath his colorless lashes, his eyes were like drops of congealed rain. An icy finger crept along Albin's spine. He'd seen painted images of the four domi and realized who this must be.

"Eol!" Waylo cried out behind him and, dismounting, drew his sword. Slashing it before him and digging in his spurs, he crashed past Albin and charged the individual on the rock. He got no more than a few steps.

With a frosty smile, Eol raised his fingers to his lips and blew lightly. A solitary wind summoned from some nether region of an arctic hell whirled around Waylo. In a second, he was frozen solid.

Albin gasped. Slipping off Grassears, he gingerly approached the soldier, who a moment before had been so vital. He touched the frosty skin, then drew back, horrified. Expecting at any moment to meet the same fate, he looked up at the domis of wind.

Eol lounged at his ease on the rock. "When I lost my stone to Brone on the throw of a die, I gambled away the source of much of my strength," he declared conversationally, "but I have not lost all my powers. Do not be so foolish as to attack me like your friend did just now."

"Is he, is he . . . ?"

"Oh, he's quite dead. When he thaws out in the spring, the crows will pick him clean. They will leave his bones as a warning to servants of Brone that they may not pass through these mountains until he's rectified the wrong he did the domi." Eol leaned forward and pointed a long white finger. "Oh, yes, I know who you are and what you carry." His laughter sounded like the clinking of ice cubes and summoned another freezing wind. It whipped open the leather pouch secured around Albin's waist and scattered the documents inside. The boy tried snatching at them, but they eluded his cold-stiffened hands and flew down the side of the mountain as if they were doves chased by a bloodthirsty hawk.

"Your king grows weary of the burden he carries around his head," Eol said. "No wonder, for it is sucking the life from him. He directs you to Peneto with a petition for Faring. He begs the wizard to send some magical balm that will relieve him of his pain. Well, now I turn you back with a message from Eol. Tell your king that the only way he can rid himself of the torment the stones are causing him is to journey here himself and give them back to their rightful heirs. Failing that, the stones will kill him long before his time. Every day he wears them illegitimately will be more of an agony than the last."

* * * * *

Many leagues to the north, perched high atop Dragon's Beak, the most inaccessible mountain bordering the Peninsula, lay Peneto. Within the ancient stronghold of wizardry, men in black robes observed their secret rituals and went about their arcane studies. One of these was Faring.

Like most of his colleagues, Faring hadn't stirred from Peneto's walls in years. Yet his peers considered him to be one of Peneto's most powerful and knowledgeable inmates. On this day, Perbledom, the elder, had called upon him to instruct a group of intended ones.

As the half dozen young men stood before Faring in the large, musty foyer of the fortress at dusk, they wore the same simple black robe as he. Otherwise, however, they couldn't have been more different from Faring. Where grim lines webbed his ascetic face, their countenances were fresh and a trifle apprehensive.

"You have studied your craft at Peneto since your parents dedicated you to us when you were children," he began. "Today marks your final testing. You are to go forth for five years with nothing to aid you but your wits. You are to immerse yourselves in the world you find outside these walls, gaining knowledge and understanding."

Some of the intended ones shuffled their feet. Others held themselves rigidly still despite the fear and excitement flickering in their downcast eyes.

"Some of you," Faring continued, "will lose your lives to the world's dangers. Others will be seduced by its beauties, luxuries, and fleshly pleasures. At the end of your trial period, very few of you will return to Peneto. Perhaps none."

Faring's stern gaze traveled from face to face and, for a brief instant, his gray eyes burned with memories. He folded his hands tightly over his flat belly. "Experience will have tempered those that do return. Only by tasting the world and renouncing it can they truly be welcomed into the sacred ranks of wizardry. Only then can they be privy to our brotherhood's greatest powers. Remember, for those who make the decision to succumb to the world's temptations, there can be no turning back, no reconsidering.

"Five years from today, at twilight as it is now, the gates of Peneto will open and accept those that wait to reenter. Those who fail to appear at the gates at twilight will be forever banished."

Silently, he walked from novice to novice, making the secret sign of release above each young man's head. When the ceremony was complete, Faring, along with three other gray-bearded colleagues, followed the little group to the courtyard. Ponderously, the great metal gates swung open, and the novices straggled forth. When they were out of sight and the gates shut and barred behind them, Perbledom, Peneto's stoop-shouldered elder, turned to Faring.

"Once again, we release our young to the winds of fate. How many of them will even survive the night on Dragon's Beak, I wonder."

"All will survive if they remember what they've been taught."

"Ah, yes, but that's only the beginning. If they turn south they must contend with the wild magic in the mountains."

"No Peneton should be overcome by wild magic. It's nothing but a nuisance." Faring headed back inside the keep.

With a sigh, Perbledom followed. "I suppose you had no trouble at your trial. Truth to tell, I nearly perished that first night. I was so disoriented and frightened that all the teachings of a lifetime flew from my head. I couldn't even remember the spell for turning stones into bread."

"I, too, was frightened that first night," Faring conceded in the stiff manner that years of isolation had made natural to him. "But I had the presence of mind to remember all the basic lessons, how to warm myself with faerie fire, how to make myself invisible to predators, how to convert the materials at hand to nourishment. No wizardling, no matter how inexperienced, need ever freeze or starve if he keeps even the least of his wits about him."

"You are right, of course." Perbledom's staff clicked along the floor. With his free hand he combed gnarled fingers through his straggly beard. "For me, the years of testing were so long ago that now they hardly seem real. I went to the land of the Chee where all is sunshine and ease. I was sorely tempted to stay among them—and would have, had I been suited to that sort of life. However, I was not born for fleshly pursuits. No, my calling is a scholarly one." Faring stifled a groan as the elder showed no sign of ending his reminiscence. "I returned, and here I've been ever since, devoting my life to Peneto and to my histories. But you, Faring, you took the more difficult route and went south through the mountains, did you not?"

"Yes." Faring's patience had grown short, for the elderly wizard had taken to rambling of late—and to blundering about in matters that didn't concern him.

"Of course," Perbledom muttered into his beard. "You obviously headed south for the present king of the Peninsula is your protégé."

"You are correct," Faring said.

"How is his temperament of late, eh? Does he grow balky now that he's no longer a boy?"

Faring, irritated, turned to face the elder. "Our whole world is balky. Everywhere I look I see nothing but a patchwork of quarrelsome nations composed of even more quarrelsome individuals."

Perbledom gave a rusty laugh. "Aye, according to my research, it's been that way since the earthtenders gave us over to the domi. Over the years, they've become a sorry lot."

"That's why we must stamp out those few that are left," Faring said fiercely. "Now, if you'll excuse me, I must get back to my work. There happen to be problems in that quarter right at the moment." Faring turned on his heel and strode down the corridor, his black robe flapping about his sandaled feet.

As if he were being chased, the tall, angular wizard hurried up the winding staircase to his private quarters. These ceremonies of release always disturbed him. Though he hadn't admitted the fact to Perbledom, today's event had brought back all too vividly his own days of freedom. It made him remember the searing passion he'd felt for the woman he'd met then, and the way she'd finally scorned and rejected him.

Faring entered his rooms, leaning heavily against the wood of the door. He closed his eyes and began to mutter an incantation. As if his hands had a life of their own, they began to shape the air. A ball of translucent gray matter formed between them and spun like a miniature tornado. At the slight motion of his fingers, it lengthened, took on colors and a shape. A miniature image of a woman, beautiful and young, blond and hauntingly seductive, hung in the air between Faring's hands. It was Nioma. She smiled at him, her blue eyes shimmering in the muted light.

"Cursed whore," he muttered under his breath. With a violent motion of his arm, he brushed the image away. It broke into fragments and then dissipated like mist in a lime kiln. He flung himself away from the door and into the main room. "It's a waste of energy to think of Nioma. She's dead, and now it is the son of my teaching who rules her domain."

Still muttering, Faring went to his work table, cleared it of debris, and unwrapped a large, clear globe. "Vaar," he murmured and stroked it delicately with his forefinger. For just an instant, responsive colored lights trembled just below its surface. It was this device he used to communicate with Brone's reflector. But Vaar, the globe Faring had inherited from a legendary wizard now long dead, had powers far beyond the mere transmission of face and voice. Compared to Vaar, the reflector Brone used was but a trinket.

There were times when Faring thought of Vaar as a living creature, one with an antic sense of humor who enjoyed testing his patience as well as his skill. Sometimes Vaar brought Faring portents that hinted of future events but required subtle interpretation. Other times it formed clear images of past and future happenings, then left its master to piece together a pattern from their fragments. Most frustrating of all, there were occasions when Vaar warned of danger, yet kept its vaporous images unfathomable.

All day Faring had been plagued by the nagging feeling that something was wrong, that something needed attending to. Now, having stroked Vaar into life, he bent low over the globe. Gazing intently into its depths, he pressed his hands to its smooth shape and importuned it to reveal its secrets. "Open yourself to me, Vaar. Let me see what lies hidden beneath your veils."

Under his palms its cool surface heated. Sluggish clouds thickened in its interior. Bits of images whirled inside the clouds—a girl's gray-eyed face, a jagged streak of green flame, Brone's face, angry and tormented. As Faring strained his eyes, he thought he recognized Eol, Driona, and Taunis. Other images stirred no recognition and went past too quickly for him to study. Though Faring strained all his mental powers, Vaar's clouds stayed murky.

At last, exhausted, Faring leaned back and closed his eyes. Vaar would tell him nothing this day, except that threatening clouds loomed over the Peninsula and that events of great and frightening import readied themselves for the unfolding.

* * * * *

Far beyond the mountains and across the sea, Thropos sat high in the Sturite castle studying his own set of portents. Before him on the table sat a cage made of wicker. Inside the cage, a borset snarled and snapped. Thropos had been starving the small furbearing animal, and now it was desperate for food.

"Soon, my pet," he whispered as he sprinkled a greasy, foul-smelling powder around the outside of the cage. He muttered incantations as he uncorked a vial and shook its contents over the powder.

When he judged the mixture correct, he went to a large cage containing several doves. As they squawked in terror, Thropos reached in and seized one. Then, with the bird fluttering in his hand, the little wizard crossed back to the wicker cage on the table and thrust the dove in with the borset.

Clucking his tongue at the hullabaloo of anguished wings and squeaks and snapping and snarling, Thropos dropped a piece of carefully cured snakeskin onto the top of the wicker cage and sprinkled more powder over it. Then he picked up a lit candle and set the flame to the construction.

Ignoring the cries of the animals suffering inside the flaming wicker, Thropos studied the patterns made by the smoke rising from the cage. The time was ripe, the patterns told him.

When the cage and its contents had fallen into ash, Thropos stood, crossed his hands inside his long black sleeves, and went to the window. Grime from the castle's many chimneys outside and from the small bonfires of his experiments inside streaked the glass so thickly that he could see little. What he did see of the Sturite landscape showed him nothing that he loved. The only place Thropos had loved, the only home where he had been truly happy, had been Peneto. But he had been banished from Peneto, and it was Faring's doing.

The wheel turns and the pendulum swings, he told himself. All these many years I have been biding my time. Now the hour ripens for vengeance, and I will not turn aside from it.

Thropos left his tower room and threaded his way down the many stone steps leading to the occupied area of the castle. As his small black figure, with its twisted back and pallid visage, crept along the dank passages, the tall Sturite nobles kept their distance, some even making the sign to ward off evil. Thropos had made no friends during his many years at Yerbo's court. Every king should have the counsel of a wizard, it was believed, and therefore those such as Thropos were necessary evils. That didn't make them likable.

Purposefully, Thropos headed for the rooms where Arant had been sulking ever since his humiliation in Acuma. He found the prince alone in his gymnasium, taking his frustration out on a sawdust-filled dummy. Sweat sheened his face and naked upper body, and he grunted with rage. "Kill him," he muttered, grinding his teeth and butting the canvas figure with his lowered head. "*Kill* him!"

"Kill who, my lord? Is it Brone you speak of?"

Arant drew back from the bag and concentrated his angry gaze on Thropos. "So it's you. Did my father send you to read me another pious sermon? If so, you're wasting your time. My only regret about Acuma was that I didn't succeed in leveling the city, and Brone along with it."

"I didn't come to chastise you, though that raid was certainly ill-timed and ill-conceived."

Arant gnashed his sharp white teeth. "Why are you here, then, wizard? I warn you, I will not listen to any more of my doddering father's platitudes."

"Platitudes are not what I bring you."

"What then?" Arant's green eyes narrowed suspiciously.

"My help, prince. My guidance and counsel. You asked for these earlier. Do you still want them?"

Eyes still narrowed, Arant gazed down at Thropos. He picked up a towel and mopped his face and pulsing throat. "What brings you to this?"

"Long consideration," Thropos answered with unusual frankness. "That coupled with the realization that before I live out my span, I must taste revenge. The time to prepare for that banquet is now."

"Revenge against who? Faring?"

Thropos nodded and motioned Arant to the far end of the room, where there was no chance of anyone overhearing them. "I will give you three gifts as a surety of my loyalty to you. The first is my story. No one knows the whole of it, not even Yerbo, who has been my generous patron all these years."

Arant lounged against the wall. "Tell me then, though I think I know part of it. You and Faring were boys together at Peneto, isn't that so?"

"Yes. We were both brought there by our parents to be trained in the wizard's craft. All during our apprenticeship, we were friends and rivals. Daily, we pitted our skills against each other. Sometimes he would triumph, and sometimes I. Of our class, we were by far the most gifted. And though he was tall and strongly built and I short and frail, all agreed that in wizardly talents we matched each other evenly."

"It was a friendly rivalry?"

"At times, for we had been raised as brothers. At other times—" Thropos shrugged. "Pride and arrogance were ever Faring's besetting sins, and in those days, they were mine as well. Neither of us liked to think we might have a superior."

Arant nodded his comprehension. He was well acquainted with rivalry. "What happened?"

"The time came when our teachers released our class into the world for its testing. Each of us was to discover his own destiny. Faring and I both vowed that we would return to Peneto at the end of our trial. My purpose never wavered. I came to your father's court, spent the allotted time refining my knowledge, then set off for Peneto via the Peninsula."

Arant ground his teeth. "I know well how Faring squandered his time. He tutored Brone, inciting him to dispossess all the domi so the Peninsulan could set himself up as king."

"He did all of that, but first Faring fell in love."

"In love?" Arrested, Arant cocked his head. "With whom?"

"Nioma, the Peninsula's domis of water."

Arant's ragged red eyebrows shot up. "This I never heard before."

Thropos paced to the wall, checked himself, and limped back. "Few knew of the affair. I never saw her in the full flower of her beauty, but those who did claim she was irresistible."

"She must have been a ripe plum to tempt a bloodless hermit like Faring."

"At that time he was young and far from bloodless," Thropos retorted dryly. "And she did far more than tempt him. He fell deeply, passionately in love with her. She, however, was too light-minded to return the favor. When she tired of his slavish attentions, she rejected him cruelly."

Arant had long since cooled from his exertions with the canvas dummy. Now he flushed all over again, this time with excitement. He stepped closer to the wizard. "That explains why he troubled to set Brone on the domi. He craved vengeance." The Sturite prince worked his jaw. "How is it that you're privy to all this?"

"There's no magic involved, if that's what you're wondering. I know because Faring told me himself. On my way back to Peneto we met in the foothills of the mountains and joined forces. He was hardly a congenial traveling companion, however. He was depressed, upset. I, on the other hand, was full of joy. So glad was I to be returning to Peneto that I paid little mind to Faring's moodiness. Then it happened."

"What?" Arant licked his full lips in anticipation.

"We came upon Nioma, a withered old woman now that she had no stone to keep her young. She was dragging herself to the pool where the water domi go to die. We followed and watched its waters close over her head. At the sight, Faring broke down completely, and sobbed out his story to me like a bereft child. I, unfortunately, did not react with proper sympathy."

"No?"

Arant laughed, but Thropos expression grew grimmer. "I was young. I'd never seen Nioma in her beauty. All I'd seen was a toothless, ugly hag. The thought of my old rival madly in love with such a creature made me jeer at him. Faring reacted with the violence that is part of his nature. Before I could defend myself, he threw me down the side of the mountain and left me for dead. My twisted back is the result."

"But you did not die."

"No." Thropos's shook his head. "Driona found me and nursed me back to a semblance of health. Of course, by the time I recovered enough to travel, it was too late for me to return to Peneto at the appointed hour. Its gates closed to me forever. I returned to your father's castle, and here I've been ever since."

"Perfecting your art and brooding over your injuries," Arant remarked cynically.

Thropos gave a thin smile. "When Driona nursed me, she exacted a promise that I would some day help her regain her stone. Of course, at the time I was so sick I would have promised the lady anything. Lately I've been thinking of that promise, thinking that perhaps it's time to keep it."

"I agree. But you said you would give me three tokens of your loyalty. Your story about Faring is the first. What of the other two?"

Thropos gazed up at Arant shrewdly. "Do you consent to accept my guidance, then?"

The redheaded prince hesitated, then nodded. "I consent. So long as our aims coincide, whatever instruction you give me, I will carry it out."

"Very well, then my second token is this. Recently, I've received word from Taunis and Driona that they seek an alliance against Brone."

Arant's green eyes glittered. "And the third?"

"The third is perhaps the most intriguing of all. It is a young woman nesting like a cuckoo in the bosom of Brone's court, a young woman named Reawen."

Chapter Six

Brone had not been back at the Plat six days when word arrived that a Sturite delegation would visit him. Yerbo, angered and embarrassed by his son's unauthorized raid on Acuma, hoped to smooth over the unpleasant incident. Though he couldn't come himself, he planned to send his eleven-year-old daughter, Fidacia, as ambassador.

"So, you're to meet my intended at last," Brone told his mother. They had just breakfasted together and now lingered over a final cup of hot cider. Since returning from Acuma, Brone had spent more time than usual at the Zeleta. His mother had needed no urging to allow Reawen to return to service there, and after dinner, Brone always asked to hear her play.

"When you came back from that mission to Zica, you described Fidacia as charming," said Killip.

"She is a striking little creature," Brone agreed. "Great wads of red hair, huge green eyes, a high-spirited manner. Obviously, her father considers her a wonder. Yerbo's letter implies that once I lay eyes on her again I'll be so enchanted I'll forget the atrocities at Acuma entirely."

"I hope he's right, but somehow, from your tone, I get the impression that's unlikely. When you returned from Zica those many months ago, quite apart from regarding marriage to Fidacia as politically helpful, you seemed taken with the girl."

"I was. She's a charmer. But she's also a child. It'll be years before our marriage can be consummated. I'm beginning to realize that I want a real wife now."

Killip frowned delicately. "If Fidacia is as irresistible as you say, surely she's worth waiting for."

"A man doesn't really know what he finds irresistible until the right woman comes along. Only then does he know."

"Are you telling me that you've seen another who strikes your fancy more?"

Brone played with the handle of his cup. "I am a king, and a king knows his duty. If the breach with the Sturites can be mended, I'm still prepared to take their princess as my bride."

Killip sighed. "I hope the minute you lay eyes on her again, she'll delight you so that you will claim her for your wife, and all this strife and tension will disappear. It seems that, since Leana died, you've been beset by worries."

Brone laughed harshly. "And like all women, you imagine that a good wife will soothe all such problems away." Unconsciously, his hand lifted to his brow where he touched the circlet around his head. He knew Leana's death wasn't behind his problems. No, it was the stone-laden band that had grown so burdensome.

Striving for lightness, he said, "Well, perhaps Fidacia will tease me out of my moodiness." He moved his spoon a half inch to the right and then pushed it back again. "Speaking of charming women, I don't suppose your reed player is about?"

"Reawen?" Killip looked amused. "I never ask her to entertain me at breakfast, if that's what you're wondering. She has other duties in the morning."

"Have you forgiven her for running off to have a look at the war in Acuma?"

"Of course. Reawen's not a slave, you know. She's young and spirited, perhaps too spirited for the quiet life we lead here. I fear she finds my household rather dull, poor child. But I should be very sorry to lose her. Not only is she a pleasure to listen to, she's a pleasure to look at as well."

Brone cleared his throat. "I'd like to borrow her to entertain the Sturite delegation when it arrives, if you don't mind."

"Of course I don't mind." The queen mother cocked her handsome head. "You have your eye on her, don't you?"

A faint redness crept up the back of Brone's neck. "I think she's a fine musician."

"Oh, you think more about her than that," Killip replied archly. "I'm not so old that I don't recognize the look you get when Reawen's about. And I agree, she's a lovely creature. But she's very young."

"I know she's young. Fidacia is even younger."

"Yes, but that will be a marriage of state, quite a different matter."

"I am not precisely in my dotage, you know."

"No, of course you're not." As Killip gazed at her son, a frown tugged at her pale brows. Brone was still a young man, in the prime of his life. Yet he looked much older than his years. Just in the last few months, his forehead had become deeply lined. Now, for the first time, she noticed sprinklings of silver in his golden hair. "When you mentioned meeting a woman you found irresistible, I suspect you were speaking of Reawen. If you fancy her, why don't you make her your mistress? I will not object."

"Perhaps you will not object, but the same isn't true of the lady herself. I've already asked and she's said no."

Killip stared. "She actually said no?"

"Yes, Mother, she actually refused. And you know I have never been one to force a woman."

"Perhaps that's because you never needed to. They've always come running at your slightest nod," Killip replied tartly. She laughed. "My little Reawen actually refused you. How very interesting."

A quarter of an hour later, Brone left his mother and strode rapidly along the stone path across the gardens toward his palace. Since returning from Acuma, he'd been anxious and irritable. Breakfast with Killip that morning had done nothing to improve his mood.

"Any sign of Albin?" he asked Pib when he reached the tables.

The strawberry-blond stablehand pointed at Grassears's empty stall. "No word yet, Sire. Hope he hasn't run into trouble."

Brone's expression darkened. "I hope so, too." He turned and strode from the stables, musing.

Back in his rooms, the king went to his cabinet and withdrew the leather case containing the reflector. Several times since Faring had warned him about the attack on Acuma he'd tried communicating with his mentor. But, for the first time since Faring had given him the reflector, all his attempts had been unsuccessful. It was his mentor's silence that had made Brone decide to send Albin to Peneto.

In pain from the stones and distressed at being unable to raise anything but clouds with the reflector, he'd wanted Faring's opinion on the Sturite raid. At the time, sending Albin had seemed reasonable. But the route was dangerous. Brone was fond of his young messenger and didn't relish the thought that he might be harmed.

Now the king bent over the reflector once more and struggled to clear his mind for another try at communication. He had been too long without Faring's counsel and sensed danger coming at him from every quarter.

For long, frustrating minutes, the glass remained clear. Finally clouds gathered within it. They swirled and thickened, went dark and then light again, but revealed nothing. What was wrong? Brone wondered. It was almost as if something standing between Peneto and Jedestrom was deliberately interfering. One of the domi? He hadn't thought they had the strength. Could one of them have gained some new power? Or was it something else entirely? Some other mighty wizard, perhaps?

Touching the stones and pressing his hands to his aching temples, Brone concentrated his call to Faring. To his surprise and relief, the mists within the disc parted abruptly, and he saw the wizard's haughty face.

"Finally!" Faring exclaimed. "I've been calling to you for

many days now, but you've refused to answer."

"On the contrary. I've been trying to get through to you. I've raised nothing but fog. Has my emissary arrived at Peneto?"

"Emissary?"

"A messenger named Albin. I sent him to beg you for some spell to relieve the pain of the stones. They grow unbearable."

"No emissary has arrived at Peneto. As for the stones, they are the price you pay for your power. You knew that when you sought to wear them."

"I was an ignorant boy. Now I am a man, who's beginning to think that the price of power is too high. They torment me, Faring, and every day the agony grows worse."

For an instant compassion flickered in the wizard's gray eyes. Then he shook his head. "I have no spell that can help you. The domi stones are a law unto themselves. They were passed to the domi by the earthtenders. As for this Albin of yours, if he went through the mountains, he's probably dead."

"Dead!"

"Have you forgotten the wild magic? When you went into the mountains to steal the stones, I gave you a charm against the magic. Has your Albin such a charm?"

Brone pounded his fist into his palm. "I'd forgotten the wild magic. It's been so long, and I was distracted with the Sturites."

"If the wild magic left by the earthtenders didn't get him, the domi may have. They still roam there, you know, along with wolves and other predators. A lone traveler would be in great danger these days."

"He's not alone. I sent a soldier to protect him."

Faring merely shrugged. Then his eyes narrowed. "I too have had trouble. Vaar, who always sees so clearly, has shown me only clouds and confusion. However, several things have appeared briefly out of the mists, and I should tell you of them before this image fades. One is a girl's face."

"A girl's face?"

"Yes." Faring looked perplexed. "Dark hair, silvery eyes, young and pretty. I know her not, but I do know that if Vaar shows her to me, she must hold some key."

Brone opened his mouth to reply, but at that instant Faring's image vanished. Turgid darkness replaced it. Try as Brone might, he couldn't break through. Finally, he gave up the effort, leaned back, and massaged his aching forehead. A girl with dark hair and silvery eyes, he thought. Who else could it be but Reawen? And, according to Faring, she holds a key to the future.

Faring would have been surprised to see that the thought made him smile.

* * * * *

The sun shone in Jedestrom, but Albin had not seen its face in the mountains since before his encounter with Eol. For a day and a night, freezing rain had leaked from the sullen sky, icing the all but impassable path. Wet, cold to the bone, frightened, and miserable, Albin and Grassears struggled to find their way out of a maze of dizzying crevasses and rocky precipices.

"I think the wolves are still following," Albin whispered into one of his horse's hairy ears. "If we can't find wood dry enough to build us a good fire tonight, they'll have us for dinner."

Grassears snorted and quickened his pace. But the frozen path made speed treacherous—not to mention the crafty and malicious trees, which lashed their leafless branches out like living whips and sometimes even whispered insults from mouths hidden in their bark. And it wasn't just the trees. Twice already the shaggy little horse had stumbled to his knees in fright when eerie laughter had boomed out from what appeared to be a solid wall of rock.

Albin was a mass of cuts, bruises, and sore muscles. As shadows gathered and the sleet continued to dribble down, he became so anxious that he finally guided Grassears off the trail and into a stand of evergreens. He waited anxiously to see if any would speak to him or try to stab him with their needled boughs. When they did not, he breathed a small sigh of relief and patted his horse's head. "We have to find dry wood and get a fire going," he muttered. "If we don't have a blaze by nightfall to warm and protect us, we're finished for sure."

After such a long, unbroken rain, scaring up fuel that might ignite was no easy task. Tying his horse where he could crop grass, Albin spent the next hour searching. Frustrated after working for some time with no success over a small pile of tinder, he pushed a strand of wet hair off his face and glanced up. A faint light glowed in the distance.

"Now what could that be?" he asked himself, lifting his head and squinting. Untying Grassears—for he knew he couldn't leave the horse alone and unprotected—Albin threaded his way through the woods toward the glow.

"A fire," he whispered to the horse. "A big one. Maybe we're in luck. If someone friendly built it, we might find warmth for our frozen hides and food for our empty bellies."

On the other hand, chances were better than good that whoever commanded the fire was not friendly in the least. Tying Grassears to a tree at a distance, Albin approached cautiously.

The word "big" was inadequate to describe the bonfire raging in the center of the large clearing. So great was its heat and intensity that it warmed Albin's cheeks, even though he'd hidden himself well among the trees at a distance of at least fifty paces. Who in the world could have started such a magnificent blaze in this sort of weather? he wondered. Then a fox-faced figure dressed in bright red strode forth from the shadows, and Albin had his answer.

Taunis! Stunned, the young messenger clung to his tree. Now he was glad that he'd been so careful, for Taunis mustn't see him. Eol had spared him only so he could report to Brone. And Eol, though ruthless and capricious, had the reputation of being a hundred times better natured than Taunis.

Albin took a step backward, hoping to sneak away undetected. He stopped. Out of the corner of his eye he'd caught a flicker of movement. Though the stormy night ringed the firelit clearing, a particularly dense darkness loomed on the side opposite Albin's hiding place.

It grew larger and blacker. Then it bulged into the simmering light like the shiny black egg case of some monstrous, many-legged insect. Even Taunis appeared taken aback by this apparition. He'd stopped pacing around his bonfire and turned to stare open-mouthed at the egg case.

The shiny thing grew so swollen that it looked as if it must burst and spew out a horde of hungry spiders. A crack appeared at its rounded top and traveled down its length. Above the roar of the flames, Albin heard a faint but spine-tingling tearing sound. He turned away from the clearing, prepared to run, but his eyes stayed fixed on the horrible capsule.

The crack widened into a gap and then swung open neatly. But instead of the insects Albin feared would scramble from it, a lone man stepped out. "Thropos," Albin breathed, recognizing the wizard he'd seen on his visit to the Sturite court with King Brone. Then he clapped a hand over his mouth and stared anxiously, fearing that one of the two in the clearing might have heard him.

Fortunately, they were far too intent on their meeting to pay attention to anything else. Taunis stepped forward and spread his arms wide, obviously greeting Thropos. As they drew close, the two made a dramatic contrast. Thropos—small, wizened, misshapen, dressed in dusty black. Taunis—tall and erect, foxfaced, aswirl in crimson robes.

Fascinated, Albin watched Taunis lead the Sturite wizard closer to his bonfire. For several seconds they stood talking. Then Taunis stretched his long arm, pointed at the flames, and made a slow circular motion.

Albin's eyes widened. The blaze changed color and texture,

darkened and took on a thick viscosity. Suddenly, sparks leaped from it. They burned brighter, shot upward, then congealed into figures with legs and arms and pointed candleflame heads. At Taunis's direction, they twirled and danced, somersaulted and leapfrogged.

Why, they're creatures made of flame, Albin thought, and they're putting on a show for Thropos!

But the Sturite wizard was not to be outdone. After watching for several minutes and then clapping his hands politely, he straightened and then stretched out a bony finger. He appeared to chant something, though Albin couldn't make out the words.

Again, the black canopy of night above the dancing flames seemed to gather itself and grow denser. From it, beaked, dragonlike creatures with sooty wings exploded into the firelight. They circled above the flamedancers, screaming silently from distended beaks. Then they dived directly into the pirouetting flamedancers, apparently immolating themselves.

But that was not the case. A moment later the winged beings shot out of the heads of the flamedancers. They rocketed up and exploded against the stormy night sky with a sound like thunderclaps, showering the clearing with many-colored sparks.

Dumbfounded, Albin watched all this. What in the world was going on? He focused his attention back on Taunis and Thropos, and suddenly he knew. The fire domis's flamedancers and the wizard's miniature dragons had been shows of strength. In the guise of cordiality, Taunis and Thropos each had paraded his strength for the other's benefit. This was the opening round in a secret negotiation of some sort.

Albin wished he could hear what the two were saying, but that was impossible. Whatever they were discussing, he felt sure they were plotting treason against King Brone. Albin dared not watch any longer. Somehow, he had to steal away from this spot and make it back to Jedestrom to warn the king.

* * * * *

As the day of the banquet for the Sturite delegation drew close, rumors hatched inside the Zeleta like gnats in spring. Reawen could hear them buzzing throughout the palace.

"*Fidacia is still a child..*"

" *. . . so lovely . . .*"

"*She hates her brother, that marauding . . .*"

"*The king is besotted!*"

"*Would he break tradition?*"

" *. . . announcing his engagement before the Choosing!*"

Reawen had no way of gauging the truth of all this tattle. She did know that many days had passed since Brone had bothered to visit the Zeleta. When she'd ridden back with his army from Acuma, she'd told herself to be patient, to bide her time and wait for the right opportunity. But what if the right opportunity for regaining her stone didn't present itself in time?

When Brone's secretary had come to question her about her background, she'd given him a story that would not be easy to discredit. Still, what if the runners he'd sent out managed to uncover her deception sooner than she expected? Even if they never stumbled on the truth, what if, after Brone married Fidacia, she ceased to see him except on public occasions? What if she lived out the rest of her life in the Zeleta, tantalizingly close to the stone but never able to regain it?

No, Reawen decided. Better to take the offensive, to act boldly and have the issue resolved. And the banquet might provide a chance to do exactly that.

By the night of her performance, Reawen had made a plan. To be sure, with only her small store of knowledge about Brone's household to go on, her scheme was chancy. Yet, it was the best she could devise, so she steeled herself to see it through.

That evening, the king's steward collected Reawen along with the other performers selected to entertain Brone's guests.

The banquet hall was a huge room alight with the flames of a thousand candles and awash with sound and color.

Looking around, Reawen felt dazzled. While she was dressed in a lavish—or so it seemed to her—lilac gown with an embroidered bodice, she felt drab compared to the hundred chattering guests garbed in exotic costumes of every hue and description. They sat at long tables carved from lanken and covered with platters of meat, steaming vegetables, and jellied fruits. As the people gorged, the painted beams on the ceilings echoed with titters, roars of rough laughter, and the clank of dishes and cutlery.

Reawen spied Brone immediately. He sat facing the assembled guests at a long table carved more magnificently than all the others. The king's dark blue velvet tunic opened at the throat and boasted full sleeves, which fell back at the wrists to reveal a white silk underblouse. Brone looked handsome and noble. His only ornaments, she noted with a tightening in her chest, were the stones. In the artificial light, they glowed softly on the gold band that seemed almost indistinguishable from the gilded glitter of his hair.

The young domis tightened her fingers on her reed until they ached from pressure. Surely, she told herself, he must take the crown off at night to sleep. Her scheme depended on that.

On either side of the king, ladies and lords in silks, velvets, and winking jewels talked and quaffed goblets of wine. As they laughed and smiled, they gnawed at joints of meat, picked at bowls of fruit, and sank their teeth into slices from crusty loaves of freshly baked bread.

Reawen picked out Fidacia at once. She was a glowing young creature with a pointed chin and a pretty mouth. Above her slanted eyebrows, masses of flame-red hair set off her creamy skin. Her apple-green silk dress underlined the brilliance of her wide green eyes. Anyone could see that very soon she would mature into a striking beauty.

In the cleared space facing the royal table, a troop of jugglers performed. They tossed first balls, then knives, then finally a dizzying succession of lit torches. Amazing though their feats seemed to Reawen, none of the other diners paid attention. Was skill of this kind so commonplace that no one even bothered to look? she wondered.

Servers outfitted in the royal colors of blue and gold came bearing more platters heaped with food. Reawen tracked the progress of a tray loaded with uncooked meat. A young boy with short legs and a worried expression carried it to a table at the far end of the hall.

When he reached his destination, Reawen realized why he seemed nervous. Though the creatures standing around the table had arms and legs like men, their bodies were covered with a greenish-gray, snakelike skin. Ornamental gold bands coiled up their arms. She stared. They were the odd creatures named Gutaini she'd first seen with Albin on the highway into Jedestrom.

To her amazement, they ate standing up, tearing at their food and peering around them suspiciously. When the boy reached them with the tray, they seized it from him roughly and discourteously turned their backs. With their sloping foreheads, scaly flesh, and heavy-lidded eyes, they didn't seem human at all, Reawen thought. Their clannish rudeness reinforced the impression.

The serving lad hurried away, and Reawen averted her eyes. She found herself gazing at Albin, who stood at attention in the retinue behind the king. This was the first time she'd laid eyes on him since he'd returned from his mission in the mountains. She had been worried about him and was pleased to see that he'd returned safely.

It must have been a difficult journey, Reawen thought. Albin looked thin and pale, and there were dark shadows under his eyes, as though he'd gone days without sleep. He smiled at her, and she smiled back, warmed by the sight of a friend in this alien crowd.

When the jugglers left the floor, Fidacia suddenly stood. After announcing in a childish voice that she would dance for the king, she walked around the head table to the open area in front. The lines of her body, trembling on the edge of budding womanhood, were clearly visible beneath her tight gown. After shooting a dazzling smile at Brone, she began to sway. Her slender hips vibrated while her fingers clicked a slow rhythm. On cue, a Sturite musician appeared out of the crowd and began to beat a drum. Another blew a melody on a set of pipes. Against its spiraling song, Fidacia's arms twined around her torso in languorous weavings.

All at once, the musicians' rhythms gathered speed, and the Sturite princess began to writhe and twist, riveting everyone's attention. As her grace gave way to abandoned energy, the dance climaxed in a frenzy of motion. Suddenly, the music ended, and Fidacia arched backward, sinking to the floor amid thunderous applause.

After taking many bows, she returned to the king's table, and the steward signaled Reawen. Quite certain that after Fidacia's flamboyant performance, hers could only be anticlimactic, Reawen took the floor. Though she did not look directly at Brone or Albin, she sensed their eyes on her. Tonight, she repeated over and over in her mind as she found her place on the floor and lifted the reed to her lips. *Tonight.*

With the first few notes from her reed, Reawen lost herself in her music. The raucous noise of the banquet hall flowed around her unheeded; she found herself once again in the world of undersea wonder she had discovered beneath the ocean off Acuma's shore. Her music swelled and rolled with the tales from the old man's storyrocks. Her notes raced at the terrific speed of a larfin through sun-glinted waters and trebled and trilled with the songs of the Pleons, those laughing foam mistresses. Reawen's melody washed over all who were gathered in the hall that night, nobles and servants alike, taking them to cool rivers and sun-splashed pools. As the last lingering notes ebbed gently away, her audience felt the pull of an emotion they didn't quite understand; they shared in the longing of a young water domis afraid of never again knowing the pure joys of her realm.

The applause of the diners brought Reawen back to herself. Dashing away the last of the magical memories her music had awakened, she bowed to the head table without really seeing it. She quickly left the hall, her thoughts all on her plan. Somehow she had to hide herself inside the king's private chamber. But first she had to find it.

Several minutes and several hallways later, Reawen looked nervously to either side of yet another corridor. She advanced cautiously down the empty hall. If anyone discovered her in this area of the Plat, she would surely be ejected and her plan ruined.

"I've never seen the cook in such a temper. He nearly killed that apprentice who dropped the peacock pudding."

At the sound of the petulant voice, Reawen slipped into a shadowy alcove and willed the passers-by not to see her. Gris had tried to teach her how to create an illusion of invisibility, but she was even less adept at it than at the mindtouch. In fact, she'd only resorted to it once before, when she'd come upon a mother bear with her cubs in the forest. And that was a long time ago. Now Reawen closed her eyes and visualized Gris standing before her.

"Make of yourself a clear pool," she instructed. "Create such a stillness within you and around you that, for others, you cease to be."

The technique apparently succeeded, for the two servants strolled past without looking her way. Reawen decided to press her advantage. Tentatively, she reached out mentally to the one carrying a stack of towels and began the mindtouch. A few seconds later, she smiled in relief. Luck was with her; he'd shown her the route to Brone's chambers.

Still, it wouldn't be easy to get there unseen. Another

servant, carrying a tray loaded with goblets, swung around the corner. Hastily regathering her mental forces, Reawen concentrated on becoming a clear, still pool once again, and he passed her by. After his footsteps died away, she slumped against the wall. Her hands trembled. I can't lose my nerve, or I'll surely fail, she told herself. Tonight I have to be stronger than I have ever been before.

Reawen continued down the corridor, then turned to her right down another passageway. The closer she got to the king's quarters, the more servants she had to fool. The supreme test came when she met the sentry standing at attention outside Brone's door. She hung back, waiting for a servant to give her the opportunity she needed. After a few eternal moments, a maid approached the sentry carrying a pitcher and wine goblet on a tray. As the guard treated her to a grin and loud greeting, Reawen mustered all her strength and skill, placed herself squarely inside a waveless pool, and followed the maid into the room. She stood stock-still as the maid set the pitcher and goblet on a small table in the sitting room, then turned to leave. When Reawen saw the king's door close behind her and heard the jovial voice of the sentry bid the maid good night, she wanted to shout. If only Gris could see this! she thought. She'd be proud of me.

As Reawen reminded herself what she still had to do, the feeling of triumph fled all too quickly. She began inspecting Brone's sitting room with a racing heart. Though it was large, it was furnished simply. Reawen tiptoed to a doorway and found a large, but equally plain bedroom. Really, for a king's private quarters, these rooms didn't seem all that magnificent, she thought. The queen mother lived in far greater luxury. Adjoining the sitting room on the opposite wall was a map room, Reawen discovered, with much finer appointments.

Reawen crossed the bare wood floor back to the bedchamber and halted at a table next to the bed. The table held a painted bowl and a pitcher filled with water. Much of her plan had depended on finding water in Brone's room. Now that she had discovered it, she took heart.

Delicately, Reawen dipped her fingers into the water, forming it into a ball. When the round shape lay quivering in her palm, she moved to the dark red curtains drawn tight against the night. She concealed herself within their folds, parting them just enough to provide her a view of the door.

Hour after hour crawled by, and Reawen waited tensely. Several times she heard voices in the hall, but no one entered. She could only stand in the dark, reviewing her plan and thinking of all the things that might go wrong. Should she attempt to make herself invisible again when the king arrived? She decided against the idea; she doubted she could sustain the concentration that long. What if Brone brought a woman back to his rooms with him? It would matter not, she told herself sternly. Hadn't she watched him with Nioma in the water images? If she could do that, she had the stomach for anything.

Nevertheless, she was very glad that, when the king finally came to his chambers, he was alone. She heard him dismiss a servant and shut the door to the hall. Through the crack in the draperies, she watched Brone stride across the sitting room into the bedchamber, remove the gold band from his head, and set it on the table next to the basin with a loud clank. Reawen almost gasped with relief and pent-up excitement. So far, so good.

However, late though it was, he seemed in no hurry to retire. Prowling to the window, he pulled the heavy curtain back. Mere inches from where Reawen had hidden herself, he stood looking out into the darkness. She shrank inward, barely managing to throw up her protective illusion in time.

Her control was on the point of snapping when he finally moved away. But then it was only to go to the sitting room to retrieve the goblet of wine and throw himself into a chair close to a pair of candles. Their flames sent shifting patterns of light trembling like frightened thieves around the far corners of the room and across the doorjamb. Brone stretched out his long legs and sighed heavily. For many minutes he sat swirling the bowled shape of the goblet between his hands.

Reawen wondered what he thought about. From his expression, something troubled him deeply. It was strange to see Brone like this, his face naked and brooding. She acknowledged to herself that he was a very attractive man. Instantly, however, she rebelled against the admission, closed her eyes, and wished the night were over. She hated the intimacy of this situation, the humiliation of playing the spy.

At last the king stirred. He set his drained goblet on the table, rose, and crossed to the bedchamber, carrying the candle-holder. Reawen's eyelids flew up as she watched him strip off his clothing and drop it in a careless heap on the floor. She'd never seen a naked man before. This broad-shouldered warrior was so different from the boy who had made love to Nioma. Yet they were one and the same, she reminded herself, and her gaze left him and sought out the gold band next to the water pitcher.

With another heavy groan, Brone doused the candles and flung himself down. The room folded into a close, velvet darkness. Yet he didn't sleep. Even in the dark Reawen's keen gaze saw him lying faceup on the bed, staring open-eyed at the ceiling. Her shoulders cramped with tension. Why didn't he sleep? she wondered. Surely during the evening he'd drunk enough wine to put an ox into a stupor. Yet, even without trying mind-touch, she sensed his thoughts humming. Finally, however, he closed his eyes, and the night curled its hand around him.

When she knew that he was asleep, Reawen exhaled a slow breath. All of her body ached now. Gingerly, she eased from her hiding place. Her legs felt so stiff that she feared she might stumble and fall. She waited, breathing deeply and flexing her knees slightly, until she felt strength and control return.

After a last worried glance at the sleeping king, Reawen focused on the crown on the table next to him. Brone had told her it was protected by a binding and couldn't be touched. There was no way to know the exact nature of the spell, which had probably been cast by Faring. Still, there were more ways than one to pick up a crown. She didn't have to use her hands. Uncurling her fingers, she looked down at the ball of water glimmering in her palm.

Softly, Reawen approached the table. When she stood at its edge, she turned her attention to the water. Between her hands she stretched it into a thin sheet, then spun it into gossamer threads. Deftly, she wove the threads into a fine, flexible net. Spinning water webs had been one of the first skills Gris had taught her. Often as a child, Reawen had captured birds with water nets and then laughingly set the birds free. Now she intended recapturing what Nioma had so carelessly lost. And once I have the stone back, she told herself, I'll never let it go.

As Reawen prepared to drop the net, she worried about what might happen when it touched the crown. What if it flashed, shot sparks, or warned Brone in some other way? Even if none of that occurred, what if dragging the heavy crown off the table made a noise that woke him up? She cast a quick, fearful look in his direction, then firmed her shoulders. It was too late to turn back now.

Standing directly over the crown with her back to Brone— but vividly aware of his regular breathing—she stretched the net wide. She was flexing her fingers to release it when her ears picked up a peculiar rustling. Reawen froze. She inched her gaze around, searching the darkness for the source of the noise. For a beat of time, her heart seemed to turn to ice in her breast. The rustle came from something on the floor, something crawling toward the king's bed.

As she strained to see through the shadows, she spied a sort of snake. Growing up in the mountains, Reawen had seen many serpents, and had even made casual pets of some less poisonous ones. She knew the different species native to the Peninsula, but this thing squirming past her feet was like nothing she had ever encountered.

It isn't alive, she realized as she watched it coil itself around the leg of Brone's bed and inch up the post. It was some sort of mechanical device. With a flash of memory, she realized it resembled the ornaments she'd seen twined around the scaly arms of the Gutaini banquet guests. Now, however, it had a hideously menacing animation.

Having achieved the top of the post, it began to writhe along the platform, toward where the king lay, naked and defenseless. As Reawen watched in horror, it crawled near his head, and a tiny needlelike tongue slid from its metal jaws. It did not stop at Brone's head, or at his arm, which was flung back against the pillow. Instead it homed in on his exposed throat.

With every instinct, Reawen knew it had been sent to kill him. The question was what her reaction should be. Despicable as the thing was, it didn't appear to threaten her. In fact, it had slithered past her feet without even appearing to notice. What's more, if Brone were dead—and not by her hand—retrieving the crown would be much easier. But, as she stared at the evil thing's rearing head and saw it prepare to strike, her hands assumed a will of their own. Swiftly, they dropped the net of water over the vile contrivance and pulled the web tight.

The instant the water net touched the mechanical serpent, the device began to sizzle and smoke. Brone jerked to a sitting position as a shower of sparks exploded. With a cry, he seized Reawen's arm and very nearly snapped it at the shoulder.

A second later, his door crashed open and the sword-brandishing sentry erupted into the bedchamber. Running feet echoed in the corridor, and several other guards shot into the sitting room. Behind them, Albin darted in and approached the king, carrying a torch that lit up the bizarre scene.

Brone, naked, every taut muscle defined in the torchlight, held tight to Reawen's arm. They stared into each other's faces, while flickering shadows carved their features into masks.

Between them lay the shell of the Gutaini snake. Its acrid odor fouled the air.

"It's one of their damned filthy assassinators!" the first sentry cried out, gesturing at the smoldering piece of metal.

With his free hand, Brone flung the deadly thing away from his bed. His hard blue eyes stayed fixed on Reawen. "What were you doing in my room?" At her silence, he tightened his fingers so that she gasped. "Answer me!"

"I left my reed in the banquet hall," she improvised, "but when I came back to find it, I lost my way. The corridors here are a maze."

Brone looked disbelieving. "Go on."

Reawen's glance wavered, and she caught sight of Albin's shocked expression. Throwing back her head she turned to Brone and went on in a steadier voice. "I passed by your door and saw the thing crawl beneath. It looked dangerous, so I followed. When it crept up onto your bed and reared to strike, I threw water on it."

She indicated the bedclothes, and Brone's eyes followed, noting the water spots on them. His grip lessened slightly. "Why weren't you stopped by my sentry?"

Reawen shrugged. "He was asleep, so I walked right past."

The man flushed a dark red. He could hardly deny her claim for, after all, she was in the room, and he hadn't waylaid her.

"Perhaps I was under a spell, my lord," he interrupted. "Perhaps whoever set the assassinator in motion had the power of blinding me."

"Or perhaps you were asleep, just as she claims," Brone retorted. Casually pulling the bed cover over the lower portion of his body, he continued to survey Reawen. Suddenly, all remaining traces of anger left his face, and he looked amused. He released her hand and turned to Albin.

"Escort the lady back to her quarters, and, when you've done that, return here. I'm going to dress and call on our Gutaini visitors. I'm curious to know who's missing an arm bracelet."

Albin led Reawen past the murmuring guards and out of the king's rooms. As she followed him from the Plat and across to the Zeleta, she realized that he was upset about something more than what had just happened to the king. But she was far too miserable over her failure to recover her stone to pay much attention to Albin.

"Here's your room." He stopped in front of her door and thrust it open.

Surprised by his tone, she looked up and saw him glaring at her. "I'm sorry about the snake, but it was a lucky coincidence that I saw it."

"Coincidence? Do you think I don't know what you were doing? You were in that corridor in the middle of the night, creeping to his room like a . . . like a . . ." Albin strangled on the words. For a moment he stood clenching and unclenching his fists, apparently speechless with strong emotion.

Glaring at Reawen and breathing hard, he said, "You can have no idea what I've just been through. I almost died in the mountains! Once I was almost ripped to pieces by a pack of hungry wolves. Another time I nearly froze to death. Two things kept me going—duty to my king and the knowledge that you would be here waiting for me when I came back." Snapping his jaws shut as if biting back an even greater torrent of angry words, he stalked quickly away, leaving Reawen standing there with her mouth open.

Chapter Seven

Later in the week, Brone stood at the map room window, contemplating the river. He watched boatmen pole a gaudy pleasure craft bearing a contingent of foreign diplomats. Though the Choosing was weeks away, already foreigners crowded the city.

A knock sounded. "Come in," Brone said gruffly and turned to face the door.

Albin opened it. "You sent for me, Sire?"

"Indeed, I did. It's time we talked again about this business in the mountains."

Albin bowed and took a step forward. But resentment glowed in his eyes and stiffened his shoulders. Albin still hadn't recovered from the shock of finding Reawen in King Brone's bedroom. Though he had been warned by the unfortunate Waylo, it had come as a terrible shock.

The king, caught up in his own concerns, didn't notice. "We haven't had a proper discussion since the discovery of the Gutaini assassinator."

"No, Sire."

Arms akimbo, Brone began to pace. "Do you know that we found one of the Gutaini emissaries dead of a knife wound? He had been stripped of his bracelet."

"Everyone knows that, Sire. The Gutaini trumpeted it throughout the city. Have you caught the outlander's murderer?"

"We have not, Albin. But I suspect it was someone in the Sturite entourage, some agent of Arant's, no doubt."

Albin watched as the king rubbed the deep crease between his brows. He looked tired, but not unhappy—as if he had a secret that buoyed his spirits. Bitterly, Albin thought about Reawen. He knew he had no right to feel angry because she preferred to king to him.

Yet, he couldn't help himself. All the way through the mountains, as he fled the wild-magic and the minions his panicked mind imagined Taunis would send after him, the thought of her had been at the back of his mind, lending him strength. He'd even considered asking her if she'd like to become promised to him. Then, to arrive home and find that she'd been sneaking off to King Brone's chambers—it was almost more than Albin could do to relax and stop glaring at the king he'd worshipped as a hero for so many years.

"As you can imagine, all this makes it awkward to accept the peace negotiations the Sturites came to offer."

Albin nodded. "Where are the Sturites now?"

"Still housed in the royal compound, but under guard. I don't care to find any more death devices in my sleeping quarters." The corners of Brone's mouth lifted. "Though I would certainly not object to my lady mother's lovely reed player saving me again." He turned a bemused countenance to Albin. "Have you seen Reawen?"

Albin answered sullenly. "Not since the night of the assassination attempt, Sire."

The king shook his head. "A shy and lovely creature. It's been a busy week. Even so, I've walked to the Zeleta on several occasions in hopes of finding her alone. I've been wanting to give her my special thanks. Each time, she's hidden herself away like a fawn from a huntsman."

Albin had been too angry and jealous to seek Reawen out himself. Even so, he was glad to hear she'd been avoiding the king. At least that meant she was modest enough to feel some shame at her wanton behavior.

Shrugging the subject off, Brone planted himself in front of the map of the Peninsula. "These are perilous times, my boy."

Albin nodded and drew near. With these sentiments he

could sympathize all too well. "My liege, have you given thought to the news I brought about the domi?"

"I have, and it only confirms my fears. Enemies surround us, enemies who plot against us. We have no proof, but it's certain that Thropos is helping to brew up some evil. I had hoped that a marriage to Fidacia would change a foe into a strong ally. Now I question the wisdom of that strategy.

"It's possible that by choosing the Sturite princess—whose brother, my sworn enemy, will soon come to power—I will only anger the other nations who put forth their princesses as bridal candidates. What's more, it's time to provide myself and the Peninsula with an heir. Fidacia will not be of childbearing age for years." Brone shot Albin a quizzical look. "What would you do in my place?"

The messenger's jaw dropped. Never before had the king asked advice from so lowly a person as he. To hear him asking it now on a matter of such intimacy and importance—"Sire I . . . I . . ."

The king smiled indulgently. "There are times when you remind me of myself."

"I do?" Albin's hazel eyes dilated.

"Oh, not in looks, or even in demeanor. But there is a quality about you . . ." Brone sighed. "It reminds me of my youth, when all things seemed much simpler. 'Tis not particularly logical, I suppose, but I would trust you with my life, Albin. Give me your honest opinion, were you in my place, what would you do?"

Albin drew himself up. "From what I've seen, marriage is a tricky business, one that's as like to create foes as friends. I wouldn't rely on it to bring peace. Instead, I would seek out a new strategy or weapon with which to confound my enemies." He glanced at the band of stones around his monarch's head, for what he really meant was that the king should defend the Peninsula by calling up their power.

Brone's face lit. "Exactly what I have been thinking myself.

Better yet, I believe that I may have just such a device. Come with me, Albin, and if you will vow to keep mum about what you see, I will show you."

Puzzled, Albin followed the king out of the Plat and down the raked path that led to the armorer's quarters.

"Buw has set up a secret demonstration in this storeroom," Brone told him when they arrived at a squat stone building. He knocked, then pushed open the door.

The moment they crossed its threshold, Buw hurried out of the gloom. The old weapons master and commander of Jedestrom's army thrust closed the heavy metal-studded lanken door behind them, securing it with bolts. "For safety and secrecy, my liege," he murmured, turning his bald head to shoot Albin an uncertain glance.

Brone placed a hand on the boy's shoulder. "I've decided to acquaint my personal messenger with this weapon," he told the armorer. "He's as close to me as anyone at court, and I will need a dependable confidante."

Buw ran a forbidding eye over Albin's gangly length. "If the king trusts you, that's good enough for me. But heed me. Tell no one else of what you see here. Its whole effect may depend on surprise."

Wondering what this mystery could be, Albin nodded and followed a step behind the king as the heavyset warrior led them both to a large table. For the first time, Albin noticed the man who stood at its head. "Phen!"

"You know this fellow?" Brone demanded.

Albin nodded. "I met him at a tavern near Acuma."

The king frowned. "A strange coincidence."

"Far stranger things happen in war," Phen countered with a laugh. He addressed Brone as easily and confidently as he had Albin weeks earlier. And as before, something in his bluff manner commanded both liking and trust. "Happened your messenger and I shared a cup of ale and a few words about the Sturite invasion, nothing more. If you harbor any doubts about the likes of me, you can ask Buw here to vouch for my character."

"Phen and I were boys together," Buw spoke up sturdily. "With him at my back, I would not hesitate to charge an army of Sturites." His leather tunic creaked as he leaned confidentially close to the king. "He has traveled much and seen things that will amaze your ears. Better yet, he's brought back a wonder from the far corner of the world—a wonder that may be the saving of us one day. Already I have described it to you. But words mean nothing, Sire. Now you will see it and judge for yourself."

With unconcealed excitement, Buw gestured at Phen. The bearded adventurer opened a leather pouch attached to the side of his belt. From it, he took a wad of thick, absorbent cloth. This he carefully unwrapped to reveal a metal box sealed with pine gum. As he set the box on the table, stripping the gum from it with the point of an ivory-handled knife, his audience of three watched closely.

Finally Phen lifted the lid. What he withdrew was another cloth-wrapped box, identically sealed.

Albin blinked and the king lifted an eyebrow. "What is this? A game of nesting boxes?"

"You will see the reason soon," Buw promised. The armorer kept his gaze riveted to the lid of the second box, which Phen was now cautiously opening. Inside lay a sealed glass vial containing a gray powder.

"I begin to suspect you have brought me the residue of some hag's potion," Brone remarked.

Though Albin said nothing, he was irritated by the suspense Buw and Phen were so clearly enjoying.

"Perhaps it is a witch's potion, but one I'll wager you'll find of interest," Phen remarked. He unstoppered the bottle. With agonizing care, he dipped a slender metal spike into it, lightly coating the point with the substance. This done, he quickly resealed the vial.

The king looked a question at his weapons master. "And now?"

"Now Phen will sprinkle a few drops of water at one end of the table and moisten the spike at the other." Buw pointed to a flask of liquid near Phen's elbow.

The king began to tap his foot. Next to him, Albin shifted impatiently. An instant later, however, both their gazes became intent. As Phen immersed the spike, it began to glow with a greenish phosphorescence. Gradually, the glow intensified and expanded into a halo of bright emerald light. An acrid aroma filled the air.

Turning the tip downward, Phen laid the spike to rest. At once, the green halo abandoned its host and, with a threatening crackle, crept across the table leaving the surface behind it charred. Its slow, destructive progress did not waver until it reached the moisture at the opposite end. Only then did its fierce light fade and die.

"Behold greenfire!" Phen cried and hoisted the innocent-looking vial of powder. "Happen now you ken why I packed it so carefully. To bring this treasure back to the Peninsula, I had to travel many months over land and water. Had moisture gotten at it, I would have been incinerated before I could yank the pouch away from my belt."

"Picture its effect on the tip of an arrow!" Buw injected. "In large quantities, strategically placed, it could drive an invading army off the coast. Ignited, the powder will march directly to the next nearest water before extinguishing itself."

Brone gazed at the charcoaled table, his eyes bright with calculation. "One would have to store it with great care and guard it more fiercely than a dragon's horde." He shot Phen a hard look. "Why have you brought this substance to me and not some other, more powerful king?"

Phen shrugged. "You are rich enough to reward me as well as any, and the Peninsula is the land of my birth. Isn't that reason enough?"

"It is, but just what have you brought me? Do you have the formula for this amazing powder?"

Phen shook his head. "The country from which I stole greenfire was called Claymia. It's a fabulously wealthy, but isolated land with few enemies. To the Claymians, greenfire is an interesting but dangerous toy. They regard it as far too unstable to keep in enough quantity for military use. And since they are so well secured by mountains and ocean, they have little need for its protection." Phen paused. A reminiscent smile lifted his firm mouth. "The Claymians are a gentle, good-natured people. I spent many happy years in their land."

"If it was such a paradise, why did you leave?" Brone demanded.

Albin listened carefully. Hearing Phen speak of this strange and fabulous land filled him with excitement. He felt a rush of envy for the other man's adventures. What a life he'd led!

Phen shrugged. "I was born with wandering feet, Sire. No place, no matter how magical, has held me longer than Claymia. But even there I grew restless and began looking for an excuse to leave. When one of their magicians demonstrated greenfire during a public entertainment, I saw its potential. I hoped that if I smuggled a sample out, your alchemists could copy it. I felt sure that Buw here could figure out a system for storing it safely."

"Buw and my alchemists shall certainly try," Brone muttered. "They shall certainly try."

* * * * *

From a nearby tree an owl hunting for careless mice hooted through the dusk. Hardly more than a shadow, Turlip slunk through the undergrowth. He looked nervously from side to side. Then he picked up a stick and, with many low curses, crawled in among a stand of prickly holly. From the outside, it appeared a natural part of the forest. Inside, it was a wall of green surrounding a perfectly circular cleared space, obviously a creation that had little to do with nature.

Muttering under his breath as he massaged the places where the prickles had stung him, Turlip crept to the point on the circle that faced south. There he knelt and used the stick to make signs in the packed earth—an inverted triangle, an elaborate crosshatched device, a series of lopsided concentric circles.

Sitting back on his haunches, he stared at his markings. Anxiously, he glanced about him. Then he drew several considerably more complicated symbols. As he struggled to form these with the tip of his stick, his tongue lolled out from one side of his slack mouth. He began to snort and snuffle, as though the simple act of breathing was almost too much.

He finished the final sign, and the stick burst into orange flame. With a scream of terror, Turlip fell back. Gasping, he clutched at his heart. The signs he'd scratched changed shape, began to writhe and crawl like worms. The sky directly over the circle went from blue to a viscous gray. A chill wind snapped through the top of the enclosure. Petrified, Turlip stared up as a black cloud formed.

The cloud funneled downward, touched a solid black tip to the center of the space, then whirled upward. A shape defined itself where the cloud had touched, and then quickly congealed. A moment later Thropos stepped forward.

"What's wrong? You look as if you're in pain."

"I—I—" Turlip gagged. He struggled to right himself. "Every time I does it, it gets harder. And it's always different. You never does it the same."

Thropos dismissed that with an imperious wave of his bony hand. "What news? Be quick about it. There's a limit to how long I can stay in this spot without dematerializing."

"Dema . . ."

"For sky's sake, man, stop wasting my time and spit it out. What have you learned?"

"I only hears what they say down in the kitchen when I

carries the scraps out to the pigs," Turlip answered with more than a touch of resentment. "That assassinator you had me set loose didn't kill the king, but everything else's goin' according to your other plan, just the way you wanted."

"Brone suspects the Sturites? He's lost his enthusiasm for a wedding with Fidacia?"

"He's got Fidacia and her crew all tucked away where he can keep a close eye on their doings. Word is, he don't even visit the poor young princess."

Thropos rubbed his bony hands together. "What of our hopeful little water domis?" A cackle of laughter burst from his bloodless lips. "Oh, when Taunis told me who she really was, I could hardly believe my good fortune. Then, to have her discovered in Brone's rooms before she could take her stone back—it's almost better than if the assassinator had done its work."

From his kneeling position, Turlip peered up at the magician craftily. "The king has eyes for her, all right. Right now she's hiding away in that Zeleta, but I sees him look her way, and I knows what's in his mind." Turlip licked his lips. "He wants her."

"And he shall have her," Thropos said through his sharp teeth. "You and I will see to that."

At this, Turlip reared up like a garden snake provoked beyond fear. "What about me? I wants the little lady, meself. What's me reward to be for doin' your dirty work? You can't just toss a few coins me way, this time. What you're havin' me do is all too big and too dangerous!"

Thropos gazed down at the thief in disdain. His pinched nostrils flared, and his mouth twisted into a cruel parody of a smile. "You don't show me the proper respect—and fear—my friend. Perhaps it's time I taught you." Thropos pointed a long finger at the thief, and suddenly Turlip went whiter than snow. Clutching at his throat, he gagged and struggled.

"Do not try to bargain with me. Keep in mind that if you

anger me, I can easily end our arrangement. And I can end it in a way you will not enjoy. There are worse things than death," Thropos added silkily. With a faint half-smile, he watched Turlip kick in the dirt, gagging and snorting for air. Finally, he lifted his hand and waited for the thief to recover himself.

"For . . . forgive me, my lord," Turlip finally gurgled. He lay rubbing his grimy throat. "I didn't mean . . ."

"We both know what you meant, my nasty little compatriot," Thropos answered. "Now that we understand each other, I'm prepared to answer your request. If all goes according to my scheme, you may have the little Reawen and do with her what you please. But only when she has served my purpose. Is that clear?"

"Perfectly," Turlip answered with a groan.

"Now—" Thropos massaged his pale hands, stroking them as if he were washing them clean. "About this pillawn of hers. I believe I might enjoy having a pillawn for my collection. Yes, I think I might enjoy that greatly. See to it."

* * * * *

"So that's what Queen Fidacia will look like." Quista pointed at the portrait displayed in the Plat's central reception hall.

Reawen studied the image. It showed a beautiful young woman with a thick mane of reddish golden hair, taunting emerald eyes, a full bosom, and a provocative smile. "That's no eleven-year-old."

Quista laughed. "No, it's the artist's conception of what she'll be like at sixteen. Imaginative, wasn't he? She's nothing but a flat-chested hoyden now. That picture is all King Brone will have to comfort him nights until she's of age." The serving girl sighed. "Of course, he's not marrying for love. Needs be policy must govern all the king's important decisions."

Quista moved to the next painting, but Reawen stood a

moment longer eyeing Fidacia's bright head. If the Sturite child blossomed to look anything like this, she would be worth waiting for. Irrationally depressed by the thought, Reawen turned to find Quista staring in fascination at a portrait of a lady in an elaborate headdress. The lady smiled seductively through thick, heavily painted lips.

"A Threbian woman who's already been married twice," Quista muttered maliciously. "Never in a million years would Brone choose her. None of these girls have a chance," she added, sweeping a hand at the long line of portraits on display.

Reawen gave her friend's shoulder a warning touch. It would not do to be overheard by any of the people milling about. Some of them were the foreign ambassadors who had brought these portraits representing their country's candidate for the king's hand. There was even a painting of a Gutaini princess.

"Hideous, isn't she?" Quista whispered. "Brone will never, never choose her. Can you imagine our handsome king coupling with such a creature? Phaww!"

Reawen eyed the reptilian princess. Did the Gutaini really wish to mate her with Brone?

Just that morning, the Plat's main hall had been thrown open so Jedestrom's populace could see and admire the paintings. The Choosing would not take place for another several weeks, and, until the disastrous banquet night, everyone had assumed that Fidacia would be the next queen. Now the trouble with the Sturites and the attempt on Brone's life threw that into doubt.

Strangely, the uncertainty only seemed to add to the festive atmosphere. Already people were placing bets on their favorites and even wearing candidates' colors on their sleeves. Outlandishly dressed ambassadors strutted about, lobbying for their princesses. Speculation and gossip ran riot. The women in the Zeleta talked of nothing else.

"If Brone doesn't choose Fidacia—or one of us—" Quista whispered with a giggle, "I hope he picks the Chee princess."

She pointed at a painting of a voluptuous creature in diaphanous pantaloons and a bejeweled breastplate. "She'd add a little color to the place, don't you think?"

"Undoubtedly." Reawen nudged Quista's shoulder. "Listen, I think I'll go back to the Zeleta. It's so hot and crowded in here, I'm getting a headache."

"We haven't inspected half of the portraits yet," Quista protested.

"I know, but for now I've seen enough. You stay, and I'll meet you later."

"Oh, all right." Quista hailed a chattering group at the opposite end of the large room.

Reawen watched the serving girl shoulder a path toward her friends, then turned away. If I try to escape out the main entrance, I'll have to spend the next quarter hour pushing through a sweating multitude, she thought. Glancing around, she spied a small door behind a column. More than likely it joined a hall running to the arcade, which connected the Zeleta to the Plat, she thought and decided to try it.

As Reawen hurried along the narrow, deserted passageway, she darted uneasy glances at the doors on either side and worried that someone might discover her trespassing. She didn't like the attention she'd drawn to herself the night of the Gutaini assassinator. Though people seemed to accept her story, she'd seen the sly looks they shot at her. She knew they talked about her behind her back.

Quista had spoken her thoughts plainly. "Aren't you the cunning one," she'd snickered, "pretending to be so innocent and high-minded and all the time tiptoeing around to the king's rooms."

"I wasn't tiptoeing to his room!" Reawen had protested. Quista only winked. Reawen already knew what Albin thought. It didn't take much guesswork to figure out what was going through the king's mind. Now, not wanting to have to repulse his amorous overtures a third time, she'd been taking care to stay out of his way, at least until she'd decided on her next move.

Reawen glided quickly past a series of closed doors. Just ahead she could see the place where the corridor widened into an octagon. The connecting hall would take her to the Zeleta. But even as she heaved a small sigh of relief, her sharp ears picked up something that brought her feet to an abrupt stop.

"The heat grows stifling, and I fear weather for the festivities that precede the Choosing may not be favorable. Is it not in your power to bring a cooling wind, Highness?" inquired a disembodied voice that Reawen recognized as belonging to Brone's steward.

"It is," the king's retort rumbled through the door, "but it is not my wish to command the stones for such trivial purposes, Stry."

Electrified, Reawen pressed her palms together. He won't use the stones for such "trivial" purposes because they take too much out of him, she thought. Probably he's been wearing them so long that it makes him physically ill to use them at all.

Abruptly, the door opened and Brone stepped out, followed by Stry. Both men looked as taken aback to see her as she was to encounter them. The king paused, his blue eyes sharpening. Reawen tried to hurry around him, but he blocked her and ordered his steward to leave. When the man had disappeared, Brone said, "What are you doing here? This passage is forbidden to any but my servants."

"I was trying to find my way back to the Zeleta from your reception hall," Reawen told him truthfully. Instead of meeting his eyes, she gazed down at the gold bracelet on his arm.

Brone's expression softened and grew playful. He slipped a finger under her chin. "Look at me, Reawen, and tell me why you've been avoiding me. We both know that you were coming to me that night when you saved my life, and I would have welcomed you. I've been looking for you since, waiting to take you in my arms. Will you come to me tonight?"

Reawen shot him an angry glance. His arrogance and her own unwilling response to his nearness infuriated her. "You are wrong. I was not coming to you that night. I was doing exactly what I claimed."

He ran a caressing thumb along the line of her jaw. "There's nothing to be ashamed of. Come to me, and I'll give you a place of honor. You must know I desired you the moment I looked on you."

"You say that to me when you are about to marry another!" She couldn't keep anger and a touch of jealousy out of her voice.

"There's no shame in being a king's mistress. Come to me tonight, Reawen. Or, if you are too shy to slip into my room, meet me in the garden and let me show you there how much I care for you," he said. As he spoke he bent a look of hot desire on her that left no doubt as to his meaning.

"No!" Reawen cried and fled away down the passage.

As she turned into the octagon, she stumbled, and the short hairs on the back of her neck quivered. A servant dressed in a shapeless gardener's smock was dusting a torch holder. She passed him by quickly, never looking his way and never seeing that the ferrety eyes that followed her belonged to Turlip the thief.

Once in the Zeleta's garden, Reawen dropped onto a bench and covered her face with her hands.

What's wrong? Are you jealous of all the king's lemans?

Reawen looked up in time to see Cel light on a nearby branch. The pillawn dug her golden claws into the bark and folded her wings down against her fluffy chest.

"No, I'm not jealous," Reawen snapped and then described what had just passed between herself and Brone.

Why didn't you agree to his proposition? Cel inquired.

Reawen scowled at her pet. "I've told you before I don't want to make love with him. The very thought gives me the shivers."

If you're clever, you won't have to go that far, Cel pointed out practically. *For sky's sake, girl, we've been here months now.*

"I know how long we've been here. I can't leave, but you could. Why don't you?" Reawen threw this out in sheer frustration.

Why don't I leave? Cel rolled her purple eyes and clicked her sharp golden beak. *I don't leave, my dear Reawen, because I'm here to watch over you.*

"Watch over me?" Reawen gaped. "I thought you came along because you were my friend."

That, too. So why don't you listen to your best friend's advice? We have been here many weeks, and you have had many chances to get back your stone. But you've muffed them all.

"Muffed!"

Muffed them all, and we're no closer to having the stone than we were in the mountains.

Reawen flushed. Cel referred, of course, to the incident with the Gutaini assassinator. Instead of letting the thing kill Brone so she could regain her stone, she had saved the man.

They'll discover who you are one of these days," Cel clucked in the girl's mind, *and then it will be too late.*

Reawen had to admit that all the pillawn said was true. "Oh, Cel, I know you're tired of hanging around here. I don't blame you, not one bit."

Cel fluffed her pinfeathers. *It's not so bad. This garden is very pretty and these roses smell sweet. But . . .*

"But it's boring," Reawen completed the thought. "At least you're free to fly around when you want. I'm stuck in that house full of women who do nothing but gossip and admire themselves. I long to be back in the forest with Gris. I miss her, and I worry about her being all alone for so long."

Then stop being a silly child and do what you must, Cel urged. *Brone was the death of Nioma, and without your stone you will wither just as surely. Don't let him be the death of you. Meet him in the garden and convince him to give you what is rightfully yours.*

"But how?"

Meaningfully, Cel blinked. *If you don't possess instincts that will show the way, you aren't your mother's daughter. It's high time you learned to bend a man to your will.*

Reawen left the garden to return to her duties in the Zeleta, her pet's words still ringing inside her head. Cel stayed on her branch. She fluffed her feathers around her and chattered to herself. *Silly child. Foolish, impetuous. Too proud for her own good.*

Gradually, Cel slipped into a contented half-doze in the warm sun. Despite her show of irritation, she was pleased with herself, pleased that she'd egged Reawen into considering another avenue to the stone. Reawen was far more cautious than Nioma, and generally that was good. But sometimes caution was a trap. There were times when one just had to go ahead and do what needed to be done.

As Cel mused thus, she sank her head into her feathers and closed her purple eyes. Around her the scent of roses was thick. Bees buzzed a sleepy song in the sun-warmed breeze. Cel sighed, dreaming of another garden and another time. She saw herself riding the wind on a mountaintop, answering the call of an ancient awaiting her amid crystal pillars. She was unaware of the dark shadow lurking behind a fat yew, unaware as Turlip fitted a tiny poisoned dart into a miniature bow, unaware as he took aim at the plump white target she presented and then, with an evil grin, fired.

Chapter Eight

Reawen paced in front of her window. The queen mother had a sick headache and would not require entertainment that afternoon. There was really nothing for Reawen to do for the rest of the day but fret over her meeting with Brone and the argument she'd had with Cel.

She turned to her bed and picked up the iridescent blue dress Quista had designed for her. She was to wear it for the first time tomorrow and during the whole week of festivities preceding the Choosing. She held the gown to her shoulders, wondering what Gris would think of it.

For a moment, she could almost hear her aunt grumbling. "Just the sort of ridiculous outfit a man likes to see a woman get herself up in," Gris might say.

As an image of Gris formed in Reawen's mind, pain squeezed at her heart. Oh, how she missed her and the simplicity of their life in the mountains. Homesickness washed over Reawen. She missed her sparkling forest pools. She missed the woodland spirits she'd played with as a child. She even missed the wild magic that could trick and entrap the unwary. You couldn't always believe what you saw and heard in the mountains, and sometimes you had to fend off the powers that roamed there with powers of your own.

But Reawen understood the wild magic. She knew how to channel it. She knew how to communicate with the spirits of her mountains and felt comfortable there, despite the danger. Indeed, in a way, she was part of it herself. How clean and unfettered all that seemed in contrast to the complications besetting her here in Jedestrom—problems of duty and obligation, decisions that made her feel either foolish or unclean.

Now she had to decide whether or not to follow Cel's advice. Should she meet Brone in the garden tonight?

He might not come there, she told herself. After all, she'd refused his invitation. But deep inside she knew he would be there regardless of her rebuff and that he would wait for her.

Still clutching the silken dress to her bosom, Reawen sank down on her bed. For many weeks now, she'd known it must come to this. Cel was right, of course. To win back her stone, she must have the strength to grasp the opportunities fate offered and use the weapons she possessed—women's weapons.

She'd failed trying to seize the stone openly. She'd failed with guile and stealth and couldn't risk failing again. Logic dictated that she must meet the king and somehow seduce the stone from him as he had seduced it from her mother.

Yet the prospect made her stomach clench. Perhaps it was because she did find Brone physically appealing, she thought. Though years of bearing the weight of the stones had destroyed the smooth beauty of his youth, he was still a fine-looking man. She couldn't help admiring his kingly bearing and the just and intelligent way in which he ruled the Peninsula. He had integrity and generosity. How could she not see that and appreciate it?

Although she found him attractive, the image of Brone and Nioma together never left her mind. The combination of her attraction and that image filled her with horror. I know that if I meet him as Cel advises, I will never be the same again, she thought. I will have lost something I prize, and it's not just my virginity. It's my integrity. She frowned. Was any sacrifice too great to regain the stone?

Deeply troubled, Reawen wandered from her room back out into the gardens. She trod the paths hoping to find Cel, but the pillawn was nowhere in sight. In the distance Reawen heard ripples of laughter, for everyone in the palace was in a holiday mood over the Choosing. Everyone but me, she thought grimly.

She'd skipped the midday meal, and now hunger directed her steps to the kitchen. But the thick stew the cook had prepared turned her stomach. With a grimace, Reawen returned to the garden and perched on a bench, where she stared moodily at the playing fountains. As twilight gathered, their spray became a pale glitter sparkling on Reawen's face, and she asked herself over and over what she should do.

I won't meet him, she finally decided. I can't meet him and be true to myself. She knew that, no matter what Cel said, she was not born to be a seductress. If I play that role with Brone, I will never feel clean again, she thought. I must win my stone back in some other fashion.

The decision made, Reawen hurried back to her room. She half expected to find Cel waiting for her, but the pillawn's perch was empty. "Probably still out catching fireflies," Reawen muttered to herself.

She went to the window and gazed out, silently communing with the river Har flowing in the distance. If only she were in it instead of locked away here in this airless room, torn by frustration and doubt!

A sharp tap broke into her reverie. Reawen opened her door, but the dimly lit passageway outside was empty. Frowning, she glanced down and then gave a little cry. A basket attractively lined with dark green leaves and heaped to the top with glistening emberries lay at her feet. Quista must have left it, she thought, and felt her empty stomach contract in happy anticipation. Or perhaps the king had sent it.

Reawen frowned, hesitating. So what if he had sent the basket? she asked herself. Eating a gift of emberries from him wasn't the same as agreeing to become his mistress. With a last glance down the empty corridor, Reawen picked up the container and carried it into her room. She'd expected to go to bed hungry. Now she'd have a feast!

* * * * *

Smiling cruelly, Thropos listened to the baby rabbit's dying squeak of agony and fingered a beaker filled with its fresh warm blood. He turned to contemplate the unconscious pillawn in the cage opposite his work table. "Ah, my beauty," he whispered. "Soon we'll be getting to know each other."

Turlip had summoned Thropos to a magic circle and delivered the unconscious creature just that afternoon. In return, Thropos had given the thief a talisman allowing him to locate the water domis and a carefully prepared basket of emberries. Special emberries for a greedy little water witch, he thought. His small dark eyes glittered with amusement.

All the pieces were falling into place. Now only one more thing remained to be done before the little wizard set into motion the plan he'd formulated.

Pursing his lips in concentration, Thropos began to mix ingredients from the dried herbs hanging from the rafters and the jumble of jars on the shelves behind him. Many unappetizing items floated in the containers he uncapped—bits of toad and snake, the preserved embryos of bats, unrecognizable slivers of flesh that the uninitiated could only guess at and shiver. When all the horrid ingredients were in place, he pounded them to a murky consistency in his mortar. Chanting tunelessly, he blended them with an oily liquid and carefully poured the mixture into a small vial. Where he spilled a drop on the table, a small, bright red hole appeared, and a poisonous-smelling steam rose.

Thropos had just slipped the sealed vial into his pocket when the peremptory sound of boots thudded up the stone steps. As if he owned it, Arant strode into the tower room. He wore his leather exercise armor, and his heavy face gleamed with sweat. "I am no errand boy, wizard. How dare you send one of your mechanical squirrels to order me to wait on you?"

"I didn't order you," Thropos replied mildly, "merely sent word I'd like you to visit me in secret. And the squirrels aren't mechanical. They're only creatures I've performed a bit of brain surgery on. My, ah, adjustments make them obedient to my command."

"Whatever they are, I don't like 'em. Their dead eyes give me the creeps." Arant's gaze fell on the golden cage containing the pillawn. "What's this big white bird, another of your victims?"

Thropos unlocked the cage and lifted Cel out of it. With obvious enjoyment, he ran his hands over her soft, inert body. "Not a victim," he murmured, "but a spoil of war, a reward for a job well done." He slid a forefinger over the perfect curve of her small head and then stroked the silken down covering her breast. "Tell me, my prince, what do you think of my prize?"

Arant stepped toward the table. "If its another animal for your experiments, it looks dead already."

"Merely drugged. She will wake up within the hour."

"She? What is it? Some sort of albino owl?"

Thropos chuckled. "Not an owl, my prince, but a pillawn. A rare and wondrous creature, perhaps the last of its kind left alive."

"Well, it won't stay that way long if you've got it." Arant shrugged and turned away. "It's pretty enough, but of what use?"

"You think too much of war and violence, my lord. Pretty things can be very useful. Take your sister, for instance. Right now, she is a very valuable commodity."

Arant showed his teeth. "Not if I can help it. I'll tear Fidacia limb from limb before I see her married and whelping a set of princelings for Brone."

Thropos chuckled again. He was in a rare good humor this day. "Be easy, my lord. It is precisely that problem that prompted me to summon you here."

"No one *summons* me, wizard! Dare to send one of those damn unnatural squirrels to my rooms again, and I'll boil it and have it sent up in your stew!"

Thropos blinked, then smiled toothily. "Pardon, my lord. I

meant to say *invite*." After clearing his throat, he moved to lock Cel's body back up in its cage.

"As I said before, pretty things can be useful. Sometimes they may accomplish what war cannot. There is an ancient spell that requires the blood of a pillawn. For years now, I have studied it with the longing of a frustrated lover, for it is a spell that could crush a strong enemy. However, I never thought to wield the power of that spell—I never expected fate to bring a pillawn to my hand. Fate has surprised me, in this case pleasantly." As he spoke, Thropos picked out the vial of murky liquid he had prepared. He rotated it between his bony fingers. Arant found his green eyes fastening onto it, despite himself.

"Stop speaking in riddles. What's that you hold?"

The wizard smiled thinly. "Kindly, fate has chosen to place before us a banquet of opportunities, my prince. But if we are to feast, we must first make certain preparations. And we must act boldly and without the anchor of conscience to hold us down. To speak very plainly, do you still seek my help in the matter of your sister's proposed marriage?"

Arant nodded. "As I have already told you, wizard, I wish to rule the Sturite nation and crush my enemy Brone beneath my heel. Help me to these twin goals, and I will do anything you ask—never mind the anchor of conscience. What's more, when success is mine, you shall have any reward I am capable of giving."

"You are powerful, my liege. But not powerful enough to give me the vengeance I crave. Yet, you can help me to it." Thropos pressed his fingertips together. "Before you can crush Brone, you must first set yourself up as king here. To do that, there is an obstacle you must remove from your path." Thropos handed Arant the small vial. "The next time you dine with Yerbo, slip this potion into his wine goblet. Do it without being detected, and you will be safe from suspicion. It takes its time to kill. He will not know its effect for at least a day and a night."

The wizard and the redheaded prince stared hard at each other. "You ask me to poison my father?"

Thropos lifted his shoulders. "It's a decision only you can make, my liege."

"But he will die soon in any case."

"He could live for years, and by that time it may be too late for our purposes."

Arant stood frozen with shock. "A patricide calls down the curses of the gods upon his head."

"You do not believe in the gods, and even if you did, you've already violated their tenets so many times that once more can make little difference."

"Can't you do it?" Scowling, Arant thrust the vial back at Thropos, but the wizard refused to accept it.

"Yerbo has been my friend. I will not sully my hands with his murder. It's your part to decide how badly you wish to rule in his stead and to wreak vengeance on Brone. But if you do go ahead with your half of the bargain we make here, you may be sure I will fulfill mine."

* * * * *

An hour later, Arant's wistite spurs rang against the stone of the corridor that led to the Sturite king's quarters.

"I wish to see my father," he said to the guard who moved to bar his path.

"I cannot let you pass without first asking the king's permission, my lord" the man declared. Though he blanched with fear, he stood his ground.

"If you know what's good for you, you'll get out of my way," Arant muttered through gritted teeth.

The door fell open, and Yerbo stuck out his graying head. "For the love of hawks, what's going on out here?" He saw Arant and his eyes narrowed. "Oh, it's you. I might have guessed. You've been a troublemaker since the moment of conception, and your disposition hasn't sweetened yet. Come in, if you want to talk with me; I want to talk with you as badly."

Red-faced with irritation, Arant followed his father into the room. "I came to inquire after your health."

Yerbo dropped into a chair, groaned, then shot his son a disbelieving look. "You astonish me. Since when have you shown the slightest interest in anyone's health but your own? Just consider the health of those men who were hanged for your foolishness at Acuma."

"They were soldiers. It's a soldier's lot to die in battle."

"They didn't die in battle. They were strung up like chickens."

Arant's teeth met. "Acuma is past. I've admitted my mistake, so let it die there."

"I'd be willing enough to hear the last of it if I thought you were, too." Yerbo sighed. "My son, I see a bitter brew of hatred simmering inside you. I recognize the acrid smell of it, for I was much the same when I was young. If I imagined myself insulted, I wouldn't rest until I'd avenged myself. But the years have taught me more wisdom than that. I've learned there is more to gain through peace than war."

"I would rather slit Brone's throat than sit down to sup with him."

"I had similar feelings when I was a hotheaded youth. But consider the facts. Brone, for all he may stick in your craw, is a strong king and a competent warrior. If he were removed from the Peninsula, the domi would regain their power. Then where would we be?"

"Free to strike a deal with Taunis and Driona, who, from all reports, are both eminently bribable. Free to plunder all the wistite we can use and trade."

"Not with the Gutaini hovering so close to the Peninsula's border. It's only Brone's might that keeps them at bay. Remove him, and they'd swoop down to gobble up the Peninsula's riches for themselves."

"I'm not afraid of those scaly-skinned freaks."

"You should be. I've seen them in battle. They're formidable." When Arant opened his mouth to protest, Yerbo raised a hand and sighed heavily. "Don't you see? Marrying your sister to Brone will make it unnecessary to fear such as the Gutaini. Once she's borne him a son, we'll have favorable trade agreements and an ally so powerful that every other nation will fear us. And it can all be done without shedding blood."

Arant gazed for a long moment at his gray-haired sire. "How can you bear to part with her? I know she's your favorite child. You've always loved her more than me."

"More than you?" Yerbo stared. "How little you understand me. No man loves his daughter more than his son, least of all a man such as I am. You are my only male heir, Arant. When you were born, my heart rejoiced. In you I place my hopes and the hopes of the Sturites. It's partly for you and your future that I have taken such pains to negotiate this truce with Brone. If it goes forward, you will one day preside over a prosperous and well-protected kingdom."

Arant bowed his head. "Father, forgive me. Your ungrateful son has been foolish and quarrelsome. But now that he understands you better, he will mend his ways." Arant went to a cabinet and brought out two goblets, which he filled with wine from an earthen decanter. "To a bright future," he said and smiled as he handed over one of the brimming winecups. "You'll hear no more protests from me. Now, let us drink a toast on it."

Yerbo looked first confounded, then delighted. "I never thought to hear you speak such honeyed words, my son."

"You misjudge me, Father. I love you too well and respect your judgment too deeply to argue with you more." Arant lifted his cup to his lips. "To Fidacia and the peace and prosperity she will bring to us."

"To your sister," Yerbo agreed enthusiastically. He drained the cup his son had given him.

* * * * *

In her room, Reawen lay collapsed on her bed. Her slim arms were flung above her. Next to them sat the empty emberry basket. Inside her head was a darkness thicker than that which obscured her window. Weighty mists writhed and coiled within it. Finally, out of those mists came a chilling voice.

As it whispered instructions to her, she rose up from her bed and pressed her sharp knife into her palm.

"When he takes you into his arms, kill him," the voice hissed.

"Kill him," Reawen repeated, then turned and walked out her door into the night. As she moved, she felt weightless, almost as if she were floating. For a long time she stood alone, statue-still, uncaring and unmoving. Then she was gazing through the moonlight at a lover. She saw his shoulders gleam in the pale light. Her mouth went dry, and she looked up into his face. Shadows carved his features, so familiar, and yet those of a stranger. He did not speak. Silently, his arms went around her and held her firmly against his chest. The beating of their two hearts stirred her blood, and she felt the knife's sharp edge creasing her palm.

Her stranger-lover carried her to the edge of a river and laid her gently down on its mossy bank. His hands began to stroke her body. Softly and sweetly he slipped the shift from it until she lay naked on the grass, shivering with pleasure and anticipation.

Her eyes remained closed. She could not look up into her lover's face, but it didn't seem to matter. All that mattered were the pleasurable sensations.

His warm lips pressed down on hers, and his fingers tangled in her loose hair. Then she felt the length of his body press down. His mouth touched her throat, then her breasts. He took her hand, uncurled her fingers, and, with a little chuckle, dropped the knife into the grass so that it was lost to her.

Reawen felt a sharp pain that made her gasp and cleared her head for an instant. Then the fog clouded everything again. Her lover wrapped her firmly in his arms and whispered promises in her ear, promises she couldn't quite comprehend. Like everything else, their meaning faded into the mist that filled her head. Reawen sank into a velvet darkness and felt nothing more. She didn't even awake when Brone carried her back to her room and laid her gently on her bed.

Late in the night, a cool wind from the north cleared the sultry haze from Jedestrom's sky and refreshed its air. But when Reawen came back to consciousness, her forehead was damp, and her tongue felt as if it had grown moss. Pools of light spilled across her floor, but as she gazed up at the ceiling she saw only black mist. Images from a dream she'd had took shape just behind the mist, and she broke out in another damp sweat.

Moving her head stiffly, she spotted the empty emberry basket lying on the floor. Nausea washed up her throat along with a horrible suspicion. Abruptly, she sat up, moaning at the sharp pain stabbing at her head.

Then she blinked. Grass stains streaked her hands and her white shift. A small leaf clung to the garment's hem. She stared at it, and her throat constricted.

"Cel?" The pillawn's perch was bare. When Reawen saw that, she leaped off the bed. This was the first time since she'd come to Jedestrom that Cel hadn't flown in to spend the night. "Could she have left without telling me?" Reawen asked herself aloud. But no, Cel would never do that. What then? A chill spread through her. Could someone have harmed her?

Reawen looked around wildly, but saw no evidence of an intruder. The oil lamp had burned itself out, and her clothes lay tumbled on the stool just as she'd left them. Still, there was the dream and the grass stains. Shakily, Reawen paced. She stared from the basket to the bed to the empty perch and then pulled off the shift and wrapped her body in a clean gown.

Most of the household still slept, so the gardens were

deserted. Quietly, she slipped through the hall and out a back entrance toward the river. "Cel?" she whispered, "Cel!" But Cel didn't answer.

Reawen hadn't paid much attention to where she was going. Suddenly she found herself in a spot on the riverbank that seemed all too familiar, a spot she remembered from her dream. Reawen gave a little cry of horror. Her knife lay in the grass, grass that was still crushed by the imprint of her body and another's—Brone's. Reawen collapsed onto the ground. What she remembered from the night hadn't been a dream, it had been real.

Reawen lay still as death for almost an hour. Gradually, however, the puddle of hot light that the rising sun spilled on her cheek began to burn her skin. She sat up. Through the sparse trunks of the hedge she glimpsed servants hurrying past the garden to the Plat. Already, preparations for the day's festivities were underway. If she lingered here much longer, she'd be discovered and reprimanded. Grimly, she stood and made her way back to the Zeleta.

Somehow she managed to gain the shelter of her room without calling attention to her tear-streaked face. She washed carefully, combed back her hair and donned the blue dress Quista had laid out for her.

When Reawen looked at herself in the mirror, she saw that she was still close to tears. Fiercely, she forced her lips into a straight line. I have to behave as if nothing happened, she told herself. She would not give Brone the satisfaction of seeing her acknowledge his triumph. She would keep to herself and hold her head high. But secretly she would watch for an opportunity to revenge herself on Jedestrom's golden-haired king. For he had drugged and raped her, she was convinced, and somehow she would make him pay dearly.

The next few weeks preceding the Choosing were to be filled with merrymaking. Reawen had been assigned five stations, places in the gardens and halls of the Plat where she was to entertain guests. The first of these was in the rose garden. There, with the scent of flowers filling the air, she played. With her reed at her lips and her head bent, Reawen hardly saw those in the brightly dressed throng who gaped at her as they passed or stopped to listen to the mournful web of intricate sound that flowed from her reed.

"Don't play such sad songs," a festival manager warned one day as he directed her on to her next station. "This is a time of joy. Make your music reflect that."

Nodding, she walked toward the fountain where she was to spend the afternoon. As she moved through the crowd, voices remarked on the beauty of the gardens, crowed over the change in weather, and expressed gratitude to the king for all the benefits of the day. Tumblers and clowns darted across the path. They turned somersaults and cartwheels and made the children squeal with joy.

A grinning juggler moved beside Reawen and said in a stage whisper that all could hear, "Beautiful lady, I will juggle these daggers just for you. If, entranced by your face, I misjudge and a knife plunges into my heart, it will be your loveliness that I die for."

The crowd laughed, but Reawen gave him a look that changed his teasing face and made him reach out to her. "What's wrong? What have I said?" But she tore past and ran until she gained the security of the fountain and her music.

The festival time drifted past in a blur of pain. Days Reawen moved through her duties as though she were made of stone. In the evenings, she walked in the gardens calling for Cel. Nights she lay awake staring at the pillawn's empty perch or tossing through nightmares that left her wan and drained.

"What's wrong?" Quista finally asked her. "Every time I catch sight of you, you look pale as death. You walk around as if half of you were somewhere else."

Reawen looked at her friend and smiled wanly. "I've been having nightmares, and my stomach is upset."

"Well thank goodness the Choosing is tonight, and we have only this day to get through." She patted Reawen's shoulder and then went to entertain in another part of the garden.

As evening drew near, Reawen moved to her last station, a corner in the Plat's main reception hall. Anticipating the hour when the royal entourage would arrive and Brone would announce his choice of bride, crowds swarmed like picnicking ants.

Everyone was happy but Reawen. At the thought of seeing the king, her throat burned with anger and humiliation. Twice while she'd been playing this week she'd looked up to find him gazing at her from a distance. But they hadn't met, and half of her never wanted to see him again. Another part of her, however, knew she must and longed for the moment when she would have the revenge she craved. She fingered the knife she'd retrieved from the grass after that night, now hidden in the folds of her belt.

The hour of the Choosing drew near, and guards began clearing a path from the main interior doors of the hall to the raised platform, where Brone and Killip would sit when he made his announcement. All day the ambassadors had waited before the portraits they represented. Now they stiffened, and, throughout the hall, voices rose in speculation.

"You can stop playing now," an entertainment director whispered in Reawen's ear. "In fact, it would be best if you left. We won't require your services again until later tonight. Why don't you go get yourself something to eat—you look pale."

"And miss the ceremony?" Reawen protested, her eyes ironic.

He shrugged. "Do as you wish."

Reawen pressed herself against a wall in the far corner and waited with her arms crossed over her chest and a fevered glitter in her eyes. Around her, people whispered about Brone and Fidacia and craned their heads to see if any of the royal party had arrived. Another group of guards marched past, calling for silence. They halted and stood shoulder to shoulder, forming a human barrier on either side of the path they had cleared to the thrones.

Smothered as she was by the press of bodies, Reawen could see none of this. She could only hear and feel the ripple of interest from the crowd. Yet, as if there were a current connecting them, she sensed Brone's presence the moment he came into the room.

Sick with tension, Reawen closed her eyes. Her inner eye could see him as if he stood before her, the tight golden curls lifted over the band set with stones, the flickering blue gaze beneath it. She imagined his gaze mocking her, and her hands clenched at her sides into tight fists and then felt again for the shape of the knife she carried.

The Ceremony of Choosing was a long, involved affair. Every ambassador had to present his candidate's portrait and make a speech extolling her virtues, and some ambassadors went on for what seemed like hours. It would take all night to work through the lineup. What a farce this all is, Reawen thought. Everyone knows he will choose Fidacia.

Though Reawen could see little, murmurings of admiration told her when the Sturite princess's portrait had been brought forth. By this time, the reed player's head throbbed unmercifully. To ease the pain, she closed her eyes and let her mind drift out to the river. How she longed to be soothed and cleansed by it and to float away from this place.

Another eternity crawled by. Then a hush descended over the crowd and, with a sense of foreboding, Reawen's eyes snapped open.

"Open your ears. The king is going to make his announcement," the man next to her whispered down to his short, plump wife.

Reawen straightened. Suddenly, all present in the hall held their breath. Though Reawen couldn't see Brone through the forest of heads, she could hear his every word.

In a firm voice he said, "The time has come for me to choose a wife. Beautiful and virtuous though the ladies are who have been presented to me, I have not yet seen a portrait of the woman I would take for my queen."

A gasp of surprise and dismay rippled forth from the assemblage, but Brone's deep voice cut through it. "Yet the lady I would wed is in this room. She is Reawen, my mother's reed player. It is she I would have for my wife, and no other."

Rigid with shock, Reawen stared blindly before her. It was a mistake. Surely it had to be a mistake! Brone's audience clearly thought so, too. They muttered and shuffled. Some raised their voices in surprise.

Ignoring them, Brone stepped easily off the raised platform holding the thrones and began, despite his guards' objections, to shoulder his way through the crowd. Parting it like a knife through butter, he cleared a path directly to Reawen.

As Brone strode to her, she stared wildly. He gave her a flashing smile and held his hands out to her. When she did not respond, he seized her cold wrists and led her out of the throng. Seeing how numb she was, he threw a protective arm around her waist and squeezed her reassuringly. At that, she stared up into his face and was astonished by the recklessness she saw there. For the first time since she had met him, the king looked both young and happy.

Chapter Nine

Thropos placed Cel's cage in the center of his work table and sat down before it. "Now, my pretty ladybird, it's time we had a conversation."

Cel huddled at the bottom of the enclosure. Her feathers drooped, but her eyes glared defiance at her captor.

"You needn't pretend that you can't speak," Thropos went on. "I know what you are. If the legends are to be believed, and apparently they are, your kind was made to be the companions of the domi. You must be quite ancient."

Older than such as you can imagine. Cel spat the words into his mind.

"Ah." Thropos fingered the tip of Cel's wing. When she drew it back from the edge of her bars, he smiled nastily. "Never underestimate my imagination. It might surprise you. Tell me, lovely and venerable bird, what is the secret of your longevity. Is it a special sort of food you eat?"

Cel hooted.

"Well, then is it a spell?"

No spell of a black-robed magician's making, Cel retorted haughtily. *I was created in the time of light. In my childhood, the streams ran with song. Magic fluttered in the crystalline air like a precious banner. The grass and earth and trees were infused with spirit. To be alive was to experience joy.*

"There's little enough of that left now."

Not in your part of the world, at any rate, Cel agreed. *Darkness and heaviness have crowded it all out.*

"Then why are you here, pillawn?"

Because I choose to be.

"That is not a good enough answer."

It will have to do.

Thropos tapped an impatient finger. "What of your fellows?"

All dead or flown away.

Thropos's eyes slitted. "Flown away where?"

To another place, wizard. There are many places you know nothing about. This one is far beyond your reach. On this world, I am the last of my kind.

Thropos studied his prisoner. "You must be rather unusual to have stayed on when all your fellows have fled."

Unusual, Cel agreed.

"Perhaps it is loyalty to your mistress that has kept you here."

Cel merely blinked her large purple eyes scornfully.

"Then what a shame it is that I may have to sacrifice you." Again, he reached a finger through Cel's bars to touch one of her feathers. She darted her golden beak, and he quickly withdrew. "Now, now, pretty pillawn, be nice and perhaps your life will be lengthened. Who knows, perhaps I will even spare you so you can fly away and join your playmates."

I am not such a fool as to believe anything you say, wizard. You mean to slaughter me for one of your vile experiments. Cel cast a meaningful glance at the other cages lining the walls. Many stood empty now, for Thropos had been busy hatching spells and potions of late to block all communication between Peneto and Jedestrom. Cel had witnessed dreadful sights.

"Perhaps not," Thropos said smoothly, "not if you tell me what I need to know willingly. For instance, this charming little mistress of yours, Reawen, what can you tell me of her?"

Cel gazed back at him in suspicious silence.

"Oh, you needn't fear that you're going to give away a great secret, my pretty and very loyal pillawn. I already know that she's Nioma's daughter. I also know what she's doing tootling her reed in Jedestrom—trying to steal back her domi stone, isn't that so?"

Again, Cel blinked her great purple eyes, but said nothing.

Thropos chuckled. "Perhaps it is I who should tell you about your young mistress. You may be interested to know, for instance, that she's about to wed Brone. Oh, yes, you may well look astonished, but I assure you it's true. The Peninsulan king is quite besotted with her and has chosen her for his bride over all the other candidates. Not a wise move in the least, I'm afraid, for in doing so he's offended all his neighbors. What's more, by humiliating our little Fidacia so publicly he's provided our new young king, Arant, with a very good excuse to demonstrate his displeasure."

I can't believe Reawen would marry Brone, Cel burst out. *She hates him!*

Thropos chuckled again. "She hates him so much, she's willing to wed him to steal her stone away from him. More power to her, I say. In fact, by providing the lovestruck Peninsulan king with a most romantic opportunity to sample her toothsome young body, I've helped her to her goal. It will be most interesting to see what occurs when she attains it. But that's not what I wish to question you about, my pretty pillawn."

I'm not your pretty anything, and I will answer none of your loathsome questions, Cel retorted scornfully.

"Not even about your Reawen's parentage?" Thropos wheedled. When Cel blinked in surprise, he added, "Oh, I've deduced that Nioma bore her. It's the identity of her father that whets my curiosity. For you see, when I conjured up a picture of your mistress in my seeing glass, I was most struck by her eyes. I've the most tantalizing conviction that I've seen those gray eyes on another." Thropos wet the narrow slit of his mouth with a grayish tongue. "I had a boyhood friend of whom your Reawen reminds me."

When Cel remained speechless, Thropos gave his thin-lipped smile. "Now I know that Nioma was, not to put it too indelicately, an amorous lady. Reawen's father might have been one of a veritable flock of possible lovers. But it so happens that my friend was smitten with her at just about the time that

Reawen, if I've calculated her age correctly, must have been conceived. Isn't that interesting?"

What can it matter to you who Reawen's father is? Cel demanded angrily.

"Oh, it matters." Thropos folded his hands over his stomach. "It matters greatly. Now, for your amusement and mine, pillawn, I intend to show you your mistress's wedding night."

Cel's eyes opened wide, and she let out an outraged squawk.

"Oh, yes. No point pretending to false modesty. We are both sophisticated creatures of the world, are we not?"

Laughing, Thropos stood up and brought a wide crystal bowl to the table. After he carefully placed it next to Cel's cage, he unstoppered a flagon. As he poured a clear blue liquid from it into the bowl, he said, "This medium is precious and rare, so I do not make use of it lightly. But for this particular occasion, I think it's worth the expense." The liquid began to give off a luminous vapor. "Ah yes, yes indeed. Watch carefully, and you shall see our happy couple's nuptial celebrations."

* * * * *

Brone paced the length of his bedroom. At one end he stopped to adjust the set of the candles glowing on the tall wardrobe. At the other end of the room, he moved a tray holding wine glasses to a different angle on a table. He checked the hourglass and then locked his hands behind his back. Soon, he told himself, Reawen's serving women would deliver her to him. Before the ceremony earlier today, they had been apart far too long, he thought, cursing the weeks of preparation tradition required between the Choosing and the wedding.

He guessed that, at this moment, she must be finishing the elaborate ceremonial bath that would prepare her for the pleasures of their wedding night. He didn't know the precise details of the ritual, but guessed it must be similar to what he'd just gone through.

Brone smiled as he recalled the joking among the serving men at his own bath. Only Albin had hung back with an austere face. By now, Brone had guessed that his messenger was infatuated with Reawen, so he'd taken pity on the lad and sent him away to cure his heartsickness in private.

Brone inhaled the sweet fragrance of the bouquet of white roses arranged near his bed. The roses brought to mind the petal smoothness of Reawen's skin. Impatiently, he glanced at the door. Soon she would come, arrayed in the same white silk that clothed him, he mused longingly. In his mind's eye, he saw the satin cloud of her dark hair against her ivory neck.

Grass and wind had scented it that night in the garden. He'd waited long for her there, half thinking she would not come. But he had determined to stay until dawn to test the issue. And at last Reawen had rewarded his patience. She had glided over the grass like a sleepwalker. In the silvered moonlight, it had all taken on the fantastic quality of a dream. She had come into his arms so silently, but with such hunger that his passion had overcome him entirely.

Brone dropped into a chair and leaned his golden head back on the polished wood rest. That night in the garden he had realized it was Reawen he must have for his queen.

Before he'd met her, the betrothal to Fidacia had seemed politic. Now, other considerations took precedence. The stones were draining his vitality, and he must face the fact squarely. He was still strong and virile, but for how long? What if, by the time Fidacia came of age, he was incapable of siring the heir the Peninsula needed to maintain its stability?

Then there was the Peninsula's defense to weigh. He had always distrusted the Sturites. Now, with Acuma sticking in his craw, his distrust combined with an active hatred. It will take more than a barbarian bride to make my kingdom safe, he thought. The Peninsula must learn to protect itself.

Brone locked his fingers together and stared off into space. He had considered the problem long and hard and now thought he might have the solution. Given the mountain chain guarding its back, the Peninsula was vulnerable to attack only from water. To the north, its east and west coastlines were so rockbound that a fleet would dash itself to pieces trying to gain access. Below Jedestrom, shoals of sand and mud would make landing a large war party treacherous.

Only the deep waters of Acuma and its sister port to the west, Avera, were negotiable by warships such as the Sturites used. Brone had discussed with his advisors and architects a plan to seal these two deep harbors with a barricade of water gates and surround their backs with high walls to contain an attack, making it easy to repel. The design was almost completed, and he hoped by the following summer to have it in place.

He tapped his fingers restlessly. His army, though small, was well on the way to matching any on the continent for efficiency. Perhaps Peninsulan warriors would never be as fierce as Sturite or Gutaini, or as ruthless and clever as Chee. Yet Brone was convinced that good training might make them equally effective.

Three days before the Choosing, his alchemists had dropped the decisive piece into the puzzle. Wyar, his chief alchemist, had appeared before him with downcast eyes but a smug smile.

"I think I have news that will please you, Sire," he'd murmured.

"What news is that? Have you ferreted out the formula for greenfire?" Brone remembered well his hopeful excitement as he'd asked the question.

"We have, Sire," Wyar had retorted with the confidence that only complete success could allow. "If you will accompany me to our workroom, I will demonstrate what our science has wrought."

Brone soon confirmed Wyar's claim, as he'd witnessed the dull powder his alchemists concocted spark to life exactly as Phen's had done during his demonstration in the storeroom.

Small green flames had danced toward a bit of water on the worktable before Brone's grateful eyes. They had, indeed, unlocked the formula for greenfire. With that weapon in his arsenal, Brone believed he could drive almost any invasion back to the sea.

Even now, the king's engineers were devising metal canisters for the containment of the deadly substance. In the old stone keep, which looked down on the newer parts of the city from a hill near the eastern wall, a sealed storage room was being constructed to shield the canisters from moisture, so the powder could be safely stored. Brone frowned. Greenfire must, of course, be kept secret, for its effectiveness would depend on surprise.

Brone poured himself a glass of wine and glanced at the door again. Reawen's bridal bath must be complicated indeed. How much longer would he have to wait? Tenderly, he imagined his bride in the perfumed water. Her skin would be rosy from its warmth. Her hair would glisten like wet black silk. He compared the seductive image with his memory of her as she had looked that morning, when he had come upon her in the river. Perhaps he had fallen in love with her then.

Ironic, he reflected, that greenfire should free him to marry where he chose. He had never expected to have that luxury. To be sure, there had been unpleasant repercussions after the Choosing. The Sturites had stamped out, threatening to wreak vengeance for this insult. Good riddance, Brone thought and laughed. The happiness he felt colored everything.

He looked consideringly at the broad bed with its dark red coverlet. Was Reawen happy, too? he wondered. That night when she'd met him in the garden, he had thought she returned his feeling. Yet her behavior since the Choosing had disturbed him. Of course, he hadn't seen much of her. Chosen brides stayed sequestered until their marriage day. But during their wedding ceremony, though he had gazed down on her warmly while he snapped the heavy wedding bracelet in place on her arm, she had avoided his eyes.

Perhaps she didn't love him yet, he conceded. But women tended to give back feeling when it was received. Surely after tonight, when she knew the strength of his love for her, she would return it.

The ceremonial knock resounded, and Brone leaped to his feet, crossing the sitting room to open the door. Flanked on either side by torchbearers and trailed by serving women, Reawen stood on the other side of the threshold. Wrought golden clasps adorned the waist and shoulders of the white gown she wore. On her narrow feet she wore delicate embroidered sandals. A wreath of freshly picked flowers decorated her curls.

As Brone looked down at her, his blue eyes turned smoky. He waved away her attendants, seized her wrist, and drew her inside. When he felt her cold hand tremble in his, a wave of tenderness swept over him. "Reawen," he whispered triumphantly and shut the door.

The moment they were alone, Brone turned her toward him and threaded his fingers through her dark hair. He touched his lips to her neck and, with a shock of pleasure, inhaled the fresh scent that always clung to her. In the garden he had thought it was the grass and the night air. Now he realized that it was Reawen.

She was standing stock still and staring straight ahead. "Are you frightened?" he whispered, tightening his embrace. "You have nothing to fear. Tonight we have all the time in the world."

She gave a little squeak of surprise when he scooped her up and carried her to the bedchamber. When he laid her down, she struggled to rise, but his hand pushed her gently but firmly to the bed. While she stared up at him, he sank next to her and covered her lips with his. "You are so sweet, Reawen. I've been longing for you all these weeks. Were you surprised when I chose you?"

"Astonished," she whispered faintly.

He chuckled. "Ever since you gave yourself to me in the garden, I've wanted to put my bracelet around your wrist.

She stiffened when he mentioned the garden, but Brone supposed that was because of her shyness. Once again his head descended, and his mouth covered hers hungrily. His fingers tracked a path across her collarbone, moved gently down her rib cage and closed on her breast. He expected her to respond with some of the passion she had shown him in the garden, but she did not.

Coaxingly, he moved his lips from her mouth to the hollow of her throat. Softly, he slipped her loose gown from her shoulders so that he could caress the valley between her breasts. "Beautiful, beautiful Reawen," he murmured. "I'm aching to make love to you."

When she didn't reply, he lifted his head. "But I want you to make love to me, too. Tell me you desire me."

Expressionlessly, as if repeating a speech by rote, she said, "How can I believe that you truly love me? Jedestrom is full of women who've shared your bed. I don't know why you've married me, but it can't have been for love."

At first Brone was impatient. This was childishness, he thought. Then, looking at his bride, he realized how young she was, how fresh and naive. He told himself that jealousy was a good sign, for it meant she cared.

He touched her cheek and stroked the soft curve. "I'm not a boy. Of course there have been other women, Reawen. But if I'd had hundreds, it would mean nothing. I've made you my queen, you and no other."

Instead of responding by throwing her arms around him as he'd hoped, she closed her eyes and turned her face away.

Baffled and frustrated, Brone said, "Reawen, this is foolishness. What more can I do to prove how much I care for you?"

As if nerving herself to leap a chasm, she took a deep breath. Then she opened her eyes and turned. For a long moment her gaze rested on his crown.

"You can let me hold the green stone." She said it defiantly, as if she had no real hope of his complying. "If you did that, it would prove you love me."

Brone stared at her coldly. He felt angry and disappointed that she'd made this silly demand. Yet, she looked so lovely lying there that his heart melted. "You're a hard woman to please, but tonight I intend to please you. And," he added, grinning as he took the band from his head, "I intend for you to please me."

Manipulating a catch, Brone took the stone from its resting place and playfully slid it into Reawen's palm. Before her fingers could close over it, however, he snatched it back. "First you must kiss me for it."

She gazed at him uneasily.

Laughing at the look on her face, he said, "Sit up, that's right. Now put your arms around my neck and kiss me. No, don't try to cover yourself with your gown. I like it where it is."

As Reawen regarded him warily, his smile widened. "You don't fool me," he chided gently. "You're pretending you don't wish to kiss your husband, but I know better. I'll prove my love to you by letting you hold the green stone, but before I do, you'll have to admit you feel something for me. Now, get on with it. Sit up and kiss me."

Reawen struggled to a sitting position, put her hands on his shoulder, and touched her lips to his. When she drew back, Brone laughed at her, laughter that sprang from the well of jubilant love brimming inside him.

Still holding the stone out of her reach, he mocked lightly, "Not like that. That was hardly a kiss at all. I mean a real kiss. Kiss me deeply. Then tell me that you love me and want me. Only then will I let you hold the stone."

Quick as a reflex, Reawen lowered her black lashes. Something about the way she'd done it jarred Brone, and he watched her intently. Her timidity was beyond reason after what they'd shared in the garden, he thought. He was determined to break through her shyness and teach her not to be afraid of him.

With her lashes still lowered, she put her arms around his neck. With a little sigh, she pressed her breasts to him and kissed him hard. One hand moved up to the back of his head where his hair curled around her fingers and clung. His lips parted slightly and he waited. He could feel her breathing unevenly against him. Tentatively, she touched his teeth with her tongue. He drew a ragged breath, seized her waist, and pressed her hard against him.

"I love you," he whispered as he lay her flat against the pillow, his chest on hers. Urgency flamed through his groin, but he wanted her on fire as well. It was only when he felt her finally respond to his caresses that he pulled his tunic off. Naked, the mat of gold hairs on his chest glinting in the candlelight, he dragged her gown off as well. For a long moment his eyes drank her in.

"Now say it, Reawen. Tell me you love me. Tell me you want me!"

She seemed to be staring up at him in desperation, and he wondered why it was so hard for her to speak the words he longed to hear. In a desperation of his own, he wedged her face between his hands and lifted it close to his. "Say it!"

"I love you, I want you," she gasped out.

He pressed his body on hers. "Tell me again, Reawen. The words are like wine to me. I've wanted you for so long."

When she dragged air through her lungs and forced out her declaration once again, he kissed her breast, took her hand softly in his, and uncurled her fingers. Dropping a kiss in the palm, he murmured, "Then you are my queen and have the right to share my power." A moment later he pressed the green stone into her hand and closed her fingers around it.

"Now you must know that I love you," Brone murmured as he lowered his mouth to Reawen's.

His bride didn't hear. She was hardly even conscious of his

presence. In the candlelight her eyes had grown silvery and secret. Suddenly Brone cried out in shock. The body he held in his arms shimmered like foggy water through moonlight and vanished.

* * * * *

"In the seductress category your Reawen is not in her mother's league," Thropos commented. He sat back and regarded the blue liquid in his bowl. It had cleared and then become opaque.

She's young, inexperienced, snapped the captive pillawn.

"Even so, any village maiden would have shown more enthusiasm with an ardent and handsome groom such as Brone."

She has too much integrity to be an easy liar. She hates him, I tell you.

Thropos sneered. "Of that, my pretty pillawn, I'm not so sure. I know little of women, but to me it appeared that in their last embrace she gave back some of the fire burning so hotly in her suitor."

When you say you know little of women, you only concede an obvious truth. What does it matter that Reawen is not like her wanton mother? She got what she was after. Cel puffed out her feathers.

"Indeed, she did. Now the green stone is hers." The wizard's eyes narrowed. "I hadn't realized it would give her the cloak of invisibility. To my knowledge it has never conferred that power on Brone."

The king is not of the domi line. The stones are not sympathetic to him. He can wield their power if he chooses, but each time he does he pays a terrible price in vitality, and he knows it.

Thropos stroked his chin. "That must be why he stopped using them so early in his reign."

Of course. They were sucking the life out of him. Just wearing them is killing him. For Reawen it is entirely different. She, like the other domi before her, resonates sympathetically with her stone. It will lengthen her life, not shorten it.

"Could Nioma make herself invisible?" Thropos demanded sharply.

No, but Nioma was never the strongest in her line. They were all different, you know. Some could command much more than others.

"And from what we've seen, it looks as if your Reawen will be among those who make the most of the stone."

The longer it's with her, the more it will enhance her power, declared Cel defiantly.

"And just what are these mysterious powers? How overwhelming will your virginal little Reawen become?"

Behind the bars of her cage Cel gazed out at the wizard warily. *Already you've tricked me into telling you more than I intended. You will have to answer that question yourself.*

Thropos's thin lips curled back, and he cackled with amusement. "Clever pillawn! I have ways to learn whatever I wish from you."

I've seen the way you like to torment the poor, helpless creatures in your cages. Do your worst to me. I'll tell you nothing.

"Oh, I doubt that." He leaned forward and stared insolently at his captive. "If I were to do my worst, you'd soon beg to answer my questions. But perhaps such unpleasantness won't be necessary just yet. Perhaps someone else will tell me what I wish to know."

Drawing back, Thropos passed his hand over the liquid in the bowl. An image appeared. It showed a dark little man sneaking along the edge of the river beyond Jedestrom's gates.

Cel's round eyes dilated. *Who's that?*

"Don't you recognize the tramp who attacked your mistress just before she met the accommodating Albin? Tsk, tsk. You should remember him, for it was you who fought him off."

Vile scum! Cel exclaimed.

"An accurate description, I fear. But his name is actually Turlip," Thropos said mildly. "He works for me and has been quite useful in a number of matters, including your capture.

Alas, no service is rendered without a price. I've had to promise
him a reward. The reward is your Reawen."

Monster! Cel shrieked. *You'll not have your way. Reawen's invisible now. Your servant won't be able to find her.*

"Ah, but I've given him a device with which to track her,
invisible or not." Thropos shot Cel a sly look and then returned
his avid gaze to the bowl. "He's hot on her trail right now. I
look forward to seeing what happens when he locates her. Perhaps then we'll get some notion of this new-hatched water
domis's talents."

* * * * *

Reawen slipped past the first trees that straggled down the
slopes where the forest began. The thin dress she'd stolen from
a washline was in tatters, and her bare feet were bloody. But she
was free, free of Jedestrom, free of cowardly pretense, free of
Brone and his disturbing declarations of love.

Clutched in her hand was her stone. As her fingers tightened
on it, she cast a last worried glance over her shoulder and hurried into the woods that she knew would offer her shelter on
the long journey back to the mountains.

Reawen had been following the river northward for no more
than a day when she acknowledged to herself that she must risk
stopping somewhere. She needed shoes, clothing, food, and
some means of carrying her stone more safely.

Sighting a likely village, she hid herself in the forest until
dusk. When the moon began to glimmer in the treetops, she
held the stone between her palms, squeezed her eyes shut, and
called on its power to make herself invisible. Against her skin,
she felt the stone grow warm. There was a rushing feeling, as if
her body were turning to wind. She looked down at her hands
and saw nothing. She was invisible, even to her own eyes.

Reawen's heart pounded painfully. It was all so new and
alarming. She didn't feel fully in control of the stone. It was

like holding something wild and dangerous in her hand. What if she made a mistake? Might she not disappear so thoroughly that she was lost even to herself?

For so many months she had longed for the stone. Now that she had it, she was half frightened of it. Yet, she felt in her bones that it was meant for her.

Reawen's thoughts went back to her wedding night, and she winced with pain. "I love you," she'd said to Brone. If only he hadn't made her say it. Never would she forget the tender expression she'd seen come into his eyes. His image with the band around his head seemed to pierce her, and she clutched the stone as if it were an anchor.

Brone would never have felt that it was anything but his enemy, she reflected. How had he ever had the courage to wield it? How could he have the strength of will to wear all four stones for so many years? It would be like spending your life wrestling with a foe who would eventually kill you. Only now did Reawen begin to fully understand that he must love his people very much to make such a sacrifice.

Reawen slipped into the village. With nothing but the imprints of her bare feet in the dust to mark her passage, she explored its dirt-packed streets. Finally, she found what she sought. Taking a deep breath, she wished herself visible. When she looked down and saw that her arms were solid and real, she sighed with relief and stepped out of the shadows.

"I wish to buy a neck chain," she told a burly fellow hammering at a forge on the outskirts of the settlement.

Suspiciously, he looked her up and down, making her conscious of her disreputable appearance. She guessed that her dark curls were matted, her cheeks streaked with grime. "I be no fancy lady's jewelry maker, only a blacksmith."

"A simple chain is all I require, and I will pay you for it well."

Again he looked her up and down. "With what?"

"With this." Reawen unclasped the wedding bracelet that

had been Brone's bridal gift and handed it over.

When he felt its weight, the blacksmith's craggy eyebrows lifted. "This be solid gold. Where did ye get it, if I might be so bold as to ask?"

"It was a gift, and that's all I'll tell you," Reawen said firmly. "Will you take it in trade?"

The man stared down at the bracelet. "Whoever gave ye this must have thought high of ye. Sure ye want to give it up?"

A flush rose up Reawen's neck, and for a moment she felt a mad impulse to snatch the bracelet back. But that couldn't be. "I'm sure," she answered expressionlessly. "Will you have it?"

"Only a fool would say nay . . . but it's worth much more than an iron chain."

"Is it worth an iron chain and the price of a cloak, new sandals, and enough coin to buy a week's supply of bread and cheese?"

At that, he barked a laugh. "If such is all ye wish, ye've struck a bargain, little lady."

By nightfall Reawen had a full stomach. She also had shoes to protect her feet, warm garments, and a pack loaded with food. As she faded back into the woods outside the village, she smiled. By the time the first autumn leaf touches earth, I'll be back in the mountains with Gris, she thought.

After all, who could stop her flight now? She'd managed to elude all the guards who'd chased after her that first harrowing night when, naked and terrified, she'd fled Jedestrom. If they hadn't been able to find her then, they certainly wouldn't be able to track her down now—not with her stone safely suspended between her breasts on its new chain and all the new and rather upsetting powers it seemed to have bestowed on her.

Reawen's fingers went to the bodice of her rough gown and sought the oval shape of the stone beneath it. It seemed to vibrate, almost as if it was a second heart. It felt like part of her against her skin. It *was* part of her. She'd known that from the moment she'd touched it.

Yet, it continued to terrify her. For, in some strange way, it seemed to have ideas of its own. "It's changing me," she murmured aloud. "With every day I wear it, it will change me more."

Oh, how I wish Cel were here to advise me, Reawen thought. Her eyes grew wet as she pictured the pillawn. Anguished, she glanced skyward in the vain hopes of spotting the flutter of white wings. What had happened to Cel? Many times Reawen had tried to find her in water images, but she'd been unsuccessful.

She brought a hand to her forehead and thought, Cel would tease me out of this strange mood I'm in. She would tell me to stop fretting because I told Brone I loved him. I couldn't help it. He forced me to say the words. What did it matter that they hadn't meant any more than the declarations he'd made to her? For surely he hadn't really been sincere when he'd told her that he loved her. No, he'd merely desired her, she reassured herself. Desire and love were two different things.

As darkness fell, Reawen took shelter in a protected spot on the riverbank. After she'd nibbled her bread and cheese, she curled up inside the warmth of her new green woolen cloak. Clasping a hand tight around her stone, she fell into the deep sleep of exhaustion. Gradually, she began to dream that a golden-haired king embraced her and looked down at her with tender blue eyes. "I love you, I love you, I love you," she heard herself say.

If Cel had been with Reawen, she might have given warning when a dark shape slunk behind a nearby bush. In the distance, a field mouse squeaked in pain and terror as an owl descended on it with slashing claws. But that wasn't enough to jar Reawen from her dream of Brone.

There you are, my pretty, Turlip thought, and rubbed his hands together gleefully. For three days now he'd followed Reawen. Always keeping a respectful distance, so as not to alarm her, he'd been hard on her trail as a hungry ferret. The invisibility she'd assumed during the first day of her escape had confounded the king's pursuers, but it hadn't mattered to him—not with Thropos's talisman to point her out. Turlip had been close enough to spy on her when she'd snatched a gown from a washline to cover her nakedness. He'd hovered like a bloodthirsty bat outside the village where she'd traded away her bracelet. Now, after all these weeks of frustration, he intended to claim his tender, black-haired prize.

Silently, he darted out from behind his bush, slunk up a mossy slope, and seized Reawen's shoulders. "You're mine, now, and no nasty white bird about to help you!"

Reawen awoke with a gasp. The dream she'd been struggling through had turned into horror. Instead of Brone's handsome face, she saw Turlip's oily one. It leered down at her like something out of a nightmare. With a shriek, she tried to free herself, and almost succeeded. But Turlip was as strong as he was unsavory. Grinning with snaggle-toothed anticipation, he dug his fingers into her arms. Planting a knee between her legs, he forced her back against the hump of mossy ground where she'd been curled.

"Don't think you can escape me, sweetling," he hissed, his face so close to hers that she could smell his sour breath. "I've been lickin' me chops after you fer too long. Oh, I'm good and hungry, I am, an' I don't even mind takin' a king's leavings."

Reawen, now fully alive to her danger, began to struggle in earnest. The stone gave her strength she hadn't had before. She punched viciously at Turlip's chest.

"Ow!" he howled and fell back.

Scrambling from beneath him, she jumped up to flee. But the thief had recovered quickly. Cursing, he snatched at her arm with one hand and grabbed up a stout length of fallen branch with another. "Tricksy little bitch! Time you was taught a lesson!" He raised it over his head and swung a vicious blow.

Reawen managed to dodge. Turlip hit at her again. This time, instead of evading the blow, Reawen seized the branch.

As she matched her strength with Turlip's, the thief stared at her in amazement. For a long, agonizing moment, it was a standoff. Then the stone grew warm against her breast. Suddenly it was easy for Reawen to drag the weapon away from Turlip. Lightly she tossed it into the brush. Then she drew herself up and stared hard at her assailant.

Turlip froze. "What's goin' on? What yer, no, no . . ." he began to whine. But it was too late. A tingling power waterfalled through Reawen, a power she couldn't stop. In her need, she had unconsciously summoned the stone, and now the stone controlled her.

Turlip's body began to glow. His features contorted in agony. All at once he sagged, melted, flowed downward. Then he was no more, and Reawen found herself gazing down in horror at a puddle of murky, foul-smelling water.

Chapter Ten

"I used ter think you was a good-natured boykin. Not no more," Pib complained as he watched Albin curry Grassears's rough coat.

"What is there to be good-natured about these days?" Albin snapped. He looked as if he could use a good combing himself. His rumpled clothes looked slept in and probably had been. His straight brown hair stuck out in points around his head, and he wore a perpetual frown.

"True enough, what with the king so sore-headed because his new bride gave him the slip on his wedding night." Pib cocked his shaggy, strawberry-blond head. "Guess you have special reasons for bein' in such a blather, since you was sweet on Reawen yerself."

Albin threw his currycomb so hard that it bounced against the stall door with a resounding thwack. "I've got good reasons to be upset! The king blames me for what's happened. He thinks I smuggled a spy into his household."

Pib's pale green eyes widened. "Meaning Reawen?"

"No, Grassears here. Of course, meaning Reawen! Who else?"

Pib stood blinking for a moment. "'As he said so? The king, I mean."

"He hasn't said a thing. King Brone's been so busy trying to track Reawen down that he hasn't got around to calling me into his presence yet. But mark my words, he will. When it happens, I'll be lucky to walk away with a whole skin."

As if on cue, Brone's secretary poked his balding head into the stable. When he spotted Albin, his mouth pursed. "You are to come with me, young master. The king wishes a private

163

word with you."

After shooting the briefest of I-told-you-so glances at Pib, Albin tugged his rumpled tunic into place. Resignedly, he ran a nervous hand through his unkempt hair, then followed the fussy little bureaucrat back through the palace grounds.

All the paths were crowded. Soldiers and servants scurried back and forth on a multitude of tasks. Military and civilian alike wore somber expressions, for, since Brone's disastrous wedding night, the Plat had not been a pleasant place to be.

Albin remembered well the moment when the alarm had sounded. He'd been hunched in misery on the edge of his bunk, trying not to think of Reawen and Brone together. The news of her disappearance had hit him, and everyone else who lived on the palace grounds, like a bolt of lightning.

In the days since, things had only gotten worse. Brone wore the tight face of a man simmering in a stew of rage and humiliation. With each report that his soldiers had failed to find his runaway bride and bring her back, his fury deepened. And others at the Plat shared his anger.

"To think that I dressed her up to please the king's eye," Quista had thrown at Albin when she'd caught him in the garden, wandering disconsolately. "If I'd known what she was I wouldn't have given her anything but the back of my hand. And it was you, you great stupid donkeyhead, it was you who brought her here and begged me to treat her like a sister. Sister, pah!"

Now, as Albin tapped on the king's door, he braced himself for a much worse rebuke.

"Come in," he heard Brone's voice snap.

After taking a deep breath, Albin entered. At the far end of the map room, the king sat at a low table scattered with papers.

"See this?" he asked without looking Albin's way. He held up a wide gold bracelet. "Recognize it?"

Albin swallowed. "It's a wedding bracelet."

"It's the one I put on Reawen's wrist. I'd know it anywhere.

It was my grandmother's, and it's made of solid gold."

"Does . . . does that mean . . ." Albin couldn't bring himself to say the words. In his mind he pictured Reawen's dead body lying sprawled in some wilderness spot. How else could the king have retrieved the ornament? Surely she wouldn't have parted easily with such a treasure.

"I haven't found my elusive bride, if that's what you're thinking. This morning, a blacksmith brought the bracelet to my steward. When my tender consort passed through the smith's village, she traded my gift for a loaf of bread and a collection of rags." For the first time, Brone looked up. Albin met his gaze and stepped back as if from a physical blow. In the king's blue eyes he saw desolation, a wasteland of blasted hopes.

"Come close," Brone said. "I won't bite you."

"It's my fault. I . . . I'm the one who brought her here," Albin stammered. "Truly, I had no idea."

"Of course you had no idea. She fooled us all. How were any of us to guess that such a guileless young woman was one of them."

"One of them?"

"The domi, Albin," Brone snapped impatiently. "By now you must have heard the rumors. Well, they're true. She came here to steal the green stone."

"One of them." Albin shook his head.

"Besotted as I was," Brone muttered, "such a possibility never occurred to me. But now that I look back on everything that happened, it's obvious."

"One of the domi—" Albin continued shaking his head as if trying to clear it. "Oh, Sire, I never dreamed—"

"None of us dreamed. That's how she managed to do what she has done." Brone pounded a balled fist into the palm of his hand. "She can't be allowed to succeed."

Albin stood before him in silence, shoulders drooping, hazel eyes welling with confused emotions. He felt guilty, sorry, hurt, and betrayed. He was also alarmed. What did it really mean that Brone no longer had the green stone?

"You're thinking, of course, that she's already succeeded," Brone said cynically. "She's made fools of my best trackers, and by now she's well on her way to the mountains." He shoved the bracelet to one side and paid no attention when it rolled from his table and fell to the floor. "For there's no question now—that's where she's headed. She's going back to those infernal mountains, where she can hide with the rest of her scheming, conniving tribe. I can't let her succeed, and I won't!"

Brone surged up out of his chair. Tigerishly, he paced to the right of the large wall map of the Peninsula. "I'd like nothing better than to take an army with me to the mountains and flush the lot of them out of their hiding holes."

Albin clenched his hands. "Is that what you intend to do, Sire, fight the domi?"

"It's what I'd like, not what's possible." Brone whirled and faced Albin. "Only today I've had news that Sturite warships are heading for our coast. They come to launch another attack."

"Another!" Albin went white.

"Yerbo is dead, and Arant wears his father's crown. He's declared that I dishonored his sister when I married Reawen. He says he has no choice but to avenge Fidacia." Brone's mouth twisted. "It seems that, by choosing Reawen, I've brought trouble down from more than one quarter. Let that be a lesson to you, Albin. When it comes to women, be guided by your head and nothing less."

Brone laughed, but the rough sound held pain, not humor. "I have to ride with my army south to meet the Sturites," he said. "It won't be as simple to settle this matter as it was at Acuma. This time, Arant plans a long siege, and he'll have the whole might of his army at his back. Given the time of year, there's little likelihood of my invading the mountains until spring." Brone's fist thunked into his open palm. "But I'm determined to lay the groundwork for that now." The king took several prowling steps toward his messenger. "Albin, you're one of the few around me in whose loyalty I have absolute confidence."

The boy bowed his head. "You can always trust me to serve your interests and the interests of the Peninsula, my lord."

"I know that's true. In this desperate hour, I'm prepared to trust you in a way that I would no other." His mouth grim, Brone gazed down at Albin's bent head. "Like a lovesick fool, I gave the green stone from my crown to Reawen. Now I intend giving you the white stone."

Albin started, hardly believing his ears. "Sire!" His eyes widened as he watched the king lift the gold band from his head. Brone undid a catch and slipped the wind domis's gem from its socket.

"This is no token of my affection, Albin. Nor is it a whim. I have a serious purpose. Difficult times lie ahead for the Peninsula and its people. To beat off the Sturites and the domi and whoever else plans to attack us, we will need help. I have to speak with my mentor, Faring. Some interference lies between us, and I have not been able to make contact. Much as I regret it, I'm afraid I must send you into the mountains again."

Albin felt the blood drain from his head. A few weeks earlier, he'd thought he was going to die in those craggy cliffs. The only things that had sustained him. . . . He swallowed, trying not to think of the water domis he had so longed for. Go back! More than likely, if he went back he'd never come out alive.

"I know what you're thinking," Brone said, "and even if I didn't, I could guess from the color of your skin. You've gone pale as death."

"It's . . . it's not just the wolves, the magic, and the cold," Albin stammered. "It's the domi. Taunis didn't see me, but the wind domis did. If I meet Eol again, he'll turn me into an icicle."

"Not if you carry his stone. Oh, I don't doubt that you'll meet him, for he'll sense the stone on you and so, very likely,

will the others. They'll gather around you like hungry hyenas."
Brone's mouth twisted. "But no matter what they do, they
can't take Eol's stone away from you by force. You have to give
it. If you refuse to give it, if you hold tight to it, it must protect you."

Albin thrust his hands behind his back. "The green stone's
gone, Sire. What if I'm tricked out of the white? The domi will
have half their powers back."

"You won't let them trick you, Albin. You're far too sensible.
I have perfect confidence that, before winter ends, you will have
delivered my message in Peneto and returned to give me back
Eol's trinket." With a sudden smile, Brone pulled Albin's arm
free, unclenched his fist and lay the white stone in his palm.

A quarter of an hour later, Albin was back in the stable
watching Pib make his way out. "Now what can the king want
with me?" Pib muttered.

"It's probably just something about the horses."

Pib looked doubtful. "I don't think so. Yesterday his secretary was here askin' about my Sturite grandma. Wanted to
know if I had any Sturite relatives left. Now the king wants to
speak with me. You don't think as how Brone suspects me of
spyin', do you? It ain't my fault my grandpa fell in love with a
redheaded wench he met on a tradin' trip."

Albin patted Pib's broad shoulder. "No one thinks you're a
spy. Maybe the king's hoping your grandmother told you something useful about the Sturites."

Pib frowned. "Wish she did. But I can't think of anything.
She was just my old grandma, you know. Never said much
about her homeland. Never said much of anything, come to
think on it."

"Well, you never know. You might have picked up something useful from her and not realize it."

Pib brightened. "Mebbe. I'd like that. Now, what about you,
Albin. Will you still be hangin' around when I come back from
talking with Brone?"

Albin shook his head. "He's sending me away on another mission. As soon as I've got provisions, I'll leave."

"Off adventuring again, eh?"

Pib's eyes glowed with envy, but Albin didn't notice. "Yes, lucky me," he muttered.

"Well don't look so glum about it. Wish I was goin' on a mission. Gets awful borin' stayin' here in the stable all the time," Pib grumbled. "I'd like to do something for my country and be a hero. That would stop the tongues waggin' about my grandma. But Brone will never send me on a mission. All I'll ever get to do around here is shovel manure."

Albin chuckled as Pib strode off for his appointment with the king. When he'd rounded the corner and was out of sight, Albin's smile faded. He turned to Grassears. "Well old friend," he told the little horse, "we're heading up into the mountains again. What do you think of that?"

Grassears stared at his master and flinched.

* * * * *

Many miles to the north, Reawen slid to her knees. She had come to an outcropping of rock sugared with golden fern. Tears started from her eyes, for she knew this place. Expectantly, she looked around. For a moment she held herself still, listening intently. Then she closed her eyes and took several deep breaths.

In a low, clear voice, she began to chant. "Wild magic, hill magic, leaf, bird, and rill. Come Lawen, come Batin, come Mrimrill."

When Reawen heard a high-pitched giggle, her lashes parted, and she looked into the faces of three of her childhood playmates. Regarding her solemnly, Lawen sat with his short, furred legs crossed. Everything about him was brown: his hair, his eyes, his nut-colored skin, and the tiny horns that jutted from his forehead.

Next to him, Batin lay flat on his stomach, his pointed chin resting impudently between his cradled hands. His slanted eyes glowed with mischief. A leafy green suit clung so tightly to his slender body that it seemed to be part of him. The wings growing out of his back were a lighter shade shot with gold.

There was another giggle and Mrimrill danced forward. She was tiny—hardly the length of a raised forefinger—and quite lovely in her gossamer blue gown. An aureole of shimmering silver curls framed her heart-shaped face. Poised on the edge of a fern, she could easily have been mistaken for a flower.

"Friends of my childhood, I have returned to live among you in peace and harmony," Reawen said softly. "To show my goodwill, I bring gifts."

Ceremoniously, she laid a carefully selected object at the feet of each of the ancient forest spirits. Before Lawen, she set a polished nut she'd found among the roots of a giant tree growing along the river's edge. Before Batin, she placed the iridescent feather of a jet black crow. And Mrimrill received a tiny, perfect pink rose. It was one of summer's last.

"Do you accept my offerings?" Reawen asked anxiously. She wondered at the serious looks on their ageless faces, as they each gazed at her intently. Did they not see before them the same girl that had departed the woods so many months before?

The threesome vanished along with Reawen's gifts. Laughter bubbled in the air. Reawen felt a soft kiss on her cheek. "Welcome home, domis of water," Mrimrill whispered from nowhere and everywhere. Batin lightly pinched her earlobe. "Hail, mother . . . of the waves," he teased. Reawen felt her hand warmly squeezed and knew it was Lawen quietly renewing his friendship—and something more. As the laughter faded away to nothing, Reawen smiled and wept, all at the same time. Reflecting fondly on her childhood comrades and their strange behavior, she wished she could join in the games they still played. Suddenly, the realization dawned on her that she had indeed left her girlhood behind her forever.

The cave that was journey's end for Reawen lay hidden in the side of a thickly wooded hill, screened on all sides by tall pines and an unkempt growth of holly. Nearby, a stream, choked in places with fallen leaves, gurgled through mossy soil. Earlier that day, Reawen had come upon the stream. Now she followed it to the place where Gris liked to wash the herbs she sometimes traded for wool and other necessaries on her travels south for festival days.

Reawen saw the imprint of a naked foot deep in the mud. So, Gris had been there recently, she thought joyfully as she hurried up the track. On the other side of a bend she found the older woman standing, as if waiting for her. She was thinner. The bones in her wrists stood out starkly under her weathered skin. Her hair hung in lank skeins about her stooped shoulders.

"Gris?"

"So you've come back." Gris's voice sounded rusty—she probably hadn't spoken to a soul in weeks, Reawen thought. "I knew you would. Still, I was afraid you might change your mind." She began trembling violently. Her head dropped forward on her bony chest, and she covered her face with her rough hands. Then she crumpled to the ground. "Reawen, it seems so long that I've been waiting."

Reawen flung herself down beside her aunt. "What's wrong? Has something happened? You don't look well."

Gris didn't answer, only moaned and kept her hands pressed to her face. Then Reawen saw that her twisted fingers were damp with tears.

"Gris, you're crying. Don't cry!" Tenderly, Reawen wrapped her arms around her aunt's shoulders. "Oh, Gris," she murmured into the graying hair, "of course I came back. How could you think I wouldn't?"

Gris quieted and lifted her lined, tear-tracked face. "In the water images, I watched you when I could. I saw how Brone made love to you, and that you were not unaffected. I thought you might choose to stay with him, and I couldn't bear the thought of losing you forever. You're right, Reawen. I haven't been well. Perhaps it's just loneliness. I'll begin to feel better if you're back to stay."

"Of course I'm back to stay. Never would I leave you and not return. My place is here with you."

"Reawen, are you sure?"

"Of course I'm sure." Shaking slightly, Reawen found the chain and lifted it from beneath her neckline. "You see? I've brought the stone."

Gris squeezed her hands together and gazed at it in silence. Then both women began to cry and laugh and hug each other with joy and relief.

That evening, bathed and rested, Reawen sat opposite Gris. Between them was a small fire over which a fragrant pot of soup bubbled. As they watched it, they talked.

"Did you bring gifts for the spirits of the forest?" Gris asked.

"I did, and they accepted them."

"Well, of course they would." She smiled. "They have always loved you. What of the wild magic? Did any of the trees or rocks trouble you?"

"Not at all. In fact, an oak greeted me kindly, and a birch sang me a song of welcome and then blew a shower of gold leaves at me."

Gris laughed. "The wild magic is gentle in these parts. It's only in the high mountains that it can grow vexatious. You have always been beloved here. And now that you are truly water domis, you will be honored as well." Gris studied Reawen intently. "Do you know what it means to be domis of water?"

Reawen got up and peered into the pot. She ladled some steaming soup and handed the wooden bowl to her aunt. "I thought I knew, until I wore the stone. Now I'm not sure."

Gris gazed at Reawen wisely. "Often we think we know something until something happens to show us we were wrong all along. Tell me what you mean."

"Oh, Gris, I always knew that the stone belonged to me. But the moment it touched my hand, I began to realize that I belonged to it also. I can wield its power. But it also has power over me." Reawen settled back and laced her hands around her upraised knee. "On the way home, a tramp assaulted me, a very nasty fellow. I wanted to fight him off, but I never intended to kill him."

Gris's spoon paused midair. "What happened?"

"I was losing the fight, when suddenly the stone took over. I felt a force flowing through me, the like of which I've never felt before." She shook her head. "The tramp literally dissolved before my eyes."

"He became water?"

When Reawen nodded, Gris set the bowl down and leaned forward to poke the fire. "I saw Nioma do it once. The human body is mostly water, you know. The stone simply broke it into its basic ingredients."

"It was a terrible thing to see it happen so suddenly like that and to know I had caused it."

"Not you alone. If this villain had never attacked you, he'd be whole and hearty." Gris's hand crept to her breast and then dropped back to her lap. "The stone will protect its own. As long as you wear it, you're safe from violence. You're also safe from disease. The ills of the flesh will not touch you. Think of that."

But Reawen couldn't get her mind off what had happened to Turlip. "When the stone destroyed the tramp, it commanded me, not the other way around. I was completely in its grip."

"You're a novice yet," Gris explained gently. "You must use the winter months ahead to gain mastery over your stone. For when spring comes . . ." Her voice trailed off, and her eyes grew dull.

"Yes?" Reawen questioned.

"Spring may bring new challenges to us both."

For a long moment, Reawen gazed silently through the fire's

flickering light. "You know, don't you?"

"Know what?"

"I—" Reawen bit her lip.

A new alertness came into the older woman's expression. She studied Reawen's averted profile. Her eyes widened. "You are more than what you were, and it's not just the stone."

"I am two. I carry a child in my womb."

"Brone's child?"

"Yes, it's his. Who else's?" The girl hid her face in her hands. Her shoulders shook. "Oh, Gris," she sobbed, "I never intended it. Truly, I don't even know how it happened." Haltingly, she described the strange, dreamlike night in which she'd met Brone in the garden and made love with him. "I know the emberries I ate were drugged. He must have sent them and then raped me."

Thoughtfully, Gris shook her head. "That does not sound to me like Brone's work. Oh, I know he must have wanted you, else he wouldn't have made you his queen and given you the stone. But drugging and raping—" She shook her head again. "No, that's the work of dark magic."

"Magic?"

"Reawen, for weeks now I've sensed there's more afoot here than just your vow to regain your stone. Whether it be our fellow domi or some foreign wizard or both, I don't know. But other forces are at work. I fear those other forces will make themselves felt to us come spring."

"What do you think that spring will bring besides the birth of my child?"

Gris folded her mouth into a grim line. "For one, I think the king will want to capture you and take you back to Jedestrom. Certainly when he learns that you carry his babe, he'll try to claim his own. And there's another thing."

"Yes?"

"Reawen, as your babe develops, the stone will balk at your commands. A time will come when you are not one person, but two. It will sense this and rebel. It may even act unpredictably. That will be a perilous time for you, for your powers will be weak, and it will be dangerous to you and to the child to use them at all."

"What can I do?"

"You can keep yourself strong and learn to master your stone now, while it's still your eager servant. Every day you must practice. I'll help you."

"What of my child? Will I be able to bequeath the stone to it?"

Gris shook her head. "Only if it is born in the true line of the domi. And only time and the testing at the sacred pool will reveal that." With an effort, Gris pushed herself to her feet. She walked around the edge of the fire and took Reawen's hand. "Now is not the hour to worry over bequeathing the stone to anyone. Trust me on that, child, for now we have troubles enough to worry our heads over. We must strengthen ourselves over the winter. Come spring, we must be ready for the trials that lie ahead of us."

* * * * *

"Steady now," Albin told Grassears. They were picking their way across a stream. Though narrow, it had a treacherously rocky bed and a fast-running flow of ice-cold water. On the other side, the first frost of the season had firmed the earth, touching the trees with flame.

Albin looked around, appreciating the seductive autumnal beauty. It tempted him to linger over this part of his journey. Even though he was deep in the wooded foothills, he still felt safe. If there was wild magic here, it seemed benign. Once he thought he heard a tree laughing at him, but when he jerked around to defend himself, it only sent a shower of aspen leaves falling around him like soft gold coins.

Even as Albin drank in the splendid woodland scenery

surrounding him, a faint frown puckered his brow. The tall trees screened out the mountains. But he knew they lay ahead of him.

"We have to get through them before winter sets in," he told his horse after the animal had stepped safely up on the bank. With a shudder, Albin remembered the freezing cold of the mountain passes when he'd tried to navigate them. And that had been in summer.

Of course, much of that travail had been the work of Eol. "Please the lucky spirits, let me not meet up with him again," Albin prayed.

Nudging Grassears with a practiced knee, Albin followed the stream northward. Two days earlier, he'd spent the night at the last inn along his route. It was so far north of the Peninsula's southern coast that news of the war with the Sturites was scant. What he had heard boded ill.

"This ain't no little raid like the king put down so easy before," one road-weary merchant had told the group of farmers who'd gathered around the tap in the common room. "This time they come equipped with all their best warriors and battleships. I heard tell the king's army is taking terrible losses." He'd shaken a grizzled head. "Anyhow, I still puts my money on Brone. But mark my words, he ain't going to see the last of them devils until winter ice storms help him drive them off."

Albin had felt almost disloyal when he'd risen early the next morning to guide his pony north into the mountains instead of south, where he knew that awesome battles raged. But his instructions from Brone were all too clear. Somehow he had to reach Peneto.

Suddenly the trees parted, giving him a brief glimpse of Dragon's Beak. The tall crag was the highest point between the range of barrier mountains and the wizards' no-man's-land beyond. A chilling premonitory shiver rippled up Albin's thin back. It was on this peak that he'd met Eol. Before he gained Peneto, he would have to climb Dragon's Beak again.

The stream shot northward like a bright silver arrow. All the next day and the days after, Albin followed its course. As he left the foothills for higher ground, trees grew less thickly, and sheltered camping places became a little harder to find. Thankfully, the sun continued to shine, and—during daylight hours—the air stayed warm.

Nights, however, Albin chafed his hands in front of his fire, thankful for his waterproof bedroll and the thick sheepskin coat he'd brought with him. Sometimes he peered out into the darkness, feeling that eyes watched him. Once he even thought he heard airy laughter. Fortunately, the eyes and the laughter didn't feel threatening. Not yet.

"The sun's getting ready to hide his face," Albin told Grassears late one afternoon. "We'd best keep an eye out for a good camping spot with lots of deadwood for a roaring fire. We're getting pretty high up now. Who knows when wolves may decide to drop in on us, wanting a bite to eat?"

As he spoke, Albin glanced down at the gurgling stream to his right. All at once he sensed a change in it, a new brightness, a slight lowering of the temperature. The hairs on the back of his neck stood up. "Something funny's going on," he whispered to Grassears, slipping silently off the pony's back. After he'd tied his animal to a stump, he crept on alone. He pushed warily past a flame-red pyracantha and peered around a rock flanked by a thick stand of evergreen. "Reawen!" he breathed.

She was clad in a long green cloak over a shift of roughly woven white wool. Her hair, grown to a mass of ebony curls, swirled around her neck. She stood very still, her hands outstretched and clasping something between them.

Albin felt the temperature lower another degree and then gasped as he saw water leap upward from the stream in a reverse waterfall. At what was clearly Reawen's command, the unnatural flow stopped in midair and began to take on a new shape. First it was just a seething ball, whirling in layers on itself. Then wings grew out from its sides.

A bird, Albin thought numbly. She's made a bird out of water!

The bird went dark and fell apart. Reawen's eyes opened, a bleak expression in them. Suddenly, she snapped her head to the right. Albin tried to dart behind the rock, but he was too late.

"At last, Albin," she said sternly. "It certainly took you long enough. What are you doing there? Spying on me?"

With his heart in his mouth, he came out. "Reawen," he whispered, "is it really you?"

"Yes, it's really me."

Yet she didn't seem much like the girl he'd met in the woods only a few months earlier. The black-haired beauty who regarded him with stern, silvery eyes was not a girl, but a woman. More than that, she was a woman who controlled a power that he couldn't even begin to understand. At one time, he'd dreamed of asking Reawen to promise herself to him. How ridiculous that seemed now.

"Did you know that I was coming?" he asked.

"Of course I knew. I saw it in the water images. I've been waiting for you. To pass the time, I've been doing a bit of practicing. How long have you been watching me?"

"Long enough to see you make a bird out of water. What was it?"

Reawen slipped whatever she'd been holding down inside her neckline, and Albin realized what it was. The green stone. So she really was domis of water. All this time, he'd hoped the speculations running riot in the Plat weren't true. Now that hope finally died.

"I suppose it won't hurt to tell you," Reawen said, taking a step toward him and smiling tentatively. "The bird was my pillawn, Cel. For weeks now I've been trying to find her. Something—some power—blocks me."

"Pillawn?" Albin blinked. What was that? Dimly, he remembered a fairy story about such a creature.

"She's a pet. I'm terribly worried about her. But you don't know Cel, so you couldn't understand. Come, Albin, tell me what you're doing here."

"The king sent me."

"Did Brone send you to find me? If that's so, it won't do him any good. There's nothing you can say that will persuade me to go back to Jedestrom or to give back my stone. It *is* mine, you know. It was never his." She closed the distance between them. As she held out her hand, she suddenly seemed more like the spirited but gentle girl Albin had thought he'd known.

"It was only chance that I found you, Reawen," he explained. "King Brone didn't send me for you, but to cross the mountains to Peneto. Since you left Jedestrom, we've gone to war with the Sturites, and the king needs the counsel of his mentor, Faring."

Frowning, Reawen indicated a flat place amid the rocks where Albin had tried to hide himself. "Be easy, Albin. You looked frightened when I first saw you, and it hurt me. Surely you must know that I mean you no harm. Sit down with me and tell me all that's happened."

Albin did as she asked and for the next hour they sat talking. He told her all that had happened since she'd fled the king's marriage bed, and she explained who she was and why she'd come to Jedestrom in the first place.

"So you knew that I was searching for a reed player because you read my mind," Albin mused. He remembered well that enchanted moment when he'd awakened to the rising thread of her music. No wonder it had sounded so sweet. "To think, I believed you were a village girl not much different from me, and all the time you were a goddess."

"Not a goddess, really," Reawen corrected, "just a dispossessed orphan of the stones who was hoping to right the wrong done her."

"You must have been angry when I talked about the domi. I'm surprised you don't strike me down now."

Reawen looked hurt. "How can you think that? You were a friend. Perhaps you don't regard me as a friend now, but I still think of you that way. Besides . . ." She hesitated. "Besides, now that I've seen Jedestrom and all that Brone managed to do while he carried the stones, I can understand some of what you told me."

"You mean you won't punish us in the spring with floods?"

"Of course not."

"You don't plan on joining forces with the other domi to regain their stones?"

"I don't even know them. I only saw Driona once in my life, and that was when I was very young. I'm not in league with the others. I owe them nothing and feel nothing for them. All I want is to live here in peace with the stone that is my birthright. You and the people of the Peninsula have no reason to fear me. In fact, I wish you all well."

Solemnly, Albin gazed at Reawen. Things could never fall out in the peaceful way she hoped, he thought, not with war raging in the south and the king beside himself with anger and humiliation over her desertion. Not now that she was carrying his child. For Albin had noticed the slight fullness in her waistline and guessed the significance of it.

"What about the king?" he asked. "Do you hate him?"

Reawen turned her head, hiding the expression in her eyes. "I don't hate him."

Albin leaned forward. He wanted to take her by the shoulders and shake her, but he was afraid to touch her. "Reawen, he loves you."

"Oh, Albin—"

"He does. I saw him the morning after you left. He was beside himself."

"With rage, I'm sure."

"With hurt. You hurt him by what you did."

"Yes, I deceived him in exactly the way he deceived my mother. I made a fool of him." Reawen gave a bleak little laugh. "Albin, I don't wish to discuss Brone with you. When you see him again, tell him I wish him and the people of the Peninsula no harm. Tell him that if he leaves me alone, all will be as it was before. No floods will come down to ruin crops or drown livestock. I intend to manage the Peninsula's water for everyone's good. Let's not talk of Brone anymore, Albin. Let's talk about you. What is it about you that's different?"

"Different?" He tried to look innocent.

Reawen's clear gray eyes searched his face. "You can't hide it from me. My stone tells me you're carrying its fellow. This very minute I feel them reaching out to each other."

The messenger sighed. "I hope you're not going to try to take it away from me."

"Of course I'm not. What would I want with another stone? Besides, stones can't be taken. Now, what's going on? What are you up to?"

Albin described his last disastrous encounter with Eol. "Brone gave me the white stone to use as protection this time," he said.

Reawen lifted her brows. "Then the king trusts you as he does no other."

"I only hope that his trust isn't misplaced. What if I don't have the strength to get past Eol, even with the stone? So far it's done nothing for me except make me feel frightened."

Reawen gazed at him consideringly. "Eol can be cruel, I've heard. If you're going to deal with him, you'll need all the help you can get." Her grim expression lightened and she chuckled. "Maybe there is something I can give you."

"What?"

"Eol loves games of chance. He'll bet on anything. And I've heard he's not above cheating." She reached into the pocket of her cloak and drew out a pair of ivory dice. "A gambler friend gave these to me. He's a rogue named Batin. Cheating is his favorite pastime. Here, try them."

"What?" Reawen dropped the dice into Albin's palm, and he

stared down at them in confusion.

"Think of a number and roll them. Go on," Reawen urged.

Albin shrugged. "All right. Eight." He rolled, and two fours came up.

She grinned. "Whatever number you think of, that's the number you'll get. Batin won three of my best reeds before I realized what he was up to. He gave me the dice to show he was only joking. But I don't need them. You keep them. Who knows? They might come in handy."

Albin would have treasured any gift from Reawen. He closed his fingers over the dice. "Thank you."

"You're welcome, Albin. I only wish I could give you more. I've missed you."

"I've missed you, too." He swallowed. If only he could tell her how much.

They gazed at each other, then Reawen rose and held out her hand. "Goodbye, Albin. May luck and all that's right and good go with you."

* * * * *

"Seeds from the gardener's most splendid sunflowers, berries picked from the king's own hothouses, freshly harvested grains, choice meats, and still you won't eat?" Grinding his teeth, Thropos used a stick to slide the untouched pan of food out of the bottom of Cel's cage, letting it drop onto the table with a loud clank.

In the back of her barred prison, Cel huddled, a disconsolate heap of white feathers.

"I see you've decided to let yourself die rather than serve my purposes. Well, I'll not allow it!" Thropos raged.

When Cel made no answer, he thrust his face close to her bars and hissed, "There's a spell that calls for a pillawn's living heart. Do you want me to work it now? Do you want me to cut you open and yank out your innards?"

When she only closed her purple eyes and turned her head away, his sharp teeth met. "Fortunately for you, I'm not ready to set that spell in motion. I'll not let you die on me just yet, pillawn. Besides, you brighten the place up." He considered her. "You think that because your mistress has her stone and is back home with the old hag who raised her, she's safe. That's not the case. It so happens that Reawen's beloved auntie has a sickness in her bony breast, a sickness that will soon kill her.

At that, Cel opened her eyes.

"Aha! So now I have your attention. Well, there's more. It's a pity Gris isn't long for this world, because your pretty child Reawen is with child herself. She'll soon need a babyminder." Thropos leered. "Yes, my pet, she's pregnant."

How do you know this? Cel interrupted.

"Ah, you'd be surprised what I know. If you're not already aware of it, let me inform you of something. When a woman is pregnant, she's vulnerable. A wizard possesses many spells that will affect a living fetus. I could deafen it, make it blind, twist its tiny body. I could do any of those things with ease. And any woman, no matter whether she is a domis or not, can have trouble in childbirth." Thropos rubbed his hands together. "She can even die."

You are a monster, Cel's voice croaked in his head.

"I am a kind monster," Thropos replied with a smirk. "For I've brought you a delicious dinner. If you don't want Reawen or her child hurt, you'd better eat it." With that he pushed the dish back into Cel's cage and watched with satisfaction as she began to peck up a few grains of corn.

Chapter Eleven

"Now we're in for it," Albin told Grassears. Ahead of them loomed the ragged crags of Dragon's Beak.

It had been two days since Albin's meeting with Reawen. All that time he and his pony had enjoyed fine weather. The sky was a bowl of perfect cloudless blue, and below it the mountainsides blazed with autumn color. Luckily, Albin had seen no wolves. Only the birds and an occasional shy deer or surefooted goat interrupted the solitude of his journey.

Still, he knew such luck couldn't hold. Indeed, as he started up the final ascent toward Dragon's Beak, an eerie hush fell over the rugged landscape, almost as if something was waiting for him—and gloating.

Eol's up there somewhere, Albin thought. I can feel his cold eyes on me. Albin reached into his pocket and touched the dice Reawen had given him for luck. They were probably worthless, but knowing they had come with her good wishes brought him comfort.

All the rest of that day, he and his stout pony climbed the rocky trail that led through Dragon's Beak's narrow passes. Much to Albin's relief, the weather held, with no cloud in the sky—not even a wind that could be called more than a breeze.

So it shocked Albin down to the soles of his feet when he rounded a bend and found Eol. He was perched on a rock, waiting with an air of patient amusement. At his right hand sat a huge white wolf with ice-blue eyes.

"Greetings, messenger. So we meet again." The tall, impossibly slender domis of wind was clad in a tight-fitting garment of gray. Albin noticed that it was cunningly woven to be streaked like wind on water under an overcast sky. A thick, dark cloak swirled around his shoulders, and his feet were shod in soft leather boots. A silver belt set with gems hung low on his narrow hips. The scabbard dangling from it held a short silver sword. As before, his white hair rayed out around his head in a pale nimbus. His colorless eyes regarded Albin cynically.

The boy stood frozen in the middle of the track. For long seconds his heart seemed to stop beating altogether. Then it started up, thumping against his rib cage so wildly that he was sure the wind domis must be able to hear it. "I'm on a peaceful mission for the king," he said. "Will you let me pass?"

"Now, that all depends," Eol drawled. He reached down to stroke his wolf's head. The animal never moved so much as a muscle, but Albin felt the bunched ferocity behind its stillness. "I must say I don't consider visiting Peneto a peaceful act. Stirring up that hornet's nest of busybody wizards invariably brings trouble. But let's allow that to drop for the moment."

He stood, dusted himself off, then approached Albin leisurely. "Perhaps I'll let you pass, but only if you pay my price."

"What price?" Albin felt the stone he carried in his pouch grow heavy and hot. For a moment he feared it might burn right through his leather pouch and drop out on the ground at Eol's feet.

Eol smiled thinly. "You're carrying something that belongs to me. I want it, boy. You'll not get by me or Lii here until I have it. Now, hand over my stone."

Albin shook his head. "I cannot."

Eol's eyes slitted so that his white lashes all but met. The wolf named Lii got up off his haunches and began to circle Albin in the same way a hungry tiger might a tethered goat.

"Don't refuse me, my fine little messenger," Eol snarled. "If you do, you'll never leave the spot you occupy now. Lii will tear out your throat."

"He can't as long as I carry the stone." Albin tried to sound brave though he was shaking, and his knees felt like a poorly thickened jelly.

"Do you dare to tell me what can or can't be done?" Eol snapped his fingers, and the wolf growled and leaped. Albin could see its long yellow fangs, feel the heat of its breath. Waiting for a violent, bloody death, he closed his eyes. But it was as if the wolf had jumped at an invisible shield. It yelped and fell back, confused.

Eol screamed with rage. "I'll freeze you and your horse in place, and you'll stand there until you're both no more than bones!"

Albin slipped his hand into his pouch and wrapped his fingers around the white stone. It burned and throbbed. Doubtless, it was eager to return to its true master. But as long as I hold it, Albin told himself, it must protect me.

"I'm sorry, but I cannot give you your stone. Now, please let me go my way in peace," he said respectfully.

In answer, Eol made a pass with his pale hand, and a frigid wind shredded the sunny afternoon. It whirled around Albin but never touched him. A thin envelope of warm air shielded him from its icy fury. The stone, he thought. It *is* protecting me.

When Eol realized what was happening, his white face flushed with rage. "Maybe Lii can't tear you to pieces, and I can't freeze you, but I can certainly keep you standing there until you go mad from the sound of this!" he cried. Raising his hand, he lifted the wind to a screaming pitch. It howled and wailed like a thousand crazed demons.

Holding tight to the stone, Albin stood trapped inside its whirling fury. He was unable to move and hardly able to think. Eol's right, he admitted to himself. If I have to stay here listening to this hideous howling, I'll lose my wits. I'll eventually starve. Still, he held fast and gritted his teeth, enduring the torture.

It went on all the rest of that afternoon. Knowing it had to be almost as terrible a torment for the wind domis as for him was Albin's only consolation. It soon became obvious that Eol couldn't just go away and leave the winds to do their work. Without his stone, he couldn't control the whirling wind unless he stayed close to it.

As dusk began to fall, the twisting storm dropped to nothing, and Albin found himself staring into Eol's angry and impatient face.

"I grow bored, messenger."

"That's no . . . nothing to what I feel," Albin stammered. He felt dizzy and sick. Stiffly, he flexed his numbed fingers and knees, rubbed his buzzing ears, then glanced over his shoulder. Grassears had moved off and was cropping grass. He appeared unharmed.

"You're stubborn," Eol spat. "But so am I, and I can outlast you. I assure you, there's no way you'll get by me until you give me back what's rightfully mine."

"The stone isn't rightfully yours," Albin protested. "You gambled it away. Brone cast the dice with you for it, isn't that right? And he won."

Again, Eol narrowed his pale eyes. "Are you a gamester yourself, boy?"

"I roll dice with the stablehands on occasion," Albin conceded warily.

"Ah, then we have something in common, for I like to test my luck on occasion as well."

Albin said nothing. Reawen hadn't been the first to talk about the fondness the domis of wind had for gambling. Albin had heard many stories. If a fraction of the tales were true, gambling was Eol's greatest weakness.

Eol shot the boy a cunning smile. "Since we seem to have reached an impasse here, what say you that we cut through all this nonsense with a wager?"

"On what?"

"On my stone, of course."

Albin shook his head. The king had trusted him. He couldn't

betray that trust.

"Ah, here's where it will pay to consider your options. For you haven't any, really. If you refuse to yield to me, I'll use my power to make you stay here until your flesh drops from your bones. I'll have the stone when it rolls to the ground from your lifeless hand. Try your luck, and your chances improve."

"In what way?"

"If I win the stone, you go free with your skin intact."

"And if I win?"

Eol tried to look guileless. "If you win, you go on your way and nothing lost."

"What about when I come back from Peneto? Would I be able to pass safely even then?"

Eol gritted his teeth. "Even then."

"How do I know you'll keep your word?" Albin asked, stalling for time while his thoughts raced.

Eol drew himself up. "I have many faults, but treachery is not among them. If I give you my pledge, you can be sure I'll keep it."

"And do you give me your pledge?"

"You have it, messenger."

Still, Albin hesitated. How could he risk the stone when he had promised Brone never to part with it? Yet, what could he do? If Eol detained him indefinitely he might well go mad and would certainly die of starvation, and then the stone would be lost anyway. At least as long as he kept talking to the white-haired domis, he didn't have the hideous wind howling around him.

"If I risk all on a wager and win, I only get to keep what I already had before I met you."

"That's right," Eol agreed silkily. "Since your life is part of the bargain, isn't that inducement enough?"

"You might make it more appealing. After all, you must want your stone very badly."

Eol gazed at Albin while he considered. "You're right, I do.

There's more to you than first appears, isn't there? Come with me, messenger, and we'll see what we can find to tempt you."

Eol strode away with Lii at his heels. Albin hesitated, but when the huge wolf turned and looked at him with its unblinking eyes, he quickly went to retrieve Grassears and followed.

After many twistings and turnings, the wind domis led him to the mouth of a cave that lay hidden behind a stand of stunted pine.

"I would never have guessed this was here," Albin commented.

Eol looked at him coldly. "You weren't meant to. And when you leave here, you won't be able to find it again."

"Why not?"

"You won't because I won't wish it."

Inside, the cave was blacker than the night rapidly gathering its forces outside. Eol lit a pair of torches fixed to the walls, and, for a long minute, Albin stood blinking.

When his eyes finally adjusted, he gazed around in amazement. Eol's cave was as luxurious as a Chee trader's city palace. Bright-patterned rugs covered the stone floors. Painted murals representing scenes from the distant past streaked the walls with color. Chairs and cushions had been arranged to invite comfort. However, most striking of all was the treasure that lay heaped in every corner.

Albin walked over to a chest. Half open, it was spilling over with gold and jewels. From the cave's stone floor, he plucked up a ring set with a huge emerald. "Where did you get this?"

Eol, who'd been watching closely, shrugged. "Who can say? My ancestors accumulated the baubles you see here. I really have no idea where most of them came from."

"Many generations of wind domi have lived in this cave?"

"Many, messenger. I come from a long line. We go back to the time of the earthtenders, when life was a very different matter from the paltry thing it is now."

Though Eol had made his remark with a sneer, he'd piqued

Albin's curiosity. He'd heard tales of the time when earthtenders had ruled. The domi were one of the few remaining remnants of that mystery-shrouded period. But this treasure—what tales it could tell if it could only speak!

Frowning, Albin asked, "It's said that when Nioma lost her stone, she lost her youth as well. She died almost immediately of old age. That hasn't happened to you."

"No, nor to Taunis or Driona. Fortunately for us, we were all relatively young when we were deprived of our birthrights. So we're all still alive." Eol chuckled at a private joke. "I'm very much alive." He went to Albin's side. "Now, what do you see that takes your eye? What do you see that will make our gamble seem worthwhile to you?"

Albin's eyes widened. "Do you mean I can choose something here?"

"That's exactly what I mean. There's nothing in this cave that I value so much that I couldn't part with it for the sake of my stone. Take your pick."

Nervously, Albin looked around. He saw objects of incredible richness and beauty. There were musical instruments made of fine inlaid wood, dishes and goblets fashioned from silver or gold and set with gems, strings of pearls, rubies, sapphires, and diamonds, armor the like of which even Brone did not possess. Yet none of it tempted him. All he really cared about was keeping his skin and the king's stone.

When he said as much to Eol, the wind domis stared at him curiously. "Are you so loyal to your king that you want nothing at all for yourself?"

"You make me sound like a saint or a fool. I'm neither. Of course I want things for myself."

"What?" Eol challenged.

Albin opened his mouth, but nothing came out. He thought of his boyhood dreams of riding champion horses. Those fancies seemed ridiculous to him now. *What I really want is Reawen,* Albin thought, *and now I'll never have her.* Still, that didn't mean his life was over—at least, he hoped it wasn't.

"Well," Eol prompted, "choose something."

Albin focused his attention on the treasure pile. "There's so much, and it's all in such a jumble. It's confusing."

With an impatient snort, Eol walked past Albin and kicked at a mound of precious objects, scattering them. "Any one of these things," he said, holding up a solid gold ewer, "would make your fortune. If you were to take this back to Jedestrom, you could live in ease for the rest of your life."

"A life of indolence is not what I seek."

Eol studied him. "Then what do you seek, messenger? What is your heart's desire?"

Albin blinked. If Reawen could never again be his heart's desire, than what should take her place? He'd never really asked himself that. Yet, now that Eol had put the question so baldly, he realized he knew the answer. His response, as well as his future, lay in service to his king. "I want honor, adventure, high purpose, the thrill of a great victory for King Brone."

It was an answer that obviously surprised the wind domis. Eol laughed so loud that the cave rang. "Honor, adventure, high purpose! If only your king could hear you now. You want to be a hero. You want to be like him, only greater."

Albin knew how absurd he must appear. "I admire Brone more than anyone," he defended. "Why shouldn't I want to emulate him?"

"No reason at all. Doubtless, it's a great compliment to him," Eol conceded between chuckles. "It's just that coming from a sprig of a boykin like you it's—"

"Ridiculous?" Albin hung his head. How foolish he must look and sound, dreaming of becoming a hero.

For the first time since they had met each other, Eol looked at him almost sympathetically. "Well then, if victory and high purpose are really your heart's desires, I have just the thing for you. Its name is Victory."

He went to a stone ledge and took down a worked leather

scabbard. Inside was a short sword with a dull metal hilt. Compared to the other bright objects littering Eol's cave, it was unprepossessing.

Eol handed Albin the sword, and the young man gazed down at it suspiciously. "Why do you give me this?"

Eol grinned, showing teeth that were sharp and white. "Why do you ask so many questions? Unless I'm mistaken, you are just the sort of hopeful embryo warrior for which Victory was forged. I can't remember when it hasn't been gathering dust in that corner. And I'll grant it has lost some of its looks in the process. But if the legends I heard at my mother's knee are correct, it will come to life in the hands of the right man. Are you willing to take a chance that you are he?"

Albin slid the sword from its scabbard and hefted it. Where the leather had shielded the blade, it was mirror-bright and reflected sparks from the firelight of the torches. The weapon's weight and balance felt right—not that he knew very much of such things. Suddenly Albin wanted this sword for his own, wanted it so much that he heard himself say, "Yes, I am."

Again, Eol showed his teeth in a sharp smile. "Then we are ready to wager?"

Albin swallowed. Reluctantly he set down the sword. "What game do you want to play?"

"Oh, nothing complicated," said Eol. "Nothing that requires skill or daring. That wouldn't be fair to you."

Humbly, Albin agreed. He knew that in a fight or a race, he couldn't best the wind domis.

"Let's rely on pure luck."

Again, Albin humbly agreed.

"Very well, what do you suggest—a toss of a coin, the bounce of a ball, the roll of the dice?"

Albin, thinking of the dice in his pocket, was about to answer "dice" when he noticed the expression on Eol's face. The domis was watching him like a cat stalking a baby bird. "The toss of a coin," Albin said, "only it must be a coin of my choosing." He reached into his pocket and withdrew a flat bronze penny.

Eol took it from his hand and sneered. "A two-headed penny. You must think me a fool to fall for a trick so old." He tossed the penny aside. "Now, what about the bounce of a ball? I have a fine one woven of golden threads."

Albin shook his head. "If you can control the wind you can control the way a ball bounces. I don't trust your golden threads."

Again, Eol burst into wild laughter. "What a crafty little messenger you are. Your king would be proud of you. Very well, what's left? Dice, I'm afraid. And since it's unlikely you carry any with you, I'll have to supply them. Now let me see, do I have any?"

While Albin watched suspiciously, Eol tapped his chin in a show of thought. "Why, yes, I do believe I may. It will take me a moment to find them, though. Lii here will keep you company while I look."

Grinning, Eol disappeared into the shadowy depths of his cave. Albin looked over at the wolf. The enormous animal was sitting on its haunches staring at him hungrily out of its strange pale eyes. What was it thinking? Albin wondered. Was it even really a wolf? What if it was some spirit in a wolf's body—a spirit that was even now reading his mind?

Fervently, Albin hoped not. With the wolf eyeing him, he reached into his pocket. As he withdrew the dice and slipped them into the fold of his sleeve, the wolf growled low in its throat. Trembling, Albin waited for it to leap at him. When it didn't, he asked himself what he intended to do. It all depended on Eol's dice.

"Well, here we are," Eol said as he came striding back into the light. "I just happened to have these. What do you say? Do these meet with your approval?" Eol opened his palm and held out dice that looked exactly like the ones Albin had just hidden. It seemed almost too good to be true. Had Reawen known somehow? And what would happen if he managed to substitute his dice for Eol's and win?

Albin looked at the wolf and then nodded warily. "I guess they're all right."

Eagerly, Eol rubbed his hands together. "Very well then. Let's get on with it. I suggest five rolls. Whoever gets the highest score wins. I'll go first."

* * * * *

"A stranger comes!" The lookout posted on Peneto's topmost tower beat a gong, the sound reverberating in the courtyard below.

"Be he friend or foe?" asked the fresh-faced novice on duty below. He and his younger companion had been assigned to the gate only a week earlier and were none too sure of their duties.

"Go find out from Perbledom, you ninny!"

"Oh—oh, yes. I forgot." The smaller of the two boys gathered up the skirts of his black robe and pelted across the cobblestones. After taking the steps of a winding staircase two at a time, he pounded vigorously on a stout oak door.

"Come in, come in, come in!" the elderly wizard on the other side croaked irritably. "Where did you learn your manners? From a blacksmith? I need peace and quiet if I'm to complete this manuscript."

"Begging your pardon, Master," the youngster piped apologetically. He stepped in and paused a second to catch his breath. "There's a stranger at the gate. Should I let him in?"

Looking highly put out by the disturbance to his studies, Perbledom raked a hand through his scraggly beard. A stuffed owl covered with dust peered over his shoulder from a corner of the room, and several dried bats hung from a beam. "Well, of course you must let him in. Egad, boy, we're in a wilderness. What do you propose to do? Leave him outside to be eaten by wolves or driven mad by wild magic?"

Perbledom scratched at his left temple. "Though, I suppose

if he's got this far, he's already survived wolves and magic. He doesn't look mad, does he? We can't have madmen wandering about the corridors. Though, in all truth, the way some of our brothers behave, I suppose a madman would hardly be noticed."

"Begging your pardon, sir, he doesn't look mad. But my instructions were that you're supposed to . . ."

"Yes, yes, yes, of course. I remember now. I'm supposed to look into my glass and check out his credentials." Perbledom pushed up his spectacles, rose, and began shuffling through the crowded and wildly disorganized shelves next to his chamber's one tiny window. "Now, where did I put that dratted thing? Never can find it when I want it, but always stumbling over it when I don't. Ah," he cried, holding aloft a grimy crystal ball. "There it is at last. Now we shall see about this stranger who's come calling."

After trailing a tea-stained sleeve over the top of the ball to dislodge the worst of the dirt, he plunked it down on his table. He pushed his sleeves up to his elbows, cleared his throat, repositioned his glasses yet again, and peered into the ball. Beneath its dusty coat it came to life, glowed, and produced a picture.

"Ah, yes, yes, yes, there he is. Quite a nice-looking young fellow, though a bit peaked. I should say he hasn't had a pleasant trip through the mountains. No, not a bit of it, though how is a body likely to enjoy such a journey, with all the nonsense afoot out there?" He paused. "You know, there's something about him." Perbledom cocked his head. "He's carrying something, something powerful. Can't see where it's inimical to us, however. In fact, I divine that he's here to confer with Faring on a matter of some importance. Yes," he concluded, suddenly recalling the novice awaiting his response. "Let him in, and do it at once, before the wolves eat that wretched little pony of his."

A few minutes later, Albin and Grassears clopped into Peneto's courtyard. "Faring," Albin whispered hoarsely to the wide-eyed lad who'd seized his horse's reins. "I've come all the way from Jedestrom to speak with Faring." And with that, he slumped over the pommel in a dead faint.

When he returned to consciousness, he was lying on a narrow cot in a chill, high-ceilinged stone room. A thin shaft of light from the keystone-shaped window opposite lit the small table next to his bed. On it someone had set a tray containing gruel and tea. Steam still rose from the tea.

The door opened, and a tall thin man with an austere face and penetrating gray eyes entered the room. "Awake, I see. Well, young man, you'd best sit up and get some of what's on that tray into your belly. Then we talk."

Something about this gray-eyed individual brooked no opposition. Besides, Albin felt starved. He pushed himself into a sitting position and lifted the tray onto his lap. Then he dug into the unappetizing but hot and filling gruel as if it were a delicacy. When he'd emptied the bowl and set it aside, he sipped at his tea and gazed with wary expectancy at his silent host. "Sir, you're Faring, aren't you?"

The wizard nodded. "That is my name. And you are Albin, Brone's favorite and most trusted messenger." He observed the boy intently. "Well, tell me your story, Albin, though I think I can guess at most of it. You're on a mission from your king. Tell me how you got past Eol without handing over his stone, for that's what you've managed to do, isn't it?"

Quickly, Albin reached for his pouch. It still hung from the belt at his waist and inside he could feel the solid shape of the white stone. "Yes," he admitted, "I still carry the domi stone my master gave me for protection. I also carry a sword that I won from the wind domis."

While Faring listened closely, Albin told how he'd shaken the dice with Eol. Albin edited the story, not mentioning how he'd switched Eol's dice with Reawen's. It wasn't that Albin didn't trust Faring. How could he not trust his king's mentor? It was just that Albin didn't like Faring. There was something grim and fanatic in his unblinking stare, in the flare of his aquiline nostrils. And for some inexplicable reason, Albin didn't want to mention his meeting with Reawen to the man.

"Each time you shook the dice, they favored you?" Faring queried sharply.

"Yes."

Faring shook his head. "You have a fool's luck. Considering the pledge you gave your master, you took a terrible risk."

Albin nodded soberly. "I know, and now that it's over, I don't know how I could have done such a thing. All I can say is that at the time it seemed I had no choice. It was either that or die of exposure on the mountaintop, for Eol would never have let me pass."

Faring arched a challenging black eyebrow. "Well, you came away with a whole skin and the stone, so I'll not burden you further with my chastisements. Now, deliver me the news you bear. Some darkness has descended over Vaar and clouded her vision. For weeks now, I've heard nothing of doings in the Peninsula. I've grown concerned."

Albin remembered the old saying about a messenger bearing bad news and took a deep breath. Reluctantly, he described the Choosing, Reawen's theft of the stone, and her disappearance. As he spoke, he watched the wizard closely. A strange expression had come into Faring's eyes. His thin nostrils twitched as if he were scenting some evocative, far-off fragrance. As Albin went on to describe the attack of the Sturites, who Brone was even now fending off, the wizard seemed to barely listen.

"Describe this girl to me again."

"Slender, dark hair, gray eyes, very beautiful."

"Beautiful goes without saying, since Brone chose her to be his bride against all logic and reason. How old?"

"Oh, somewhere near my years."

"You can't say precisely?"

"No, not precisely. We never talked about our ages."

"Something in the way you say that leads me to think that you and this Reawen were on close terms."

"It was I who found her and brought her to Jedestrom," Albin admitted.

Faring's stare bored into him. "I agree it's nothing to be proud of, given the events you describe. Tell me how you came to meet her."

Lowering his eyes, Albin described awakening to the enchantment of Reawen's reed.

Faring listened and nodded. "How fortuitous, since you'd been sent to find a reed player for Killip. Why, it's almost as if this Reawen read your mind because she wanted you to inveigle her into the Plat."

Albin shot the wizard a startled look. "She did read my mind."

He seized on that. "How do you know? Is there something you haven't told me about her?"

Albin wavered. He still hadn't mentioned his most recent meeting with Reawen in the mountains. Unfortunately, his hesitation had given his secret away.

"You're holding back, aren't you? I warn you, young man, it's best not to do that with me. What you don't give me willingly, I can take—and not always pleasantly."

For the first time, Albin felt threatened by the force of Faring's personality. Still, he couldn't bring himself to betray Reawen. He felt that their meeting in the foothills had been a private matter between her and him.

Faring gave a thin-lipped grin. "Not talking, eh? Well, we'll see what we can do about that. There are other ways of drawing information from a reluctant witness. For instance—"

Faring went to a cupboard and took out a vial of powder. Glancing from time to time at Albin, he sprinkled the greenish substance over his hands. Returning, he placed a powder-filmed palm over Albin's forehead. When the boy tried to jerk away, Faring wrapped his other hand around the back of Albin's head and held him in a surprisingly powerful grip.

"Be still," he hissed. "Cooperate, and you'll not be harmed."

Albin had little choice. He couldn't get out of Faring's clutches without an open fight. Even then, he knew he'd lose. Despite his cadaverous appearance, the wizard was no weakling.

"Ah," Faring whispered. His mouth lifted in a smile that sent tremors shivering through Albin.

Suddenly, the spot on the floor in front of them began to glow with the same greenish phosphorescence that coated Faring's palms. The greenish glow thickened. Small shapes appeared and solidified. Albin gasped. The shapes were miniature versions of him and Reawen. They were talking to each other, just as they had back at the stream.

"How—" he exclaimed.

"Be quiet," Faring commanded. "I want to hear every word of this conversation."

"But—"

"Quiet, I say!" Faring gave Albin a look, which sealed his lips and congealed his blood. Then he turned his attention to the scene being played out in miniature on the floor. It was exactly as Albin remembered it.

When it was done and the phosphor glow had faded and died, Faring took his hand away from Albin's forehead. "So, she is Nioma's daughter and with child by Brone," Faring muttered explosively. "And all this time, no one even suspected that she existed. Her meddling aunt must have hidden her well."

"She grew up living in a cave," Albin injected. He rubbed his forehead, which ached. He felt as if the inside of his head had been scooped out with a soup spoon.

"An inauspicious beginning," said Faring. "Yet, it does not appear to have hampered her education. She's outwitted the king and everyone who surrounds him." As if brushing away an annoying thought, Faring passed a hand across his own broad forehead. "She does not resemble her mother in looks. Nioma was a golden beauty. Yet this daughter is dark."

"Dark and gray-eyed." Albin stared up into Faring's gray eyes. Suddenly, a strange and terrible idea glided into his mind. No, it couldn't be, he told himself. Surely it was impossible!

Abruptly, the wizard swung around and walked to the window. "You must spend a day resting and refreshing yourself. I will use that time to put my affairs in order. I intend to accompany you back to Jedestrom."

"You do?" Albin stared at Faring's rigid back.

"Yes, boy, I do. Don't sound so stricken. You should be glad to have me for a traveling companion. With me at your side, you won't be eaten by wolves or befuddled by wild magic."

Perhaps not, Albin thought. But with you at my side, I'll still be in constant danger.

* * * * *

Many miles away in Jedestrom, Pib crawled out of a stand of bushes lining the banks of the river Har. Anxiously, he looked from left to right. When he was sure there was no one to see him, he slipped down to the water and pulled a small boat out of the reeds.

For weeks now, the stablekeeper had been planning this escape. Actually, it had come into his mind on the day Albin had left for Peneto. That day Pib had been called in to Brone's office for an interview. The king had asked him questions about his Sturite relatives. Pib had answered as best he could. But he knew that his scanty replies had disappointed the king. When he'd left the Plat, Pib had felt disappointed with himself.

"I am the dullest fellow in the world," he told himself. "Why, here is young Albin, off helping the king and having a real adventure. What am I doing? Spending my days taking care of dumb animals. If I go on this way, I'll be nothing but a dumb animal myself."

That's when he got the idea. Maybe he could do something to help the king. After all, he had red hair and green eyes just like a Sturite, didn't he? Everyone said he was the spitting image of one. And he'd learned a bit of the Sturite lingo from his grandma. Why couldn't he go to their land, pass himself off as one of them, and learn something to help the king? Well, why not? All it would take was a bit of courage. High time he showed the world he had some of that.

The idea had taken hold of him, and he'd begun to make plans. He'd bought this small boat, provisioned it, and hidden it away. And now, the time had come to set his plan into action. "Now or never," he whispered to himself as he pushed the little craft out into deeper water, toward the cargo ship that would carry him to foreign shores. "Now or never." With a last backward glance, Pib scrambled in and began to row.

* * * * *

It was two months since Reawen's encounter with Albin. Gris and Reawen sat before a low fire, which flickered uncertainly in the melted snow.

"Do you begin to understand the stone's powers? Do you sense its possibilities?" Gris asked.

"I think so," Reawen replied a trifle uncertainly. She wasn't wholly confident with the stone yet, and she wasn't quite sure what Gris meant by "possibilities."

"There are many things you can do with the stone when you have absorbed its patterns," Gris continued. "You can send floods. For instance, in spring you will want to flood the plains to renew the soil. They haven't been inundated over a decade, and by now they will need it badly."

"But people have built settlements all up and down the rivers. I know because I had to travel past them. Sometimes at night I even stole food from them. A flood would ruin those villages. A flood would kill their livestock. People might be drowned as well."

Gris shrugged. "Peninsulans will learn all over again not to build so close to the banks. It was never done before Brone took the stone. The last years under him have made them careless."

Reawen scowled, and Gris gave her a sharp look. "You cannot have human concerns and be water domis. The two are not compatible. It is humans who must adjust to the necessities of nature, not the other way around."

Reawen supposed that Gris was right. Still, she didn't like to think of flooding all those hopeful villages.

Once again the older woman broke into Reawen's troubled thoughts. "There are other things you can do with the stone. You have used watercraft to look into the past and the present. The stone will let you look into the future."

Reawen lifted her head. "How?"

"Since I never held the green stone, and Nioma didn't control it as masterfully as our mother before her, I don't know. But I do remember that it's possible. Perhaps it's something you should try to learn. If Nioma had bothered to acquire the skill, she might not have made such a fool of herself."

Reawen smiled sadly at her aunt. "What kind of domis would you have made if the pool had chosen you?"

The muscles in Gris's jaw tightened. "I don't know. Better than your mother, I think." She sighed. "But Grizala did not find favor with the pool."

"Grizala?"

Gris laughed harshly. "It was my name until the pool rejected me. Afterward, I shortened it to Gris."

Reawen's eyes clouded with sympathy. "The pool can choose only one from each generation, and it had already chosen my mother," she said softly. "If I had had a sister, she might have been chosen over me."

"Yes, but because your mother met Brone, you were an only child."

"Tell me of my father, Gris. Why did Nioma send him away?"

"She was fickle."

Reawen looked out beyond the sputtering campfire. "I wonder who he was, and whether I will ever meet him."

"I hope you never do," Gris replied. "I hope that with all my being."

Snow fell daily, clotting the trees and wrapping the air outside the cave in an eerie stillness. The mountains were impassable and the forest almost equally so. Yet Reawen was restless. She pushed her way through the white drifts, sometimes playing her reed and sometimes just gazing blankly at the intricate web the barren branches etched against the winter sky.

At night, strange dreams troubled her, dreams about Brone that were mixed with worried dreams about Gris. For, though Gris wouldn't discuss her health, it was obvious to Reawen that her aunt wasn't well. Often Reawen would awaken with a start and then lie staring up into the cave's darkness as she listened to Gris's snores, interspersed with soft moans of pain. The time she'd gone to her aunt's side to ask what was wrong, Gris had angrily denied her pain. "Stop imagining things and leave me alone so I can get some sleep!" she cried.

Nothing is the same, Reawen thought. Gris is changed and so am I. I'm not the same girl I was before I went to Jedestrom. And then she placed a hand on her belly, where Brone's child was steadily growing. No, I'm not the same at all.

One day, she decided to try challenging the stone's energy to look into the future. It proved to be very difficult. Searching for the future was like trying to find a sliver of wood drifting in a sea obscured by fog, Reawen thought. Sometimes in the grayness she could make out dim outlines. But, when she tried to fix on them, they eluded her. Reawen frowned, discouraged with her struggles. Though she felt the stone's power coursing through her, she was unable to focus it. She shook her head to clear it and bent to gaze into the pool one last time. As she fought her way through the smoky barriers of time, something concrete finally washed into view.

The water darkened and bulged. An image formed. Holding

her breath, Reawen gazed down at it. The picture that came into sharp focus was of a boy, a lad of no more than ten. He was thin and wiry with a mop of thick black hair. He had a face cut on sensitive but firmly modeled lines that seemed familiar.

What struck Reawen most forcefully was the expression of terror and pain in his wide blue eyes. It wrenched her heart, parched her mouth, and knotted her chest. She cried out and reached to the image, but it faded away. It left her kneeling by the water's edge while her breath came in harsh gasps.

What was the boy to her that she should have torn his image from the future and been moved to despair by his expression? With another cry, she covered her face and decided never again to seek her future. She was afraid of what she might find.

Chapter Twelve

An early thaw left patches of rotting snow only in deeply shaded valleys. Along the sunny section of the stream where Gris and Reawen walked, the ground had softened to mud.

"Spring's not far off," Gris announced and gave the younger woman at her side a pointed look. "You've stopped using the stone, haven't you?"

Reawen nodded. "It's drawn back from me."

"The babe throws it off, no doubt." Gris shook her head. "A pity, for that makes you vulnerable just when you may need to be strong."

Instead of responding, Reawen stopped and turned. "Someone's coming."

A twig snapped and branches parted. A short, rounded figure stood framed in shadow.

"Driona!" Gris exclaimed.

"No other."

Reawen stared at the woman who stepped forward. She wore her rich brown hair coiled on either side of her handsome head. Below the creamy rounded column of her throat, her loose brown cloak draped in such a way as to suggest a more than luxurious body lurking beneath its folds. As she regarded Reawen, a slow smile spread across the moist bloom of her full mouth.

"We meet at last," she murmured in a throaty voice. She took another step forward so that she stood fully revealed in the thin, late-winter sunlight. "Doubtless, you're wondering what brings me. It's very simple. I'm here to congratulate you on the recovery of your stone."

The back of Reawen's neck prickled. "How did you know?"

Driona's full red lips curved upward. "Such things cannot be hidden from me, my child. I felt the shift of power in the earth, of course." Her broad, shoeless feet sank lightly into the soft mud. "I rejoice for you and in you. You are clever enough to make a worthy domis. The others agree. We all request a meeting."

"We?"

"Taunis and Eol, the domi of fire and air."

Though Reawen kept her face blank, her mind was leaping. She knew almost nothing of the other domi, and, until her journey to Jedestrom, had given them little thought. On the rare occasions when Gris had spoken of the others, it had been scornfully.

Despite all they had in common, they were traditional antagonists. Though earth was not antithetical to Reawen, fire and water were dangerous to one another and so were earth and air. In the past, they'd held their rare meetings under rigid conditions of truce. It had been at least a century since the last one.

"You and I are not opposed," Driona drawled in her warm, heavy voice, "so I have come to you as an ambassador." She opened the soft palms of her hands in a conciliatory gesture. "I propose we meet on the plateau above the tree line where the four have met in times past and where we can be safe from each other." Her velvety eyes drifted down to Reawen's breast and then to her belly, now rounded with child. "Is Brone still as handsome as he was when he seduced me?" she murmured wryly.

"Reawen, don't go!" Gris interrupted. "You can't trust their tricks. They'll be jealous now because you have more power."

Driona's dark eyes clashed with Gris's. "You are a stupid old woman," the earth domis hissed. "The green stone is only one of four. This child cannot hold it independently. If she had left the four with the usurper, they would have destroyed him, and we would have reclaimed our property. Now she has upset that balance. She has no choice but to negotiate with us." Her eyes, which seemed to have hardened into chunks of coal, swiveled to

Reawen's. "Come in a week's time," she commanded and then
turned on her heel.

Gris spent the rest of that day sputtering over Driona's pre-
sumption. "Don't let her intimidate you into meeting with
them in that unprotected spot. Your powers are at low ebb. You
mustn't put yourself in jeopardy when the child in your belly
makes your stone a stranger to you."

"Oh, Gris, how can I refuse?"

"Nioma never met with them. She would never have anything to do with them."

"Maybe that's one of the reasons why she came to grief,"
Reawen argued. "Driona is no fool. The four stones do create a
balance. They are like the four points of a compass, opposed
and yet connected and necessary to each other. The domi held
them in a balance and so, in his own way, did Brone. Now there
is an imbalance, a discord. I feel it in my bones, and I have been
feeling this uneasiness—this sense of wrongness—all winter."

Gris's eyebrows lowered. "Perhaps what you're feeling is
something much simpler. Perhaps you've been missing your
handsome husband. Perhaps, even now, you're longing for him
and thinking of going back to return the stone."

"No! I will never do that! Even if I wanted to go back, Brone
would probably kill me for what I did to him."

"Not while you carry his child." Gris put a hand to her heart
and labored to steady her breathing. "And perhaps not after it
is born, either."

* * * * *

"If we're not burned to charcoal before the night's out, it'll
be the biggest miracle since this planet was set spinning
between the stars," Phen grumbled. He and Albin perched atop
a cartload of metal canisters. It was after midnight, when none
of the Plat's busybodies was likely to catch them at their secret
task.

Nevertheless, as their powerful team of workhorses labored to drag their heavily laden cart to the moonlit tower at the top of the hill, both kept a wary eye out for spies. Now that Albin knew that Pib had been a spy, he seemed to see traitors behind every corner and bush.

"You can't be certain the stablekeeper was a betrayer," Phen argued.

"Everyone says it. Even the king thinks so. Why else would he have sneaked away like that? And I thought Pib was my friend."

"Lad, don't lose faith in a friend so easily. I've learned things happen for a lot of different reasons. There's no knowing the human heart."

While they mulled that over, they kept an anxious silence. Finally, Albin whispered, "Surely we're far enough from the river."

" 'Tisn't the river that has me worried, lad. Greenfire's sensitive to water of any kind. There's dew in the grass at our feet, sap in the trees. It might start to rain, and they say we're nine-tenths water ourselves."

"There's not a cloud in the sky and hasn't been for a week. It's been dry enough so the dew doesn't amount to much. These canisters are so thick and so well lined, they'll protect the powder. If that isn't enough, Faring's wrapped the bed of our wagon in one of his spells."

"Wizards!" Phen made as if to spit and then thought better of it. "I know you think you did us all a big favor when you brought that stone-faced crow back with you, but I have my doubts. I'd as soon trust the rats that haunt the wharves as put my faith in one of his tribe."

"What have you got against wizards?"

"I've seen enough of them in my travels to know a thing or two about them. They're power mad. Why else would they run around in those black robes and mix up potions from every nasty thing that creeps and crawls?"

"They're scholars, interested in the why and how of things?"

"Hah! They're puppetmasters who enjoy watching the likes of us dance while they twiddle the strings."

Perbledom hadn't been like that, Albin thought. Though Albin hadn't spent much time in Peneto, he'd grown fond of kindly old Perbledom.

"You're prejudiced, Phen. Faring helped the king drive off the Sturites so we'd have the winter to prepare for their next attack. And he's pledged to stay and help until things are back to normal. You'd rather he were on our side than theirs, wouldn't you?"

"Oh, aye, especially when Arant's already got that little weasel, Thropos, backing him. If we're to keep that pack of redheaded devils at bay 'til this business with Brone's witch of a wife is settled, we'll need every advantage we can get." Phen whistled through his teeth. "I only hope the greenfire lives up to my promises."

"Do you have doubts?" Albin asked in surprise.

"I came here on a whim, lad." Phen sighed. "I'll be honest with you. I thought, after all my wandering, I'd like to go back to my homeland and rest my bones. Maybe even find me a wife and a spot to settle down. The greenfire was just an excuse, a ticket into the king's favor. I hoped it would buy me a new life. Truth is, it's never been tried in warfare. How can I be sure it will work the way we all think?"

"It will. It has to." Albin smiled at the adventurer's rough profile. When Phen had decided to stay on and take the post of Brone's military advisor, Albin had been glad. From the beginning, he'd liked and trusted the man. Now that Phen had chosen him to be his helper, a strong friendship had grown up between them. Albin had learned a lot from him. Just hearing Phen talk about the lands he'd visited was an education.

"You and Quista seem to be hitting it off," Albin remarked. "Do you think she's someone you might settle down with?"

Phen shook his head. "Quista's a likely lass and a luscious

morsel between the sheets, but I haven't yet met the woman who'll keep me coming back on a permanent basis. Truth is, I'm beginning to think I never will. Well, here we are. So far, so good," Phen added as the horses drew up to the watchtower. He frowned up at it. "Can't say I agree with the king that this is going to be as good a place to store the powder as the keep was."

"So long as no one guesses it's here, it should be safe enough."

"When it comes to greenfire, I don't like 'should be's' or 'guesses,'" Phen grumbled. He unlocked the heavy door to the tower. After a last look around to make sure they were unobserved, he and Albin began carting the canisters inside the previously deserted building.

"You see," Albin said, "it's dry as dust in here, and those stones have to be at least two feet thick."

Phen's expression didn't lighten. "The keep was still better. For one, this place is outside the city gates and could get cut off."

"Never! Anyhow, greenfire won't be here long. Once the new building is finished, we can move the canisters there. In the meantime, our warning system is foolproof."

Phen groaned. "Nothing is foolproof, lad. You'll learn that when you've been out in the world a bit longer."

"The king has another purpose for the keep."

"Aye, he's fitting it out in hopes of bottling up that pretty little schemer of a bride inside it. Well, more the fool, he! Since she made a ninny of him in his marriage bed, the man's been more ill-tempered than a bear with a rusty nail in his toe. He's better off letting her go, I say."

Albin kept his back to Phen so the older man wouldn't see the wistful expression that he knew had come into his eyes. "Even if Reawen hadn't stolen the stone, forgetting her wouldn't be an easy matter, Phen," he muttered.

* * * * *

Reawen set off for the plateau alone, for Gris had stubbornly refused to keep her company. "What do you want me for?" she'd grumbled. "It's two days' hard climbing, and I'm not up to it."

"It's more than a week's climb to the pool, and you never balked at that."

"That happened a long time ago."

"Less than a year."

Gris eyed Reawen's swelling belly. "A long enough time to make different people out of both of us, girl."

"Oh, Gris, I know you haven't been feeling well all winter. Won't you please tell me how I can help you?" The older woman had only turned away and refused to discuss the matter.

If only I knew what was wrong with her, Reawen fretted as she scaled the almost vertical, rocky trail. *Lately she's so crotchety and ill-tempered, as if something's paining her all the time.* The change in her aunt worried Reawen, but she didn't understand it or know what to do about it. *Maybe it's really me who's changed,* she thought. *Maybe now I see things in Gris that I didn't notice before.*

Reawen skirted a large boulder and then stared up, shading her eyes against the brilliant sun. Winter had definitely worn itself out. Below, the tree line had blurred with new green buds. Even the dried tufts of grass poking through tiny crevices in the rock had a more hopeful look.

Another half hour's hard work brought Reawen to the shadow of the overhang on the lip of the plateau. At one side a narrow path wound up to the back of it. The roundabout passage meant she wouldn't know what waited at the top until it was too late to turn back. Taking a deep breath, Reawen began the steep scramble.

Atop the table of bald rock two figures stood observing her approach. When she hauled herself up onto the meeting place, Driona slid her a smile. "You are prompt. Unfortunately, Eol is not. He was always unpredictable, and since he wagered away his stone he's become even more capricious. To be honest, I'm not sure he'll come at all. Taunis, however, is here."

Reawen studied the red-robed figure hovering at the far edge of the plateau. He had orangy, fox-colored hair and a short, pointed orange beard. His eyebrows swept up at sharp angles. Beneath them, his yellow eyes bit into her. Controlling a shudder, she drew back. Fire was her foe, his powers directly opposed to hers. It was Taunis's gem on Brone's crown that had burned her. The sight of him made the pain of that contact blaze over her afresh. But now, she reminded herself with a certain satisfaction, she held the green stone while his clenched fists were empty.

"You're not as beautiful as your mother," he remarked in a whispery voice that set Reawen's teeth on edge. "Apparently, however, you're much cleverer."

"What do you want of me?" Reawen demanded.

"Our stones."

Driona, whose eyes were black as night in her fleshy face, nodded. "Our stones."

Reawen drew herself up. "Then get them. Alone, I went to Jedestrom and retrieved mine. Why don't you do the same?"

"How, when our faces are known? You were successful only because Brone didn't realize you existed."

Out of the corner of her eye Reawen caught a slight movement. Suddenly another figure stood poised on the plateau's edge, a tall, amazingly slender man with colorless eyes and a cloudy mass of white hair.

"So you've joined us at last," Driona said acidly. "How kind of you."

"Not kind at all, dear lady," he replied suavely. "After all, I, too, have something at stake here."

"One wouldn't know it from your behavior." Driona sniffed. "If you had even so much as the patience of a frightened clodle, you could have taken your stone back from that boy. Instead, you let him walk through our mountains as if they were a well-guarded stretch of the king's highway."

"Ah, but I haven't got the mentality of a clodle. That, thankfully, is what sets me apart from my colleagues."

Reawen watched as the three glared at each other. Taunis seethed openly. Driona's sensual mouth pouted, and Eol looked coldly amused. Reawen began to wish that she'd followed Gris's advice and refused to attend this hateful meeting. She was considering simply turning around and leaving when Taunis appeared to read her mind.

"It was selfish and shortsighted of you to take only your own stone. You should have brought back all," he accused.

"I couldn't. Brone's crown had a binding. It burned my hand. Besides, it's too late for that. I can never return to Jedestrom."

"You can do your duty by us without going back," Taunis purred. "Now that your power is restored, use it."

Reawen's hands clenched. "How?"

"Drown Jedestrom. Destroy Brone's palace and his people. When the spring rains come, use your might to swell the tributaries and wash the Peninsula clean. After that it will be easy enough to take back what is rightfully ours."

Reawen saw desire for vengeance leap in Taunis's yellow eyes like a hot storm. He cared for nothing and no one but himself. The other two domi were much the same, she thought as she looked at each with a deep sense of shock. All were thoughtless and vengeful. Perhaps what Albin had said about the cruel reign of the domi was true, after all.

What about me? Reawen asked herself. How do I fit into this unpleasant quartet? "Why should I do what you ask?" she demanded.

"Tell her," Taunis snapped at Driona.

The earth domis stepped forward. "You imagine yourself safe. But so long as Brone commands the other three stones, you will never be safe. You, and yours," she gazed pointedly at Reawen's swelling belly, "will always be at risk. If you don't destroy Brone and restore the balance of power among the four of us, he will surely destroy you. You shake your head, but only because you are young and naive. When you seek to bring spring floods to nourish the earth, his engineers will build dams to control you. They will move in on your forest and cut it down. It would be madness to let his strength grow while you still have the chance to stop him."

A cold wind bit into Reawen's cheek, and her eye sought the spot where Eol had stood. The rock was bare, for the wind domis had left as silently and scornfully as he had come. The others stood their ground and watched her like birds of prey.

In her heart, Reawen knew that what Driona said was true. Now that Brone knew what she was, he could not ignore her existence. At this very moment he might be laying plans to harass her. She had been stupid to imagine that taking the green stone would end her difficulties. Now was the time to ensure her own safety and that of her child. Yet, even if she had wanted to agree to Taunis and Driona's demands, she couldn't. With the baby inside her grown so large, the stone had become uncooperative. Somehow she had to lie low and protect herself until her child was born.

"I must think on it," she muttered as she turned on her heel. "In two week's time, I will give you my decision." The water domis departed down the slope.

In silence, Taunis and Driona watched. "Well," Driona said when the black-haired girl was out of sight and out of hearing. "What do you think?"

"What should I think?" Taunis snapped. "She's no more cooperative than her slut of a mother."

"Ah, but she's intelligent," Driona countered. "Reason is on our side, or we can make it seem so."

Taunis shot the earth domis a curious look. "What will you do when you have your stone?"

Driona smiled slyly. "First tell me what you will do with yours."

"That's easy." Taunis's crimson robes turned a brighter red. He pointed a finger at a stunted bush that had managed to grow out of a crevice in the rock and watched in satisfaction as it burst into flame. "I will scorch Jedestrom to the ground," he rasped. "When I'm finished, it and its king will be nothing but ashes. I will sear this upstart Brone like meat on a spit and watch his handsome face shrivel and blacken."

Driona tsk-tsked. "Such a violent nature you have, Taunis. There is no subtlety in it."

The fire domis glared at his companion. "Why? What do you have in store for our fine blond king and his ungrateful, renegade people?"

"Something far more interesting and longer-lasting than what you propose. Would you like to see?"

Taunis eyed Driona warily. "What is it?"

"Come with me and I'll show you."

She led him off the plateau and down into a richly wooded valley below. The trees smelled ripe with rising sap and new green. The earth beneath their feet was soft and rich. As Driona passed by, its loamy fragrance intensified, hanging in the air so thickly that it dizzied even Taunis. Driona paused in a clearing. She pressed a toe into the ground and whispered a barely audible word. Obediently, the earth began to part. The opening widened until it became a passage.

Driona looked over at Taunis. "Come with me."

"Into the ground?" He shook his head. "Do you think I'm a fool? Fire can be smothered by dirt."

"Taunis, my dear cousin, I realize you are claustrophobic, but find your courage. I have no wish to harm you. Indeed, I would be a fool to harm my ally. We are stronger together than apart. I merely want to show you what I've been doing with my time all these years since I lost my stone."

Taunis continued to eye his cohort suspiciously. Then he shrugged. "Very well then, I'll risk it. Show me."

She led him down the passage, through slick walls of earth

and rock. Down and down they went until the air seemed heavy and stale in their lungs.

"How do you stand this infernal darkness?" Taunis snapped his fingers, and a flame glowed at the ends of them. He swung his hands, lighting their passage. "There are veins of gold and silver in your walls," he commented as he followed reluctantly after Driona.

His normally ruddy complexion had gone waxy. Driona, on the other hand, seemed to revel in their close quarters and the pressure of earth and rock over their heads. If anything, her curves grew more lush. Her cheeks bloomed.

"There is every kind of treasure in my walls," she agreed. "Those of you who live only on the surface have no idea what riches I possess. The earth hides her greatest glories from prying eyes."

"Yet you lost the prize you cherished most to a pretty stripling," Taunis pointed out petulantly. "Did Brone coax it out of you in the same way he coaxed it from that slut, Nioma?"

Driona turned a cold eye on her cohort. "I'll tell you my story if you'll tell me yours, Taunis. How did he get your stone from you? By outwitting you?" At Taunis's angry expression, she smiled. "Ah, I see that's the case. But why do we tease each other with what's past? It's the future we must look to."

She turned down a passage, then into a chamber that stretched so far Taunis couldn't see the end of it. Torches flickered above the doorway. By the dim light, he stared at the wall opposite. "By the seven hells! What are they?" he exclaimed.

Tiers of narrow shelves lined the wall. Large, closely packed, whitish objects filled them. Some were egg-shaped. Others were woven of some thready substance.

Driona walked over and touched one of the monstrous, glistening cocoons. "These are my larval ant warriors."

"Ants? But they're easily the size of a man."

Driona nodded. "I've been breeding them. Those," she said, pointing at an egg, "are not yet developed. These, on the other hand, are nymphs close to hatching."

Just as she finished speaking, an ant with a body easily longer than Taunis's came hurrying in. Ignoring Taunis and Driona as if they weren't there, he tended the eggs. As his feelers wiggled, testing the air, he moistened and cleaned the white ovoids.

While he did his work, the fire domis stared open-mouthed. When the giant ant finally left, Taunis turned to Driona. "Woman, do you realize how dangerous those things could be if they hatched all at once?"

"Oh, I realize." She stroked one of the wormlike cocoons. "Did you notice the mandible on that worker? Imagine it slicing at you. Imagine a thousand of them swarming, wiggling their antennae and clicking their jaws. It would be like a nightmare come to life." She chuckled in rich amusement.

Taunis stared at the ranks of huge cocoons.

"Now, they're merely sleeping." Driona murmured. "But I have the power to wake them up."

"When?"

She shot Taunis a meaningful look. "When you and your Sturite allies march on Jedestrom. Then, an army from the underworld will erupt from the earth and attack alongside you."

* * * * *

That night Reawen was far too restless to sleep. She sat in the mouth of the cave where she'd made camp and stared out into the darkness. Nearby, she heard the gurgle of water over a rock. Normally the familiar sound would have soothed her. Now nothing could quiet the turmoil of her thoughts. Not even in her worst days in the Zeleta had she felt so much like a cornered creature. Once her child was born, it was only logical to do as the other domi asked, she acknowledged. Yet how could she wilfully destroy Jedestrom when there were so many things and people in it that she admired and even loved?

She thought of Quista, of the rose garden heady with summer perfume, of the queen mother's kindness, of Albin and Grassears. How could she bring a flood to them and then allow Taunis to sweep them with fire afterward?

Something stirred inside the cave. It was only a bat, but the whoosh of its wings made Reawen think of Cel.

"Oh, Cel," she murmured, "Where are you? So many times I've tried to find you in the water images, but they show me nothing. How I miss you, and how I wish you were here to counsel me!"

Late that night, a dream came to Reawen. She saw herself bending over the pool, passing her hand back and forth over smooth water in search of an image. With a deep sense of foreboding, she watched a picture form. Long before it solidified, Reawen knew what it would be. She saw Brone's warrior features in profile. Slowly, he turned his head and stared at her with icy, implacable blue eyes.

The next afternoon, on the way home, Reawen trudged past a familiar birch grove. She quickened her pace and then, despite her tired muscles, broke into a trot. It will be good to talk all of this over with Gris, she thought. She'll have something sensible to say, something that will help me see my way clearly.

"Gris!" Reawen called as she hurried through the aspens. "I'm back, and I have a lot to tell you!"

"I will be more than glad to listen to anything you have to say, wife!" a deep voice rang out harshly.

Reawen froze in horror. "Brone!"

Attended by a half dozen armored soldiers, the king came out from the shadows where he'd been waiting. He wore leather armor, and the gilded helm that covered his head hid much of his face as well. All Reawen really saw were his eyes, and they were as angry and implacable as the caustic blue eyes that had accused her in last night's dream.

"So, what Albin told me is true. You really are with child."

Protectively, Reawen crossed her arms over her belly. "Where's my aunt? What have you done with her?"

"The hag who occupied this cave is safe enough. She's in the custody of my soldiers."

"Your soldiers!" Reawen's fists clenched, and she controlled her trembling with an effort. "You must make them release her at once. She's sick!"

"She's a conspirator," Brone countered in the grating tone he'd taken from the first. "She conspired with you to rob me. I should throw her into a dungeon along with you, her well-schooled deceiver."

"Are you so bitter that you would take out your anger with me on a sick and helpless old woman?" Reawen asked with scorn.

Brone took a menacing step forward, and for the first time Reawen saw the stones in his crown begin to glow, fueled by the heat of his emotions. So he *was* capable of activating them. She hadn't been sure of that before.

Her husband's nearness affected her powerfully. She thought of the anger and fear he had stirred in her from the first. But she also remembered the sweetness of his lovemaking on their wedding night. She had dreaded a meeting such as this, not alone because of his hatred, but because of her own guilty and confused emotions as well.

"I am more than bitter, my sweet bride. Your treachery has eaten away all the love I had for you. Don't imagine that I have come all this way out of longing for the sight of your face or the joy of your company. All I feel for you now is hatred and distrust. But, so long as you have the green stone, you pose a threat to the Peninsula. What's more, you carry my child." Once again, his gaze swept over her burgeoning belly. "I have no choice but to take you back to Jedestrom, where you can be watched so you will do no further harm."

Reawen marshaled her strength. "You forget that I'm no

longer a helpless servant in your mother's household. You cannot give me orders."

At that moment Reawen felt the stone's faint call and knew
that she could use it to protect herself against Brone. But at
what cost to her child? And what would happen if she did use
it? She remembered only too well the fate of the vagrant who'd
attacked her in the woods. She had no wish to see Brone melt
into a puddle of water at her feet. Nor was she sure that her
stone would be effective against the three he carried. Surely
they would protect him.

Clearly, Brone thought so, too. He reached forward and
caught her wrist. "No, you are no servant. You are my wife, and
I mean to take you with me, wife."

As Reawen struggled against him, she considered her
options. If she joined with the other domi, she could wreak
havoc on all Brone's works. But she distrusted Driona, Taunis,
and Eol. She had no desire to ally herself with them and did not
wish to destroy Jedestrom and all the things and people she
had come to admire.

She could do battle with Brone here and now, pitting her
stone's strength against his. Perhaps, despite her pregnancy, she
would win. Perhaps she would kill him as she had the vagrant.
But this was the father of her child, a man to whom she was
still drawn, despite the insurmountable barriers between them.
And what if their struggle harmed the child? Always, her mind
came back to that.

Reawen lowered her eyes. "What are your plans for my
aunt?"

"She will accompany you to Jedestrom."

Reawen gave a little cry. "You can't drag Gris to your city.
She's lived here all her life. Away from these woods and this
cave she would surely die."

Almost imperceptibly, Brone's steely grip on Reawen's wrist
lessened. "I did not come here to harm your aunt. If you will do
as I ask and make no trouble, I will release her."

Reawen gazed down at her feet. Again, she studied her alternatives. Inside her belly, her child stirred. Soon the time would come for it to be born. The thought frightened her as nothing else did. At least if it were born in Jedestrom it would be safe for a time, safe from Brone's wrath and the machinations of the other domi. Then, when she had regained her strength, she would be able to decide what to do.

"All right," she said. "Free Gris, and I will go with you."

Chapter Thirteen

Arant prowled alongside the piles of armaments stacked on the practice field. Shields, swords, bows and arrows, maces and every manner of cruel device designed to maim or—preferably—kill lay ready for distribution to the recruits he'd been training.

Periodically, Arant stopped to push his thumb against the wistite tip of a lance or to test the spring on a crossbow. When he finally came to the end of the formidable collection, he turned and eyed Thropos, who had silently accompanied him on his review.

"Very impressive," the wizard allowed. "Considering the disarray in which your forces scuttled back from their last attack on the Peninsula, your armament makers have wrought miracles. You must have driven them hard."

"I promised to have their legs torn out by the roots if they didn't produce to my specifications," the young Sturite king snapped. "As for the disarray of my troops, they were unprepared for Brone's cowardly tactics."

You mean their commander was unaccustomed to employing his brains instead of his hot temper, Thropos thought sourly. But he had learned to curb his tongue with Arant. Honesty simply wasn't worth the price.

"Now that spring's upon us, we will serve up some surprises to the Peninsula. Brone hasn't bested us yet. Isn't that right, my pretty?" Thropos added, looking fondly down at the cage he carried in his left hand.

"Lately, you tote that ridiculous bird around with you everywhere you go. You talk to it as if it were your leman," Arant observed scornfully.

"Cel is my sweeting," Thropos agreed almost humorously. He returned his gaze to the pillawn, who shot him a tired look with one purple eye. "She's the prettiest female Thropos has ever had under his thumb."

Arant snickered. "No, I don't imagine many women fancy you. You're not the handsomest of men."

"Nor ever was," Thropos retorted with a sharp edge to his voice, "though, before Faring twisted my back, I was passable enough."

"No need to let your looks hold you back. If you want a woman, you have my leave to take one. All told, there's more pleasure in rape than in making eyes and trading lies."

Arant should know, Thropos thought. He never bothered with courtship. When he wanted a woman in his bed, he grabbed the nearest wench, whether she be serving maid or highborn lady, and dragged her off.

"Wizards were meant for a solitary life," Thropos said aloud. "I accepted that long ago. Yet it doesn't mean I'm incapable of appreciating beauty where I see it. Cel here is one of this earth's true beauties."

Thropos set the pillawn's cage on a stump and stood back to regard its shivering inmate with the air of a connoisseur. "Just look at those eyes, the color and clarity of amethysts. And her feathers, as pure a white as the most unsullied snow. It pleasures my eye to gaze upon her."

Arant listened to this panegyric contemptuously. "I hear you even talk to her."

"Some of my more intelligent conversations are ones I've held with Cel," Thropos agreed. "She's a wise philosopher, a seasoned traveler, a female of wide experience."

"I thought you intended sacrificing the bird for one of your spells."

"Oh, I do—a very special spell. You shall see when the time comes."

"Take care you don't get so softhearted over her beauty and

philosophy you can't slit her throat," Arant mocked.

"Never fear, my hasty young king, Thropos's heart will never again be so soft as that," the wizard retorted, taking hold of Cel's cage once more. "Now, where is this spy you've caught?"

"Come right this way."

Arant led Thropos past the practice field to a rocky stretch of coastline on the north side of the castle. There, a half dozen soldiers stood guarding something.

Thropos squinted. "What have you done with him?"

"Staked him out on the shale, the better to tickle the truth out of him." Arant laughed nastily.

Thropos lifted an eyebrow. He knew what Arant meant by "tickling."

"Who is this unfortunate creature?" Thropos inquired.

"A Peninsulan bumpkin named Pib, with more gut than wit. From what we can learn, he imagined that the red hair and green eyes he got from a Sturite grandmother would allow him to pass among us and spy. Of course his accent gave him away within hours." Arant rolled his eyes. "He had some crackbrained notion of gathering information for Brone."

"Did Brone send him?"

Arant guffawed. "That's the most amusing thing of all. Apparently this fool decided to play the spy on his own. I daresay by now he regrets the notion."

As they stopped at the foot of Pib's mangled body, the truth of that seemed obvious. Blood caked his once shining strawberry-blond hair and streaked what was left of his face. His eyes had been gouged out. His hands and feet had been cut off.

"This lad will tell you nothing more," Thropos observed dryly.

"No," Arant agreed. "Shall I draw out his torment or end it?"

For the first time, Cel spoke to the men from her cage. *End it, wizard,* she cried. *For sky's sake, end it!*

"If I were you, and that were my bird, I would do the opposite of what she says," Arant sneered.

"Ah, but you are not me," Thropos replied. "As a matter of fact, I think she's right. End his misery now by cutting off his head. Not for reasons of mercy, you understand, but because I wish to take it with me on my journey."

"For what purpose?" Arant queried.

Thropos smiled. "I think it might be a nice touch to leave it for one of our Peninsulan friends."

Arant laughed at that. Grinning, he gave the order to one of his men. The Sturite soldier lifted his axe, and, seconds later, Pib's headless body lay jerking on the stones.

Turning away, Thropos said, "And now, my lord, it is time for my departure."

"You intend taking the bird with you?"

"Indeed I do."

"No supplies? No food, no weapons, no water?"

"I'll have need of none of those."

Arant looked puzzled, but he put forth no further protests. "You know your business, I suppose."

"You must trust that I do, for all our enterprise depends upon it."

The two walked beyond the field to a beach, where soldiers were in the process of dragging a small boat with a triangular sail up onto the sand. "Do you know anything about handling a sail?" Arant inquired.

"All I need to know."

The Sturite king shrugged his thick shoulders. "Very well, then, wizard, climb in and I'll shove you off."

Without another word, Thropos stepped into the small craft. He settled himself and the pillawn's cage and waited expectantly.

"In two weeks' time, we'll meet on the shores of the Peninsula."

"In two weeks' time," Thropos agreed.

Arant gave another careless shrug and put his shoulder to the bow of the boat. Smoothly, it slid over the hard-packed sand and slipped with a light splash into the water. As of its own volition, it righted itself, turned and headed toward the mouth of the harbor. Halfway there its sail ran up its rough mast and caught the wind. Through all this, the wizard never moved a finger.

You expect to sail to the Peninsula with no food or water and no compass? Cel questioned.

"At last. I wondered when you would deign to speak again."

That cruel redheaded oaf makes my tongue stick like pine sap, Cel said bleakly.

Thropos gave his thin smile. "Arant is an oaf, you're quite correct."

And a murderer and patricide into the bargain. The two of you make such an evil pair it takes my breath away.

Thropos shrugged. "Nobody's perfect. You should be grateful to me. Just now I did your bidding and saved that Peninsulan idiot further pain."

You didn't do it to please me. You have some foul plan for his poor head. Cel had been avoiding looking at Pib's bloody head, which sat dripping on the transom seat. Now she glanced at it and looked quickly away. Horror filled her purple eyes.

"Whatever my plans," Thropos commented, "I had nothing to do with that silly boy's death. It wasn't I who persuaded him to play the spy."

No, but it was you who tempted Arant to poison his own father.

"One man's temptation is another man's unthinkable deed. Arant found his own level. I only supplied the means."

Cel squawked. *What monstrous depravity do you have up your sleeve? The Peninsula is at least a two-day sail from Sturite shores, and in this little boat it will take far longer.*

"You are mistaken, my beauteous pet. It will take no time at all to reach the Peninsula. Just watch." As he spoke, Thropos lifted his hands. The weather had been clear, the sky an unsullied blue. Suddenly, a dozen clouds appeared and scudded toward the small craft. An instant later they had enveloped it in a thick fog.

Ignoring Cel's cry of alarm, Thropos stood. His face darkened with the weather, and his eyes seemed to look at something deep inside the clouds, something the bird could not see. In a guttural chant, he began muttering. With every unintelligible word, the fog that curtained his craft from the world coagulated and roiled.

Flickers of lightning flashed inside it, growing louder and brighter. Then, with one ear-splitting clap, the cloud dispersed and the boat sailed into clear weather once again. However, it no longer headed into open sea. Instead, it sped smoothly and purposefully into a tiny cove sheltered on three sides by tall headlands of rock. On one of those rocky promontories, Taunis and Driona stood waiting.

*   *   *   *   *

"Do you realize how dangerous she can be to you here?" Faring sat very still, his critical gray eyes never leaving Brone.

Tangled in his own thoughts, the king paced back and forth. "Of course, I know she's dangerous. That's one of the reasons why I brought her back."

"One of the reasons, perhaps, but not the only reason."

Brone reacted like a stung bear. "I don't deny that I chose Reawen for my wife because I wanted her. I'm not like you, Faring. You taught me how to be a king, but you never succeeded in teaching me how not to be a man, how not to be human."

Faring's smile was self-mocking. "You won't be the first to have made a fool of himself over a beautiful woman. Don't go on being a fool. I repeat, Reawen is dangerous to you."

"I have her under guard in the keep. Its stones are two feet thick."

"I know a thing or two about her kind. Doubtless, she's staying put because she wants to, not because of your precautions. When she decides to leave, she will, and your guards won't be able to do a thing about it."

Brone pressed his fists to his head as if it were paining him. "What would you have me do? She carries my child!"

"Is that so important?"

"Yes!" It was a cry from the soul. Before Faring could find a reply to it, Brone strode from the room. Rapidly, he walked down the corridor that led from the Plat to the gardens. Face set, he waved away the courtiers who made to follow him, and quickened his pace. He strode past the stables to the empty field where the old keep sat far removed from the other royal buildings.

The guards jerked to attention when he tramped past them. Ignoring the officious steward who followed at his heels like a yapping lapdog, Brone climbed several flights of stairs. On the top landing he pointed at the sturdy metal door behind which he'd sequestered Reawen. "Unlock that."

A moment later he strode into his wife's apartments and slammed the door behind him. He stopped short when he saw her. She sat embroidering beside one of the slits that served as windows.

"Greetings, Wife."

"Greetings, Husband."

"What do you make?"

"A gown for my child," she replied peacefully.

She was beautiful, he thought. Sitting there with the sunlight playing over her busy hands, she looked anything but threatening. Her pregnancy had imbued her ivory beauty with softness. Her hair had grown past her shoulders and fell in smooth waves. She now wore her stone in a silver band on her forehead. It seemed to wink at him tauntingly.

"Reawen, I must talk with you."

"Yes?" She looked up expectantly, and Brone felt his heart

tighten. If only she had been as she seemed when he wed her. Right now he might have been the happiest of men instead of the most miserable.

He swallowed and looked about the room. "Are you comfortable here?" He had given his servants orders to provide her with every luxury. A thick, many-hued carpet lay at their feet. Silk cushions softened the furniture, and tapestries covered all the stone walls.

"Oh, yes. I miss the out-of-doors, I miss seeing the spring. But except perhaps for the food, I have no other complaints."

"The food?"

"The meals you send me are too elaborate. I'm accustomed to simple fare."

"I send what my physician says a birthing woman needs. Of course," he added with an edge of bitterness, "you are no ordinary woman." He began to walk about the room, touching a table here, an embroidered cushion there, picking up a carved alabaster bowl and then setting it down. "The child you carry is mine, is it not?"

She watched him carefully. "Yes, of course it is, Brone. I've known no other man."

At that, his head lifted slightly. "Then it must have been conceived that night in the garden."

"Yes, the night you raped me."

He looked surprise. "There was no rape. You met me willingly."

"The emberries you sent drugged me."

"I sent no berries."

They looked at each other, both wrinkling their brows. Before Reawen could decide whether she believed him, Brone went on. "I've always thought there was something strange about that night. We were like passionate ghosts in a play written by another. I'll speak with Faring on it."

"Yes, your wizard. I heard he had come to stay with you."

"He's here to counsel me. These are difficult times. I managed to beat off Arant's army before winter set in. But there's little doubt he'll attack again, perhaps aided by your domi friends."

"They are no friends of mine. I wouldn't be here if they were." Quietly, she told him of the proposition Taunis and Driona had put to her and her decision not to accept it. "I let you bring me here for two reasons," she concluded, "to give Gris her freedom and to allow myself some time for thought. You might as well know, Brone. I will stay here until my child is born. After that I will leave."

"The child is mine," he retorted fiercely. "It will be my heir."

"I have thought of that. The child is also my heir. It's more important that it be trained in domi ways than brought up to wear your crown. If, when it is old enough to make the decision, it wishes to return to Jedestrom—" She shrugged.

"I won't let you take it."

"You can't stop me." She smiled at him almost pityingly. "You imagine you can hold me here with thick walls. Obviously, you don't understand the nature of my power. Everything on this earth is composed in part of water, and that means I can control it."

"Why, then, don't you?"

"I don't choose to, now."

His teeth met. "I have the other stones."

"And they will protect you. But you can't use them against me."

Brone's features hardened, became masklike. "You are wrong about the domi stones protecting me. They do not love me the way yours seems to love you. They are eating me alive."

"I know that," Reawen agreed with real sympathy, for there were times when she did sympathize with Brone. There were more such times than she cared to admit, even to herself. The image of his former beauty would always be emblazoned on her memory. Now she saw before her a tired man weighed down by care and pain. "I can see it," she said in a gentler voice. "It's because you were never meant to wear them. Take them off, and you will recover."

"I can't take them off and do my duty to the Peninsula. That means I will die young," Brone said. "I must think of leaving an heir. The child you carry, if it's a boy, must become king in my place."

Reawen's eyes widened. Suddenly she remembered the vision she'd had of a dark-haired boy crying out in fear and pain. She was certain now that it had been the babe in her womb. "No! The child I bear will be raised in the mountains, a free spirit as are all the children of domi. If later he should choose—"

Impatiently, Brone interrupted. "The child must be raised here and taught how to be a good king." He stepped closer. "You admit yourself that this land has grown kinder to its people under my stewardship. The Peninsula needs a legitimate successor. Beyond that, it needs a ruler who can command the stones as I have never been able to do. A child of yours and mine could do both."

Emphatically, Reawen shook her head. "You don't understand the ways of the domi. Very few of us are born to the stones. Most likely this child will not be one of the chosen. Even if he is, he could never wear the other stones. They would be an agony to him."

"You say 'him.'" Brone's expression grew eager, and he stepped closer. "So you know that the child you bear will be a boy?" When she didn't answer, he seized her hands. "You never loved me, did you?"

At the sound of his voice and the look in his blue eyes, Reawen felt as if something inside her were being torn apart. "I—I admired you. It was impossible not to. But, from the first, I knew you were my enemy and that you had seduced and robbed my mother. No, I never loved you. How could I?"

"Reawen, what happened with Nioma was all so very long ago. It hardly seems real to me. I was another person then—a boy, under the sway of a wizard. Faring had complete control over me."

"And still does."

"If that were so, I would never have chosen you for my bride. I am a man now, but then I was a fatherless lad, easily persuaded by such as Faring. Can you not understand that and forgive me?"

She drew away and crossed her hands over her breasts. "Possibly, I can forgive you. But I can never forget. How can I love you when I know what you were to my mother?"

"Perhaps you don't need to love me. Perhaps it is enough that I love you, and have almost from the first. Knowing what you are hasn't changed that. Reawen, despite everything, we have made a child together. Could we not make a future together, as well?" He reached out to touch her shoulder, but at the frozen expression on her face, he drew back. "I will leave you now, my wife, but for my sake, and for our son's, think on it."

* * * * *

Over the Sturite castle, the dull sky brewed an angry storm. It seemed a fitting complement to the military scene on shore. Armored swordsmen toting spears or axes and wearing hooded war eagles on their shoulders stalked the length of the beach. Some galloped the stretch with their horses. Foot soldiers polished shields, cleaned heavy cannons, and tried to avoid being trampled. Along the rocky fringes, archers with crossbows huddled in front of smoky fires and muttered amongst themselves.

"Just catch a gander at Arant," whispered one bearded veteran. "The way he struts about, you'd never think he ran for home while Brone hacked our army to bits last time we tried this."

"If good old Yerbo were still alive, we'd be sitting home by our own fires 'stead of freezing our arses," agreed the man at his side.

"I still say it was mighty convenient the way Yerbo keeled over just when it was most handy for Arant," hissed a spindly individual wedged between them. No sooner had he spoken than a heavy hand came down on his shoulder and yanked him back roughly. The fire scattered into red-hot brands, and his horrified companions jumped back, yelping.

"Talking treason about the king begs death," a grim-faced guard snarled. He hauled the luckless archer down the beach to the hillock where Arant stood, preparing to address his assembled forces.

With his red braids whipped by the wind and the polished studs on his black leather armor flashing against the gray sky, the young king was an impressive sight. His color, already high, darkened visibly when he heard what the archer had been saying to his compatriots. Drawing out his sword, Arant used two strokes to hack the man in half.

Turning away from the twitching remnants of the body and the blood that poured into the sand, Arant waved a hand for silence. He got it. Only the wind and the birds disturbed the sudden hush.

Slowly, his narrowed green eyes surveyed the impressive army he had assembled. "Sturites!" he finally shouted above the thin screech of the gulls. "Twice we have hurled ourselves against the Peninsula's shores, and twice we have been repulsed. But Brone's army is small, and we have bled it until it is weak. This time, I promise you, we will win! When we do, we shall exact a rich and satisfying vengeance! You saw what I just did to a traitor. That and worse we shall do to every Peninsulan man who opposes us and all their male offspring as well."

A roar of approval rose up from the flame-haired assemblage. When it finally died down, Arant continued. "Brone's kingdom grows fat on its wealth. Its women wear jeweled combs in their hair and dresses of silk that caress their thighs." Arant leered. "The thighs of those women shall soon know a rougher touch!"

Another shout of approval rose up from the Sturite soldiers, and they shuffled their heavy-booted feet eagerly.

"Warriors," Arant cried hoarsely, "I promise you that when we touch these shores again, Jedestrom will lie in ashes, and you will each have pockets stuffed with Peninsulan riches and a Peninsulan woman for your plaything!"

*   *   *   *   *

What was it? Faring asked himself. Never before had Vaar failed him. But since the appearance of this troublemaker, Reawen, in Brone's life, the glass had been as obscure as a miasma-shrouded swamp. Even now—though Faring had been trying to see his way for the past hour—roiling clouds swirled within Vaar's depths, obscuring all.

Was it the girl herself doing this? Faring wondered. No, that was unlikely. This was wizard's work, this fog of obscurity that blinded Vaar's searching eye. What wizard could be so strong— as learned as he, perhaps even more proficient?

In answer to this question, the mist cleared from Vaar's eye as if blown by a robust wind. "Thropos!"

Thropos smiled thinly out of the crystal orb. "So, the great Faring recognizes his humble childhood friend even after all these years. I'm flattered. Especially since you may have thought me dead."

"I knew you were alive and in the Sturite court," Faring replied stiffly. The hairs on the back of his neck stood upright, and a chill rippled up his spine. Seeing how Thropos had changed unnerved him. Thropos had never been handsome, but now he was a twisted caricature of his boyhood self. His mouth, which had once found occasion to smile, had become a cruel slash in his fleshless face, and a demonic gleam shone in his eyes.

"I was glad that you survived your fall," Faring added. "It troubled me that I had to leave before I could determine your condition."

At that, Thropos's laughter chimed out hysterically. "Do not insult my intelligence, Faring. After you pushed me over that cliff, you never gave a thought to my condition. By injuring me, you made sure I would never be able to return to Peneto in time. You left me for dead and good riddance to the only rival you ever really had!"

"It was never that, Thropos. I never feared you as a rival. It was my temper and your tongue that was your undoing. You should never have taunted me so cruelly."

Thropos's lips curled up into a cunning smile. "No, I should never have teased you about your haggish ladylove. But I did, and that was my mistake. Your mistake was in not making sure that you had killed me. All these years that I have hated you, Faring, I have not been idle. I have been nursing my strength for the day when I could revenge myself. I have been growing and learning and waiting—waiting for the hour that is upon us."

Thropos's wild laughter rang out. "As you have no doubt surmised by now, it is I who have blinded Vaar's eye. It is I who have arranged for your daughter to be Brone's nemesis. For the charming Reawen *is* your daughter. No doubt, by now you've guessed that, too. It is I who have set a noose around you and yours, and now it is I who will tighten the noose until it chokes the life out of all it encompasses." Again, Thropos cackled crazily, hardly able to contain his mad glee.

Faring, however, grew more stern, and his eyes turned flinty. "You forget that you still have me to deal with. In our boyhood contests, you rarely bested me, Thropos."

The laughter wiped itself from the smaller wizard's weasel face. His eyes turned into deadly balls of venom. "Arrogant, as always, Faring. Though I have changed from the days of my youth, you have not. Now, at last, the time has come when I shall crush your arrogance! Meet me, if you have the stomach for it. Let us test our skills against each other for the last time."

"Done," Faring hissed. "Only name the time and place!"

Smiling crookedly, Thropos's acid-filled visage gave him instructions, then faded. For long minutes, Faring sat still as stone before Vaar. His eyes stared ahead blankly. His vision had turned inward to scenes of the past.

He remembered sunny days when, under the watchful eyes of older novices, he and Thropos had played in the highland meadow outside Peneto's gates. They had romped and wrestled like newborn lambs, never imagining that their destiny was to be anything but brothers.

Then Faring thought of his affair with Nioma. Strange that a few brief weeks with a lightminded woman should change the course of so many fates. Those weeks had sent a shock wave into the future.

As his mind chewed on this, Faring rose and locked Vaar away. Then he tucked his gaunt hands into his long black sleeves and strode out of the Plat and across the courtyard. When he arrived at the keep, he curtly addressed the soldiers on guard there.

"I wish to speak with the lady Reawen."

They gazed at him in awe and terror, and the one in charge spoke up nervously. "The king has instructed us that no one except himself shall see his queen without his express permission."

Faring raised a finger, and the soldier's eyes glazed over, as did those of all his compatriots. While the guards stood like living statues, he walked calmly past them up the winding staircase leading to Reawen's tower chamber. He did her the courtesy to knock. When he heard her voice, he knew she had felt his advent and was waiting for him with a mixture of curiosity and barely controlled hostility.

He walked in and found her standing with a window slit at her back and her hands folded over her rounded belly. He had seen her image in Vaar, yet the sight of her in the flesh shocked him. Though very beautiful, she bore no resemblance to Nioma. No, she was not her mother's daughter, she was his.

And as he acknowledged this fact, a bitter humor rose up inside him. Fate, as always, would have the last laugh.

"Good morrow, Daughter," he said ironically.

She stared back at him with eyes that, though far more beautiful than his, ringed as they were in silky black lashes, were exactly the same intelligent and uncompromising shade of gray. "You will excuse me if I cannot bring myself to address you as father. One who has set out to destroy all the family left to me does not seem worthy of the title."

"Since domi females traditionally shuck off their mates as squirrels do walnut shells once the fruit inside has been tasted, I cannot believe that my presence or absence during your childhood, supposing I had even known that you existed, would have been of much consequence. It is true that I am the enemy of your lawless breed, and you have reason to hate me. Yet you must be curious about me, as well."

She inclined her head, and despite himself he admired the way the sunlight brought out the iridescence in her long black hair. "I admit to that. Yet, plainly, you have no curiosity concerning your daughter. Otherwise, you would have visited me long before this."

Faring eyed her thoughtfully. He had not come here to speak kindly to this meddlesome young woman, yet he found himself softening. In a voice that was almost gentle, he said, "Sit down, Reawen. You are heavy with child, and what I have to say will take some time." When she had stiffly obeyed, he continued. "I have not seen you before now because I could not bring myself to face my past.

"When I was young," he explained, "I was passionate. Passion thwarted breeds gall. It is like a force of nature, and when it rages inside you, you are as helpless before it as a bird in the whirlwind. In my youth, I fell in love with your mother. She was unworthy of my love, and when she cast me out, I swore vengeance against her and all her breed."

"You schooled Brone to take that vengeance for you!"

Faring merely nodded. "He was my tool. Through him I changed the Peninsula and the forces governing it. No matter what you may imagine, no matter what your scheming compatriots and the Sturites may conspire to do, it cannot be changed back into what it was."

Reawen stared up at the tall, gaunt wizard. Standing still before her, he did not look at her as a father might. His gaze held no pride or love. In it, she saw something else far more disturbing.

"Why are you here?"

"To help you with the decision you must make. You have retaken your green stone, and with it you assume great power. But it is too late for that power, Reawen. What Brone has brought to the Peninsula, you and your kind cannot turn back. The days of the domi are finished."

"I am not finished, and neither is my child!" Reawen cried out.

"Your child and Brone's, a child destined to heal the breach between the past and the future. Accept that fact, Reawen."

"You mean accept the king as my husband, stay here and be his queen—even if I do not care for him?"

"You care for him quite enough, Reawen. That much you cannot hide from me. It is only your stubbornness, because of the part he played in your mother's destruction, that makes you draw back from him. You must be more reasonable. In that time, he was merely my puppet. Hate me if you must, but accept him. Do not attempt to stand in the path of this destiny, Reawen. If you do, only tragedy can result. The days of the domi are all but done, and the Peninsula is marching forward to something new. You bear a son who was meant to be a great king. If you try to deny him that providence you will only bring disaster on him, on the Peninsula, and on yourself."

Two bright coins of angry color glowed in Reawen's pale cheeks, and she drew herself up proudly. "You cannot use Brone to make me and my child into your puppets, wizard! Tell the king that I will not stay here. When the time is right, I will leave for the mountains where I belong, and I will take my child with me where I can raise him in the domi fashion—wild and free."

Faring swiveled on his heel and stalked to the door. Before he disappeared through it, however, he turned back one last time. "You are a foolish girl, Reawen, and fools deserve no quarter."

Faring stepped from the tower and waved a hand at Reawen's guards. They blinked and looked around stupidly. In another moment they'd be as they were before, quite oblivious that they'd just spent part of an hour frozen like living statues.

Muttering angrily to himself, Faring strode back toward the Plat. "Stubborn, foolish girl," he kept saying over and over again.

As he was passing the stables, he heard an anguished cry. Jarred from his furious thoughts by the sound, Faring walked toward it. Inside the stable, he found Albin staring at something round propped atop Grassears's stall.

"What is it?" the wizard asked, squinting through the shadows.

"By all the stars that shine," the boy whispered. "It's Pib's head!"

* * * * *

The king was walking the garden paths some hours later. Faring had informed him of his talk with Reawen. "After the child is born, you must devise some way to kill her," he'd warned. "I will help you in this."

"But you say yourself that she's your daughter!"

Faring's long face had only grown grayer. "It matters not. The child must stay here and be raised up with you. As long as his renegade mother lives, she will endanger it and the future of this land."

Brone's response had been to turn his back on his mentor and hurry away. All afternoon he had paced alone in the garden, his mind a ferment of painful thoughts. Moments earlier he had paused at the spot where he and Reawen had made love, where the child she carried had been conceived. Would he ever forget that strange, enchanted night? Would he ever forget how she had floated across the grass and come into his arms like a sleepwalking goddess? How could he conspire to kill her, even for the safety of his child? No, it was impossible!

Rounding a corner, Brone came upon one of the gardeners. He was patting a bed of early spring flowers into place. The man glanced up, his face shadowed by the broad brim of his hat, and then clipped one of the blossoms and handed it to Brone.

"What is this?" Brone said, gazing down at the flower. "It almost looks like a rose, but surely roses don't bloom so early."

"These do, my liege," the gardener said. "They're a special hybrid. Smell the fragrance."

Brone lifted his hand and inhaled the rose's intoxicating sweetness. It made him think of Reawen, of her grace and the fleeting joy he had found within the clasp of her white arms. "Thank you," he told the gardener, "I'll press this rose in one of my books."

The man nodded, gathered up his tools, and glided away through the foliage. Brone had not been alone more than a moment when he heard the thump of hurrying feet. Flushed and wild-eyed, his steward rounded the corner. "The Sturites are at the walls of the city!" Stry cried. "Somehow they've managed to sneak up the Har!"

Turning on his heel, the king was already making plans to mobilize his army. As he hastened down the path, his hand closed hard on the stem of the white rose. One of its thorns pierced his skin, and a moment later he tottered, clutching at his heart, and fell to the ground.

Chapter Fourteen

"It's that damnable Thropos!" Phen cursed. "Alone, Arant hasn't the brains to take us by surprise."

"I still don't understand how it happened," Albin said. All day he'd been running errands for Faring and had only a sketchy idea of the disaster taking place outside Jedestrom. When he'd been able to snatch a moment to breathe, he'd hurried to find Phen. The military advisor was commanding a work crew fortifying a weak spot in the city's wall.

"Clever bastards built shallow-draft boats and sneaked them up the Har's eastern branch through the marshes under cover of night." Phen grunted as he hefted a sandbag.

Albin dragged another bag off the wagon Phen was unloading. "Taunis and Driona must have had something to do with that," he ventured. "They're the ones who would know all the best places to hide." Albin remembered well that night in the mountains when he'd spied Taunis and Thropos with their heads together. This sneak attack must have been part of what they'd been plotting."

"Well, they fooled us." Phen kicked a booted foot at the barricade of sandbags he'd erected. "All along, we've put so much stock in greenfire, but we can't get to it. I knew it was a mistake to move the powder to that tower so Brone could jail up his bride in the keep. Now the powder is on the other side of the Sturites, and I only pray they don't sniff it out."

Brone's military advisor wiped the sweat from his face and picked up a shovel. "Ah, but it wouldn't be so bad if that decoy party of Sturites to the west hadn't lured off our army with the false news of an attack on Avera. I warned Buw not to send the troops out there, but the old goat wouldn't take orders from me. Now he's in a fix. Arant's got us roped in with our best fighting men chasing shadows, and with greenfire out of reach."

"It wouldn't have happened if the king had been in command!"

"Aye, boy, but he wasn't." Phen's thick brows snapped together. "How is he? Any sign of coming around?"

Albin shook his head sadly. "Faring's tried everything, but King Brone just lies there."

"Oh, surely it's not as bad as that, is it? He's not dead."

"No, but he might as well be, for all the sign of life in him. Faring says it's a poison of some kind. It's made a living corpse of him."

"Thropos again, no doubt. How I'd like to wring that black crow's spindly throat!" Phen paused to tug at his thick brown beard. "Or maybe now it's not Thropos we have to blame, but that witch in the keep."

"Reawen?" Albin's head jerked up. "Oh, no, Reawen wouldn't poison the king."

"What makes you so sure of that, lad? Seems to me the lady has no great liking for her husband, or us for that matter. Maybe she's in league with Taunis and Driona. They're her kind, so it makes sense. Maybe she's even behind what happened to that friend of yours, Pib."

At Pib's name, Albin stumbled and dropped a sandbag. Tears flooded his eyes and threatened to overflow. "Reawen didn't have anything to do with what happened to Pib. It was the Sturites who tortured him and then cut off his head. And it must have been Thropos who left the head for me to find." Albin's throat worked. "Phen, when I think how Pib must have suffered—how could I have ever thought he was a spy?"

"Now, now, lad." Phen patted Albin's trembling shoulder. "We all misjudge our fellows sometimes. You mustn't blame yourself."

"But I do. When I left for Peneto, Pib said something about wanting to have an adventure. I should have paid attention and warned him."

"It wasn't you who killed him so cruel, lad."

"And it wasn't Reawen, either," Albin asserted forcefully. "She's not in league with the other domi. She's not like them! She's told me so herself!"

Phen laughed cynically. "I hate to get you any more riled up, but maybe she's pulled the wool over your eyes just the way she has the king's. You've had a case on her all along, and it's plain you'd believe anything she chose to say."

Albin turned bright red. He let another sandbag drop and seized Phen by his muscular shoulders. "You've never even met Reawen, so how would you know?"

"I've heard enough about her from you, and I know the ways of the domi. They're not to be trusted, lad. No matter how fair they may seem on the surface, they're pure devilment under-neath."

"You're wrong, I tell you. I can prove it. Why don't we ask Reawen to help us get to the greenfire?"

Phen's eyebrows shot up to his hairline. "Now that's an interestin' idea. What makes you think she would?"

"She doesn't want to see Jedestrom or the king harmed. I'm sure of it! The child she bears is Brone's. Oh, I know she'd help us if we asked her."

Absently, Phen mopped at his sweaty brow. "Whether you're right or wrong, I can't say. But it's certain we haven't the authority to meddle with arrangements at the keep. The king's locked her in there because he wants her to stay. For all I know, letting her out would only make this damnable situation worse—that is, if it can get any worse," he added darkly.

But it did get worse. The Sturites surrounded the city and prepared for a long siege. From the walls, Phen and Albin watched them set up tents, dig trenches, and prepare batter-ing rams. The insolent pace at which they went about their preparations was somehow more chilling than if they'd rushed the walls in a berserker frenzy. It showed the depth of their confidence in the ultimate outcome.

"Can we keep them out?" Albin asked Phen.

The older man shook his head. "For a while, maybe. But these walls won't withstand a full-blown assault by thousands of redheaded devils. We'll do our best. But unless the king comes to or that wizard of his performs some miracle, I'm afraid things look bad. What does Faring say, by the by? Any hope from that quarter?"

Albin grimaced. "He keeps his own counsel. I know there's something on his mind, some plan. So far as I can tell, he's told no one what it might be."

Phen nodded curtly. "One thing I've learned: in the end, a man must stand on his own two legs and rely on himself, not the magic of crazy wizards. A man's got to cock his toes up sometime. The thing is to go down fighting and to die with honor."

"If we had greenfire, we might not have to fight at all," Albin countered. He was young, his whole life before him, and he didn't like this talk of death with honor. What good was honor if you were cold and stiff as yesterday's porridge? "Phen, let's go speak to Reawen. With the king sleeping like one of the dead, she may be our only chance. It's at least worth trying."

Phen shook his head, but Albin wouldn't give up. All that afternoon, as Phen helped organize the city's ragged defenses, he had to listen to the boy argue his case until finally, as evening shadows thickened, the old veteran agreed to accompany him to the keep.

"We shouldn't even go near her," Phen grumbled, muttering about domi powers.

They started across the meadow that led to the ancient structure and found it unguarded. "Buw must have ordered Brone's guards to man the walls," Albin said, and shook his head. "We have so few fighting men left in the city."

Phen spotted Reawen watching their approach from the topmost window slit. "Maybe the witch already knows what we've come for," he speculated.

"Stop talking about her that way," Albin hissed fiercely. "She's not like that, I tell you!"

"Well, well, so the baby boy has teeth. Then what is she like, lad?"

"Like you and me, only caught in a terrible situation that was not of her making."

"That describes the human condition down to a tittle. Her situation can't be more terrible than the one we'll all be ground up in when the Sturites leap over those walls swinging their battle-axes," Phen grumbled.

Yet a few minutes later when Phen stood before Reawen, his attitude changed. The rugged adventurer's language smoothed out, and he became polite—even gallant. With amusement, Albin thought that if his rough-hewn friend had been wearing a hat, he would surely have doffed it to Reawen—witch or no witch.

Albin, on the other hand, was all but struck dumb by the sight of her. Though her belly swelled beneath her loose gown, it was her face that captured his complete attention. Instead of dimming its beauty, her pregnancy seemed to ignite it. Her ivory skin glowed incandescent. Her gray eyes shone like bright water. And her black hair swept her shoulders in a tumble of richest ebony. Accenting her loveliness was the green stone centered on the silver band across her forehead.

"Albin, I'm so glad to see you!" she cried, reaching her hands out and clasping his fingers in hers. "I've missed you, but I know you haven't come to talk over old times. What is it? What's going on?"

"You don't know?" he asked cautiously and shot a sideways glance at Phen.

"Of course I don't know. No one's visited me, even to bring food, for two days. I can hear the noise outside, but that window slit gives me no view. I've tried to see what's happening through water images. Yet I'm allowed so little water, I can't make sense of what it shows me."

"Reawen, the king's ill, and we're besieged!" In a rush of words, Albin explained the situation to her. Occasionally, Phen would add a phrase or two. Mostly he kept silent while the boy spilled out their mutual distress.

As she listened Reawen's expression stilled and then grew anxious. "You say Brone hasn't wakened or even moved in two days?"

Albin shook his head. "Faring thinks it must be something that Thropos has done to him."

Reawen knew nothing of Thropos, so Albin had to do even more explaining. When he had finished, she grew thoughtful. "I wonder if this Sturite magician could have had anything to do with Cel's disappearance."

"Cel?"

Reawen noted Albin's confusion. "Of course, you never saw her, because I kept her hidden. When I first came to Jedestrom, I had a bird, a wonderful bird named Cel. She disappeared from the gardens outside the Zeleta, and I've mourned her ever since." Reawen pressed her hands together. "I don't know if I can help you, Albin. Now that my pregnancy is advanced, my powers don't come to me so easily. There are times when my stone feels almost unfriendly. When it does work, I can't predict just what it will do. Sometimes it does things contrary to what I've willed. My aunt explained to me that it's because the stone knows that I'm no longer one person and hasn't decided about the other person my body is growing."

"Reawen, you may be our only hope!" Albin exclaimed.

Distressed, she gazed at him. "All right. I'm willing to try, if you understand the risk. What is your plan?"

Albin didn't really have a plan. All he knew was that somehow they must leave the protection of the city, sneak past the Sturite lines and get to the tower.

When Phen explained the properties of greenfire to Reawen, her eyes widened. "You say there's no water anywhere near this storage place?"

"No, that's why the king picked it. Until the spring rains come next month, it's dry as a bone. If only we could spread greenfire so it encircled the Sturites and then bring water to it, it would run straight through the enemy until it found the river. I tell you my worst fear, lady, is that the Sturites will break open that tower and find what's stored inside. If that wizard's involved, the seven hells only know what will happen next."

Reawen nodded and extended her hands to both Phen and Albin. "I'm not sure if I can bring the water you need, but I'm willing to try on one condition."

"And what might that be, milady?" Phen asked suspiciously.

"That if we succeed, you and Albin will take me away from Jedestrom and return me to my mountains."

The two looked at each other. "She's the king's wife. They'll accuse us of treason if we help her escape," the older man warned.

Albin lifted his shoulders. "What choice do we have?"

Phen glanced out the window. From this height he could see over the city walls to the angry threads of smoke rising from Sturite fires. "None, I'll warrant." The scars on his leather vest rippled as he shrugged his own agreement. "All right, then it's a bargain. If we're going to try and get past those devils out there before they find the greenfire themselves, I think we'd better do it tonight."

* * * * *

Faring gazed down at the king's body. Brone's servants had placed his bed in the center of his sleeping room. There, except for the band of jewels on his head, he lay naked. His physicians had examined him to no avail, and Faring had dismissed them as a pack of useless quacks.

Slowly, he prowled the perimeter of the king's bed looking for some clue to what had made a barely breathing marble effigy of what had been a strong and active man. Faring knew the cause had to be poison, and he suspected Thropos of administering it. Even as a boy, Thropos had been a master of disguises and deception. Poison—slow and deadly—was his style. Somehow he must have insinuated himself into the royal household to do this deed.

As Faring's gaze swept the king's form, he found himself remembering Brone as a boy. He had been eager, intelligent, and handsome. Having just lost his own father, he had been hungry for a substitute and, thus, easily taken over. All of these qualities had made him a perfect tool.

And that had been precisely how Faring had regarded him— as a tool to be honed sharp, guided to its target, and then controlled. Faring had never returned the affection or admiration that the boy had showered on him. During all these years such a thing had never even occurred to him.

Now, however, he found himself viewing Brone differently. The divine beauty he had possessed as a boy had changed into something quite different. Now his was the body of a magnificent man in his prime, and it showed no sign of deterioration. Deep lines grooved his face, however, and silver had begun to dim the gold of his hair. In one still so young, this had to be the effect of the stones, Faring mused. That Brone should be so ravaged struck the wizard as a great waste, for there was much to admire in the man. Except for his occasional willfulness and his weakness for beautiful women, he was honest and well-intentioned. Nobility rested on his shoulders like a richly deserved mantle.

For the first time, pity and a touch of remorse stirred in the gaunt mage's vindictive heart. Brone's lot had not been an easy one, and then to have had the misfortune to have fallen in love with such as Reawen—

Faring set his mouth, realizing that, though the girl was intelligent, loyal, honest, even noble, she was much like him— unforgiving and unwilling to compromise. That flintiness in her will be her downfall, he thought.

And what of the child she bears? he asked himself. It will be the child of my daughter and my surrogate son. If Thropos has his way, he will destroy it, too, in his mad revenge. I cannot let that happen.

Revenge. Faring understood its coin well. Only now was he beginning to comprehend its true price.

A timid tap on the door sounded, and a second later a physician cracked the barrier and showed a hesitant face. "I have a tray of food, m'lord Faring, if you wish to eat."

"I wish nothing."

"There's cider. Perhaps it would be well to moisten the king's mouth with it?"

"Perhaps." Faring watched as the physician minced in carrying a mug brimming with the sweet brew. "Let me try that first." After tasting it and finding it wholesome, he handed it back to the apprehensive little man.

"I'll just moisten the kings lips with it," the man said and then, in his nervousness at the wizard's disapproving look, tripped over his own feet and splashed half the liquid onto the king's left arm. "I'm sorry! Oh, dear, oh, dear!"

Angrily, Faring snatched the cup away from the distraught physician, who'd started dabbing at the king's drenched arm with the edge of his trailing sleeve. "Get out! Get out, you and your clumsiness. I'll see to him."

Muttering imprecations, Faring waited until the door closed and he was again alone with Brone. Then he set about cleaning the sticky liquid off the king's skin. As he worked between Brone's fingers the sharp crease dividing the wizard's black brows suddenly deepened. "What's this?"

He leaned forward, staring intently at a tiny spot of pink. "Now, what could be causing that?" Faring took a magnifying glass out of one of his deep pockets and placed it over the spot. "Ahhh!" he murmured on a long exhalation. "So that explains it." A moment later he had withdrawn an almost imperceptible thorn from the king's left thumb.

* * * * *

"I hope you know what you're doing, lad," Phen grumbled. He, Albin, and Reawen gazed at the depression, which lay a few feet from a deserted section of the city walls. Darkness had fallen an hour since. Luckily, it promised to be a murky night. The moon and stars were hidden under a thick cover of clouds.

"I tell you, if we follow this trench, we'll find a spot where we can burrow under the wall. I used to exercise the horses around here with Pib." For a second, Albin's voice caught. Steadying, he went on. "Pib showed it to me."

"If we can burrow out, the Sturites can burrow in," Phen pointed out.

"Only if they know the place, which I'm sure they cannot."

Phen puckered his lips. "Who knows what secrets they bandy about among themselves? Though your Pib was no spy, I've no doubt they've had a bucketful of such in and out of Jedestrom to pick up just such tidbits as this. We may burrow out to find a redheaded welcoming party." He turned to Reawen. "What think you, my lady?"

She gazed dubiously at the trough. "It may do for you and Albin. You're both thin and athletic. But in my condition—"

"If you won't fit, we'll widen it for you," Albin injected. "Come, the only way to find out is to try."

For want of a better plan, the two followed him. The trough led to a hollowed-out spot beneath an older section of wall. Weed choked it, but once they'd pulled away the greenery and sent all the worms and insects living within scuttling, Albin and even Phen were able to squeeze through. For Reawen, however, such tight quarters were impossible. Whispering and grunting, the two males set to work scraping at the earth with Albin's knife and Phen's small axe.

"That wee toy of a knife is useless. Why don't you try pryin' up these rocks with that great sword dangling on your hip?" Phen suggested.

Albin stuck his knife back into his belt and took out the weapon he'd won from Eol. After much inner debate, he'd decided to bring Victory along, even though he had only a rudimentary idea of how to use it effectively. Sword fighting hadn't been part of his training. At least the blade had a hopeful name, he'd told himself.

Now he was glad he'd decided to wear Victory at his belt, for it proved surprisingly effective as a digging tool. A half hour later, Reawen was able to join them on the other side of the city wall.

"Are you all right?" Albin whispered anxiously after they'd dragged her through.

"Passable," she said wryly, stopping herself from chuckling at the pun. "I only hope the child doing cartwheels in my womb doesn't decide to be born this very minute."

The inky darkness hid Albin's and Phen's horrified expressions. Until that instant, neither had considered this possibility. "Balls of ice," Phen muttered.

As silently as possible, the threesome scrambled up an incline and then across a flat area of scrub. In the distance, Sturite fires brushed the night, each a tongue of flame licking at the gloom.

"Loud doings with our friends out there," Phen commented ironically. "Just listen to all the drunken shouting and laughing. You'd think they were at a feast."

"That's because Arant believes he's already won. He's celebrating early," answered Albin.

Reawen cocked her head. "Arant is Fidacia's brother, of course."

"Yes, lady, and present king in Zica. He's a mean bastard, begging your pardon. If he catches us out here, he'll use us to bait his war eagles."

"Not so long as I have my stone."

"I thought you said you weren't sure of your powers," Albin put in anxiously.

"I think the stone will answer me if I call on it hard enough. It's just that——" Reawen flattened her hands before her and rubbed her palms together lightly. "It's just that I'd rather not call on it unless I have to. And, as I said before, I'm not always sure what will happen when I do call on it."

"Well, tonight I'll be surprised if you don't have to," said Phen. "For one thing, needs we must pass mighty close to the Sturite camp if we're to reach the tower on the other side with enough time to spare to get our work done before dawn. Have you the stomach for it, my lady?"

Reawen chuckled low and patted her protruding belly. "Another bad pun. Yes, Phen, I have the stomach for it."

With that, the little band set off across the field, doing their best to pick their way over the moonless terrain without stumbling or, worse, breaking an ankle. As they drew close to the Sturite camp, they could see the firelit faces of their enemies all too clearly.

When they passed close to one particularly bright fire, Reawen tugged at Albin's sleeve. "Look, that's Taunis and Driona!"

The boy shuddered. "I was hoping you wouldn't notice. You're not going to betray us and join them, are you?"

Insulted, Reawen glared at him. "Of course I'm not going to join them. I would never betray you. I've had enough of deceit. Besides, I don't like either Taunis or Driona. They would as soon crush me and mine as they would anyone else. Please believe me, Albin. I don't want them to destroy Jedestrom and all the good that Brone has wrought in the years of his rule."

Albin breathed easier, but his relief was short-lived.

"Who's that bent little man in the dark cloak talking with them?" Reawen demanded.

Phen answered. "It's Thropos, my lady, Arant's wizard."

"He looks familiar. I feel I've seen him someplace before, perhaps even at the Plat."

"It wouldn't surprise me. When it comes to that one, nothing would surprise me. Lucky they're so busy jawin'.

Maybe we can sneak past."

But when Albin took Reawen's hand, she pulled back. "He's carrying a cage. It's got a white bird inside it." She flattened her palm over her breast. "It's Cel!"

"My lady, we must get on while we're able."

"I can't leave knowing Cel's here."

"But—"

Reawen's gaze stayed fixed on the firelit scene in the distance. "I'm sorry, but I can't go with you until I've found out what they're doing with Cel. Go on to the tower without me."

"We can't leave you here," Albin whispered angrily. His words were lost on Reawen. She was already creeping forward.

"Now we're in for it," Phen hissed. "She's fooled us and plans to join them."

"She isn't! She's going to get her bird."

"Either way, it's certain they'll catch us and cook us for Thropos's supper. Might as well die a hero as a yellow-livered craven," he added and began to follow Reawen.

When they were so close that the heat from Taunis's fire warmed their cheeks, they took shelter behind a bush. As Phen and Albin dropped down beside Reawen, they could make out some of what Thropos was saying.

"He's bragging to Taunis about his nasty accomplishments," Reawen whispered angrily. "It was he who put that Gutaini snake into action and poisoned the emberries I ate." Ignoring the uncomprehending look her two companions gave each other, she hurried on. "Thropos poisoned the king, as well."

"That much I already guessed," Phen gritted. "Now what, my lady? That big fire's so bright it's chasing away the night. We're as close as we're going to get without being seen. Indeed, we're mighty lucky that wizard has been distracted by his boasts. Otherwise he would have picked us out, sure."

Reawen fingered her stone. "I must get to Cel. Just look at her in that cage. All this time Thropos has kept her a prisoner. I must set her free."

"But—" Albin started to protest. Then he noticed the expression on Reawen's face. She had closed her eyes as if preparing for an ordeal. "Reawen, you said you didn't want to use your power unless you had to!"

"I think it's necessary," she replied between gritted teeth. Then she vanished.

"Glory be!" The astonished Phen hissed on a little puff of air. "I was lookin' right at her, and she disappeared. Where'd she get to?"

"Isn't it obvious?" Albin replied grimly. "She's made herself invisible and gone into the Sturite camp after that bird."

Chapter Fifteen

As Reawen crossed behind Thropos, she kept a careful eye on the wizard. He might have ways of seeing through the cloak of invisibility she'd assumed. Despite her assurances to Albin and Phen, she didn't know how long the green stone would let her maintain it. This late stage of pregnancy made her a weak and vulnerable creature.

Inside her belly, her child moved in protest, clearly disliking the strain on both their systems. There's no help for it, my little one, she whispered in her mind. I can't leave Cel to whatever fate this evil wizard has in store for her.

Thankfully, Thropos was so deep into his bragging conversation with Taunis and Driona that he appeared oblivious of all else. "I hear she's big as a house with Brone's brat," Reawen heard Driona sneer.

"A brat he'll never live to see," Thropos answered.

At the cackle of delight from Taunis, Reawen shivered and hurried past.

Thropos had set Cel's cage on a stump some ten yards away from the gossiping threesome. All the other Sturites were keeping to their own campfires, so Reawen began to hope that she'd be able to free Cel before anyone noticed or interfered.

"Cel," she whispered, squatting down in back of the cage and pressing her face close to it.

The bird, a doleful lump of crumpled white feathers, had been dozing. At the sound of her mistress's voice, her purple eyes popped open.

"It's me, Reawen. You can't see me, but I'm here, and I'm going to help you."

Merciful dragonflies!

"Just be still and pretend nothing's happening." Reawen tested the cage's lock. "Do you know where Thropos keeps the key to this?"

On a chain around his scrawny neck, worse luck. Even you could not take it from him without his noticing.

"There are other ways to open a lock." With the tip of her finger, Reawen removed a drop of water from the dish just inside Cel's cage. After she'd placed the drop on the lock, she closed her eyes and willed it into a thread, hard as wire, yet flexible. At her direction, it burrowed inside the lock. Seconds later there was a tiny click, and the mechanism inside the lock released.

Bravo, my sweetling, Cel cooed in Reawen's mind. *You are the best and most talented mistress in all the world.*

"Oh, but you're not free yet. Now I'll open the cage so you can fly away."

And what will happen to you when Thropos sees the flutter of my wings? That one might see through your invisibility.

"I have my stone for protection. I'll be all right."

Cel twitched her head. *You are pregnant, and your stone is in revolt. Yes, I know your state. You are heavy with Brone's child and therefore vulnerable. Besides, if I flew out now, the Sturite war eagles would shred me.*

"Oh, Cel, the Sturites have caged their eagles for the night. See, they're all locked away."

The pillawn only fluttered her dainty white head once more. *No, I have a score to settle with yon wizard. Sweet child, you've done all you can for Cel. Leave the cage unlocked and slip out of this cursed camp while you can.*

Reawen argued, but Cel stayed adamant. She would not fly from the cage, and nothing her mistress could say or do would change her mind. Inside her belly, Reawen felt her infant kick and turn, protesting the strain of invisibility. Suddenly she saw her hand appear, transparent yet discernible to an alert eye.

Depart! Cel commanded. *If you are caught and killed, so is your child. You haven't the right to risk its life!*

Head bowed in defeat, tears blinding her, Reawen slipped back out of the enemy camp.

"Are you crazy?" Albin hissed when she gave up what was left of her invisibility and sank down, exhausted, behind the bushes where he and Phen were hiding. "If Thropos or Taunis or Driona had looked up, they would have seen you. Even I could see you!"

"You just don't understand. I had to try and help my pillawn."

"What's more important, a bird or our safety and that of all of Jedestrom?"

Phen lay a warning hand on Albin's elbow. "Quiet, boy! Looks like our little lady here got out just in time."

"Balls of ice! What's that?" Albin exclaimed.

A thick black cloud had whirled out of the darkness. As Reawen, Albin, and Phen watched in galvanized silence, it oozed up in front of Thropos. When it had the Sturite wizard's attention, it lengthened into an inky column and coalesced into Faring.

The firelight flickered over his cadaverous features and set small red lights dancing in the depths of his eyes. With mock civility, he bowed to Thropos. "I come to accept your challenge, old friend."

Still perched in front of the fire with Taunis and Driona, the Sturite wizard paled and seemed to shrivel. Instantly, however, he recovered himself. He jerked to his feet and regarded his childhood rival scornfully. "Whirling about in black clouds is a childish trick that any apprentice of our guild might play at. I had thought better of you."

"You have thought too long and too hard on me, Thropos. It's time to test the potency of the acid bubbling and hissing inside you."

As Faring's sharp words spat from his mouth like well-aimed darts, Taunis and Driona stared from wizard to wizard. With almost comic unity, they scrambled back and out of the way. The Sturites, too, looked on with open-mouthed fascination but kept their distance. Arant, who'd been gaming with some of his nobles, staggered drunkenly out of a tent to investigate the commotion. He froze when he saw what was afoot. Even he knew better than to interfere with the two black-robed figures squaring off against each other.

"So be it," Thropos declared. "I have a score to settle, Faring. This is a victory I have waited many years to taste. Pleasure long delayed is all the more agreeable. I expect when I taste it at last, it will be sweet."

Smiling grimly, he lifted a finger. The coals of the fire around which he, Taunis, and Driona had been conferring scattered to four corners. They hissed, pulsed red, and then, with a deafening roar, flamed up. The flames sizzled along the ground and met to describe a burning circle. Inside its simmering wall, the two rivals faced each other. "Let the games begin," Thropos intoned.

"Let them begin, indeed," Faring replied composedly. "Do you remember the trinkets of our boyhood?" he queried with mock innocence. A red-eyed demon materialized in front of him. Sweat oozed from its warty green skin and flecks of foam dripped down from its glistening fangs.

"I have not forgotten our childish toys," Thropos cried. Effortlessly, he materialized a like creature, only uglier. Its fingers ended in needle-sharp claws, and its mad crimson eyes blazed.

Slavering and howling, the two monsters circled. Each was obviously prepared to murder the other to protect its black-robed master. With hideous shrieks, they closed, clawing and biting, scratching and rending. Black blood flowed from the wounds they dealt each other, yet neither slackened the viciousness of its attack.

"Are those things real?" Albin whispered in wide-eyed horror.

"Real enough so you wouldn't want one sinking its fangs into you," answered Phen.

"If I understand it aright, they're solid projections from each wizard's mind," Reawen injected *sotto voce*. "It's a matter of how long each can keep it up and equal the ferocity of his rival's horrid invention."

"Well, the two appear evenly matched and neither less nasty than the other," commented Phen.

As he spoke, the two demons rolled on the ground between Thropos and Faring, locked in a death grip. Abandoning his first creation exactly as a bored child might a toy that no longer amused, Faring muttered three short words. With stunning abruptness, a mechanical giant wielding a dagger-studded mace sprang up from his demon's dying body. Quick as a thought, a like warrior rose up from his twin, and a fresh battle began.

It ran the same course as the other. The instant its fury showed the slightest sign of abating, new horrors took up the warfare. Hideous serpents, monster toads, slime creatures that filled the air with a choking stench—each was more terrifying and repellant than the last, and each wrought its worst in the fiery circle. Yet, neither Thropos nor Faring could best the evil magic of the other. The contest between the wizards continued to be a draw.

When this impasse became obvious to all, Thropos took a new tack. Abandoning his latest creation—a huge white worm that secreted acid from the countless tentacles covering its coiled length—he stood, human, before Faring and smiled.

Then he metamorphosed into a dragon.

Like a nightmare version of one of the shapeshifting, undersea Pleons, Thropos's twisted form suddenly stretched skyward and turned blacker than the wizard's robes. Snout, tail, wings, and claws erupted from the monstrous body, and the man's skin hardened into metallic scales. The creature—no longer recognizable as Thropos—lowered its head, firing a blast of scorching breath at its opponent.

But Faring's body had shimmered and reformed as well, into the form of a blood-red dragon. Shrieking, it launched itself at the sky, evading the fiery assault. The black beast, too, rose into the air. Wheeling, they flapped great wings in a wide circle and then, claws outstretched, made a raking pass at each other. Flames shot from their nostrils. The hot wind from their leathery wings shriveled the grass below and collapsed some of the Sturite tents.

"I wouldn't like to meet one of those when it's feeling out of sorts," Phen muttered. Hardly hearing him, Albin and Reawen stared up at the battle in the sky in amazement.

The dragons wheeled, screamed, and made another pass. The red dived toward the earth, then shot back up again, the black soaring right after. The red spun, and the two beasts faced off again, tearing at each other with vicious swipes that made all who watched shudder and flinch. Still, neither combatant gained ground. Finally, exhausted and bloodied, both sank to the earth within the boundary fires, and the beastlike forms cracked and fell away, revealing the two wizards in their original shapes.

"Die!" Thropos cried, as he rose from the remnants of his dragon body. Long streamers of blue lightning crackled from his outstretched fingers and struck his opponent with such impact that they knocked Faring back almost into the flames of the circle.

Faring's recovery was instantaneous. Yellow bolts of storm energy flowed from him. The blue and the yellow clashed, spitting clouds of sizzling sparks. They jammed the fiery magic compass with such explosions of sound and color that the wizards themselves seemed lost in the dazzling melee. Yet neither let up. Again and again, they smote each other.

"How long can they go on like this!" Albin exclaimed.

"Not forever lad," Phen answered. "Laying out that brand of energy has to be taking its toll on the both of them. But better they should beat each other into smithereens than that they should be doing it to us."

"I think that last lightning blast hurt Faring," Reawen whispered through whitened lips. Her face expressed her horror. "See how he doubled over and dropped to his knees when it struck?"

Thropos, too, saw that he'd finally delivered a telling blow. "Now," he shrieked maniacally, "for the *coup d'grace*."

As he spoke, a dagger appeared in one of his blackened hands. Cel's cage, which had been sitting on the stump outside the circle of flame, flew into the other hand. "It's a pillawn," Thropos screeched, holding the cage aloft. "Remember the spell that Perbledom told us of, the spell that would crumble a wizard—any wizard—into dust? Only it was out of reach, because it required an ingredient impossibly rare, the living heart of a pillawn!"

"He's going to kill Cel!" Reawen cried, and started up to rush forward. Phen and Albin dragged her down by the arms, and just in time. For at that very instant Cel, who'd been listening to all this with an unnatural calm, bolted from her unlocked cage. With an unearthly cry, she plunged her razor-sharp talons into Thropos's startled face.

"Aiiiiiii!" he screamed as the pillawn darted away. Then he screamed again, a long hideous wail. Bolts of yellow death streamed out from the fallen Faring's fingertips and ignited the vindictive little wizard. Before the goggling eyes of the Sturites, he burst into a ball of oily flame.

"Cel!" Reawen cried.

"She flew to safety. Now we must away from here, my lady," Phen whispered urgently. He shot a meaningful look at Albin.

"Are you sure? Did you see?" Reawen demanded.

"Sure as I can be. Now's the time to get ourselves to the tower, before the Sturites recover from these doings and decide to have a look around. In a way, it was bad luck that Faring should decide to have at Thropos tonight. After Arant's had time to think it over, he might wonder if that show wasn't meant to distract him from something else that was going on. Now, take our arms and let us help you over this patch of rough ground here."

With the hubbub of the Sturite camp ringing in their ears and the acrid stench of the battle filling their nostrils, the three scurried back into the night past the enemy outpost.

"What do you suppose happened to Faring?" Reawen whispered when they were well clear of the nightmarish scene.

Albin looked at her sympathetically. He'd long suspected that Brone's mentor was also Reawen's father. Now, something in her expression told him she knew it to be true.

"I don't know," said Phen. "He took some terrible punishment. But if any mortal can turn up whole after such a beating, it'd be that wizard."

The domis of water stopped in her tracks. "I shouldn't be walking away from him like this. I should go back."

Albin grabbed her wrist. "Reawen, you can't. You just absolutely can't. If we're to save Jedestrom, we cannot think of him now. If Thropos has killed him, there's nothing you can do. If he hasn't, there's probably still nothing you can do, and he'll take care of himself. We've a terrible task before us, and already the night is half over."

Reawen stood for a long moment, debating. At last, reluctantly, she nodded and started forward. Soon the tower where Phen and Albin had stored the greenfire loomed before them.

"It looks deserted," Reawen said. "Isn't anyone guarding it?"

"Brone set guards," Phen answered, "but if they had any sense at all, they fled when the Sturites came."

"Let's hope Arant hasn't posted men there himself," said Albin.

"He might have," Phen admitted. "My suspicion is he hasn't found the greenfire yet. If he had, I think we'd know by now."

Chewing on that thought, the three cautiously made their way up the slope to the tower.

"I don't see anyone at all."

"Nor I," Phen agreed with Albin, "I think we may be in luck." He turned to Reawen, who showed unmistakable signs of strain. Her breathing was labored and so were her steps. Under the moon her skin was waxen. "I know it's a lot to ask after what ye've been through," Phen began sympathetically, "but before we start, I must know if you still think you can bring water to the top of that hill."

"There are no active wells or streams nearby."

"I know that, lady. I know I'm askin' the impossible. So I must have your answer before we dare try to set this thing in motion. For if there's no hope of water, we're defeated before we even begin."

Wearily, Reawen nodded, then closed her eyes. For several minutes she stood in silence, apparently communing with some unseen force. When she finally opened her eyes again she said, "There's an inactive spring on the other side of this hill. It's been dried up for centuries, but it may be possible to reawaken it."

Phen rubbed his nose unhappily. "May be?"

"May be," Reawen repeated. "I won't know until I try. And if I understand the nature of your greenfire correctly, I may not do that until all is ready."

Phen nodded his understanding. "It'll take a bit of time for the lad and me to cart the greenfire down and spread it aright. Sit here and take some ease, my lady, while we work. I'll lay my leather vest on the grass to keep the dew from your gown."

Gratefully, Reawen accepted Phen's gallantry. While she rested and searched for strength, Albin scaled the outside of the locked watchtower. He wriggled in through a window slit and, using a rope sling, began lowering barrel after barrel packed with the volatile greenfire powder.

"Aren't you afraid the dew will set it off?" Reawen asked. She watched Phen begin to sprinkle the innocent-looking substance in a line paralleling the Sturite camp and the river.

"Not enough wet here to set it on the march, I judge," Phen grunted. "Though, we may see a sparkle or two."

Sure enough, flares of green light began to leap up here and there along the trail Phen and Albin were creating. Fortunately, it had been very dry in recent days. The dew on the grass was slight, so the flares quickly died away. Still, they were alarming and highly conspicuous.

"What if the Sturites see those flashes and come to investigate?" Reawen hissed after a particularly bright one.

"Let's hope they're either asleep, too drunk, or too busy sweeping up what's left of their wizard's ashes to see straight by now," Phen answered. But he shot Albin a worried look. "Best step it up passing those canisters, so you can climb back down and help me, lad. The sooner we get this job done, the more likely we are to pull it off and keep our skins whole into the bargain."

As the night wore on, Reawen sat on the grass wringing her hands and brooding. She stewed about everything—the well-being of the babe moving fretfully within her, Brone, Faring, the project at hand, and Cel. The last of these worries was relieved when white wings showed up in the dark sky. A plump white body dropped like a weighted cushion to Reawen's shoulder.

Are you well, mistress? the pillawn inquired sweetly.

"Cel! Oh, Cel! You almost frightened me to death back there! Where have you been?"

Washing my talons clean of a cruel wizard's blood. The pillawn chittered deep in her throat and then nuzzled her mistress's hair. *I did frighten Thropos to death, and that is what matters, my sweetling. For he was an evil, nasty man, and the world will be a better place without him. Now, tell Cel what dangerous and ill-advised thing you and your friends are about here.*

* * * * *

On the other side of Jedestrom's beleaguered walls, deep within the Plat, Brone stirred. Posted to watch at his bedside while Faring went off on some unexplained mission was Halow, the physician. Halow cocked his balding head.

A moment later the physician opened the door, peered out, and said to the guard posted there, "Awaken Sepok and Crai. I think I just saw the king move his hand."

After the soldier scurried off, Halow went back inside to stand watch. The king lay still as death, and the nervous little physician began to wonder if he'd been imagining things. If that was the case, his colleagues would not be happy at being awakened at this absurd hour. However, just as he bit his nails and looked anxiously at the door, Brone stirred again. The king's hands opened and flexed, and he turned his head back and forth, as if fighting away some troublesome dream. A low groan escaped his lips, and his burnished eyelashes fluttered.

Eagerly, Halow hurried forward. He put an exploratory hand on Brone's forehead and then pressed his ear to the king's broad chest.

"What are you doing? What's happened?" Brone said distinctly.

Startled, Halow looked up to see the king gazing at him. When their eyes met, Brone tried pushing himself into a sitting position. He fell back with a hoarse cry of frustration.

"No, no, my liege. You mustn't move! You've been very ill!" Incoherently, and with much fluttering of his hands, Halow explained what had happened. When he came to the part about the Sturites encamped outside the walls of Jedestrom and preparing to lay siege to the city, Brone's blue eyes, which had been rather unfocused, narrowed to sapphire slashes. He cursed long and hard, then demanded, "Where is Faring?"

"I do not know, Sire. He would not say where he was going."

"What of my wife? Is she still well guarded in the keep?"

"I know nothing of her, either, I'm afraid. Since you fell into a coma, all has been at sixes and sevens. And with the Sturites

preparing to batter down the walls and kill us in our beds . . ."
Halow's voice trailed off, and he clasped his hands together, for
the king had succeeded in sitting up and was swinging his long
legs over the side of the bed.

"If we stay in our beds, they certainly will kill us. Get my
clothes and my sword and help me dress!"

"Oh, no, Sire, you're too . . ." At the withering look he
received from Brone, the physician swallowed, then scurried to
carry out his orders.

A few minutes later, Brone brushed past Halow's blinking,
freshly awakened colleagues. Ignoring them, he strode down
the corridor and out to the stables. The first thing he did, after
leaping astride his favorite white stallion, was ride to the city
walls where astonished soldiers welcomed him. When he
shouted for Buw and Phen, several soldiers and citizens scurried to find the commander and the king's advisor. While they
were gone, an officer informed the king of how Arant had lured
the better part of the army out of the city, where they were
presently chasing a will-o'-the-wisp too far to the west to be of
any use during the imminent siege.

When the men returned with Buw, reporting that Phen was
nowhere to be found, the king dispensed with greeting the
exhausted commander. "How long do you think we have?"
Brone questioned grimly.

The answer was bleaker yet. "They'll come at us by morning's my guess," the old weapons master allowed. "There's
something happening out there, and it doesn't bode well.
Flashes of fire and light such as you wouldn't believe."

"Where's Albin?" Brone asked.

"He hasn't been seen for hours," Buw replied gruffly. "Trust
him and Phen to go out there to reconnoiter and get themselves in trouble."

Brone's scowl deepened. He thought of the greenfire and
cursed himself for allowing it to be stored outside the city
walls. It wouldn't surprise him if Phen and Albin had risked

capture by the Sturites, a fate literally worse than death, to try to recover the volatile powder.

With a curt but encouraging word to his soldiers and a nod to Buw, he remounted his horse and headed toward the keep. As he rode, a wave of nausea swept through him. Groaning, he clung to the saddle to keep from toppling. I feel like a sick babe, he thought with disgust. My muscles have gone soft as an invalid's. But there was no time for weakness now. Whatever had put him in a coma for two days—and was still sapping his strength—would have to be ignored.

Brone found the keep deserted. Hurling an oath at the open door, he knocked it to one side and rushed upstairs to Reawen's quarters. As he had suspected, they were empty. For long minutes he stood staring around at the signs of her habitation—her abandoned embroidery, the chair where she had liked to sit by the window tending her hair, the silver combs and brushes he had gifted her with. He picked one up and touched his finger to an ebony strand caught in the bristles. Where had his reluctant wife flown to? he wondered. Was she now in the Sturite camp, an ally of the domi after all? Was she happily plotting his overthrow with them?

The whoosh of wings yanked him from his bitter reverie. A plump white bird sailed through the window and landed on the backrail of Reawen's chair. There it folded its wings and gazed out at him from improbable purple eyes. *If you are looking for your leman, you will not find her here.*

Brone's jaw sagged. "It talked! In my mind!" His expression went from astonishment to suspicion. "What are you, bird? Some shapechanging witch, or perhaps a wizard in disguise?"

I am a pillawn, Cel said with dignity. *Pillawns knew speech when you humans were still grunting and throwing sticks.*

"But pillawns are . . ."

We are not extinct. Merely extremely scarce. Indeed, I am the last of my race, she added with a trace of sadness. *However, I did not come here to speak of myself, but of your wife.*

Brone took a step forward. "You know where my wife is, pillawn?"

Indeed I do, and so should you. For you love her, do you not? Oh, yes, I could see that from the first.

"It matters not what I feel for her," Brone retorted stiffly. "She hates me."

A woman's heart is not always so easy to read. How can Reawen hate you when she bears your child and even now is doing a dangerous deed to help you? She's at the tower, preparing to bring water to greenfire. Cel brushed Brone's forehead with a soft white wing. *If you want your wife and child to survive, you must help her.*

Chapter Sixteen

"Quietly now." Brone motioned to the small party of mounted soldiers and citizens behind him. After he'd left the minimum of troops behind to defend Jedestrom's walls, there'd been precious few to spare for this foray. These he'd led through a secret passageway behind the Plat. Now, with their horses' hooves muffled, they followed him around the outside of the city.

"We'll circle to the left of the Sturite camp," he'd explained to Buw when they set off. "If we can pass without them seeing us and get to the tower—"

Buw shook his head. "Not much chance of that."

Brone's mouth hardened. "Maybe not, but we'll have to try. Small as our numbers are, we can't challenge them openly. If we stay holed up in Jedestrom, we and our people will be slaughtered like rats. This is our only other option."

Now, as they came around the curve of the western wall, they stopped to take stock.

"The seven hells!" Buw muttered. "Those Sturites are swarming like dung beetles. Just look, they've got every square foot of space to either side of the north road covered."

"They're making ready to attack," said Brone.

"And it looks as if it's going to be a damned nasty battle," Buw agreed.

Behind them, the other Peninsulans murmured uneasily. They were loyal, well-trained men. But even the bravest of them had to be dismayed by the scene before them. The Sturites were assembling a massive, well-armed force.

To see their way, the invaders had appointed boys to carry lanterns. Their lights moved and swayed across the field in front of the city gates like a vast blanket of candle points. The lights showed off dense ranks of archers and foot soldiers. Above their heads, dark clouds of war eagles circled and dipped ominously. As Brone listened to their harsh cries, he thought of gentle Cel and hoped she'd flown to safety.

"That rumbling we hear must be chariots," Buw commented. "I've seen Sturite attack chariots. The armor on them will slice an enemy's horse to pieces. There must be hundreds of the things rolling about out there to make such a noise. Why, the very ground is shaking. If they come on us, we haven't a prayer against them."

"Then we'll have to try to avoid them," Brone answered in a steady voice. "Come, we'll lead our horses and veer far to the west, where we can get some protection from hills and trees. If we can get around behind the bulk of the Sturite forces, we can pick a path to the tower." As Brone spoke, he gazed off in the direction he knew the tower lay. A faint flash of green caught his eye and made his heart stutter.

It captured Buw's attention as well. "Dragon breath! What was that?"

"Reawen, Phen, and Albin," Brone answered shortly. "They must have reached the tower. I'd wager they are bringing out the greenfire."

"You mean, you think they're scattering it about?" Buw's question came in a muffled roar.

"That must have been their purpose in going," Brone retorted sternly. "Let's hope that flash came from them and not our enemies."

"Balls of flame, it won't matter if they get the stuff lit when we're halfway there. We'll be caught between the greenfire and the Sturites."

"We have to risk it. More likely, the Sturites will see those sparks and head for the tower themselves." As he spoke, Brone gave the signal. His men dismounted and, looking nervously from right to left, led their horses through the shadows.

Stealthily, they moved around the Sturite lights. As they crept along, several parties of Sturites passed within yards. Somehow the Peninsulans went undetected.

"That was close," Buw whispered when the last of the enemy had disappeared over a rise. "For a minute there, I could smell Sturite sweat. If one of our horses had whickered, it would have been all over with us. Luck is with you tonight."

"I hope so," Brone said through his teeth. He glanced toward the tower, now a dark shape blending with the night sky. Again, a flicker of green gave warning that it wasn't deserted. What were Phen and Albin doing? And Reawen—would he see her before long? Would he be able to defend her, as Cel had told him he must? He passed a hand over his brow and smothered a curse. He felt weak still. Beneath him, his legs trembled slightly. He glanced back to make sure none of his men had seen, and then steadied himself. This was no time for weakness.

They had gained another fifty yards, and Brone was beginning to hope they might win through undetected. As they rounded a low rise, a throaty voice seemed to rip away the cloak of night.

"I do believe it's Brone and a party of soldiers. Well, well, well."

The king and his men froze.

"That was a woman's voice!" Buw exclaimed. "Whose?"

As they stared into the darkness, the moon emerged from behind a cloud and spotlighted a sensuously rounded shape. "Driona!" Brone exclaimed.

She stepped forward into full view. "Yes, it is I. After all these years, we finally meet once more. How poetic."

Smiling broadly, the earth domis opened her arms wide and displayed a full bosom only lightly covered by her red silk gown. She was dressed as if for a celebration. She wore her dark hair coiled high on her head and studded with diamonds. A rich velvet cloak hung from her shoulders to her feet which, as always, were bare. Her broad toes were planted firmly in the ground. "Have you missed me, Brone?" she murmured.

"What is it you want, Driona?"

Instead of answering, she stood looking him up and down. An amused half-smile played on her full lips, but there was interest and hunger in her eyes. "You've changed, and not for the better, my love. When I knew you, you were the most beautiful youth. Now—" She shook her head and clicked her tongue. "Still, you've turned into a handsome enough man. I remember well what we shared before you played me that mean trick and stole my stone." She gave a throaty laugh. "You can't have forgotten, either. Come with me, Brone. It's quite useless for you to stay here trying to defend Jedestrom. In the morning, the Sturites will take it. Save yourself and come with me," she crooned. "I can hide you away from everyone. With me you will be safe."

The king drew his sword. "I don't wish to harm you, Driona. But I must silence you. I can't allow you to give the alarm."

She drew herself up and stared at him bleakly. "Do you reject me again, then? I warn you, think carefully."

Motioning his men to stay behind him, Brone began to walk toward her. "I'm no longer a boy. I'm Jedestrom's king. Of course I must defend my city."

"Is it because of that silly girl, Reawen?" Driona's face contorted, became heavy and ugly with rage. "Oh, twice foolish man," she grated. "Reawen took only her stone from you. I will take everything you have, including your life and your kingdom!"

Imperiously, Driona stamped one broad bare foot into the earth. A cloud of dust rose up around her thick ankles. An instant later the ground rumbled. While his men stood gawking, Brone stopped and then took a wary step backward. Directly in front of him, as if an unseen hand were ripping it open, the earth muttered in protest. Then it cracked. Slowly, the breach widened and then yawned. From inside the opening, a whirring, clicking noise could suddenly be heard.

"Stand back!" Buw cried. He rushed forward, seized his king's arm and pushed him aside. Taken off guard, Brone stumbled back. He recovered himself and looked up. Then, like the soldiers surrounding him, he gaped in astonishment. Black ants the size of men were swarming up out of the hole in the earth.

"Attack!" Driona cried out to her newly hatched brood. "Kill them. Kill them all!"

Mandibles clicking, the first ant rushed at Buw. With a loud war cry, the burly arms master lopped off its head with his broadsword. But there seemed no end to the insect monsters pouring from the earth like a dark tide. Seconds later, Buw was surrounded by them. In desperation, he began to swing his mace. It whirled in a vicious circle around him. Ant heads and legs, antennae, and gasters flew in all directions. Still, they came.

Meanwhile, panicked by the unfamiliar scent and sound of the huge insects, the horses reared and flailed their legs. Seconds later they galloped off into the night, trampling many ants beneath their pounding hooves.

Signaling his men to follow him, Brone flung himself into the melee. Steering clear of Buw's whirling mace, he slashed and stabbed at insect bodies. Nothing stopped the creatures. They were like one body with many heads, one mind with many bodies. New ones merely stepped over their fallen fellows and stabbed back at him with their horned legs and clicking mandibles.

At last—though Buw defended himself bravely, slaughtering dozens of the hideous creatures with his flying mace and slashing broadsword—they overpowered him. Horrified, Brone saw one of them tear off his old friend's head and carry it away in its jaws as a prize.

With a cry of rage, Brone destroyed the creature, slashing through its cohorts until he could lop its body in two. But he could not defend all his men. They fought with great courage.

Many more ants than men fell. But Driona had created hundreds of the creatures, and none of them knew fear. As Brone's soldiers exterminated them, more simply climbed over the mangled insect bodies and took up the fight.

An hour later, Brone battled virtually alone, surrounded by the corpses of fallen ants and men. As he slashed and stabbed, he kept looking toward the tower. Reawen was up there and in danger, he kept telling himself. Somehow he had to survive this horror and get to her. The thought was like a flow of fresh adrenalin. It gave him more strength than he'd ever known. With a cry, he swung his sword in a wide, destroying arc.

* * * * *

At the tower, neither Phen and Albin nor Reawen knew of Brone's heroic battle with Driona's ants. The three were far too busy trying to accomplish the task they'd assigned themselves to give much thought to what was going on in the dark valley below. By the time Phen and Albin finally finished deploying the powder, the stars had faded, and the first faint gray fingers of dawn had begun to scratch the sky.

"Now is our most dangerous hour," Phen muttered. "If the Sturites should happen to look this direction, they could get curious about these little pops of green we're still settin' off." He turned to Reawen. "The greenfire's all laid out, milady. Are you ready to make happen what must to set it moving?"

As Phen asked his question, Albin turned to study Reawen. He had never seen her look so pale and tired. Her face was drawn. Deep shadows ringed her eyes. She had wrapped her arms around her chest, as if to shield some deep unrest within. Knowing her condition and the night she'd had, he was concerned for her. But there was nothing he could do to make her task easier. Everything depended on her now.

With a brief nod, she rose, shook the grass from her skirts and glided down the slope. Phen and Albin followed behind.

When she reached the spot where she claimed an old spring had once flowed, they stationed themselves off at a little distance and shot each other worried looks.

"Don't look like much, does it?" Phen muttered under his breath.

"If Reawen says there was water there, then there was," Albin whispered back. But he eyed the spot anxiously. Now it was nothing but a sandy trough covered over with weed.

Over her shoulder, Reawen glanced back at them. "I know it doesn't look hopeful," she said, "but deep below this spot, water still winds through the earth's bosom. I believe I can bring it to the surface. That is, I can if my stone cooperates."

"What if it doesn't?" Phen queried.

Reawen shrugged. "I can only try."

"Aye, but even if you bring the water to the surface, can you make it flow uphill and creep across this meadow until it touches the powder and sets it ablaze?"

"That I don't know. It's certain I could have a few months ago. But now with the child inside me so large and the stone in rebellion——" Reawen shook her head. "Again, I can only try and promise to do my best."

"I hope you succeed, milady, for if you don't, and Arant and his pack of hyenas find us up here come morning——" Phen didn't need to finish the thought. Everyone there understood its meaning.

Tentatively, Reawen knelt and placed her hands over the area. "The water has receded a great distance," she murmured. "I can feel it down there, but it's very faint."

Once again, Albin and Phen shot each other worried glances and then looked back at Reawen. She still knelt on the ground. Now, she straightened her upper body and took the stone from the silver band she wore. Holding it clasped between her palms, she closed her eyes.

"Looks as if she's prayin'," Phen mumbled.

"I think what she does with the stone is something like

that," Albin whispered back.

A few yards away from them, Reawen concentrated all her thoughts on her struggle to commune. She felt the green stone's power flowing all around her, yet evading her control. Of a certainty, it did not like her as she was, pregnant with another being who hadn't established a claim to its forces. As if that being knew what was happening and felt threatened, it jerked and kicked in protest.

"Be quiet, my little one, be quiet," Reawen crooned. Then, ignoring the tumult in her belly, she concentrated all her strength on her task. She pictured the dark, secret water flowing a mile deep within the earth's mysterious womb. It, too, resisted her call. For it had flowed a long time in its new haven and didn't wish to leave it. Nevertheless, Reawen implored and then exhorted.

"Rise, rise ye drowned waters. Seek the light and air, the sun and grass! Bury yourself no more!"

For many minutes Reawen knelt, locked in a battle of wills with the water and her recalcitrant stone. For several anxious minutes, she realized her prayer was having an opposite effect. Instead of bringing the water upward, the stone was sending it down deeper into the earth. Against this, Reawen struggled and fought.

"Nothing's happening," whispered Phen.

"Oh, I think it is," answered Albin. "Can't you feel the power in the air?"

"I can feel something's afoot, and I can still see them green pops going off on the hill. I just hope the Sturites aren't feeling and seeing the same things as me."

At last the water began responding properly to Reawen's call. It stopped burrowing deeper and began to seep upward. Up, up it came, finding its way through rock and stone, clay and sand.

Reawen stood, lifted her face and held her hands out over the dry sand at her feet. A moment later a dark spot appeared in the ground and a tiny gurgle of moisture bubbled forth.

"Well, I'll be," Phen exclaimed. "She did it! Now, if she can just get it up the hill."

"She can, I know she can."

Phen tapped Albin's shoulder. "Maybe we'd best leave her to it while we go up and make sure all's well. I know I'm a worrier, but still, I've got a funny feelin'."

With several backward looks at Reawen, the two hurried to the top of the slope. There they surveyed the long line of powder they'd laid during the night. Pink had replaced the streaks of gray in the sky and somewhere a bird twittered.

"Dawn's comin'," Phen muttered to himself. He jumped the powder and then strode to the other side of the tower to get a better look at the Sturite camp. As Albin followed, a premonition of danger rippled up his spine. He put his hand on the sword, which, until now, had dangled uselessly at his belt. On impulse, he drew it.

Victory leapt to his hand and fitted itself there as if it were an extension of his arm. It was as if the sword had willed him to draw it. But Albin had no time to notice or think about this phenomenon. He heard a bloodcurdling war cry and whirled to his right. Arant and a half dozen howling Sturite knights rushed toward the slope from a copse of trees. They had left their camp on a predawn patrol, noticed the flashes of green near the tower, and decided to investigate.

As they hurtled toward Phen and Albin, their red braids seemed to writhe in the wind and their faces contorted in rage. "Hack the fools to pieces!" Arant commanded between horrific battle cries. "Salt the earth with their blood!"

"We're in for it!" Phen yelled. With a bloodcurdling cry of his own, he lifted his axe and whirled it around his head. "Stand fast and give them what for!"

Albin needed no encouragement. His arm tingled with a thrilling new heat that sang through his whole body. It was as if Victory wanted to fight, needed to fight. Sword in one hand, knife in the other, Albin found himself pelting forward to meet Arant's pack of killers.

A flame-haired giant wearing an ugly snarl rushed at him. As Albin lifted his arm and brought Victory hurtling down to clash with the screaming Sturite's weapon, a fierce unfamiliar joy flooded his system. He knew nothing of swordsmanship and had never pictured himself a warrior. Yet that seemed to matter not. The sword in his arm had sprung to life. With a terrifying yet exhilarating will of its own, it slashed and cut.

Wielding the weapon with all the panache of a seasoned fighter, Albin met two more attackers and bested them with a dazzling display of skill. But even with Phen fighting stoutly at his side, it was not enough. Their enemies were formidable and outnumbered them six to one.

Suddenly, however, the odds changed. Sword upraised, Brone dashed from the shadows and joined the fray. The sight of the king, standing apparently whole and healthy, sent another thrill of power through Albin. With a joyous cry, he redoubled his efforts.

Brone's startling appearance affected the Sturite warriors as well. But it wasn't so much Brone as the horde of giant warrior ants chasing after him that unnerved them. Brone had managed to fight his way through the insects and had rushed toward the slope to the tower. Determined to hunt him down as their mistress instructed, the ants followed. But the Sturites, who knew nothing of Driona's insect army, misinterpreted what they saw. Believing the ants were with Brone, they set on them.

"Kill the insects and leave the king to me!" Arant yelled to his cohorts. "His blood is to be mine!"

While the other Sturite knights concentrated their efforts on Phen, Albin, and the ants, Arant closed with Brone.

"So, we meet again!" he snarled as he leaped at the Peninsula's ruler. He jabbed with a short but wicked-looking sword, which he held low in front of him. As he attacked, his green eyes flickered with hatred.

Brone held a similar weapon. Though his face was pale from the strain of his long ordeal battling the insects, his blue eyes glittered like the sapphires from a dragon's horde. "We meet for the final time," he agreed. Leaping forward, he parried a heavy blow and then wielded one of his own.

"You are pale as death, a man obviously unwell!" Arant taunted. "But do not look to me for quarter!"

"No quarter!" Brone gritted between his teeth.

"To the death!" Arant screamed. He struck out viciously. "You shall never see Jedestrom again. When I'm through hacking you to pieces, I promise you I'll burn it and all its people to the ground!"

Chapter Seventeen

On the other side of the hill, Reawen coaxed a trickle of water up the steep slope. She knew a battle raged out of sight. She could hear the clash of blades and the thump of blows, accompanied by bellows, curses, and screams of rage. She also knew she must block it from her mind and concentrate on her task.

If she lost concentration at this crucial time, all would be lost. The water would disappear back into its channel deep beneath the earth. Staggering with exhaustion as she was, she would not have the strength to call it forth again in time.

"Up, up," she whispered to the water. "Climb up through the grass, up toward the light." She crooned to it as if it were the restless baby turning inside her. She begged and cajoled, urged and pleaded. And all the time she fought with her recalcitrant stone, forcing it to her will.

The shrieks, howls, and clashes of metal atop the hill grew louder and more frightening. Yet Reawen refused to let them shake her. She focused all her attention on her objective. She didn't waver, even when Cel flew out of the pinkening sky and landed on her shoulder.

That's right, the pillawn's voice whispered in her head. *You can do it. Everything depends on your skill and strength now.*

Above them, Arant and Brone circled and lunged. Physically, the two matched each other well. Each was tall and muscular, each filled with rage. But Arant was healthy and well rested. Brone, badly weakened by Thropos's poison and his battle with Driona's ants, had only half his usual stamina to call upon.

Nevertheless, he returned Arant's assaults with interest. His sword flashed and sang as he dealt blow after blow.

"Hah!" the redheaded patricide yelled. He raised his sword over his head and brought it slamming down. At the last instant, Brone managed to turn it aside, but only just. Blood dripped from his shoulder where Arant had slid in under his guard during a furious exchange. But Arant, too, was freshening the earth with his blood. Sweat, mixed with blood from head wounds, half-blinded both men.

A few yards to the east of the battling kings, a wild melee raged. Albin and Phen had each killed one of their attackers and were giving a good account of themselves with the others. Fortunately, most of the Sturites were being kept busy by the ants.

Albin was in the grip of a fighting fever the likes of which he'd never even imagined before. He owed it to the sword, he vaguely realized, but as he aimed a killing thrust at one of the two Sturite giants lunging at him, he had no time to dwell on the implications of this fact.

"Good aim, lad!" Phen shouted as he landed a fatal crack with his fearsome battle-axe, earning himself a momentary respite from the melee. "I'm surprised to see you have so much steel in your spine. Truth is, I'd never have guessed you had it in you."

Twenty yards away, Arant rushed Brone in another try at slipping a stabbing blow under his guard. He failed, but managed to slash his opponent's arm. As Brone's blood pumped from this new wound, the Sturite king leered triumphantly.

Refusing to show any sign of weakness, Brone redoubled his own attack, slashing, parrying, stabbing. But he felt lightheaded and knew that his strength was ebbing fast. If he was not to be Arant's victim, he must bring this duel to a close quickly. But how, when nausea clawed at him, blood gushed from his wounds, and Arant's image was beginning to swim in his hazy vision?

At that instant, Brone caught a glimpse of Reawen from the

corner of his eye. She had just appeared on the other side of the hill.

Arant, too, had seen her. His evil leer twisted sadistically. "So your pretty wife joins our party," he sneered. "Good, for when I've done with you, I'll take her and then cut the child she carries out of her belly. After this night, there'll be nothing of yours left alive, Peninsulan!"

A hundred yards away, Reawen gasped, taking in all that was happening. Hordes of monster ants swarming up from the valley below were beginning to overcome the Sturite war party. She, Phen, Albin, and Brone would be their next victims. Phen and Albin, intent on fighting the one opponent they each had left, were surrounded by dead bodies. Her husband was white as death and covered with blood. Worse, if the king and her companions had been on the right side of the powdered line of greenfire, she might have been able to save them. But they were on the wrong side.

You can't stop now, Cel urged. *If you hesitate, the water will slip back down to its source, and all will have been in vain.*

"But if I bring water across to the greenfire, Albin, Phen, and Brone will be killed!" Reawen cried.

Do you care so much about yon king and his people? asked Cel.

Reawen gazed at the pillawn in horror. "Of course, I care!"

Then do what you must, and leave it to your husband and friends to do what they must.

Brone and Arant heard none of this. They were lost in the frenzied heat of their own private confrontation. The Sturite's threat against Reawen had released a new flame of fury in Brone. Like a berserker, he attacked Arant, his sword whirling and thrusting with his mad attacks. Despite the blood that gushed from his shoulders and arms, nothing the redheaded king did would stop his wild charge.

Phen and Albin, who had dispatched the last of their own opponents, turned to see what aid they could give their belea-guered liege. They were too late to help him. With a final

passionate cry, he buried his blade in Arant's belly. The Sturite
sank to the ground. A moment later, so did Brone.

Meanwhile, Reawen had coaxed the trickle of water to
within a few feet of the greenfire. There she stopped, unwilling
to bring it any closer and take the chance of seeing her friends
and Brone incinerated.

"There's an army of monsters from the seven hells heading
up the hill toward us!" Phen cried. "And, the stars help us,
behind them there's another army of Sturites!"

Albin saw that it was true. The sun had risen in the sky,
bathing the tower and everyone on the hill in rosy light. It
spotlighted the horde of huge black ants stampeding ever
closer. Sturites rushed up to defend their fallen king; a shower
of arrows filled the sky, arched over the swarming ants, and fell
to within inches of Brone's unconscious body.

"Quick, carry the king to the other side of the line of greenfire!" Phen ordered.

Before the words were completely out, Albin had sheathed
Victory and seized Brone's feet. Phen grabbed his arms and
together the two hefted him to safety. "Take the water to the
line, my lady!" Phen shouted, "And do it quickly, or we'll be
torn apart by ants or cut to ribbons by Sturites!"

Reawen coaxed the water to within a foot of the greenfire,
but there she hesitated again. "Shouldn't we try to save Arant?"

But already it was too late. At that instant, the water seemed
to make its own decision. It streamed toward the powder.
There was a second's hesitation, as if the greenfire were holding
its breath and marshaling its strength. Another volley of arrows
landed all around the little party of Peninsulans. One came to
within an inch of Cel, who squawked and streaked into the sky
like a shooting star.

Mere feet away, on the opposite side of the powder line, the
infuriated ants clacked their mandibles and reached with their
shiny appendages. Behind them, Sturites whirled maces and
brandished swords. Abruptly the Sturites' snarling visages and

the ants' bulging eyes and waving antennae vanished in a whooshing wall of green flame. Reawen screamed and fell back, as did Phen and Albin.

It was one thing to be told what greenfire would do or to see it in miniature, harmlessly controlled on a test table. It was quite another to witness its full destructive power unleashed on a grand scale. Even more horrifying, the ants, programmed by Driona to attack Brone, marched directly into it. Ant bodies burst into flame, their heads and legs raining down among twisted wisps of ash.

"What about the Sturites?" Albin cried as he stared awe-struck at the solid blockade of emerald flame. "Are they going to be burned alive in that, too?"

"Not if they're smart enough to drop their weapons and run in the other direction," answered Phen. "It's not moving fast, you'll notice. Slow and steady."

"And, despite the way it killed the ants, it's not particularly hot, either," Reawen observed breathlessly.

"Maybe not, but it's burning everything in its path good and proper." Phen pointed a stubby finger at the blackened area the greenfire left as it marched downhill. "I'll tell you true, until this minute, I wasn't really sure it would work."

"It's working, all right," said Albin. Whatever had stood in its path was there no longer. Arant's body was gone forever.

Reawen glanced down at Brone, bleeding and unconscious. "What if the greenfire moves toward Jedestrom instead of the river?"

"It won't, milady. It'll go straight for the Har and turn everything in between into coals. That includes the Sturite camp with all that's in it."

"What about the Sturites themselves?" Albin questioned.

"It'll drive them into the water with nothing more than they can carry. All their weapons and supplies will be gone. With Arant out of the way, they'll have no choice but to get back in their boats and give up the fight," Phen answered with satisfaction. "We've won! Just the three of us here have defeated Arant, his whole army, and a mess of monster ants to boot."

As Phen spoke, he and Albin gazed with dreadful fascination at the wall of greenfire. Remorselessly, it advanced across the field that lay between it and the enemy encampment.

Next to them, Reawen had eyes only for Brone. "We have to do something for the king," she exclaimed. Falling to her knees, she tore a strip from her gown. In a flurry of anxiety, she tried to bind up the worst of his wounds. "He's taken a terrible beating, and he's bleeding hideously!"

Albin squatted next to Reawen and pressed a hand to the king's cold forehead. "I'll run for help." He leaped back up to his feet. "There can be no danger now." It seemed he was right. Between Jedestrom's city walls and the greenfire, all was clear.

Among the invaders, however, chaos reigned.

As Phen had predicted, the Sturites were fleeing for their lives, and they were leaving behind everything they had brought for the assault on Jedestrom. However, two figures stood their ground, scornfully ignoring the mass of terrified soldiers running past them.

"It's ended," Driona said. "That whey-faced little bitch has betrayed us. There's nothing for it. We must run for the river, too."

"I can't," Taunis snarled. "Have you forgotten what I am? I can't turn tail like these other rats if water's my only salvation. Whatever this green flame is, I have to stand and fight it."

"Can you do that?" Driona queried nervously.

Despite the threat bearing down on them, Taunis shot her a scornful look. "What choice do I have? Join the Sturite vermin and save yourself, woman. Leave me to my fate!"

Driona considered. "I don't fancy the river, either. No, we are allies. If either of us is to survive to revenge ourselves on Reawen and her thieving husband, we must stand together."

Taunis hardly seemed to hear. His eyes simmered with rage

and pent-up frustration. Proudly, he faced the solid line of greenfire closing in on the abandoned Sturite camp. With a swoosh of energy, he raised his hands. Yellow flame shot up from the ground around him, and his foxlike visage darkened. The flame built higher, growing crimson tongues that licked hungrily at the acrid air. With a roar, Taunis's flame rolled forward toward the advancing greenfire.

The two conflagrations met with a deafening explosion. Yellow and red dueled with green, each apparently bent on devouring the other. For a moment it almost looked as if the green were wavering and receding. Then it glowed a deeper emerald. An instant later it had swallowed Taunis's crimson fire whole.

"You have lost!" Driona shrieked. She seized Taunis's hot hands and tried to drag him with her. "We have no choice but to run for the river."

"I cannot!" He looked first at the greenfire and then the water, and his face contorted with terror and hate. The Har boiled with thrashing Sturite soldiers. "If I must die, I'd rather die in my own element."

Now it was Driona's turn to draw herself up. "You shall not die, my friend," she declared. "You and I shall only rest a while. Deep in my earth we will be strengthened and refreshed. When we are reborn, we will be mightier and more cunning and more vengeful than we have ever been! Reawen and Brone will rue this day!"

Driona pointed a short white finger at the ground in front of her. For several seconds, nothing happened. Behind them, the greenfire advanced dangerously close. Then, with a cracking, rumbling sound, the earth bulged up and burst open. A dark passageway appeared.

Driona recaptured Taunis's hand and led him into the opening. As the two disappeared deep into the yawning darkness, the earth moved again, sealing itself. Seconds later the greenfire swept past and scorched everything beyond recognition.

* * * * *

"Leave her be to do her work, lad," Phen whispered gruffly to Albin. He put a heavy hand on the messenger's shoulder and drew him back.

The two stood at a respectful distance, watching Reawen and the desolated landscape she faced. Today, one day after the green flame had been lighted, all the land between the tower and the river was charred beyond recognition, and the stink of destruction coated the air. All the ants had been destroyed by the greenfire. Except a few bits of twisted metal that had once been wistite shields, helmets, and swords, nothing remained of the Sturites.

Many of Arant's soldiers had been drowned in the Har. Those that had survived had paddled their shallow-draft boats back to their ships and set sail for their own land with all possible speed. It would be many a year before they threatened the Peninsula again.

Reawen clasped her hands around the green stone. Closing her eyes, she communed with it in silence.

"What's she going to do?" Albin whispered.

"Heal the land, lad, heal it. Nothing is better at mending a wound than water."

The sun sparkled on the river. Only yesterday, willows had trailed their pale green hair from its mossy banks, and sweet grasses and wildflowers had bloomed. Now the water lapped at cinders and ashes.

Rise sister Har, Reawen chanted in her mind. Gather your children to sweep away this ugliness, to ease the pain of this devastation, and to breathe new life into this chaos!

The river heard its mistress's gentle plea. From distant springs, creeks, and streams, water flowed faster and harder. Tributaries gushed into the Har so that it pulsed with new vitality. While Reawen stood waiting patiently and controlling the force of its advance, it overflowed its banks and crept across the ruined landscape. By afternoon it had bathed the charred field in a shining sheet of cleansing liquid.

Reawen turned to face Albin and Phen. "The Har will stay for a week and then recede back into its bed," she told them. "By then the stink will be gone and the earth will be ready to mend itself."

As she spoke, she stumbled slightly. It had been an exhausting twenty-four hours. Though Phen and Albin, along with Brone's physicians, had repeatedly urged her to rest, she hadn't been able to. Not with so much turmoil around her and within her.

"I want to see Faring again," she told her two faithful attendants. Albin and Phen had each taken one of her arms. Gently, they helped her climb back up into the carriage in which they'd driven her out onto the battlefield. As she seated herself, she folded her hands in her lap and turned her face toward Jedestrom.

An hour later the trio were back in the Plat. Once again Albin and Phen took Reawen's arms and escorted her down the corridor to the room where Faring's body lay in state.

"He almost looks alive," Albin whispered after they crossed the threshold and stopped to gaze in some trepidation at the fallen wizard. How could they see him like this and not remember the dreadful creations of his imagination that he'd brought forth to battle with Thropos? Yet there was no sign of that hideous duel about him now.

Brone's physicians had dressed the wizard in fresh black robes and laid him on a marble altar. His bloodless features were a study in austerity, and his compelling eyes were closed forever—or so it seemed.

"I'm not so sure he's truly dead," Phen answered Albin. "I know the physicians swear to it, but with that one, a person can never be sure of anything. He must have been alive when he transported himself back here. And the doctors who dressed his body said there wasn't a mark on it." He tugged at Albin's sleeve. "Let's leave her alone with him now, lad."

After Phen and Albin had thoughtfully withdrawn, Reawen stood contemplating Faring in silence. This man was her father, she mused. Yet even before the moment of her birth, he had been her enemy. He had destroyed her mother, her heritage, and everything she had held dear. And all because Nioma's careless rejection had twisted his violent passion for her into even more violent hatred. What a strange and dangerous emotion this love between men and women could be.

Softly, Reawen stepped forward and laid a hand on Faring's. She had expected it to be cold and stiff. When she discovered that it was not, she thought of what Phen had just said. "With that one, a person can never be sure of anything."

As she gazed down at her father's frozen face, a terrible sadness washed through her, and a single crystal tear tracked down her cheek, splashing lightly onto his forehead. "Oh, Father, I wish it could have been different," she whispered. "Truly, truly I wish it."

A terrible silence filled the room and suddenly Reawen could bear it no longer. She stepped quickly back and turned to go. At that instant a low groan weighted with a terrible load of anguish assaulted her ears. With a gasp, she swiveled back just in time to see Faring's body shimmer, then fade from sight. A second later, his marble bier lay empty.

* * * * *

"I will sit with the king this night," Halow offered several days later.

Reawen shook her head. "No, I will stay up with him."

When the little physician eyed her and frowned uneasily, Reawen added, "I know you fear that I might harm him somehow. Rest easy. I want the king to recover from his hurts even more than you do, and I will do everything I can to help him, not harm him.

"You misjudge me, milady. I don't mistrust you." And it was true. Oh, Halow, like his colleagues, had been doubtful at first. When the king, feverish and unconscious from the loss of blood, had been brought back from the field of destruction outside the city walls, and they'd seen that he might well be ill unto death, they'd eyed his witch wife suspiciously. Had she not already proved treacherous? Had Brone himself not ordered that she be kept prisoner in the keep?

But during the long days and nights of his illness, Reawen had worried about him so obviously and nursed him so devotedly that even the most dubious of his other attendants had changed their minds about her. She seemed so gentle, kind, and beautiful. In Halow's opinion, she needed no magic spell to make the king fall in love with her. He thought it no mystery that Brone had chosen her for his queen over all the others who had been candidates.

"I only ask that you let me sit with Brone tonight," Halow hurried on, "because it is my duty and because you have overtired yourself during all these difficult days. And in your condition—" He let his gaze lightly skim her.

Reawen smiled for his concern. "I will not be able to sleep if I leave the king now, Halow. I feel somehow that this night is crucial and that he needs me."

When the little man continued to shuffle his feet, hemming and hawing, Reawen added, "Perhaps you would care to come back after midnight. By that time, the king may be better, and if he is, I will certainly wish to rest."

That satisfied Halow, and, with a smile, he backed out. When Reawen was alone with her husband, she drew her chair close. Since he'd fallen after slaying Arant, he'd lain for days in feverish unconsciousness. He'd tossed and turned and muttered. He couldn't be fed and never opened his eyes. At one point, he'd ripped the crown from his head and flung it away. His doctors had been horrified. Faring's binding had made it impossible for them to replace it. Now it lay on the floor next to Brone's bed.

Reawen dampened a clean cloth and dribbled moisture on his cracked lips. Then she wiped away the perspiration from his feverish brow. Lifting the cloth, she allowed herself the luxury of gazing down at his face. Taking the crown off had been good for him. Already many of the lines in his forehead had smoothed away, and she could see traces of the masculine beauty that had seduced Nioma.

Reawen hadn't permitted herself to admire Brone's hand-some looks, except in a very distant and objective way. She'd been afraid to admit to herself how pleasing he was in her sight. He'd destroyed her mother with his golden fairness, and she'd had no intention of falling victim to it herself.

But that had been when she'd considered Brone her enemy. Now she knew he was not her enemy and never had been. He was merely another victim caught in the toils of a passion that had destroyed her mother and now her father, had destroyed Thropos and Arant, Taunis and Driona, and a whole way of life. She only hoped that it wouldn't destroy Brone as well. She judged that he deserved to live and find some contentment in all that he had achieved. Long ago, Reawen had acknowledged that his people loved and needed him.

Brone began to toss, and she knew that he was fighting hard against the fever that poisoned his blood. "Reawen, Reawen!"

"Yes, my lord."

"Reawen!"

"I'm here."

"Don't leave me."

"I'm with you, my lord, and I'll stay until you are better."

He began to moan and mutter. As he rolled from side to side, he threw the covers off his broad chest. When she replaced them, tucking them firmly around him, he clutched at her hand and cried out again. "Don't leave me!"

She crooned his name until he relaxed and then patted him

gently. "I must, my lord," she whispered sadly, as tears again began to streak her face, "for when you are well and strong, you will be better off without your witch wife, and I will be better off in my mountains where I belong."

* * * * *

"This was to have been the first decent night's sleep I've had since the Sturites crept up the Har," Phen grumbled.

"The same for me," said Albin.

It was an hour past midnight. The two had been roused from their beds by Cel. Like a dream, the pillawn had flown through their windows and shaken them from their slumber. *My mistress awaits you at the keep,* she'd chirped inside their heads. *Hurry, and be secret about it.*

Now Cel fluttered overhead, leading Phen and Albin through the moonlit gardens and across the field to the darkened keep.

"It seems as if we're always stumbling around in the dark." Misstepping, Albin stopped and bent to adjust the lacing on his boot. He had dressed minus the aid of a candle and with great haste.

Phen gave him a playful thump on the shoulder that all but sent him sprawling. "You didn't bother to put your shoes on properly, but you took the time to buckle on that sword of yours, I notice."

Albin grinned sheepishly. "I don't know why it is, but ever since our battle with the Sturites, I can't seem to be without Victory. I feel naked if it's not hanging at my side."

"Interesting," Phen commented. " 'Tis a magic sword, I'll warrant."

"You think so?"

"I know so, lad. I saw you fight with it, remember? You were like one of the ancient heroes come back to life."

"Was I really?"

"That you were. Take my advice and keep that sword with you. Guard it, and it will guard you."

"I will."

"Now don't go getting a swelled head thinking your Victory there will make you into somethin' special. We have business before us that, unless I'm much mistaken, will take some clear thinkin'."

Albin nodded, but secretly gave his sword a proprietary pat. "What do you suppose Reawen wants with us at this hour?"

"I don't know, lad, but we'll soon be finding out." Phen pointed at the cloaked figure who waited for them outside the dark stone structure.

"Reawen," Albin murmured. "Do you have word about the king?" he demanded as soon as they were within whispering distance. "Is he worse?" The words caught in Albin's throat. The thought of Brone dying was terrible to him, and even more terrible because of his feelings for Reawen. What would the Peninsula be without its young golden king? Albin couldn't imagine.

"The king is well," Reawen answered. "A few minutes before midnight, his fever broke, and now he rests easily. The physicians who attend him are convinced he has begun his recovery. I know they are right, for I felt the change in him."

"I'm glad you woke us up to bring us these good tidings, milady, but why the secrecy?" Phen questioned.

Reawen stepped forward and laid a light hand on the adventurer's burly shoulder. "Even for such good news I would not have roused you from your sleep, for I know how well you deserve it." She shook her head. "Phen and Albin, the time has come when I must ask you to fulfill your part of the bargain we made. Tonight I would like to leave Jedestrom and return to my mountains. Will you help me make my escape?"

The two men stared back at her in shock. Somehow, Albin hadn't thought Reawen would want to leave Brone now. Surely she cared for him. He had seen it in her tenderness to him, in the way she had nursed him all through his weakness.

"My lady, you are so close to your time," Phen protested with a meaningful look at her belly. "To travel now would be dangerous for you."

"Good friend, that's why I ask your aid. Otherwise I wouldn't need it." Reawen gave the two a searching look. "Will you give it?"

Phen and Albin studied each other. "A promise is a promise, lad," Phen finally said wearily. "If a man doesn't keep his word, he might as well join the beasts in the forest—and they probably wouldn't want him. I'll go get a wagon and a pair of horses."

Chapter Eighteen

"Time to abandon the cart, milady." Phen unhitched the horses and then helped Reawen down from her seat.

Albin scrambled off Grassears and hurried forward to take her free arm. "Careful, careful," he murmured.

"Do you feel up to mounting one of the horses?" Phen inquired.

She glanced around tiredly. They had been traveling for almost a week now. Because of her advanced pregnancy, Reawen required the cart as long as it was possible to use it, so they had had to chance the main roads. Fortunately for them, the Sturite attack had thrown Jedestrom into such chaos that very few soldiers could be spared in the countryside. Consequently, their flight had seemed to go undetected. Still, whenever possible, Phen had avoided villages or driven through them at night.

"Do you think we might rest for a few minutes?" Reawen queried.

Phen shot an assessing look at their surroundings. "Of course, milady. We'll need our strength for this last bit of our trek. Indeed, we might as well have a bite to eat. There's some cheese and bread left in one of the saddlebags and a half bottle of mead as well. I'll go hide the cart as best I can while you and Albin take your ease."

They had paused in a clearing just at the point where the woods grew so densely on the foothills that their wagon could no longer pass between the trees. It was a pleasant spot, with a stream gurgling nearby and an outcropping of boulders that would make good backrests.

Reawen settled against one of them with a sigh. "My joints ache from that bouncing cart."

"It's not well sprung," Albin agreed. "I'm afraid you'll ache even worse after a day aboard a horse." The young man eyed her pale face and shadowed eyes with concern. She looked exhausted and unhappy, he thought, as if a great burden weighed her down. "Will you be glad to be back in your mountains?"

Reawen smiled wanly. "They are home to me. I've been worried about Gris. She wasn't well when I left her. It's not good for her to have been alone so long."

"Your aunt, that would be?"

"Yes, though she's been more of a mother to me than an aunt. It was she who raised me."

Albin gathered up the food he'd removed from the cart and settled down at Reawen's side. After he'd torn off a hunk of bread for her and cut a slice of cheese, he asked, "Was Nioma really as beautiful as they say?"

A faraway look came into Reawen's eyes. "Yes, though to tell you the truth, I saw very little of her when I was a child. She didn't live in our cave, but had her own place. A visit from her was rare. When she did come, I was enchanted. She was so very lovely with all her golden hair and her little gifts. It was she who gave me Cel." Reawen glanced up and smiled at the bird settled in a tall tree nearby.

Thoughtfully, Albin filled a cup with mead. When he had handed it to Reawen he said, "Taunis and Driona are gone, and Eol is no friend to you. You've admitted that Brone's rule has been good for the Peninsula and that its future lies with him and not the domi. If all that awaits you in the mountains is your aunt, how can you be so sure that you really want to go back to them?"

"I'm sure, for the simple reason that I have no choice."

Albin leaned toward her, his face a study in perplexity. "But why? I know Brone treated you cruelly, locking you up in the keep. But anyone can see that he still cares for you. I know he wants you and his child with him in Jedestrom."

Reawen shook her head. "You don't understand. Even if I wished to be his queen, I could not."

"Why? Is it because you are a domis? People may distrust you because of that, but when they realize how you saved us from the Sturites, they'll get over their fears."

"It's more, Albin."

"Then what? What barrier lies between you and Brone that cannot be surmounted?"

"The past," Reawen cried out. She lifted her hands and then let them fall back to her lap in a gesture of hopelessness. "The past lies between us. Brone seduced and betrayed my mother, and nothing we can do will change that. With that fact tainting any love we might discover for each other, we can have no marriage worthy of the name. I can never be Brone's queen."

"What of your child?"

"What of it?" Reawen gazed at Albin defiantly.

"He will inherit the crown. Surely he belongs in Jedestrom with his father."

Two angry spots of color showed in Reawen's pale cheeks. "Perhaps he does, and perhaps when my child is born, I should let Brone have it. But I cannot bring myself to do that. Soon the child I carry will be all I have left."

Albin met Reawen's eyes and tried desperately to think of an answer to give her that would bridge this terrible impasse. But he could think of nothing at all. "You'll still have me." He swallowed, then rushed on. "Reawen, I know this isn't what you want to hear, but I must tell you."

"Tell me what, Albin?"

He took her hand. "I love you. I always have, and I always will."

"Oh, Albin." Tears filled Reawen's eyes, and she leaned her head against his shoulder. "I love you, too, my friend." After a moment, she raised her head to look up at the youth. Albin could see in her eyes what he had realized at Eol's cave, what he had known all along—that his greatest wish in all the world could never be his.

* * * * *

"How is my lord feeling today?"

"Better, much better."

Halow studied Brone critically, noting how much his color had improved and that his eyes were now clear as newly washed blue glass.

Brone pushed away the tray containing the bowl of broth he'd been eating. He stretched until the muscles in his shoulders rippled and his joints cracked. "I'm ready to start eating real food and to get back on my feet," he said, flinging back the covers and swinging his long legs to the floor.

"Oh, Sire, be careful. 'Tis too early!" Halow hurried forward to help if need be, but Brone showed only an instant's unsteadiness when he got to his feet. A moment later, he was summoning his valet and demanding his clothes. "Where is my wife?" he asked. "I want to see her."

Halow began to wring his hands. For three days now the king had been on the mend. Twice he'd drifted out of a healing sleep to ask for Reawen. Halow had made up some excuse why she couldn't attend him. She was resting, she was being fitted for new clothes. All of Brone's physicians had agreed it would be better not to trouble him with her disappearance until he was completely recovered. Now there was no hiding the fact.

"My lord, she's gone."

"Gone?"

"She and Phen and Albin, they all disappeared the night your fever broke."

Brone stiffened. "How is that possible?"

Halow hung his head. "Your sickness, Faring's death, the Sturites—the Plat was in chaos. Otherwise, they would not have been able to slip off in the night the way they did."

"Slip off?" Resting his hands on his hips, Brone scowled. "The queen is heavy with child."

"Oh, my lord, I know, and we are all concerned for her. But the few soldiers that we've been able to spare haven't found her. However, they have brought back reports that she may have headed north."

"North?" Brone's mouth compressed into a bleak line. "Of course, she's headed north. She's gone back to her mountains and away from me."

* * * * *

"We're nearly there. The cave's just ahead."

"Beautiful spot," Phen commented as the horses picked their way across the gurgling stream.

Albin looked about, acknowledging the truth of Phen's observation. Against the rich velvet of the evergreens, the other trees had decked themselves out with lighter-hued greenery. The tender young leaves seemed to tremble and glow in the unclouded sunlight. Spring flowers dotted the mossy banks of the stream. Their fragrance sweetened the air, which hummed with the single-minded drone of busy bees.

"Oh, yes, it is beautiful, isn't it?"

Reawen was sitting straighter in the saddle, Albin noted. He had been so worried about her these last few days. The journey had been long, and she'd been in no condition to travel in the first place. But now that she was close to home, some of the sadness had left her eyes and a new eagerness infused her voice.

"That's it, that's the cave," she cried out a few minutes later. "The entrance is behind those evergreens."

Albin reined in Grassears and speculated that he might have ridden past without noticing if Reawen hadn't pointed it out.

As Phen helped her down, he seconded the thought. "I'd never have known a cave was here. Blends right in with the scenery."

Both men waited respectfully while Reawen slipped in among the evergreens. "Gris!" they heard her call out several times. Then there was a long silence.

"What d'ya expect is goin' on in there?" Phen muttered.

As Albin shook his head, Reawen re-emerged with a worried

expression. "She's not there, and she's folded all her things up and stacked them away so neatly. Gris is hardly ever neat. I'm afraid—"

"She's probably just out picking berries or something," Albin put in quickly.

"Your aunt will likely come strolling back any minute now," Phen added. "It's just a matter of waiting for her."

"Oh, I hope you're right," Reawen exclaimed. A deep frown still puckered her brow.

They waited all the rest of that day and through the night. When first light came and still no sign of Gris, Reawen woke Phen and asked that he saddle up her horse.

"Now where are you off to, milady?" he asked when he'd followed her outside. Dawn had just broken, and chilly dew showered down as they brushed past a leafy branch.

She'd set her features into grim lines. "I think I know where Gris might be."

"And where is that?"

Reawen faced the sleep-tousled adventurer. "Phen, I can't tell you, or Albin either," she added. Rubbing his eyes, the latter emerged from the evergreens shielding the cave's entrance. "Friends," she said, addressing them both, "you've kept your part of our bargain and brought me here. For that, I thank you. I will always remember and be grateful to you both. I will always pray for your health and good fortune. It pains me to say good-bye, but I must. Now you're free to go."

"Free to go!" Albin raked a hand through his unkempt locks. "Reawen, we can't leave you like this! You're all alone, with no one to help you. What will you do when the time comes to deliver your child?"

"Gris will help me."

"But you don't know where your aunt is."

"I think I do know. It's not a place where you or Phen can go, Albin. No one can go there who isn't descended from the domi."

"Are you dismissing us, just like that?"

Reawen locked her fingers together tightly and nodded. "Just like that."

"But, but . . ."

He looked at Phen for assistance, but the older man just stood there frowning. "Can't make her let us help if she don't want our company," Phen said.

At that, Reawen's expression softened, and she gave Phen an impulsive hug. "It's not that I don't want your company, or Albin's," she added, dropping an affectionate kiss on his cheek. "I love you both, really, and I shall never forget all that you've done for me. It's just that—" Her voice broke and tears began to steal down her own cheeks. "If Gris is where I'm afraid she is, I have to go to her alone. Do you understand?"

"No, I don't understand!" Albin exploded.

Quickly, Phen cut off his angry words. "Calm yourself, lad. She's right. This is domi territory, and she has to go about domi business. We have no business intrudin'."

Glumly, the three shared a meager breakfast. Afterward, Phen and Albin helped Reawen repack the saddlebags on her horse and then watched her set off.

"I hate seeing her go like this all alone," Albin said as Reawen disappeared up the trail.

"Can't force ourselves on her if she won't have us."

"Do what you want," Albin retorted, "but I'm going to follow her."

Phen clamped a hard hand around the boy's arm. "That's what I was going to suggest, but give it a minute or two. She's sure to notice if you go pelting after her now."

Albin stared at his friend and then broke into a grin of understanding. "Then we *are* going to follow her. It's what you intended all along, isn't it? But if we wait too long, we might lose her."

Suddenly, Phen's grin matched Albin's. "We won't lose her, lad. I know I've already fair dazzled you with my talents. But did I never mention that I'm the best tracker you or anyone else will ever meet?"

"No, you never did."

Phen chortled. "There's a story behind that, a little adventure I had in a rocky desert land they call Berubis. While we wait long enough to give the little lady a head start, I'll tell you about it."

* * * * *

Reawen pulled the bodice of her gown away from her perspiring bosom and mopped sweat from her brow. Her heaviness made travel difficult. Getting to the pool this time had taken much longer than that first journey she and Gris had taken together for her initiation. That seemed to have happened a lifetime ago.

Two days earlier, the climb had become so arduous that Reawen had had to leave her horse and hike the remaining distance on foot. Now she was within a half hour of her destination. She only hoped that she wouldn't be too late. "Gris," she murmured under her breath. "Please don't do anything until I can come to you. Please still be there."

Reawen was panting hard by the time she reached the crest of the rocky mount. Again, she paused to press her hand over her heart, partly to still its beating and partly because she was afraid of what she would see—or might not see—on the mountain's other side. Then, taking a deep steadying breath, she climbed the rest of the way and stood looking down. "Gris!" she cried, "Gris, wait!"

Seemingly contemplating its calm blue eye, Gris sat cross-legged in front of the sacred pool. She had exchanged the colorless, rough-woven dress she always wore for one of purest white. Her graying hair had been arranged neatly around her cadaverous shoulders.

To Reawen's eye, there was a disquieting resignation in her calm posture and serene expression. When she heard the younger woman's voice, she glanced up. But, after a moment, she turned back to the pool, as if only it could hold her attention now.

In a fever to reach her aunt, Reawen scrambled down the smooth walls of the stone bowl. At the bottom, she hurried to her side. "Oh, Gris, I've been so worried about you. Why are you here? Please, you aren't thinking about going to the pool of our mothers?"

"Aye, child, my time has come."

Reawen seized Gris's hand. It felt cool and dry as old leather. "You're so thin, nothing but skin and bones. Have you been terribly ill?"

"There's a canker in my breast, child. My sickness is unto death. But it's all right. I'm more than ready to leave this mortal body behind. My only regret is I'll miss seeing you and the babe you bear." She lifted her eyes and studied Reawen's worried features. "You shouldn't have come such a hard long journey, not when you're so close to your time."

"How could I not when I found the cave empty? I knew what you must be thinking of doing. Oh, Gris, please don't leave me!" Fresh tears gushed from Reawen's eyes, and she buried her face against her aunt's thin shoulder.

"Now, now," Gris said, stroking Reawen's silky black hair. "I know it's hard, but you won't be all alone. You'll have your child. It'll be a fine, strong lad; of that I'm certain. And anyone with eyes can see that the king is smitten with you. For all Faring stirred him up to make such trouble, Brone's a good man. He'll take care of you."

"I can't go back to Brone."

Gris felt the girl shudder with strong emotion and drew her head back slightly. With an effort, she seemed to drag her attention back from the eternal, where it had been centered a moment earlier, and bring it to the concerns of the mundane present.

"Why can't you go back to Brone? I thought you understood

how things are with the Peninsula, Reawen. It's changing. Those of our kind who want to survive at all in this new order of things will have to change with it. There's little room for the old way now, and, as time goes on, there will be less. You're young, and your life lies before you, so you must think of the future. You've stolen Brone's heart and you carry his child. It's best you share your tomorrows with him, too."

"Oh, but Gris, how can I go back to the king knowing what happened between him and my mother? It's impossible!"

As she continued to stroke Reawen's hair, the older woman's pale green eyes grew cloudy. "Is that what keeps you from him?"

"Yes!" Reawen hissed.

"But it's such a little thing, so unimportant."

"She was my mother, Gris! That picture of them together in the water image will never leave my mind."

"Would it matter so much if she hadn't been your mother?"

Puzzled, Reawen lifted her head and drew back. "No—for then she would just be another woman he had made love to. Why do you ask? Nioma *was* my mother."

Slowly, Gris shook her head. "No, Reawen, she was not."

Reawen stared at Gris, speechless.

Sighing, the older woman crossed her thin hands over her shrunken chest. "I never wanted to tell you this. Since you were the only hope for our future, Nioma and I thought it would be best if you believed yourself her daughter and therefore descended in the true line of water domi. I was so frightened when you came here to be tested. I was afraid the pool would reject you and maim you for life. But you believed yourself to be water domis, and the pool accepted you. That's all that matters. It can't hurt you or change what you've become to know the truth now. I, not Nioma, gave you life."

"You!" Reawen had been hit a stunning blow. Her mouth dropped open and she sat back on her heels.

Gris lifted a palm. "Let me explain. When I was young, I was jealous of my sister. She was water domis, and the pool had rejected me. She was so beautiful that lovers flocked to her, while I was plain by comparison, and therefore ignored. Though she was many decades older than I, who had been born in the final period of our mother's reign, Nioma looked like springtime. She possessed the stone and showed no sign of the passing years that lay heavily with me."

Gris sighed. "Yes, I was jealous." She took one of Reawen's hands and stroked it lightly. "For many years, I had resigned myself to a life of solitude. Once I accepted my state, I was happy enough, I suppose. Then one day I met Faring."

"Faring! Then Brone's wizard is *still* my father?"

"Yes, child. He was fresh out of Peneto and just beginning his five years of exile. He was young and handsome, much younger than I who, truth to tell, was getting rather long in the tooth and almost past childbearing age. But, immured in Peneto since childhood, he'd had naught to do with women. To him I seemed fair enough. I brought him to my cave, and there he lay with me. How proud and happy I was after that! For I hoped, of course, that he would stay."

Gris mused in silence for a moment, then shook her head. "My happiness lasted only a few days. The moment Faring laid eyes on Nioma, he forgot me. But I had taken his seed, and you are the result."

"Did Faring know?"

Gris shook her head. "No."

"When I spoke with him in Jedestrom, he believed I was Nioma's."

Gris's mouth twisted. "Doubtless, he did. You see, for him, it was as if I had never existed. But Nioma had no children. You are the last of our line. If the pool had rejected you, there would have been no one to carry the stone when it was retrieved from Brone. That is why I lied to you. I was afraid that if you held any doubt about your birthright, the pool would reject you as it did me."

Gris leaned forward and kissed Reawen's forehead tenderly.

Then she cupped the girl's face between her hands, searching it. "Can you forgive me?"

Reawen's eyes glistened, and her cheeks were damp. "Oh, Gris, I should have known. You were always my mother. Nioma was never anything more than a beautiful vision. You were the only one who truly loved me."

For a long moment, mother and daughter embraced. When they finally drew apart, Gris gazed at Reawen fondly. "You are all I ever could have wished in a daughter. You are beautiful and strong. You haven't always been wise, but in time, wisdom will come to you. You will make the Peninsula a fine queen. I'm sorry I shall not live to see it."

"Mother!"

Again, Gris held up her hand. "My time has come, child. The pool will accept me now, and my passage will be painless, but I cannot tarry."

*   *   *   *   *

"What are they doing?" Phen demanded.

"Just talking, so far."

Cautiously, Albin and Phen peered down over the edge of the stone bowl. Keeping a respectful distance, they had followed Reawen through the mountains. Phen's tracking abilities had amazed Albin. The faintest of heel prints on a patch of dirt, a broken branch, a spot where the brush of a skirt had disturbed loose gravel, all these things Phen had read like clearly printed road markers. Now here they were, gazing down at their quarry from a safe hiding spot.

"I've never seen a place like this before," Albin whispered.

"Fair gives a body the shivers," Phen agreed. "Tell you what, lad, it's not meant for human eyes, that's for sure. Just have a look at that pool, would you? Round as a dinner plate. Doesn't seem as if nature ever fashioned such a thing."

Silently, Albin nodded his agreement. Everything about this

place felt alien. It was as if it had been hidden here by some ancient race for reasons no one, perhaps not even the domi themselves, could clearly understand.

"Now what are they up to?"

Albin returned his attention to the two women. They had both risen to their feet. Reawen was clutching at the other one's arm.

"Appears as if milady is trying to keep her aunt from taking a swim," Phen commented, "and a good thing, too. From the looks of that old woman, I'd say she wasn't long for this world. Nothing more than a bag of bones."

"She's been ill," Albin answered distractedly.

He was focusing hard on the scene below, trying to understand what was going on. Clearly, Reawen and her aunt were having some sort of disagreement. From the way in which she gestured, pleaded, and finally wept, Reawen was trying to persuade her aunt against doing something. But, plainly, all her arguments went for nothing. Finally, bowing her head, she took several steps back and waited resignedly.

From the way the old woman turned her back on her niece and faced the pool, Albin could see that she had won their argument. She was going to have her way—whatever that might be.

She stepped to the lip of the pool and raised her arms. For what seemed like a long time, nothing happened. Then, a thick mist formed over the water's surface.

"What's going on?" Phen growled.

"It's . . . it's floating toward her," Albin hissed. He felt the tiny hairs on the back of his neck stand on end. "It's waiting for her."

Indeed, that did appear to be what was happening. The mist hovered at the water's edge, reaching long cloudlike arms out toward Gris. Like a sleepwalker, she stepped into their embrace. Slowly, she sank beneath the surface. When she had disappeared, the mist vanished with her, and the pool was as it had been before—smooth and blue as a sheet of unrippled silk.

Only Reawen's tears gave evidence that something strange and sad had occurred. She collapsed on the flat surface at the pool's edge and covered her face with her hands. Her sobs echoed against the stone walls surrounding her. They rose up so Albin and Phen could hear them clearly.

"I can't stand to hear her cry like that!" Albin exclaimed. "I'm going to go down there."

"Better not," Phen warned. "I don't think that's a spot for the likes of us."

Albin was too worried about Reawen to pay attention. Ignoring his friend, he jumped out from behind the boulders where they'd been hiding and slid and scrambled down the sheer sides of the stone bowl. He reached the bottom with a terrible clatter that made Reawen jump to her feet.

"Albin!"

"I'm sorry, Reawen," he cried breathlessly. "I know you said Phen and I shouldn't follow you, but we couldn't let you come here all alone."

"Albin! This spot is sacred. You must go away at once!"

Reawen looked truly horrified by his intrusion. But Albin had no intention of going anywhere without her. "Come with me!" he implored.

"With you?"

"Yes! You're all alone now that your aunt is gone. If you won't return to Jedestrom and the king, come with me. Reawen, I love you. I've always loved you. Come away with me, and we'll find someplace where we can live and be happy. I'll take care of your child as if he were my own. I promise!"

Vehemently, Reawen shook her head. "You must leave here at once! This place isn't safe for you." As she spoke, the pool's surface started turning an ominous gray.

"It's not safe for you, either. I saw what happened to your aunt."

"It's different for the domi, Albin. Gris went to the pool of her own free will. Now, go back, please!"

"I love you!"

"I love you, too, Albin. But not in the way you mean," Uneasily, she glanced at the pool, which had turned an even darker gray. "Truly, you will find as you grow older that I was never the one for you. But if you are to meet the future that destiny intends, you must get away from here now."

"I can't, without you!"

"Leave!" Reawen drew herself up. A power flashed from her eyes that Albin had never seen before. Suddenly, he couldn't disobey her command. With a heavy heart, he turned away and climbed back up to Phen.

"I was getting worried about you," the older man said gruffly. "That pool was taking on a right ugly look."

"She doesn't want my help," Albin muttered dejectedly. "She says we must go."

"Then mayhap we should. I still don't like the look of that pool."

"I can't leave until I see what Reawen decides to do."

"This won't be a pleasant spot to spend the night," Phen pointed out.

"No, but if we must stay the night here, then so be it—at least for me."

Phen didn't answer. He'd lifted his shaggy head and sniffed the air like a hunting dog. "We've got company."

"Company?"

"Someone's heading this way, and he's not paying much attention to the noise of his boots."

* * * * *

For several minutes, Reawen stood watching the spot where Albin had disappeared from sight. She knew he was still up there somewhere. At least he was far enough away from the pool so it wouldn't harm him. She turned toward the water and uttered some calming words. Finally, it smoothed out and took on its normal blue sheen.

"Gris," Reawen murmured as she sank wearily to the ground. "Oh, Gris!"

Reawen knew that she should leave this place now and return to her cave. Yet, somehow she couldn't. Her pain over Gris's decision was still too raw. But there was more to her deep sense of loss than even that. Gris, Reawen knew, had found peace. She, on the other hand, had not.

My mother is gone, and I never even knew she was my mother, Reawen thought tearfully. All this time she had believed she was Nioma's daughter. Never had she doubted her own right of inheritance. Did what Gris had finally revealed mean that the green stone wasn't truly hers? But no. Her hand went to the stone, and she could still feel its call deep within her, despite the presence of her unborn child. She had won it. Yet, what did even that matter when everything else was gone?

"Mother," Reawen murmured, "you are right. The world is different now. There is no place for such as us. Maybe I should join you. Perhaps the time has come to end my life, too."

As this notion passed through her head, Reawen felt a rude kick inside her belly. It was as if her child had overheard her morbid thoughts and registered his vehement protest.

Through her tears, Reawen felt herself smile. "You're telling your mother that you want to live, aren't you, my son?" The baby kicked a rough tattoo, and Reawen laughed out loud. She pushed herself back up to a sitting position. "Yes, I can see that you do. Your mother may mourn the loss of her world, but you—you're ready to meet the one that's dawning and to dream new and different dreams."

Still smiling, Reawen leaned forward and passed her hand over the water's surface. Somehow she knew that she was ready to see the future now, ready in a way that she had never been before.

Suddenly, she saw a face she instinctively knew belonged to her son. It was the same boy she'd seen in torment during her earlier vision. But now his eyes smiled hopefully back at her.

"What a beautiful boy you will be, with your black hair and sapphire eyes," Reawen whispered to the vision. "You are every bit as handsome as your father was when he stole the green stone from Nioma and set our story in motion."

At the words, the image rippled and disappeared. Another replaced it, that of Brone standing at the rim above the pool. With a gasp, Reawen turned to see that he was truly there.

"No," she whispered as he started down. "No, you mustn't! It is forbidden!"

He paid no attention to her protest. He didn't even seem to hear it. As he closed the distance between them, his intense gaze stayed fixed on Reawen's face. A moment later, he stood at her side.

"Once again, I've followed you to your mountains, Reawen. Once again, I'm asking you to come back to Jedestrom with me."

Anxiously, she pressed her hands together. "Brone, you can't stay here. This is the sacred pool of the domi, the place where we come to die."

Fiercely, he snatched her hand. "You weren't thinking of ending your life!"

"No, no!" She shook her head in denial. "For our son's sake, I want to live."

"Then live with me, Reawen. Be my queen! The people of the Peninsula need you. And I need you!" His eyes pleaded with her.

She couldn't bear to look into them. "You only want me because I am of the domi," she said, turning away. "You think that will cement your right—and our son's right—to the throne."

"Is that truly what you believe?" Brone seized her shoulders and drew her to her feet. He dragged her close and stared into her eyes deeply. "I have loved you almost from the moment I saw you. Believe only that."

She looked up into his face, marveling at its fine, stern lines.

She had thought the years had robbed him. Now she changed her mind. This man is more beautiful now than he has ever been, she thought. "How can I believe it's me you really want, when you wear those stones and expect that our son will be able to rule by wielding their power? If they are killing you, they will surely do the same to him."

"Is that what stands between us, the damnable stones?"

Slowly Reawen nodded. "Oh, Brone, they have always stood between us, and always will."

"There you are wrong," Brone said. "I sold my youth for them, and possibly even my soul. But they shall not take what's left of my life."

To her astonishment, and that of Phen and Albin watching from their hiding place, he reached up and yanked the crown from his head. With a jerk of his wrist, he hurled the crown and its winking gems into the sacred waters.

Reawen gasped. Heavy though the crown was, it floated on the water's surface. Reawen leaned forward to try snatching it back, but Brone held her shoulders. "Leave it," he ordered.

"The pool is bottomless. You'll never get them back."

"I don't want them back." A breeze whipped one of Brone's golden locks over his forehead. "I want only you and our child and the future we can make together."

She looked away from the pool and gazed up into his eyes. "Are you sure?"

"Very sure, Reawen. The stones and their powers are a legacy from the past that we no longer need. As long as we heed them, they will drag at us. Without them, we can go on and have a future of our own making. Oh, don't you see, my love? Don't you understand?"

Reawen turned her head and gazed at the pool. The crown had begun to sink. As the ornament and its stones disappeared beneath the surface, the pool shuddered. Brone had made his decision.

"There's no going back," Reawen whispered as she gazed

into his eyes.

"No," he said simply.

All at once, the green stone she wore grew heavy and warm. Her hand clutched at it, but her eyes never left her husband's. He offered her and their child a new life, she thought. And she couldn't doubt his sincerity, for he'd just made a monumental sacrifice.

Her gaze shifted to the pool. Perhaps he was right. Perhaps this day marked the end of an era and the beginning of something entirely new. Taunis, Driona, and now Gris were gone. She and Eol were the last of their breed. And Eol, unpredictable maverick that he was, might never be heard from again. Perhaps the pool was where all their stones belonged.

"Will you take me without this?" Reawen asked, as she lifted the green stone and its chain from around her neck.

Brone's gaze stayed clear as an unclouded sky. "I will take you with nothing at all, my wife. To have you at my side, I will sacrifice anything but my honor."

"Then this is the least I can do," Reawen said. Smiling at her husband with the love that she had kept hidden until this moment, she tossed the stone and chain lightly into the water. As it disappeared beneath the surface, the pool caught the sun and shimmered, opalescent.

"Gone forever," Reawen said.

"Good riddance," Brone replied. Gazing at his wife, he withdrew from a pocket of his traveling cloak a familiar gold arm band. Reawen smiled as the king once again clasped the wedding bracelet around her wrist. Behind them, sparks of light danced over the surface of the pool, and a low murmuring echoed up from its depths.

Then, as Brone took Reawen into his arms and they sealed the pledge they had made to each other with a kiss, all was still.